D0174876

THE UNQUIET

Also by Jeannine Garsee

Before, After, and Somebody In Between
Say the Word

THE UNQUIET

jeannine garsee

BLOOMSBURY

NEW YORK BERLIN LONDON SYDNEY

First published in the United States of America in July 2012
by Bloomsbury Books for Young Readers
www.bloomsburyteens.com

For information about permission to reproduce selections from this book, write to
Permissions, Bloomsbury BFYR, 175 Fifth Avenue, New York, New York 10010

Library of Congress Cataloging-in-Publication Data
Garsee, Jeannine.
The unquiet / by Jeannine Garsee. — 1st U.S. ed.
p.   cm.
Summary: When sixteen-year-old Rinn, who has bipolar disorder, and her mother move back to her
mother's hometown in Ohio and settle in a house where the previous owner hanged herself, Rinn
discovers that both the town and her mother have some uncomfortable secrets in their past and
that the ghost that supposedly haunts the school seems to be out for revenge.
ISBN 978-1-59990-723-9 (hardcover)
[1. Ghosts—Fiction. 2. Supernatural—Fiction. 3. Manic-depressive illness—Fiction.
4. Suicide—Fiction. 5. Death—Fiction. 6. High schools—Fiction. 7. Schools—Fiction.
8. Ohio—Fiction.] I. Title.
PZ7.G1875Un 2012   [Fic]—dc23   2011019559

Book design by Nicole Gastonguay
Typeset by Westchester Book Composition
Printed in the U.S.A. by Quad/Graphics, Fairfield, Pennsylvania
2 4 6 8 10 9 7 5 3 1

For Ruth Ward, who totally gets me

THE UNQUIET

Sometimes, when I dream, the deadliest moment in my life happens all over again. That's when I'm given the chance to do things differently.

When I spot the smoke from the beach, I don't stand there like a dummy, wondering if I'm dreaming. Instead, I race through the sand and up the rocky hill, slicing my feet on cinders and brush. Smoke billows from the cottage windows, clogging my throat. In spite of the steady rain, the orange flames crackle and spit. My face burns. I feel my skin melting away.

Uncaring, I fling myself into the cottage. The hammer drops from Nana's hand as she whirls from my bedroom door, alight with joy and astonishment. "Rinnie! THERE you are!"

I throw myself at her, burying my face in her neck. Hugging her. Hugging her.

I can't stop hugging her.

3 MONTHS + 13 DAYS ———————

Saturday, October 18

Mom, no service means no service. Screaming at it won't help."

Mom examines her useless cell phone. "How can this be?"

"No biggie. I'm sure we can find an old-fashioned one around. Like on *Little House on the Prairie*?" I cup one fist to my mouth and crank the air with the other. "Maw! Paw! Kin ya hear me now?"

Her murderous glare flattens me. "Hilarious, Rinn."

Well, *I* thought it was. At least *I* can maintain a sense of humor after five solid days in a cramped SUV with a mom suffering from PMS and nicotine withdrawal. Not to mention that my iPod died somewhere between Phoenix and St. Louis. For the last eight hundred miles, Mom's tortured me with talk radio.

While Mom tries to hammer more bars into her phone by brute force, I stare through the window at the town square of River Hills, Ohio. Okay, *Little House on the Prairie* may be a tiny exaggeration. No horses, no buggies, no bonnets, no boardwalks. But no traffic lights, either—and what's with that ugly red restaurant shaped like a boxcar? We're parked in front of it like we're actually going in.

"This is Millie's diner. Isn't it darling?" Mom flicks my arm. "Don't snort at me."

"I didn't snort. I'm having an allergic reaction."

"To what?"

"To all this freaking fresh air." I fake a cough. "My system can't take it. Maybe I ought to get out and suck on the tailpipe for a minute."

"Corinne, please. I don't want it to be this way for—"

"The rest of my life?"

"No, for however long we decide to stay here."

Hope flickers. "So we might go back?"

"Honey, I told you, nothing is carved in stone. Frank and I need to think things over, and you and I need to . . . well . . . be away from him for a while."

My mother's understatements never fail to blow me away. "California's pretty big. Couldn't we be *away* from him there? I mean, what's wrong with San Francisco or, or . . . ?"

"I don't know anyone in San Francisco. Here, I know Millie."

"Millie, big deal. You haven't laid eyes on her in years." Mom doesn't challenge this. "You could talk to him," I persist, fighting the too-familiar pain in my chest. "You could tell him how sorry I am. You could make him understand."

"I did. Rinn, I tried—"

"Then you didn't try hard enough!"

I throw myself out of the SUV, stalk across the street—no cars at the moment to run me over—and head toward the kind of town square you see on TV: a grassy park crisscrossed with stone walkways and a white gazebo flocked with patriotic ribbons. I could be strolling through a set from one of those old "family show" reruns I used to watch with Nana.

Nana died in July. Now that I can't bear to watch those shows, why would I want to live in one? This dinky town is too close to *Happy Days* for comfort.

I stuff my cold hands into the pockets of my heavy new jacket. Where do I think I'm running off to? To the Greyhound station to hop a bus back to La Jolla, so I can beg my stepfather to give me another chance?

Frank won't do it. Not after what I put him through.

Mom hurries up to catch my sleeve. "Rinn, I promise you. It's not the end of the world."

"Not yours, anyway."

"This isn't *all* my fault," she says softly.

She's right: it's mine, though she'll never say that to my face. She's too afraid I'll slash my throat and mess up her bathroom again.

"Honey, do you think this is easy for me? Leaving my home? My friends?" *At least you have some.* "Starting a new job in a strange town?"

"You grew *up* here. It's not like you landed from outer space."

"True, but it's been years since I left for college." College, in California, where she got pregnant with me and dropped out in her senior year.

"Yeah, lucky you," I grumble.

Mom steps around, forcing me to face her. "Okay. Did you . . . ?" She trails off the way she always does when she starts to ask this question. I know she doesn't trust me, not that I

5

blame her. But neither does she want me to feel that distrust. Like I could miss it.

"Yes, Mommy," I recite. "I took my pills like a good girl. Same way I've been taking them twice a day for the past three months and thirteen days. But you know that, right? I bet you count them. Maybe you'd like to personally *shove* them down?"

Mom spins around, hugging herself, and not because of the chilly Ohio air. A rush of shame wells up in me. I hate this awfulness between us now. I hate that I'm so bitchy to her when she's the only one who sticks by me. Unlike my real dad, the drive-by sperm donor who vanished after their one and only date. Unlike Frank, who took eight years to figure out that a bipolar stepdaughter was *not* in the contract when he said "I do" to my mom.

"I'm sorry," I mumble. *Please don't let her be crying again!*

She's not. She turns around and pulls me close to her so fast, I lose my footing. Both of us end up in a pile of leaves. "I love you, honey. We're gonna make this work, right?" She kisses my cheek and jumps up. "Come on, let's find Aunt Millie."

———◦———

I have no idea how Millie Lux suddenly turned into a long-lost relative. We find her shaking grease off a basket of sizzling onion rings, behind the U-shaped counter in the Boxcar Diner. Yep, that's the name of it.

"Millie!"

"Mo!"

Mom and the pudgy lady with the platinum perm squeeze and smooch. Mo? People who call my mother "Mo" instead of

"Monica" generally live to regret it. *I'm not one of the Three Stooges* is how she corrects the ignorant.

Mom and "Aunt" Millie jig hand in hand, oblivious to me and the one other customer in the place, a guy about my age with scruffy reddish-brown hair. For moral support if nothing else, I move casually toward his booth with the tabletop jukebox.

He nods in a friendly down-home way. "Hi, I'm Nate."

"I'm Rinn."

"You want a Coke or something?"

"Okay. Thanks."

The guy vaults the counter, grabs a glass, shoots cola into it from a spigot, then hops back over to hand it to me. Meanwhile, Mom and Aunt Millie lunge into a cheerleader routine, guaranteed to stop traffic—if there *was* any traffic:

One! Two! Three! Four! Who's the team worth fightin' for?
River Hills! River Hills! *Go*, HAWKS!

"Yikes. Laverne and Shirley," I say as scruffy guy slides back into the booth.

"Who?"

Obviously no cable TV around here, either. "Just an old show I used to watch with my grandmother."

"Used to?"

"She died." I crumple a straw wrapper.

"Sorry. When?"

"Three months and fourteen days ago."

Unfazed by my precision, he repeats, "Sorry."

Me, too.

"So, you come here often?" I bat my eyes, trying to be funny, and trying to ignore the Ya-Ya sisters.

He misses this joke, too. "Yeah, Miss Millie makes the best onion rings. Plus you get free refills on your drinks."

Oh, help. This is far worse than any *Happy Days* episode. This is Mayberry, folks, and Opie Taylor just bought me a Coke. Except Opie Taylor wasn't *nearly* this cute.

I suck my straw, thrilled that Coke tastes the same in Ohio as it does in California, then splutter when Millie swoops down and yanks me out of the booth.

"Rinn!" She crushes me in a sweaty hug. "Oh my Lord, Mo's baby girl. A spittin' image, too. Oh, just look at that *bee-yoo-ti-ful face . . .*"

Opie snorts when Millie grabs my cheeks and whips my head back and forth. Trying not to aspirate on whatever cologne she marinated in, I peel off her fingers before she detaches my skull. "Hi, Millie," I say, skipping the "aunt" nonsense. And no, I'm not a spittin' image of my mom. I'm sorry to say I look nothing like her.

"Oh, wait'll you meet my Tasha. Your ma and me, we had you two right around the same time. Of course, by then I had a ring on *my* finger."

Unperturbed, Mom makes a yammering motion with her fingers and thumb. I hide a smile by wiping my runny nose. That cologne *stinks*.

"My Tasha's a high-diving champ, the best in the county." Millie gestures to a wall covered with pictures of a girl in a swimsuit: on diving boards, thrashing through water, or displaying her trophies. "She won the district title, and regionals are comin' up. Come hell or high water, that girl's bound for the Olympics. In fact—"

"Uh, Miss Millie?" Opie raises his hand like he's in class, not in some refurbished boxcar reeking of grease and cologne. "My onion rings?"

"Oh, shoot. Well, they're no good now. Hey, what's keeping your dad?"

Reluctantly, the dude pushes himself up. "He said to bring 'em over whenever they got here." To Mom he says, "The house you're looking at is just a block from here, ma'am." He extends a hand. "I'm Nate Brenner, by the way."

Mom's own hand halts midway. "Brenner?" She turns sharply toward Millie, but not before Millie's wide rear end disappears into the kitchen. "Oh. *Now* I see."

I slit my eyes at Mom, who heads for the door without another word, then at Nate. "Don't look at me," he protests, and takes the lead.

Outside in the blessedly fresh air, I jog to keep up with Nate's long-legged stride. We catch up to Mom, whose blotchy face tells me she's extremely ticked off at something. As we cross the windy square, I marvel at Nate's choppy hair, wondering how much Clairol it'd take to transform my own black mop into that stunning shade.

"How old are you?" Nate asks.

"Sixteen."

"Junior?" Nate points when I nod. "Well, there's your new school."

Redbrick, two stories tall, River Hills High sits at the north end of the square. Around the corner from the school, Nate stops at the first house on the right: number 521 Cherry Street, a stone colonial with a gray slate roof and no front yard to speak of, only a strip of grass in front of the porch. A turret hugs one side of the house and a FOR RENT sign rattles on the porch railing.

Mom stiffens. "I know this house."

"This ugly house, you mean." Because it is.

"It's the Gibbonses' old place."

"It's still ugly."

I wait for Mom to lose patience again. To demand to know why I can't *pretend* to be excited and how long do I plan to keep this up, etc. Instead, she just stands there while Nate clatters up the steps and into the house.

"Mom?" Her spooked expression makes me nervous. "Who are the Gibbonses?"

"Mrs. Gibbons taught piano. I used to come here for lessons. Her granddaughter and I went to school together—" Abruptly, Mom shuts up, lips pursed either with thought or indecision. Then, springing to life, she trots up to the porch and stops at the door with its stained-glass window.

Bewildered, I join her. "Mom, look." I tap the arm of an old wooden chair. The bowed rockers creak against the leaf-littered porch floor. Mom's a sucker for antiques. "Isn't this great? I bet it's a hundred years—"

The door opens, cutting me off. A man appears. He stares at Mom. Mom stares back.

Then Mom, who reserves profanity for stolen parking spaces, whispers, "Oh, shit."

The man replies grimly, "Got *that* right."

————◦————

It's easy to see that this guy is Nate's dad. He's taller and heavier but with the same square, sexy chin and unruly chestnut hair.

What's not easy to figure out is his reaction to Mom. Or her reaction to *him*.

"Millie never told me this was your house," Mom says after fifteen seconds of silence. "Or that it belonged to Mrs. Gibbons."

"She also never told me the name of my new tenant," Nate's dad growls back.

"I'll kill her."

"Get in line."

Nate shuffles uncomfortably. "Uh, you two know each other?"

"Yes," Mom snaps.

"Not really," his dad snaps back.

"Honey," Mom says to me, "this is Luke Brenner. Luke, this is my daughter, Corinne." She slides her eyes back toward Nate's dad. "I thought you moved to New York."

"I did. I came back."

"Millie never told me."

"We live across the street," Nate adds.

"How nice." Mom stares desperately at me, as if *I* have a clue what's going on here. "Ah, what happened to Mrs. Gibbons?"

"She died last summer," Mr. Brenner says. "Her niece sold the house to me."

"Who are you, the local real estate mogul around here?"

"I have a few properties," Luke says coolly.

Mom replies, equally chilly, "Well, thank you so much. But I think it'd be best if my daughter and I look for another place."

He shrugs. "Suit yourself."

I can't keep quiet any longer. "Another place? We're already here! Can't we look at it at least?"

Mom shakes her head. "Absolutely not. Come on, let's go."

"You won't find anything else in town," Mr. Brenner calls as Mom heads back down the porch steps.

Nate confides to me, "He's not just saying that, either. You can't even rent a garage round these parts."

Abandoning the Brenners, I bounce down after Mom. "Wait! Didn't you hear what they said?"

"I heard." She brakes when I dance in front of her. "Well, we'll just have to drive around, then, till we—"

"Oh no. I am not spending another second in that car." *Let alone sleeping in it tonight if we can't find a place to stay.* Reading her mind, I say fiercely, "And we're not crashing at Millie's. I can't even breathe around her."

"Rinn, listen," Mom begins wearily.

"You won't even look at this house and you won't say why. I mean, it's not *that* grotesque, really. It's just . . ." I peer up at the stone turret, the porthole window near the top staring down like a mirrored eye. "Old," I finish lamely.

Mom vacillates. Luke, seemingly indifferent, waits on the porch with folded arms. Does *he* want us to leave, too? Nate, now settled on the porch railing, looks as clueless as me.

Finally, Mom sighs. "Fine. One look."

Nate winks. I don't wink back. As cute as he is, no point in cozying up if Mom plans to drag me off to the wild blue yonder again.

—◇—

"It's furnished," Mom notes. "Millie never mentioned that."

Millie never mentioned a lot of things, I think. Never mentioned who used to live here—whatever *that's* about. Never mentioned Luke. Boy, I'm glad I'm not Millie; I can tell Mom's still seething under her courteous demeanor.

The living room's small and smells funky, but is warm and pretty under the dust. A beat-up steamer trunk instead of a coffee table sits between a fireplace and a flowered sofa. My sneakers pad on the worn rug as I follow Mom, and then . . . I stop short.

A piano.

Mom stops, too, and trails her fingers across the chipped, yellowed keys. "It's the same one I took lessons on."

The keys tinkle softly. I draw a quick breath as it hits me: this is the first time since Nana died that Mom's gone *near* a piano.

Weirdness descends. I can't put a name to it. Now I'm sorry I insisted we see the inside of this place. No, I don't want to traipse around looking for somewhere else to live. But do I really want to stay in a dead woman's house? Eat off her dishes? Sleep in her bed?

Mom doesn't want to. She's made that pretty clear.

Oddly, I'm kind of liking this house. But I want, I *need*, my mom to be happy. So I poke her. "Okay. Let's go."

Nate arches his brows. Luke drums his fingers on the mantel. Mom draws away from the piano but ignores my prod. "No. Let's see the rest."

Nothing downstairs, including the kitchen, has seen any remodeling since World War II. But, all in all, it's basically livable. When we backtrack to the living room, Luke exits through the front door with an abrupt, "Take your time. I'll wait outside."

Mom sighs when we catch a whiff of cigarette smoke. "Oh God. I want one."

I scrunch my face, but not because of the cigarette. "I smell cat. Oh, *phew!*"

"Yeah, she had a bunch of them," Nate throws back as he starts upstairs.

I sneer. "Ya think?"

Pinching my nose, I plod after Mom and Nate. Two bedrooms on the second floor, both sparsely furnished, one with a canopy bed. The bathroom reeks of leftover BENGAY. Even *that* beats cat pee.

Nate notices Mom aim her radar at the clawfoot tub. "Yeah, it needs cleaning. But my dad wasn't planning on renting it out this soon."

Mom smiles thinly. "Let's see the attic."

Again last in line, I climb to the third floor fighting a rush of exhaustion. My meds do this to me around two o'clock every day, which is one of the reasons I hate taking this stuff.

An antidepressant.

A mood stabilizer.

A mild antipsychotic.

Klonopin, to prevent panic attacks.

Oh, and birth control pills so I don't present Mom with any deformed grandchildren. Not that I've had much sex lately. Or any.

I drag myself up by the wooden banister and stop in surprise. One *huuuge* room with newly painted white walls, one with built-in bookshelves, and a hardwood floor. A row of dark beams cross the peaked ceiling. The room tapers off to a rounded recess, that funny old turret I noticed outside.

"Cool!" I spring toward it. With its stone walls and cozy porthole, it's the perfect place to curl up with a book or play my guitar. As for the rest of the room, there's no furniture, no bathroom, not even a closet, but—"I love it! I can't even smell the cat pee up here."

"It's all fresh drywall," Nate says proudly. "The walls were in pretty bad shape."

"This is the best, best room!" I whirl back to Mom. "What? What're you thinking?"

"I'm not sure." Mom nibbles her lip. "It needs *so* much cleaning . . ."

"I'll help," Nate offers. "My dad and me, we can get it done in no time."

I smile sweetly. "May we have some privacy?" I don't have to ask twice. As soon as he's gone, I face Mom. "Mom, I *saw* how you looked at that piano."

"You can get a piano anywhere, honey."

"But it's like Nana's piano." Her name clings to my throat.

"No, it's not. It's only similar."

I think of Nana's, that old upright monstrosity with carved panels, scuffed pedals, and a scrolled music stand ingrained with gold. That piano swallowed up half of Nana's living room. She kept houseplants on the top, and her favorite photos. *When I die, Rinn*, she said, *this piano will go to you.*

Nana died too soon. Nobody inherited the piano.

"*Mm*, I don't know," Mom muses. "Do *you* like it?"

"Only if I get this room."

"This is an attic, not a bedroom."

"Mom, I *looove* this room. I can paint the walls myself, and there's space for my posters, and all I really need is a bed and someplace to stick my clothes, and . . ." I stop at her funny expression. "What?"

"Rinn. Did I just hear you say you 'love' this room?"

"Yes! And if we can get that cat stink out, I'll love the whole frickin' house." I bite my tongue to hold back the rest: *And since YOU'RE the one who dragged me away from my life, the least you can do is let me have it!* "Why don't you want to stay here? Is it that Luke guy?" I delight when her face flames up. "Was he your boyfriend? Did he dump you? Omigod, he did! That creep!"

Mom holds her palm out flat. "Rinn, please. Let me think about this for a minute."

◄○►

This is why I love my mom to pieces: if it were solely up to her—which technically it is—no *way* would she move into some decrepit old house where her now-dead, cat-crazy piano teacher once lived. What a contrast to our stucco ranch home in La Jolla, with its L-shaped pool surrounded by palm trees. An ultracontemporary house only minutes from civilization, meaning Nordstrom's, two bookstores, Starbucks, and the beach.

But when I said I loved that attic room, something changed in Mom's face, like she couldn't believe how psyched up I was. Like, *Who is this happy person, and what did she do with my sullen, smartass daughter?*

So, a half hour later, Mom and Luke, barely speaking, pore over legal documents while Nate and I hang around outside. I claim the porch rocker. Nate's long legs straddle the railing. "Looks like we're gonna be neighbors," he remarks.

"Don't worry. I won't make you carry my books to school."

"Thanks," he says seriously. "So, you're from California, huh? Do you surf?"

"A bit." I hug my knees, wishing I were back on the beach, in a bikini, squishing sand through my toes. It's freaking cold here and it's only October. "Did you know the lady who lived here?"

"Sure. Everyone did."

"How did she die? Old age?"

". . . Uh, yeah. Old age."

I zero in on his hesitation. "What? Was she murdered?"

"Murdered? Are you nuts?"

Don't ask me that. "Then what really happened? Or are you trying to scare us off?"

"Why would I do that?"

I jerk my chin toward the house. "Because of that stuff between your dad and my mom? Maybe your dad put you up to it, to get rid of us." Not that Nate's been alone with him since Mom and I showed up.

"I don't know anything about that, besides which I couldn't care less."

"So how *was* she murdered?" I badger, enjoying his fluster.

Nate jiggles his feet. "Anybody ever tell you what a pain in the ass you are?"

Before I can defend myself, I stop the rocker with my heels, riveted by the tinkling of piano keys: Minuet in G, flowing from Mom's fingers. I peek through the window and spy Mom, sitting in perfect position at the keyboard. She nods her head in time to the music as Nate's father gathers up the papers—a done deal, I'm sure.

This is the first time Mom's played the piano in three months and fourteen days.

This is a sign. We belong in this house.

———◄○►———

After Luke invents some excuse to drive "to the city"—which gives me hope there's humanity nearby—Nate helps us unload the SUV, lugging box after box as if they weigh nothing at all. We snipe back and forth in jest, though a voice inside me—*no, not a "voice," a "thought"*—warns me not to get too comfortable with this guy. Nate's cute, and fun, but he likes to bait me too much.

Like when he picks up my vintage guitar, a gift from Frank, ignoring my insistence that nobody touches it but me. "Ooh, possessive, are we?"

I snatch for it, but Nate's a good foot taller than me. "It's a Gibson Les Paul!"

"Get out. Do you play?"

"Duh."

He hands it back with a smile. "So play something, surfer girl."

"Sorry, farmer boy. I don't play on command."

I can't afford to let down my guard like this. Plus, what with all the miscellaneous stuff thrown around, I'm worried he'll notice something—maybe a self-help book or a prescription bottle—and put two and two together, and come up with a big fat *Oh hell, she IS nuts!*

People cannot find out about me. The idea that nobody

knows me in River Hills was the only reason I didn't complain *that* much about leaving La Jolla. Mom, on the other hand, says I shouldn't try keep my "illness" a secret. Meaning it might be wiser to give people a heads-up so they'll think twice before siccing the cops on me when they find me, oh, I don't know . . . walking naked on rooftops?

I tumble onto the sofa, leaving Nate and Mom to finish unloading. "Can we order a pizza?" I ask drowsily when the door slams one last time. "I'm starved."

"You can order one," Nate says. "Good luck getting it delivered."

Mom adds, "Millie's bringing over some sandwiches. Tomorrow we'll stock up on groceries. You're welcome to stay for dinner," she tells Nate. "You were a big help today." When Nate declines and heads for home, Mom pushes my legs aside so she can sit with me. "I didn't know Luke had a wife, let alone a son."

"All those times you talked to Millie? You never asked about him?"

Mom hesitates. "Not really. And to tell you the truth, if I'd known Luke would be our landlord, and that *this* was the house Millie meant, I might have, ah, come up with a Plan B."

"Okay, so Luke's a prick because he dumped you—"

"Rinn, your mouth."

"—but why *not* this house? I mean, once you get past the cat pee and that bathtub, it's kind of cool, right?"

"What I meant was"—she avoids my heavy-lidded stare—"maybe we'd be better off with an apartment."

I narrow my eyes. *Was* old Mrs. Gibbons murdered? Is that why Mom's so ambivalent? I wish I could ask her, but I'm afraid to mention the word "murder" or even "death." What if she thinks about Nana and loses it again?

Brightening, Mom slaps my thigh. "Why don't you go take a nap? I'll wake you when Millie gets here with the sandwiches."

"I can nap right here. I am not sleeping on somebody else's mangy old mattress."

"Fine. I'll buy you a new one tomorrow."

I hug her then. "Aw, thanks, Mommy!"

"And Monday we'll get you registered for school. Are you nervous? I am."

I bet. She's been a stay-at-home mom since I was eight, when she married Frank and let him adopt me. Frank's a retired music producer. He knows all the old rock stars, and he's the one who taught me how to play the guitar. Now she's stuck being a high school secretary. Poor Mom.

Poor me, too. Because if I get sick again, I'll go through that same old crap. People avoiding me. People talking about me. People either making fun of me to my face or too scared of me to walk down the same hall.

"If I hate it," I whisper, "can I quit?"

"No." Mom squeezes me tightly, then smooths back my hair. "You can't quit. Not this time."

———◁◇▷———

I can barely stay awake long enough to take my pills. I crawl back on the sofa while Mom putters with boxes. Just as I drift into that funny zone where you're not quite awake but not exactly asleep, Millie shows up with sandwiches and soda, which is called "pop" around here. Mom thanks Millie with a definite edge to her voice.

Snatches of their argument, taken to the front porch, penetrate my fog of exhaustion.

Stuff about Millie not being "up front" about this house *or* about Luke Brenner.

Millie ranting about how people "change" and that she and Mom are perfect examples.

Mom insisting that she *should have been told* before driving cross-country to find out, too late, for herself.

Millie then spouts some cliché about water under the bridge. Mom protests, so Millie tells her flat out, "Oh, Mo. Grow up."

How funny to hear someone say that to your mom.

3 MONTHS + 14 DAYS ——————

Sunday, October 19

No telephone service means a trip to Millie's in the morning. I wolf down orange juice and toast while Mom uses the Boxcar's phone to make calls, including one to Frank to warn him about the significant charges on his Visa. Not that Frank cares; in fact, he offered to fly us to Ohio and ship the SUV separately, but Mom thought the trip would give us some special mother-daughter time, or whatever.

I wish she'd stop feeling so guilty. Really, *none* of this is her fault.

I wait for Frank to ask to speak to me. When Mom hangs up without inviting me to the phone, the toast in my stomach forms a nasty rock.

Back at the house, we see Nate—jacketless, apparently immune to the chill—raking leaves off his lawn. When he bends over to scrape them into a Hefty bag, his shirt rides up. I stare at his bare golden back, the waistband of his shorts . . . *o-mi-god!*

"Nate!" Mom calls, startling me.

Dropping the bag, Nate approaches. I glance off to one side, wishing he weren't so dastardly adorable. Wondering if he'll be in any of my classes. If he has a girlfriend. If he *really* thinks I'm a pain in the ass, or was that his country-bumpkin way of coming on to me?

"If you're not too busy, can we borrow you for a while? Rinn needs a bed, and we could use your muscles."

Ohh, did she have to say "Rinn" and "bed" in the same sentence to some hot guy I'll be seeing in school every day?

"If it's not too much trouble," she adds sweetly.

Please, please, say no! I do not want to take a one-hour road trip to the nearest furniture store with Nate Brenner and his divinely handsome self. But Mom tosses her dark blond hair and heads for the SUV without bothering to wait for a yes or a no.

"Bossy," Nate notes. "She'll fit right in at school."

I slip into what I hope sounds like a redneck twang. "So why don'tcha tell her yah got chores to do?"

"Why, that'd be right unneighborly," he drawls back.

I hop into the front seat, Nate into the back. Nate smells like dried leaves and sweat, but nice. I send thank-you vibes to Mom for scrubbing the tub last night so I could bathe and wash my hair this morning. As I sniff my collar to see if I picked up any cat smells, Mom points to the notepad she keeps in the console. "Let's make a grocery list. There's a pen in my purse."

As I dig for the pen, the rattle of a Tylenol container almost stops my heart.

Oh, crap—my meds!

I forgot them.

Now, any other time Mom would've nagged me at least

twice. Today, the *one friggin' day* it slips my mind, she says nothing. Should I ask her to turn back? How? There's no clever way to work it into the conversation for fear it'll turn out like this:

ME: *Mom, turn around. I forgot my pills.*
NATE: *What pills?*
ME: *Oh, just all my antipsychotics so I don't, ya know, start hearing voices. Or slash my throat. Or kill somebody again.*

I clamp my mouth shut.

———◦————

In the nearby town of Westfield, we find a marked-down mattress in a family-owned "value" store, namely, a musty warehouse jammed with the leftover rejects no self-respecting retailer would stock. Mom says I can use the canopy bed if she can get "someone" to drag it up to the third floor. Of course she means Nate, who just hoisted the mattress effortlessly to the roof of the SUV and tied it with rope.

"I don't want a canopy bed." That is so not me. "I'll just put it on the floor."

We then stop at Walmart for a lamp and an extra phone for my room. Linens, pillows, and other household junk. School supplies. An iPod dock because my computer's in California. And a fake-wood desk, unassembled in a box, that Nate promises to put together for me.

"Paint," I remind Mom. "Those white walls have to go."

Nate objects, "Hey, it took me three days to paint that room."

I smile pleasantly. "Bet you can do it again in two."

After I choose a lovely shade of gray called Precious Pewter, Mom tells Nate to pick out a CD to thank him for his help. Nate protests, "Aw, that's not necessary. It was my pleasure." I smother a giggle. "What?" he asks crossly.

"You're just so gosh darn *nice*."

"Why does that sound like an insult?" he wonders.

Later, after grocery shopping, Mom asks what we want for lunch. What *I* want is to get back home so I can take those frigging pills! Will a few extra hours make a difference?

"Can't we get something to go?" I ask irritably.

"Fine with me." Nate, squashed beside me in the front seat, since there's no room left in back, studies his new CD. I don't recognize the band. I prefer Frank's music: classic rock. "I got *chores* to do, anyhow."

After a Burger King stop, I nibble a french fry and stare at the dashboard. It's 3:13—unlucky thirteen—and I'm seven hours behind on my meds. "I hope we don't have to make this trip every week. Isn't there a grocery store in town?"

"Sure there is," Nate replies. "Right on the square next to the feed store. But it's not open on Sundays."

"People in Hicksville don't eat on Sundays?"

"A'course we eat," he agrees in his fake Mayberry drawl. "Matter a'fact, soon's I git home and rustle up some grits, I got me a big ole hog I gotta butcher." He taps the back of my head. "Wanna lend me a hand, surfer girl?"

I can't even smile. *Seven hours late, eight by the time we get home. Do I double up? No, no, that's a bad idea . . .*

I cross my fingers and stare bleakly out the window.

———◦◦———

Home at last, Nate and I lug the mattress to the attic—not an easy task—and drop it on the floor. With only a screwdriver and his bare hands, he throws my new desk together, too. Then he hauls an old chair up from the cellar and wipes it down. Of course I'm grateful, but—*enough already! Go!*

When he finally leaves, I gobble my morning pills. No point in taking another dose later, or chances are I won't wake up tomorrow. Then I settle back with my guitar and strum a while.

My heart's not in it. My heart hasn't been in *anything* since Nana died.

Now Frank's gone, too. Not dead, but he might as well be.

Because I'm dead to him.

I shove my guitar into the turret and Frank out of my thoughts, then crawl under my new comforter that smells like plastic and chemicals. After my eyes adjust, I can make out the shapes of the beams crisscrossing the ceiling.

I imagine one falling on me while I'm asleep.

Did one of them just move? Was that a creak?

My windup alarm clock ticks inches from my head. The only other sounds I hear are a barking dog and a tree scraping the house.

At least I hope it's a tree.

Stop it! Just go to sleep . . .

Unnerved, I rub the scar on my neck. How long can I keep it covered before someone notices? In this climate, in the winter, I can live in turtlenecks. But what about when spring rolls around?

What'll Nate say the first time he sees it?

Oh, who cares? I don't even know if he likes me.

Scrape, scrape . . . scrape, scrape.

That tree branch again. *Or is someone breaking in?*

Is a beam breaking loose, about to slam down on my head?

I throw back my comforter and turn my Walmart lamp back on. Shadows dance. I can't sleep under these beams, not tonight, maybe not ever. I drag my makeshift bed over to the turret, the stony cubby I'd hoped to reserve for books and rainy days. No ghostly beams here, but the mattress doesn't fit.

Resigned, I drag it back. Then I move to the window on the other side of my room. From here, at the top of the house, I see the outline of my new school in the dark. A row of windows near the ground glows with murky yellow light. Then, while I watch, they blink out one by one.

Not a power failure; my own lamp burns behind me. A safe electric lamp that can't cause any fires.

A Debussy tune floats up through the heat register. I tiptoe downstairs and watch my mother's hands dance across the yellowed piano keys. Noticing me, she pats the space beside her. "Can't sleep?"

I shake my head, slide in, and rest my head on her shoulder. "You're not gonna tell them I'm crazy, are you?"

"I told them about your illness in my phone interview." I stiffen. "Honey, I had no choice. If you need a Klonopin during the day, you'll have to see the nurse. I'll give her some to keep on hand. You can't carry drugs around, especially stuff like that."

"Thanks a lot. Now everyone in school will know my business."

"It's confidential," she promises. "It's the law, Rinn. The nurse doesn't know your diagnosis. The paper from Dr. Edelstein just says 'for anxiety.'"

"*You* work in the office. Why can't I get them from you?"

"We have to follow the rules. Do you want your friends to think I'm playing favorites?"

What friends? I may not make a single one.

Mom kisses my cheek. "Go back to bed. We've got a big day tomorrow."

The melody starts up again before I reach the stairs. Keys tinkle beneath her expert fingers, and she pumps the pedals in her socks, nodding dreamily.

Instead of climbing back to my attic room, I curl up on the landing, on the newly sanitized floor, and listen to the music till I drop off to sleep.

3 MONTHS + 15 DAYS ⸻

Monday, October 20

The principal, Mr. Norman Solomon, peers curiously at Mom. "Well, Monica Parker. Seems like only yesterday you and Millie were making out with boys under the bleachers."

"Well, thank you very much," Mom says tersely. "Anything else about my sordid past you'd care to share with my daughter?" As if I don't already know how wild she was. Am I not living proof?

Thankfully, Mom and Mr. Solomon lapse into pleasantries. Bored, I yawn into my hand, and then jump when someone raps on the office door. A girl with a blond ponytail pokes her head in. "Sorry, Mr. Solomon, but Ms. Faranacci told me to hand this to you *personally*."

"Thank you, Meg." Mr. Solomon tosses the folder on his desk and scratches his heavy beard. "By the way, do me a favor? This is Miss Parker, er, Mrs. Jacobs. She's taking over for Miss

Prout. And this is her daughter, Corinne. How'd you like to show her around? I'll let Ms. Faranacci know."

"Sweet! Thanks!" Meg smiles with perfectly straight teeth, while I self-consciously poke my one crooked canine with my tongue. Still, glad to escape, even with a miniversion of my mom, I leap to my feet. She confides on the way out, "Let me tell you something, that Miss Prout was a bitch. If you called in sick? She'd call your house all day long to make sure you were there. And if you didn't answer, she'd march over and *check*."

Less leery of her now that she used the word "bitch," I follow her down a hall flanked with bland beige lockers. Big classrooms, I note, peeking into one, with real blackboards and wooden desks bolted to the floor.

Meg slaloms along, arms widespread. "Where'd you go to school before this?"

"California."

"Really? Why'd you move here?"

"It was my mom's idea."

"What about your dad?"

Questions already. It's not even officially my first day.

"I guess they're getting a divorce," I say slowly.

"That sucks. But who picked *this* place?" Meg persists as we clatter up a flight of steps. "I mean, nobody moves *to* River Hills. You live here and die here, or else you leave and don't come back."

"Well, my mom grew up here, and she kept in touch with her best friend—"

"Who?"

"Millie Lux?"

"Oh, Miss Millie, the Onion Ring Goddess. Her daughter Tasha's my best friend."

Unsure why I'm telling a perfect stranger my business, but pleased to have someone to talk to who isn't, well, Mom, I continue. "Anyway, Millie told her about this job, so Mom called up that same day and they hired her over the phone."

Meg snickers. "That's 'cause nobody else wants it."

"Next thing I know she's throwing crap into suitcases." Quickly, while I've got the chance, I ask a question of my own. "What happened to Miss Prout?"

"Beats me. She didn't show up for work one day. She just disappeared."

Interesting.

I follow Meg through the doors into the second-floor hall, and I literally trip over someone slouched on the floor. He glowers up at me through long, messy hair, iPod wires trailing from his ears.

"Whoa!" Meg feigns surprise. "Thrown out again? I bet you set a new record."

Yanking off one earbud, the guy locks onto my face with eyes blacker—and redder—than a TV vampire's. "Greetings, earthling." Sinewy, sinister, with stubble on his chin and his black hair hiding half his foxy face, *this* is the kind of guy I normally end up with. Certainly not with studly farm boys in flannel like Nate Brenner.

Meg's nudge disrupts my fascination. "Meet Dino Mancini, class idiot. Dino, this is Corinne. She starts tomorrow."

"Rinn," I correct her. I smell marijuana. I doubt it's coming from Meg.

Dino bares his teeth. "Welcome to the Underworld, *my precioussss!* Lucky for you, you missed the virgin sacrifices." He nods at Meg. "You're next, babe."

Meg flicks out her tongue. "Don't you wish?"

He pinches Meg's calf. "How come *you* get to cut and no one gives *you* a rash of shit?"

She kicks him away. "I'm not cutting. I'm showing her around."

"Cool. Don't forget to show her where Annaliese hangs out."

"Yeah, *right.*" Abandoning Dino, Meg pulls me down the hall, pointing left and right. "Okay, classroom . . . and another classroom . . . and, oh, look, another classroom!"

Surprising myself, I fall into the game. "Wow, show me more!"

"Oh, if you insist. Maybe, if we're lucky, we can find *more* rooms downstairs!"

I like this girl!

We reach the first floor again in a fit of giggles. I hug the banister, gasping for breath. "Who's Annaliese?"

"You'll find out."

Meg leads the way into a cavernous, currently unoccupied cafeteria. Neck and neck, we race across the room and burst through a pair of doors into a gym. Running through that, too, we hit another set of doors that open to an auditorium.

"We're not allowed to do this," Meg says breathlessly. "Cut through the gym like that. We're supposed to use the tunnel. C'mon, I'll show you."

We gallop down the aisle to a stage with shabby red curtains. Off to the side, because the stage area is so low, four steps lead up to the mysterious tunnel. Not a *real* tunnel, it turns out—just a narrow corridor running parallel to the auditorium, gym, and cafeteria. But the stone walls and dim lighting give it a creepy, claustrophobic effect.

Meg points to a second door directly across from the auditorium door. "The pool's in there. But they're gonna tear it all out and build a media center soon." She kicks the door open. "It's supposed to be locked, but people break in all the time, so nobody bothers to fix the lock. But if King Solomon catches you in here, you're screwed."

Snickering at the nickname, I follow her in. She flips a switch but nothing happens; the only light comes from the small windows along the far wall.

"They added on this room back in the seventies. For the pool," Meg explains.

A chain-link fence prevents us from walking more than six feet into the room. When Meg shakes it, the sound cracks the air like shattering glass. I squint through the metal links and spy the dark slash of the empty pool. "Why the fence?"

"Duh, so we don't fall in and sue?" The rattling links shiver into silence. A funny chill penetrates my sweater. "By the way," Meg whispers, "don't ever come in here alone, or even go through that tunnel. Always take someone with you."

I force a straight face. *Hello, slasher movie!* "Why?"

Meg points through the fence. "Because of Annaliese."

"What is she, a rat?" Because I definitely hear scrabbling.

"No, some girl who drowned here, like, twenty years ago, or whatever."

"Wait. You're talking about a ghost?"

Meg nods seriously. "Yeah. Her grandmother sued when it happened, so they shut down the pool for good. Anyway, her grandma died a while back, and—"

My arms prickle. *Another dead grandmother.* "Died how?"

Meg wordlessly jerks a fist above her head.

"She hung herself?"

She nods again, then rubs her arms hard. "God, it's cold in here."

"It's drafty," I say, sorry I asked how the old lady died. Now it'll stick with me all day.

"It's *freezing.*"

I shiver, too, realizing she's right. Unmoving, I feel the air around me grow colder with each passing second.

Meg cups her nose. "Rinn. What is that?" She sniffs like a puppy. "The air in here, it's like greasy or something." She touches her nose. "This is too *weird . . .*"

All *I* feel is very cold air and no, nothing greasy or weird about it. I watch her scratch her ears and then bat her hands around like she's trying to grab hold of the atmosphere. Is she playing me?

"What the hell's going on?" she quavers. "You seriously don't feel that?"

"No!" But Meg's panic is contagious; in ten seconds flat I'm out the door and across the tunnel and back in the auditorium. After that ice-cold pool room, it's like being tossed into a sauna.

Meg scampers out behind me and eyes me then with peculiar interest. "Wow, you're fast!"

"Yeah, when people scare the *hell* out of me."

"You don't do track or anything, do you? Good. So you want to try out for the squad? Cheerleading," she explains, like

I haven't already guessed. "I'm captain this year, and we could *really* use an extra body. Can you do the splits? Cartwheels? Oh, never mind, we can teach you in no time—"

Her blue eyes widen when I cup my hand over her mouth. "I can't be a cheerleader."

Her lips move. "*Whuh nuh?*"

"Because my mother was one, and I don't want to be ranting about it twenty years from now, like it was the best time of my life. And no, I can't do a cartwheel, I don't have a rah-rah personality, and I am *not* jumping around flashing my underwear. Got it?"

Meg unpeels my slick hand. "So, like, is that a definite no? Or do you want to think about it some more?"

She might be relentless, but I really do like her.

3 MONTHS + 16 DAYS ———————

Tuesday, October 21

You never told me the school's *haunted*."

"Haunted?" Mom repeats, pouring her fourth cup of coffee. She's up to two pots a day since she ditched the cancer sticks. "Not in my day."

"Well, Meg knows about it. So does some kid we met in the hall." I dribble milk over my Cocoa Puffs and swirl with my spoon. "It's, like, common knowledge."

Mom comes shockingly close to rolling her eyes, something she typically rags on me for doing. "Do you want me to remind you that ghosts don't exist? Or are you hoping I'll humor you so you won't be so nervous?"

"I am not nervous. But I will be, if you keep bringing it up."

"Sorry." She plunks her mug into the sink and grabs her sweater off the hook in the back hall. "I have to run. I should've been there ten minutes ago. Now remember, homeroom starts at seven forty-five—"

"I know, I know. You told me twenty times."

"—so don't be late."

"Why?" I drawl. "You gonna mark me tardy?"

Mom blows me a kiss and leaves. I sit there for a moment, poking at my Cocoa Puffs, then clunk down my spoon.

I lied. I'm nervous.

Upstairs, my room reeks of fresh paint; I slapped on the first coat yesterday after my school tour. I dress quickly in a black turtleneck, gray skirt, red tights, and black socks. Back downstairs, I stuff a notebook into my hobo bag, an illicit Klonopin into my pocket, and then halt, midstep, when I hear footsteps on the porch.

Creeping footsteps. Someone who knows I'm alone?

I can't even call 9-1-1. Our phone won't be turned on till later.

The rocker creaks outside. Shoe soles shuffle through stray leaves on the porch floor. I slink over to the sofa, kneel on the cushion, and part Mrs. Gibbons's lace curtains with a single fingertip. Then I hammer my fist hard—*bang-bang!*—on the windowpane.

"God*damn!*" Nate Brenner all but ducks for cover.

Triumphant, I rush to the front door. "Why're you creeping around on my porch?"

Red-faced, Nate snarls, "I'm not creeping. I'm *waiting*."

"Waiting for me? Isn't it customary around here to knock? Or at least yell 'yoo-hoo'?"

He stares incredulously. "You scared the hell out of me."

"Yeah, and I made you take the Lord's name in vain, too," I tease.

Unamused, Nate flings up a hand and clomps down to the sidewalk. Wow. He's *mad.*

I shove my feet into Mom's pointy-toed ankle boots, all I can find in our jumble of yet-unpacked boxes—anything's better than my smelly plaid Keds—and run to catch up with him. "Sorry I scared you. That was, well, right neighborly of you to wait for li'l ole me."

Instead of a snappy comeback, Nate says, "That was funny the first few times."

"Wow, aren't *you* the crabby one today?"

"Yeah, well . . ." But he can't keep a straight face, and he obviously forgives me because then he adds, "You need any help today, just gimme a holler."

"How'll I find you?"

"Easy. I'll be the dude surrounded by all the fawning chicks."

I poke him. "You're a wee bit too full of yourself, farmer boy."

"Look who's talking, in them highfalutin boots and that fancy Sunday getup."

"Guess you ain't used to citified folk," I point out.

Merrily, he agrees, "Guess I jest ain't," and steers me toward the school doors.

————◄o►————

Things don't go as horribly as I'd expected. School is school, whether it's La Jolla or River Hills or Antarctica or Belize. You file into class after class, the teacher takes attendance, and then you fall into a coma.

This year I'll try to skip the coma part. It'd be nice to receive a diploma while I'm still in my teens.

River Hills doesn't seem as cliquey as my school in La Jolla, but people do fall into certain groups. Jocks, mostly guys, with their cheerleader counterparts. A circle of preps. The obvious burnouts, including that guy from the hall, Dino Mancini. Farm kids who ride the bus in from the sticks. A couple of nobodies, ignored by everyone. No surfers, goths, Barbies, or rockers.

Rinn Jacobs, I guess, fits in nowhere.

I'm not athletic unless I'm in a saddle. My grades are average, so scratch the preps. Scratch the burnouts, too—*my* drugs are legal. And by the way people stare at my so-not-from-River Hills clothes, I know I'll never fade off into the nobody group.

Just like before, there's no Crazy Person clique.

I hate how the teachers introduce me to each class and then add that my mom's the new office secretary, like *that's* going to win me points. I make it through history with poker-faced Ms. Faranacci and then it's off to chorus with jolly Mr. Chenoweth. After that, I hit the art class I'm taking instead of Spanish or German, and this semester it's Intro to Ceramics. I spend fifteen minutes squishing clay to "get the feel of it" as Mr. Lipford puts it.

Because it's a multigrade class, Meg, who's a senior, shares a table with me. Cecilia Carpenter, a heavyset girl I recognize from chorus, is also here. So is Dino Mancini, watching me from the next table.

No, not watching: *studying* me.

Unsettled, I try to ignore him and concentrate on my clay. Eventually, though, even Meg notices. "Wow," she whispers. "He can't take his eyes off you."

Mr. Lipford picks that moment to stroll out of the room. Dino instantly hops up and slips over to Meg and me to crouch between our chairs. "Hey—Rinn, right? See, I remembered."

"Whoopee," Meg says brightly, pounding her own blob of clay.

"You got lunch next? Yeah? You want to meet me outside? I'll show you around . . ."

Meg whaps him with an elbow. "Forget it. She's eating with *us*."

Exasperated, he snaps, "I ain't *talking* to you, Carmody."

I shush them both and shoot a nervous look toward the door, never mind that everyone else is starting to act up as well. And, catching the scent of pot in Dino's dark, messy hair, I can pretty much guess what he wants to show me. "Uh, thanks. But I really need something to eat."

His disappointment is so obvious, I almost feel sorry for him—but then Mr. Lipford reappears at the door. "Back in your seat, Mancini. *Now*." Dino rises, taking his sweet time about it, and returns to his own table to stare at me some more.

———◦———

When the bell rings, Meg and I meet up with Lacy Kessler—a fellow cheerleader, with colorfully streaked hair—and Tasha Lux, Millie's high-diving darling. "Guys, this is Rinn. She's eating with us."

I smile gratefully when no one objects. I watch for Nate as we circle a table, but, sad to say, it looks like we don't share the same lunch period.

Lacy tosses her mass of curls when she learns I'm from California. "Poor you, ending up in a place like *this*."

"I'll get used to it." Though I'm not swearing on any bibles.

"Hey! Do you cheer?"

"I already asked," Meg interjects, with a reproachful look for me. "She said no."

Tasha asks, "Do you swim? Gymnastics?"

"I'm not much into sports . . ."

"What *do* you do?" Lacy demands.

"Well . . ." I can't believe I have to think so hard about this. "I play the guitar. I sing a bit."

Unimpressed, Lacy moves along. "So you guys moved into the old Gibbons house, huh?"

I nod, and the three girls exchange glances before facing me directly: Lacy, slyly; Tasha with mild alarm; and Meg, flushed, with an apologetic smile.

"Is that significant of something?" I ask Meg when nobody else speaks.

Meg's smile wavers. "I started to tell you yesterday, in the tunnel, remember? About—"

"I told you *not* to," Tasha interrupts. "My mom said to wait."

I prickle with suspicion. "What do you mean, your *mom* said to wait?"

Meg scoots closer. "Remember when I told you about Annaliese?"

"Right. The ghost." I cross my eyes. "Yeah, you won that one."

Meg insists, "Hey, I wasn't joking about that air," only to be interrupted by Lacy, who blurts out, "I can't believe nobody told you you're living in Annaliese's *house*."

"What?" I jerk to face Meg.

"Well . . . her *grandmother*'s house," Meg admits.

"But you said her grandmother—" I stop as the truth dawns. *Her granddaughter and I went to school together*, Mom had said.

"Hung herself," Lacy finishes with a satisfied grin. "Yep, she sure did. Right in the attic."

———◄○►———

I pop my contraband Klonopin under my tongue in a bathroom stall. If I wait for it to kick in, I'll be late for my next class, but at this point I don't care. I'll ask Mom for a pass.

Must. Talk. To. Her. Anyway!

But when I stop at the office, Mom's not there. Some snotty senior is manning the desk, a student assistant name badge—LINDSAY MCCORMICK—dangling from a lanyard.

"She's in a meeting with Mr. Solomon," Lindsay drones, intent on the book in her lap.

"It's urgent. I'm her daughter."

"I know who you are. I can give her a message."

"I'm sure you can," I say politely. "But I really need to speak with her myself."

Lindsay shrugs. "Come back in half an hour, they'll be done by then."

I resist the urge to fly over the counter. Instead, I turn and walk, unsteadily, out to the hall. By the time I make it to PE, I've come to my senses. If Mom doesn't know Mrs. Gibbons hung herself in our house—not just in our house, but in *my* freaking bedroom—maybe it's best she not find out while she's still on the clock.

———◄○►———

By the end of the day I have three official friends: Meg, Lacy, and Tasha. Four, if you count Nate Brenner.

Five, if you count Dino Mancini, who dogs me down the school steps after the last bell. "Hey, Rinn. Can I walk you home?"

It might be nice to have someone to hang out with after school, but I'm not sure that someone should be Dino Mancini. In the old days he'd have my pants off in a second. Why tempt fate? "Well, I just live right over there . . ."

"Yeah, I know. I'll walk you, anyhow. Nice boots," he adds, staring briefly at my feet. Then he raises his eyes slowly, too slowly. And I know that hungry look too well.

I whip my head around when someone touches my shoulder.

"Hey," Nate greets Dino. "What's up?"

Dino hesitates. "Nothin'."

Nate's hand tightens on my shoulder. Dino notices. He sends Nate a dirty look, me a sad little wave, and slouches off.

"My pleasure," Nate says, though I haven't thanked him yet. "How'd it go today?"

"Oh, just lovely. Why didn't you *tell* me she hung herself in my room?"

Happily, I caught him off guard. "You mean Mrs. Gibbons?"

"Hel-*lo*? You told me she died of old age."

"No, *you* said she died of old age. I just kind of agreed with you." I splutter, and he takes my wrist, maneuvering me away from the crowded walk. "Look, my dad asked me not to mention it, because Miss Millie asked *him* not to mention it to your mom."

"That's unethical. Can't he lose his license for misleading people? For lying by *omission*?"

Nate scoffs. "It's not like the Mansons camped out there.

Some depressed old lady committed suicide. So what? People die everywhere."

"Then why didn't Millie want my mom to know?"

"Guess you'll have to ask Miss Millie that."

"Oh, stop calling her 'Miss Millie.' That's so, so . . ."

"Hick?" he suggests. "Hayseed? Yokel?"

"All of the above. Oh, forget it." I walk away and head for the corner, but he catches up before I make the bend. *What?*"

"Rinn." He sounds tired. "Do you want me to apologize for not telling you some old lady hung herself in your attic? Okay, I apologize. Now why don't we go for a walk or something?"

"A walk?"

"A walk."

The last time I went for a "walk" with a guy I hardly knew, I woke up in City Heights, in a very bad neighborhood, minus my purse, plus the dope I'd just scored. "You just met me, Nate. Why're you hanging all over me?"

Nate clenches his jaw so hard I'm surprised he doesn't crack a tooth. "I don't know what it's like where you come from. But first of all, I'm not 'hanging all over' you—I'm headed the same way you're headed, and if you'd rather not walk with me, then say so. Second of all, I was brought up to be nice to people, which I guess is a foreign concept to you. Thirdly—"

"Is that a word? Thirdly?" I ask, hoping to temper his tirade. I didn't mean to hurt his feelings if that's what happened here.

"*Thirdly*, I . . ." He stares at the whirlpool of leaves circling our feet. "For some stupid reason I guess I kinda like you."

Startled, I blurt, "Why?"

"Beats me. Maybe because you're the only girl around

here I haven't known since kindergarten?" He nods at my un-Mayberry-like boots. "You're, uh, interesting. Some folks think that's a crime round these parts."

I'm ridiculously flattered. "You really like me?"

"If you get down off your high horse and lose the attitude, I sincerely might." A lopsided grin. "Now, do you want to take a walk or don't you? I can show you the sights."

I snicker. "Oh, golly, the *sights*! Sorry," I add quickly. "Attitude. I know."

We cross the square, pass the Boxcar Diner—*ooh, I'd like to drop in and dunk Millie's head into her famous deep fryer*—and circle down Main Street, past the high school football field, and back up Walnut Street, where Nate points out Meg's house, a cozy green bungalow. It'll be nice to have a friend who lives so close to me.

As upset as I was earlier to find out about Mrs. Gibbons, spending this time with Nate has calmed me down. Besides, he's right: people die everywhere. Is it such a big deal that somebody died in my new house?

No, not just somebody.

Somebody's *grandmother* committed suicide in my *room*.

"Mom's gonna freak," I say aloud as we cross Main Street again. "About the old lady, I mean. She knew her. She'll probably make us move again."

"I hope not."

"Me, too."

Even though I've only been here three days, the idea of leaving—of packing all those stupid boxes back into the SUV, of abandoning that big turreted room I'm in the middle of painting, not to mention the first friends I've made in years—makes me wants to rip out my hair.

"Let's find out." I break into a run.

———◦———

Mom's home from school by the time we make it back. Nate and I hear her before we even hit the porch.

Yes, she knows. How could she not? Probably the whole town is discussing it by now: *Guess who moved into the old Gibbons house? The new school secretary and that spooky daughter of hers.*

"Dammit, Millie, you had no business keeping that from me!"

I don't hear an answer, which means the phone must be working.

Mom shouts, "I'm talking about Rinn, not me. You know what I've been through with her! Do you have any idea what this might *do* to her?"

Crap, crap. And triple crap.

Nate, riveted, yelps in surprise when I almost knock him off the porch. "Go. *Go!*"

Reluctantly, he follows me to the sidewalk. It's too late, of course. He heard enough. "I'm guessin' there's more to you than meets the eye," he ventures.

"I'd say you guessed right." No point in denying it.

"Care to elucidate?"

I force a smile. "That's a mighty big word coming from you, farmer boy."

"Yup, four whole syllables. I amaze myself."

I fling down my skirt as a gust of wind shoots under my hem. It's terrible to keep such desperate secrets inside you. Worse, how long can these secrets stay secret in a town the size of a San Diego mall? Millie probably knows every sordid detail. It's just a matter of time before she opens her mouth. She'll tell Tasha first, and then Tasha will blab it, and so on and so on.

Unless people already know. *That's* occurred to me, too.

I like Nate. I'd like to be able to trust him.

"I'll tell you about me," I bargain at last, "but only if you tell me what *you* know first. No fudging it."

"Well." Nate fingers his chin. "I didn't hear all that much."

I wait.

"Um, I know your mom and dad are separated and that's why you moved here."

"And?"

"And nothing. That's it."

I blow out a sigh of relief.

"You want to talk about it?" he asks.

No, yes, no, maybe.

"My dad hates me," I say softly.

Just as expected, he argues, "Parents don't hate their kids."

"That's what you think. You don't know Frank." *Or what I did to him.*

"You call your dad Frank?"

"He's my stepdad."

"Even so. I mean, c'mon, Rinn. How could he hate *you*?"

The way Nate says "you" melts the core of my heart. "You called it," I say weakly. "I'm a pain in the ass, remember?"

Mom's distant shrill reaches us again. Nate takes my hand and leads me across the street, the imprint of his fingers warming me. "You want to come in?" he asks.

"I don't know. Am I allowed?"

"Why not?"

Because your dad's car isn't here? And my mom's got a suspicious mind? "Okay."

Nate's house is orderly, and masculine to the hilt. A set of drums takes up the dining room instead of a table. "Those yours?"

"Yep. I'm in the orchestra. Marching band, too. You're taking chorus, right? Guess we'll be seeing each other at rehearsals."

I point to the mangy deer head displayed over the fireplace. "That is *the* most disgusting thing I've ever seen."

"I shot it myself."

"Are you bragging or confessing?"

"Uh, I'll take the Fifth on that one."

On the mantel I see a photo of a woman holding a baby on her lap. The baby looks like Nate right down to the spiky hair. "Your mom? Where is she?" Not hanging out in *this* macho abode.

"New York. My dad met her in college. They moved back here when I was born, but my mom hated it. She left right after that picture was taken. Now she's remarried, has a whole 'nother family and everything."

"You ever see her?"

"Nope," he says distantly. I finger the picture frame, hating the woman who dumped baby Nate, and set it back on the mantel when Nate changes the subject. "So why are you such a pain in the ass that they threw you out of California?" Unexpectedly, he lifts the hair off my neck. "Is it because of this?"

"Don't." I push him away and smooth my hair back down.

"Are you a cutter, Rinn?" he asks gently.

"No. *God*, no. I only did it that one time."

"Why?"

I'm not sure I want to tell him. Then again, shouldn't I be the one to lay it all out, before he finds out from, say, Millie? Or the local paper?

Nate waits. I flatten my hair over my neck and stare at the fireplace, gathering up enough courage to answer his question.

And, when I do, I tell him the truth. "Because I murdered my grandmother. So I wanted to die, too."

—◦—

They diagnosed me as bipolar when I was fourteen.

At first Mom thought I was ADHD. I couldn't focus, couldn't concentrate, could barely sit through a movie. I couldn't finish a book unless I found it interesting, and whatever did interest me instantly became an addiction: ballet, guitar, astrology, you name it. World religions for a while; I was Jewish for six weeks, a Buddhist for two days. Frank drew the line when he caught me chanting on the basement floor inside a perfectly drawn pentagram.

They started me on medication. Ask me if I took it.

I loved the "high" part of being bipolar. I loved being able to research, write, and print out a term paper in one evening, not that anything I wrote made sense. I loved staying awake for days on end, talking to anyone about everything. Of course, nothing I *said* made sense, either. But you couldn't tell me that.

Most of all, I loved breaking rules. I liked cutting school. I liked getting high. I liked sex *way* too much. What's weird is that I didn't realize I was doing anything wrong. I thought everyone else simply wanted to control me.

"I used to sneak out in the middle of the night," I confide to Nate. "I'd go to the beach, or out to the stable where I took riding lessons. I'd take Mom's or Frank's car. They'd never know I was gone, unless the cops brought me back."

Who cared that the stable closed at 9:00 p.m.? Who cared that Chinook, my favorite horse, a speedy Appaloosa, belonged to the stable owners and not to me? Standing in the stirrups, crouched low over his mane, I'd ride him for hours, sailing over rows of white jumps that glowed like tombstones in the moonlight.

One night the floodlights burst on. Startled, two strides from the next jump, I yanked hard on the reins. Chinook veered, slipped in the wet grass, and next thing I knew I was flying solo over the jump. He landed on the ground with a sickening thud.

Police officers descended. If it hadn't been for Chinook, writhing and whinnying, I might've escaped; in manic mode I can outrun anyone. But I couldn't leave him behind. I blubbered into his sweaty sides, screaming *get up, get up!* I remember the pain in my shoulder when the cops hauled me up, ignoring my insistence that "my father *owns* this stable and he's gonna *sue* you pigs!"

When I lunged for an officer's gun, they slapped on the handcuffs and carted me off to jail. Then to the emergency room to fix my broken collarbone. Finally, to the psycho ward.

There, for the first time, I told people about the Voices.

————◄◊►————

So far Nate hasn't jumped off the sofa and run away in terror. "I've heard about bipolar but I didn't know it got that bad. You really hear voices?"

"Not now," I say quickly. "But when I'm really manicky, yes."
Psychotic is a better word, but how can I say *that* out loud? "It's
like, I don't know, like when you hear people talking in another
room? Sometimes they'd get louder if I'd do certain things.
Like if I put on headphones? The voices would drown out the
song. Or maybe I'd think the singer was singing to *me*." I cover
my hot face. "God. I can't believe I'm telling you this."

"So what happened to the horse?"

"Oh, he wasn't hurt. But they banned me from the stable. I
haven't been riding since."

"I have horses," Nate says calmly. "We can go riding sometime."

"You mean you're not terrified of me?"

"Should I be? I mean, you take stuff for it now, right?" I
nod. "And I didn't notice your head spinning one single time
today."

He's laughing, but not *at* me. It's like I just told him I have
mono, and yeah, he's bummed—but he can wait for our first
kiss.

Weak with relief, I lean back into the sofa. Nate's body,
beside mine, feels *sooo* comfortable. I'm not safe yet, though,
because then he asks, "What happened with your grandmother?"

I hesitate. But it's either stay here and talk to Nate, or go
home and listen to Mom's hysterics about how that dead woman
in the attic is sure to traumatize me forever. "Well, there's a few
other things first . . ."

He smiles into my eyes. "We got time."

Does he really want to know about all my so-called boyfriends? Carlos, who taught me how to pick locks and hot-wire

engines? James the dope dealer? Schizophrenic Kyle who said that psych meds were merely tools to force people to conform to society?

Or that once, out of control, I actually *hit* my own mother?

Of course he doesn't. So I skip all that. "I got into so much trouble, they kicked me out of two schools. I almost flunked tenth grade because I was in the hospital so often. When I got out last May, I was doing pretty good. But I was *so mad* at Mom and Frank for locking me up again, I . . . well, things got pretty ugly. So they sent me off to my grandmother's for the summer. She was, like, eighty, but tough, an old army nurse. They figured she'd keep a pretty good eye on me."

I *loved* staying with Nana. Her beach cottage in Carmel was peacefully isolated. Happy to be free from Mom and Frank, I stayed on my meds and did really well. Nana taught me to crochet, and we gardened, and we read books on the beach. Evenings, we'd watch those old sitcoms together. Sometimes we'd make up our own plots. Sometimes we'd even act them out.

Okay, here's the problem: when crazy people feel "good," that's when they decide they don't need drugs anymore. And, as stupid as it sounds, I missed my highs.

I wanted to be me again: the *real* Rinn Jacobs.

"So you quit taking the pills," Nate says without surprise. "Didn't she notice?"

"She trusted me." Her worst mistake ever.

Three months and seventeen days ago, a thunderstorm rolled in and the electricity went out. Nana brought me a kerosene lamp, one we used in emergencies, so I could read in my room.

"She told me to be careful, to turn it off when I was done.

Then she . . ." My throat spasms. "She said, 'See you in the morning, Rinnie, love you,' like she always did. Then she shut the door."

The Voices, strong and cruel, shrilled inside my head with every boom of thunder. Hyped up, paranoid of the shadows dancing in the lamplight, I threw open my bedroom window. Lightning crackled. Salty rain whipped my face. "I knew something terrible was about to happen. But I couldn't tell if the voices were calling me—or trying to warn me away."

"What did they say?" Nate asks quietly.

I remember the satanic chorus ringing in my ears. "They told me to run. So I did."

I climbed out my window and ran like hell. The second I reached the beach, I felt a hundred times better. I splashed through the waves, rain slashing my hair. I spun circles and leaped over rocks, my skin electrified as if by bolts of lightning. The roaring surf blocked out the Voices, and I felt safe, and alive, and positively free. Freer than I'd ever felt gulping down pills every day.

I duck my head. "I can't explain it, but it felt wonderful. Like I was *God* or something . . ." I hug myself hard, cracking my bones. "Then I saw the fire."

Nate's hand creeps closer, as if he wants to hold mine. "The house?"

I nod miserably. "The lamp. I'd left the window open and it blew over in the wind. They found her on the floor outside my room, with a hammer and screwdriver. Hammer marks everywhere. She tried to take the door off, too. She must've thought I was trapped, maybe unconscious. I hadn't answered when she called—"

A tightness in my chest cuts off my words. Wobbly, I grip the arm of the sofa. *Breathe in, breathe out . . .* In a less than gentlemanly gesture, Nate shoves my head to my knees before I can do it myself. Sorry I wasted that Klonopin at school, I squeeze my eyes shut and concentrate only on sucking in enough oxygen to keep from passing out.

It takes a while, but my galloping heart rate returns to normal. The strangling sensation disappears and the stars in my vision dissolve. I'm seriously afraid to look at Nate. I bet he thinks he's witnessing a real psychotic breakdown firsthand.

He surprises me by taking my hand, after all. "You didn't kill her, Rinn."

"Yes I did. If I hadn't snuck out, there wouldn't have *been* a fire. Frank hates me for that—and *that's* why I'm really here. My mom pretends it's to give Frank some more time. But I know he won't forgive me, no matter how sorry I am."

"But your *mom* forgave you," Nate begins.

I shake my head. "Nana was Frank's mom, not hers." I touch my scar. "That's when I did this."

———◦———

Nate offers to walk me across the street, but I tell him no. I don't want him to feel he *has* to be nice, now that he knows who he's dealing with.

"Where have you been?" are the first words out of Mom's mouth. Her fierce hug chokes off my reply. She pushes my hair aside to study my face. "We need to talk." She forces me to sit on the stairs and drops down beside me without once letting go. "Don't worry." She pats my face, my hair, like she's afraid

I'll disappear, or morph back into Psycho Daughter. "We're leaving. Thank God we didn't unpack everything yet . . ."

"But I don't *want* to leave."

"Rinn, a woman just killed herself! I never would've looked at this house if I'd known about that."

"It doesn't bother me," I insist.

"Well, it bothers *me*. Lease or no lease, we're out. We can look for something over in Westfield. It's not too far, and—"

"Westfield? You mean I'll have to change schools? Uh-uh. No way!"

"Rinn, this was only your first day."

"Yes! And I made *friends*." I jump up and point to the ceiling. "What about my room? I'm already painting it!"

"Honey, listen—"

"No, you listen. You're the one who dragged me across the whole frickin' United States. We could've stayed in California. You *wanted* to stay. I heard you tell Millie you wanted to work it out with Frank."

"Were you listening in on my calls?" Mom asks sharply.

"Right, like Millie's voice doesn't carry fifty miles? Admit it, Mom. We only moved here because *she* talked you into it."

Mom wilts under my rock-hard stare. "She thought we could use a fresh start. I *agreed* with her, Rinn. And you know she's my friend. I've missed her all these years."

I sniff. "Some friend. She didn't tell you about the house. *Or* about Nate's dad."

"Because she knew I wouldn't come."

"Do you hate her now?"

"Of course not. I love her."

"Do you love me?" I ask slyly. "Because, if you do, you'll let us stay."

Emotional blackmail. I'm not even ashamed.

Mom sighs. "Do you really want to?"

"Yes! Yes!"

One look at her face and I know I've won. When I hug her hard, she says into my hair, "We should at least move you down to one of the other bedrooms."

I set my chin. "I like my room where it is. And I *promise* not to go psycho on you again."

"Oh, Rinn—please!"

But at least she's smiling.

3 MONTHS + 18 DAYS ————

Thursday, October 23

I can hide from others what I did to Nana. Nate knows, but I doubt he'll say anything. I can tell he likes me. How is that possible?

I can hide my guilt the way I hide my past. People can't read my thoughts. Nobody here shares my memories.

What I can't hide is this stupid scar. When school started back in La Jolla this year, Mom let me take classes online. Of course "distance learning" meant I was trapped at home all day. A plus for Mom who could watch me closely, but a minus for Frank who found it impossible to avoid me.

Even if I *could* wear turtlenecks all year-round, there's this thing called PE at River Hills High. T-shirts and shorts, and no exceptions to this rule. In the stark light of the locker room where we change in and out of clothes, the damage to my neck flashes like a Broadway marquee. I know people notice, especially Tasha, who stares longer than anyone else. Luckily, nobody brings it up.

"You're going to Homecoming, right?" Lacy asks, adjusting her Wonderbra.

Meg adds, "Oh, you have to! Aside from prom, it's the biggest event of the year."

I hesitate. "Don't I need a date?"

"I don't have one," Tasha admits, struggling with a knot in her shoelaces. "Guys suck around here."

"You don't *need* a date," Meg agrees. "But I'm going with Jared O'Malley. He's a quarterback on the team."

Lacy smiles sweetly at me. "You can ask Nate, Rinn. If no one else snapped him up."

I play dumb. "Nate?"

"Yeah. I heard you guys are, you know"—Lacey wiggles both index fingers—"a *thing*."

"We are?" *Gossip at the speed of light.* "I'll think about it," I say apathetically.

"Lacy and I signed up for the decoration committee. Our first meeting's tomorrow after school. You should come," Meg begs.

"Well, I have homework and stuff . . ."

"Oh, please," Lacy drawls. "We all have homework. Don't be a drag."

Stalling, I ask, "Who are *you* going with?"

"I'm not going with anyone. I'm engaged." Lacy flaps a tiny diamond ring under my nose. I can't tell if it's real.

Nor do I care. "How can you be engaged when you're only in high school?"

"She met him online," Tasha butts in, oblivious to Lacy's

scowl. "He's a marine, in Japan. He showed up here last summer, and man, all they did was sneak here, sneak there, and dummy Meg, of course, had to cover for them, and—"

"Will you *please* stop talking?" Lacy growls. "It's none of her business. Nothing personal," she adds to me, not all that sincerely. "But I hardly know you. And I *don't* want my folks finding out about him yet."

I bite back the first cutting reply that comes to mind and instead answer nicely, "Don't worry, Lacy. Your secret's safe with me."

She looks at me as if trying to decide whether or not I'm being sarcastic—and then someone yells, "Hurry up!" from the huddle of girls waiting at the locker room door. Meg wasn't kidding when she said nobody goes through that corridor— "the tunnel"—alone. Even though it's silly, I hurry to join them so I won't be one of the brave, or stupid, ones left behind.

Before bed, I mention to Mom how I got roped into the decoration committee. "Oh, honey! I'm so happy!"

I'm shocked she doesn't launch into backflips. "Why are *you* happy?"

"Because it's hard starting a new school, and I was afraid you—" She stops guiltily.

"Afraid I'd scare everyone off again?"

"Don't be silly. I just know how difficult it can be to make new friends."

I highly doubt it. "I'm going to bed."

"Are you sleeping all right?" she calls as I drift toward the stairs. "No nightmares?"

Nightmares about Mrs. Gibbons, she means. I know she wonders if I'm *really* okay with sleeping in the attic, though she won't ask me right now, she's too afraid to discuss it, and she might never mention Mrs. Gibbons's name again. As if simply talking about the old lady might flip me out.

What Mom still doesn't get after all these years is that I can flip right out without any help from anyone. After all, nothing "brought on" my bipolar disorder in the first place. No drastic change in my life. No traumatic event. Psychosis can happen out of the blue, *to anyone*, and no one knows why. Not even the best doctors on the planet.

And *that's* why Mom is always so afraid. If we don't know what made me sick in the first place, how can anyone guarantee I *won't* flip out again?

Mom hasn't mentioned Annaliese, either. I'm more interested in her than in her dead swinging grandmother. Was my mom friends with Annaliese? Was she sad when it happened?

I'll keep my questions to myself till Mom gets past all this stuff.

3 MONTHS + 19 DAYS ———

Friday, October 24

As it turns out, aside from me, Lacy, and Meg, only pudgy Cecilia Carpenter and two other girls show up for the Homecoming decoration committee. The last two lose interest and disappear in sixty seconds. I notice Lacy eyeballing Cecilia's belly rolls. I remember that look; it's the same one *I'd* get from people when I'd start talking to my books.

"Since when are you interested in Homecoming?" she asks Cecilia.

"My mom thinks I should get involved in more activities this year," Cecilia says.

I smile my encouragement. "Mine, too." Cecilia smiles back, glad for a comrade, so I add, "I heard you singing in chorus today. You're really good." In fact, I was too busy listening to her to pay attention to myself.

Cecilia's shy smile broadens. "Thanks."

"If you're looking for something to do, Cecil," Lacy slyly inserts, "why don't you try out for the squad? We've got a couple of openings. Rinn already said no."

Cecilia flushes. "It's Cecilia. And thanks, but no thanks."

"Of course," Lacy continues, "that means you'd have to learn how to do the splits. And I don't mean, ya know, *banana* splits."

"Lacy!" Meg yelps.

"Or the seat of your pants!" Lacy finishes, laughing heartily.

Openmouthed, I watch Cecilia rise. "Never mind," she mumbles. "I'll find something else to do, I guess."

By the time I recover my wits, it's too late; Cecilia's already lumbered out.

"That," I say angrily, "was *totally* rude."

Lacy, unrepentant, lifts her hands. "Well, I *totally* do not want to hang around with that orca. Chances are she won't even go to this stupid dance."

"Why are you such a bitch?" I demand.

"Why are *you* calling me names?"

Meg and I face her with silent admonition.

Lacy bursts into tears. "Oh God. You're right. I *am* a bitch."

I watch with suspicion as Meg rushes to comfort her. *Hmm, is this one of those "passive-aggressive" ploys for attention that Frank used to accuse me of?*

Lacy snuffles into Meg's shoulder. "I wasn't gonna tell you guys. I just can't believe this is happening. But I did one of those tests?"

"Tests?" Meg repeats.

"A pregnancy test, stupid. And it, it was p-positive."

She sobs hysterically. Meg, after a stunned moment, "aw-ws"

and "c'mons" her like a mother hen. A twisted realization hits me: a creepy house, a dead body in the attic, a ghost, a sexy neighbor, and now a pregnant friend? I'm not trapped in some dinky southern Ohio town—I'm trapped in one of Nana's day-time soaps: *Will Rinn Jacobs escape her fate as a hapless member of the Homecoming decorating committee? Will she beat her way to freedom with a pair of purloined pompoms? Tune in tomorrow!*

At the clank of the janitor's cart, Meg yanks Lacy's arm—"C'mon, we can talk in there"—and pulls her to the side door of the cafeteria that leads to the tunnel. I follow doubtfully, thankful there are three of us.

Meg bangs the door shut. "Now tell us everything!"

Lacy screams and points. "A rat!"

Yes, it's a rat, curled up on the worn floor. Two more dead rodents lie motionless nearby.

"Jesus," Meg squeaks.

Shuddering in unison, we step around the furry bodies and edge farther down the tunnel. Lacy sinks to the floor and Meg crouches beside her. I simply stand there in the dim light, scoping out the nearest exit . . . *yes, the cafeteria, but the locker room might be closer . . .*

It's one thing to race through this tunnel in a group between classes. What are we doing here after hours with no one else around?

Lacy glances up at me, realizes I'm not about to politely disappear, and turns to Meg. "I missed two periods."

"*Two?* Why didn't you say something?"

"Because I was hoping it wasn't true! Oh God, what am I gonna *do?*"

Meg touches Lacy's ring. "You're engaged, right? Maybe

you guys can get married now, if your parents say it's okay. Unless . . . well, you know. Unless you want an abortion."

"I'd never murder Chad's baby. I love him! He tattooed his *ass* for me."

"Then tell him that. Tell your mom and dad, too."

Lacy breaks into fresh sobs. "Nooo, they'll *kill* me."

"No, they won't. But you have to call Chad," Meg insists.

"I can't! He's in Japan!"

"Then e-mail him." Meg hugs her. "Do it tonight and let us know what he says. Right?"

This last question, I guess, is directed at me. I force enthusiasm. "Yes, let us know. It'll be all right," I add belatedly. "If he loves you, he'll marry you." *Even though you're not even out of eleventh grade, duh.*

Lacy's green eyes glitter. "What do you mean 'if' he loves me? Don't you think he does?" Face contorted, she shuts her eyes and clasps her temples. "You don't even know him," she rasps as I back away. "You don't know *me.*"

"I only meant . . ." My words dissolve as a bone-numbing chill descends. *What the hell IS that?*

As I turn questioningly to Meg, Lacy's eyes fly open. She leaps up and plows me straight into the wall, pinning my shoulders with her iron claws. "You bitch, don't you *dare* say he doesn't love me. Who do you think you are?"

One thing I'll always be grateful to Frank for, he did teach me some self-defense. I throw my arms up between Lacy's, slamming hers to the side to break her grip. I push her away and whirl for the door—*okay, I'm officially handing over the Wacko Torch to Lacy Kessler!*—and that's when I hear it.

At the end of the tunnel, the pool room door stands open.

The distant rattling of the chain-link fence almost stops my heart.

"Who's in there?" Meg whispers, motionless except for her hand rubbing her throat.

The fence shakes again, louder, more insistent. Lacy screams, which makes *me* scream, too—and then the cafeteria door bangs open.

"What'cha all think you're doing in here, you girls?" It's Bennie Unger, the janitor, in overalls and orange knit cap.

The rattling stops.

Squinting, Bennie moves closer. I point bravely to the pool room door. "There's somebody in there, I think."

Bennie moseys around us, assaulting us with BO. He tromps down the corridor, peers into the pool room, shuts the door, and tromps right back. "Ain't nobody there *now*." I shiver at the way he stresses that word, like he knows what we heard wasn't our imaginations at all.

I think I'm the only one left who can speak. "We *heard* someone." Hopefully a human someone.

Bennie contemplates our huddle. "You all the decoratin' committee?"

Lacy and I nod. Meg, paralyzed, clamps both hands over her mouth and nose. I pray she doesn't upchuck.

"Guess you girls all best get to decorating, then." Nonchalant, Bennie shuffles off, all jangling keys and scraping soles.

Coming alive, we dash out into the welcoming light of the cafeteria. Lacy, back to her old self, leans against the wall and explodes into giggles. "Holy shit! Saved by the retard."

Meg doesn't laugh. Neither do I.

I want to know what happened to Lacy in there.

I also want to know why Bennie Unger emphasized the word "now."

⎯⎯◄◦►⎯⎯

It's funny how something can creep you out when you're there, in the moment, and everyone else is as creeped out as you.

Then, fifteen minutes later when you're safely back home and the lights are all on, and your mom's stir-frying chicken and onions, and a news anchor's yammering about another Hollywood scandal . . . well, everything's fine. Almost *painfully* normal.

I sniff. "Smells good."

"How'd it go?"

"Um, we didn't get much done." I rub my shoulder, the one that hit the wall the hardest. No point in mentioning what Lacy did to me; I don't need Mom flying over to the Kesslers' demanding to know why their nasty daughter assaulted me. I'll deal with Lacy tomorrow. "Hey, what's with that janitor guy at school?"

"Oh, Bennie." Mom shakes the wok. "He was a kid when I left. A smart one, too, till he fell off a roof, working for his brother. Millie says he's been the janitor for years." She tosses broccoli into the wok and adds a dash of salt. "Why do you ask?"

"No reason."

After dinner, I'm working on homework when my new extension phone rings. Hoping it's Nate, I almost drop the receiver when Lacy says, "It's me. Tasha gave me your number." Before I can think of a reply that doesn't involve profanity, she asks in a small voice, "Do you hate me now?"

"Is that an apology?"

"I guess so. Rinn, I swear I don't know what happened today!"

A likely story. Next she'll be pleading temporary insanity.

"It's like I went nuts, you know? I never did that before. I'm not a mean person."

"Oh, really?" I say coolly. "Is that why you treat Cecilia like crap?"

"I mean I don't beat people *up*." My silence must aggravate her. "What do you want from me? Do you want me to say I'm sorry to her, too?"

"I don't care what you do. Just keep your hands off *me*."

"Don't *you* ever lose control? You do, don't you?" she insists when I hesitate. "You know what I'm talking about."

"No, I don't. But I accept your apology." I hang up hard and turn back to my math book. The phone rings again only a few minutes later. "WHAT?"

"Hey, it's me—Meg. Why'd you hang up on Lacy?"

Why am *I* being attacked by a posse of cheerleaders? "I don't want to talk about Lacy, okay? I've been in the middle of the same math problem for ten minutes now."

"Forget her," Meg agrees. "I want to talk about that tunnel. Look, I know people have joked about it for years. But seriously, Rinn, something's wrong in there."

"Why? Because the fence shook?"

"Not just that. I didn't say anything before, but . . . remember the first time I took you in there? Something happened that day. Something tried to choke me. I *felt* it."

"Is this a joke?" I ask bluntly. "Are you guys trying to freak me out?" Maybe Lacy goaded her into it, to pay me back for slamming the phone.

"No joke. And the same thing happened today, only worse. Now my ears hurt. I'm all dizzy and nauseous. Something's not right, Rinn. It's scary."

"Maybe it's the flu."

She ignores that. "I asked Lacy if she noticed anything funny. She said no."

That's because she was too busy beating me up.

"You didn't feel anything? Really?"

"It got cold," I admit. "And I did hear that fence."

"You're not messing with me, right?"

"No, Meg. I think you're messing with *me*." Though now I'm having my doubts.

"I'm not. I totally swear." A long sigh. "Look, do me a favor— *please* don't tell anyone what I said. They'll think I'm nuts."

Yeah, they will. "My lips are sealed," I promise.

3 MONTHS + 20 DAYS ————

Saturday, October 25

As someone who's always drawn to the "bad boy" type, I can't explain my attraction to a certified band geek who'll probably major in animal husbandry and end up inseminating cows for a living.

Saturday morning, I ignore the banging at the door, figuring it's someone who hopes to convert me. Next thing I know I hear feet creeping upstairs. "Hey, surfer girl."

I pull the covers up to my chin, astonished at Nate's audacity. "Do you always break into people's homes at the crack of dawn?"

"I didn't break in. Your door wasn't locked."

"That's highly unlikely." I refuse to believe Mom would fall back so easily into that dangerous small town habit. Why not put up a sign? HOMICIDAL MANIACS WELCOME.

Nate hangs his head. "Okay, I've got a key. But that's what

you get for not changing the locks," he adds self-righteously. Before I can dispute this, he adds, "I'm off to the stable. Remember? I invited you?"

"Um, I didn't realize we had, you know, an actual date."

"Get dressed. I mean it," he adds when I scoot farther under the covers. "Don't make me come over there and get you."

"Okay! Just leave!"

The second he's gone, I jump up and wrestle into the same jeans I wore yesterday, adding a fresh shirt, a sweater, and clean pair of socks. I brush my teeth and my hair, and roll on a double-duty layer of deodorant. Tiptoeing past Mom's room, I hear her snoring. No point in waking her. I leave a note by the coffee pot.

"You could've warned me," I complain, yanking on my old Keds while Nate helps himself to some SunnyD.

"You're not much of a spontaneous gal, are you?"

I pause. "Tell me you didn't just refer to me as a gal."

"Sorry. It slipped out."

Nate drives a jeep. I don't mean the elegant, overpriced Jeeps you see cruising the sunny streets of La Jolla. I mean a *real* jeep, a muddy, battered green, decades-old relic. We take the hilly roads at a breathtaking sixty miles an hour, which for some masochistic reason happens to be the real speed limit. We turn in at a large white house with a sign—ROCKY MEADOWS FARM: PRIVATE PROPERTY—and roar down a winding drive in a blast of gravel and leaves.

When we jump out, I stand there, inhaling the scent of hay, dirt, and horses. I haven't been this close to a horse since that terrible episode with Chinook. *I missed this!* "Who owns this place?"

"Friends of my dad. They let us keep Ginger and Xan here for free, plus they pay me for mucking the stalls and turning out the horses. They're hardly ever here."

Mud sucks my shoes as we trudge uphill. Inside the L-shaped barn, horses stamp in their stalls and nicker greetings. I wander, quivering with excitement, along the row of stall doors, aware of curious snorts and clunking hooves.

Nate unlatches one stall. "Here's your big baby. Don't let his size scare you away."

I gasp as the huge black horse snuffles my hand. "What is he, a Percheron?"

Nate seems pleased that I knew this right off. "Yep. He's Dad's, really, but he never gets out here to ride him. We call him Xan, for Alexander the Great." He leads the horse out and expertly crossties him in the aisle. "A warrior horse, named after a warrior. Think you can tack him up?"

"In my sleep," I boast.

I may have spoken too soon; I can barely reach high enough to throw the blanket over his back. Nervously, I eye the bulky Western saddle. "No English saddles?"

"Nope. Sorry 'bout that, Your Highness."

He lends a hand with the saddle with no rude remarks about my lack of height. The bridle's easier; Xan obligingly lowers his head for me, while Nate tacks up Ginger. "You sure you're okay with this? I mean, after what happened . . ."

How sweet that he remembers. "I don't scare very easily."

Nate chuckles. "Fearless Rinn."

Leading Xan, I follow Ginger's shiny hindquarters out of the stable. I hop on a mounting block, step into the stirrup, and throw my leg over a back roughly the size of a speedboat.

"Good boy!" I pat Xan's glossy neck, considering the distance between my skull and the earth. I'm not used to riding without a helmet. Boots, either. But after Nate's saddle remark, I keep it to myself.

Sunlight glints through the golden canopy of leaves as we roam, side by side, first along the path, then out into an open field with mist-coated hills in the distance. When Nate clucks Ginger into a canter, Xan takes off, too. Unafraid, I sway comfortably in time to his easy rhythm, gripping his massive sides with my long-unused leg muscles.

"You're good," Nate shouts over. "You wanna race?"

I squint ahead, relishing a tingle of excitement. "You're on!"

——————<o>——————

Nate wins, but barely. After we cool down the horses and put them up, he asks if I'd like to drive the jeep home. He scoffs when I mention I don't have a license. "Kids start driving these back roads when they're nine or ten. Think you can you drive a stick?"

He demonstrates. He's surprisingly patient as I brutalize his gears: *move, jerk, stop, move, jerk, stop, JERK!* After a couple of miles I get the hang of it.

Back in his driveway, I jump out on wobbly legs and rub my sore butt. I'm *so* gonna pay for this. "Thanks for taking me, Nate. Especially after I told you all that stuff about me."

"Shucks." He climbs out, too. "Takes more'n that to scare off an ole country boy."

Before I can complain that now *he's* wearing out the joke, Nate unexpectedly touches my cheek. Is he going to kiss me now?

Instead, his fingers move down to trace my scar under my windblown hair. "Just wonderin'. Did the voices tell you to do this?"

Annoyed, I flick his hand away. "I don't want to talk about it."

"Okay," he says congenially. "Then let's talk about something else."

"Like what?"

"Like Homecoming." His lips brush my forehead. "You want to go with me?"

———◦———

Mom's eyes bug out. "He asked you to Homecoming? What did you say?"

"Nothing, really . . ."

"Well, thank goodness." Evasive, she eyes a spot on the ceiling.

"Wait. Don't you want me to go?"

"Of course I do. It's just that . . . Rinn, do you really *like* him?"

"God, Mom. First you're all bent out of shape because you think I won't make any friends. Now you're bent out of shape because I got asked to a dance?"

"I know, I know."

"Why do you care that it's Nate? Is it because of his dad?" A gruesome idea strikes me. "Is Luke my father? Is that the big secret around here?"

"Your dad?" Mom splutters. "Oh my God, no!"

"Are you sure?"

"Of course I'm sure! Luke was a year ahead of me, he went off to college, and I never saw him again. Rinn, I *told* you who your father is." *Yeah, that one-night stand.* "I'd never lie about that."

I relax. "Then why do you hate Luke?"

Mom sinks into a kitchen chair. "I don't *hate* him. Not really."

"You never did tell me why he dumped you."

"Because he found someone else." Mom whaps the table. "Oh, I could just shoot Millie for not clueing me in. Now I'm living across the street from him. I'm renting his house. My daughter's dating his son! This is just, just—"

"Ironic?" I offer. Mom covers her face. I can't tell if she's laughing or crying. "Mom, if it's gonna upset you, I don't have to go to this dance." Which, after all, means buying a dress, acting all sweet and girly, and hanging out with people I hardly know.

"No." Dry-eyed, Mom straightens up. "I want you to go. And I want you to have the time of your life. Promise me?"

"Promise I'll have a good time? Isn't that kind of a waste? I mean, what about promising not to break curfew, or do drugs, or fool around, or—"

"*Ri-i-inn . . .*"

"I solemnly promise," I recite, "to have the best time of my life."

3 MONTHS + 22 DAYS ——————

Monday, October 27

Dino Mancini is stalking me.

Well, sort of. First thing today, I find him at my locker, though he takes off down the hall when he sees me coming.

He watches me so intently during homeroom, he forgets to say "here" when Mrs. Schimmler barks his name.

He says hi to me in the hall no matter how many times we pass. Once or twice might be flattering. Six times is annoying.

In art, he asks me questions about our projects I can't even answer. He raves about my blob of gray clay that, sadly, still looks like a blob of gray clay. He makes witty remarks to get my attention and finds every excuse to brush up against the back of my chair.

Finally Meg complains, "Will you *please* knock it off?"—prompting Mr. Lipford to threaten Dino with a trip to the office.

"I'm not doin' anything," Dino protests, with a conspiratorial smile for me.

"Exactly. Get back to work, or get out."

"God," Meg murmurs when Dino slinks away. "He's, like, *obsessed* with you."

Is he? Why? Why is he bothering with *me*? Is it because I'm new, so he wants to hit on me before Meg, or anyone else, poisons my mind against him?

Or, worse, does he somehow see through me? Has he already pegged me for a girl who'd consider ditching lunch to smoke some bud, and whatever else he has in mind? Because the old Rinn, the sick Rinn, might've done exactly that.

No, she *definitely* would've done that. And enjoyed every second.

"Why don't you like him?" I ask, because it's obvious Meg doesn't.

"Because A, he's a burnout. B, he's a horn dog. C, he's trash. And D, he's Jared's cousin—which means if I marry him, I'll be related to the jerk."

"So, *why* don't you like him?"

My quip sends Meg into splutters. Mr. Lipford then levels his glare on *us*. Quickly I fake some intense interest in my project, acutely aware of Dino's eyes on me, too.

————◇————

After school, when I break for freedom, Dino steps in front of me as I trot down the steps. I slam on the brakes, losing my balance. "Hey!"

"Sorry, sorry," he stammers, catching me before I fall into

him. He adds as I hoist my book bag back up, "Hey, can I talk to you a sec?"

I glance around for Nate, who's been meeting me after school. Then I remember he has band practice tonight. "Okay," I say cautiously.

Dino guides me down the steps to the sidewalk and then stands there a moment, his hands shoved into his shabby jacket, the wind tossing his dark hair. "Okay, um, what I wanted to ask you was . . . um, about Saturday night?"

"Saturday night?" Confused, I think for a second. Then I remember. *Oh, no, no no . . . please don't ask me this.*

"Yeah, um, you know. Homecoming. So I was wonderin' . . ." Red-faced, Dino gulps hard, like he just swallowed a peach pit; I'm terrified he'll choke before he can spit out the words. "You want to go? I mean, y'know . . . like . . . go with me?"

"Oh." My own cheeks grow warm. I hate to hurt people's feelings. "I'm sorry, Dino. I'm already going with someone."

"You are?" Clearly he's astonished. "I thought, you know, you bein' new here and all, I . . . well, I just figured nobody would've asked you yet."

You thought wrong. "I'm really sorry," I repeat. "But I appreciate your asking me," I add, surprised by my own sincerity. Fine, he's a stoner. But is he as bad as Meg says?

As I turn away, he asks, "Um, who you going with?"

"Nate Brenner."

"Nate Brenner?" His unexpected smirk catches me off guard. "That figures."

Miffed now, I walk away.

3 MONTHS + 23 DAYS ——————

Tuesday, October 28

Lacy struts around my room, rubbing her flat stomach. "I e-mailed Chad ten times over the weekend and he still hasn't answered me! Now what do I do?"

"Blow your brains out?" Tasha suggests. "Oh, wait. You don't have any."

Meg slaps down her pen. "Look, we're supposed to be planning the Homecoming decorations. Can't you guys at least *pretend* to be interested?"

"Why don't you jump down Rinn's throat?" Lacy retorts. "I mean, she invites us over for this and she hasn't said a word this whole time."

Busted, I lower my paint roller. I've been rolling gray paint nonstop and the second coat's almost done.

"Homecoming's Saturday," Meg whines. "We have to do the cafeteria on *Thursday*. I can't do this by myself!"

"There's not that much to do. There's already decorations

left over from last year, right? Besides"—I aim this at Lacy—"Cecilia offered to help. Maybe we can get her back."

"Yeah," Lacy drawls. "Orca can do the refreshments. If she doesn't gobble 'em all first!"

Tasha groans. "You're so mean, Kessler."

"Shut up, Fishgills. You're not even on this committee. Why aren't you splashing around in your aquarium tonight?"

Before I can suggest that both of them shut up, Meg falls down on my mattress next to Tasha. "Oh, I'm sick of this whole thing."

Last week she was so psyched. Now she's sick of it?

"Blah-blah," Lacy says rudely. She then gestures at my walls. "Yuck, this color is *gross*. But I guess it's perfect for this room."

"Meaning?" I demand.

"Meaning, doesn't it bother you one bit that some old lady hanged herself"—she points upward—"from one of those very beams?"

She is *such* a pain. "Can we not talk about it? I have to sleep here, you know."

Tasha sits up on one elbow. "Maybe she went insane, like Miss Prout. *She* took off in the middle of the night. Never said a word. Left everything behind."

Meg speaks up in a whisper. "Maybe *she* did herself in, too." To me: "They were friends, you know, Miss Prout and Mrs. Gibbons."

Enthralled, Tasha adds, "Or maybe she never left. Maybe someone murdered her and buried her in Rinn's cellar!"

I've had enough of this. "Are you guys *trying* to freak me out?"

"You wuss." Lacy rubs her stomach one last time, then throws back her hair with an evil smile. "Okay, Rinn. Show us what you're gonna wear to the dance, then."

Rats. "I didn't buy anything."

"Are you kidding? Why not?"

"I hate shopping," I confess.

"Could've fooled me," Tasha remarks, nodding at the loaded laundry baskets and piles of clothes on the floor, all covered with sheets so I don't splatter paint on anything.

Okay, so it's not "shopping" I dislike. It's shopping for a *formal.* There is no Homecoming dress on earth that'll hide my scar. Now I'm almost sorry I agreed to go. But if I try to explain this to my friends, I'll have to explain other things, too . . .

"No biggie," Meg says, sounding enough like the old Meg to brighten me up. "We'll take you to Barney's. Everything's used, but in mint condition. Tasha got her dress there."

Tasha speaks up in a tight, funny voice. "You mean the dress I'm not wearing?"

Now we all stare at *her.* Meg asks, "What're you talking about?"

"I can't go. I'm swimming that night."

"On *Homecoming* night?" Lacy shrills.

"I have to. Nancy reserved the pool at the Aquatic Center for me." To me, Tasha adds, "Nancy's my coach. It's over in Kellersberg and it's the best pool around. I mean, Nancy really, *really* went out of her way, and—" Tasha's face falls. "I told my mom about Homecoming. But I can't get out of it."

"This is bullshit," Lacy announces.

"I bet *your* mom never missed a dance," I put in. In fact, to hear Mom talk about their old school days, she and Millie never missed a social function, period.

"I know," Tasha says sadly. "I told her that, too, and you know what she said?" She mimics Millie perfectly: "'That's different! I was popular! You don't even have a *date.*'"

"Harsh," Meg murmurs.

"Oh, and, 'If you're serious about the Olympics, then you gotta make sacrifices.'"

"She's ruining your life," Lacy says bluntly.

"Do you want to go?" I'm disliking Millie more and more.

Tasha shrugs. "Yeah, but I don't want to fight with my mom. I mean, she works her butt off to pay for my coach, and my fees, and to book these pools, and . . ." She trails off, and then abruptly lifts her chin. "Yes, I want to go. It's not fair!"

"Just tell her no," Meg suggests. "She can't drag you there, right?"

"Yeah," Lacy agrees. "You already swim, what, three or four days a week? Plus gymnastics? One night off won't kill you. It's Homecoming! Stick up for yourself!"

Tasha's huge brown eyes take us all in, one at a time. We *are* kind of ganging up on her, I guess. But it's Homecoming, a once-a-year event. How could Millie be so unfeeling, so unreasonable?

Then Tasha's elfin face breaks into a shaky grin. "You guys are right. Screw the pool—I'm going to Homecoming! It's my life, right? Who cares what she says?"

High fives all around.

———◄○►———

After dinner, I relate Tasha's dilemma to Mom as we carve pumpkins together. "And can you believe what she said about how Tasha's not popular, so why bother going?"

Mom says neutrally, "Maybe Tasha's exaggerating."

"Or maybe Millie's a bitch," I grumble.

Mom opens her mouth, then changes her mind. "Well, I guess she can be. At times."

I don't repeat the earlier part of our conversation, how my friends kept harping about Mrs. Gibbons hanging herself in my room. I don't want her to suspect that, yes, maybe I *am* a bit paranoid about sleeping upstairs, after all. I wasn't before. But they sure got to me today.

I jab the knife into my pumpkin to scrape out an eye socket, wondering suddenly about Frank and if he's called here lately. Or, if I called him, if he'd hang up on me.

Probably. The day Mom and I left California, he ducked away from me when I tried to hug him. He barely said good-bye. It still hurts me to think about it.

But I bet it doesn't hurt me as much as what I did to him.

3 MONTHS + 24 DAYS ——————

Wednesday, October 29

In my dream, I'm playing my guitar onstage in front of the whole student body. Halfway through whatever I'm playing—it's not even clear in my dream—someone in the audience yells: "MURDERER!"

One by one they all take up the chant: "MURDERER! MURDERER! MURDERER!"

I jump off the stage and try to run, but the mob surrounds me, smothering me, slashing me with their claws, and I can't escape . . . can't escape!

————◄○►————

The thing about dreams is that they're only dreams. If you don't dream, Dr. Edelstein once explained, you can develop emotional problems. At best, you can't concentrate. At worst, you hallucinate. Dreaming is how people cleanse their brains. A "cerebral enema" was her exact description.

At breakfast, the first thing Mom says is, "I heard you talking in your sleep. Another bad dream?"

"All my dreams are bad." Seriously, they are.

Mom bangs silverware into a drawer. "I can't believe he's making you wait till January for an appointment." She means the new psychiatrist Dr. Edelstein referred me to. Someone in Cincinnati, not here in town, thank goodness.

"I could threaten to bomb the school. That'd get me in quicker."

"Don't even joke about that!"

Well, isn't she in a delightful mood? Days like this I wish she'd go back to smoking.

———◀◦▶———

In art, when I see Cecilia Carpenter, I'm not sure how to approach her. Lacy was so nasty to her; what if Cecilia takes it out on me?

Taking a chance, I pop out of my chair and slide in next to Cecilia, two tables away. "Hey." Yes, I'm saying "hey" like everyone else around here. "Sorry about the other day. You know, with Lacy?"

Cecilia smirks. "Why are you apologizing for Lacy?"

"Because Lacy won't." When her smirk spreads to a smile, I add, "I should've stuck up for you. I guess I wasn't expecting it."

"*I* should have expected it. She's so, she's such a—"

"Shrew?"

Cecilia giggles. "Yeah. Too bad, because I really like Meg. Tasha, too. Tash and I took gymnastics together, and then"— she gestures downward—"I got fat. And please don't say anything stupid like 'Oh, you're not that fat.' It's no big deal. I know what I look like."

Relieved by her candor, I plunge right in. "Why don't you change your mind about helping us out? Seriously, we need you. Tomorrow, in fact."

"Are you guys that desperate?"

That's when Mr. Lipford catches on that I'm at the wrong table: "Well, Corinne. I take it you're ready to add your final coat of paint?"

"Uh, yeah." I hop up and whisper, "Eat with us!" to Cecilia, and scurry back to my own hard lump of clay.

"What was that about?" Meg whispers, paint brush poised.

I pretend not to hear her and hold up my project instead. "So what do you think this is?" It started *out* as a bowl, but . . .

Meg examines my work of wonder. "Ashtray? Candleholder?"

"Okay. Candleholder."

Whatever. It's almost done.

———◄◦►———

Circled around our usual lunch table, Meg, Lacy, and Tasha watch as Cecilia and I approach. That's when it hits me: they won't welcome her one bit. Especially not Lacy. Do I really want to see her humiliated again?

I nod toward a different table. "Let's go sit there."

She does so, with aplomb. "I get it."

"Get what?"

"Why you dragged me over here instead of sitting with your friends."

I start to say they're not really my friends, that I hardly know them. But that feels like a lie. "Maybe I'm trolling for more friends?"

Cecilia ruffles her dark hair. I notice for the first time how pretty she is. How, if she slimmed down a bit—okay, a *lot*—Lacy might consider her a serious rival. "Sure. You breeze into town, like out of nowhere, right? And already you're hanging out with the queens. Plus, rumor has it"—she twirls a foil-wrapped corn dog—"you've got a boyfriend already. You know some girls would draw blood just to get Nate to *look* at them?"

"We're neighbors, that's all." *So far, anyway.* "Maybe people are only nice to me because my mom works in the office. Friends in high places and all that."

Unconvinced, Cecilia unwraps her corn dogs. I do the same. Hate to say it, but I'm loving this new high-fat diet of mine. Back in California we mostly had stuff like salads, fresh fruit, and tofu burgers on the menu. Of course, back then, off my meds, I refused to eat anything I didn't make with my own hands. Poison, you know.

I break the cap off my Snapple. "Who do you usually eat with?"

"Pat Schmidt, but she's out with mono. And Stacy Winkler"—she nods toward another table where Stacy, running for student council, or possibly Dork of the Year judging from her OshKosh B'goshes, campaigns to a bunch of bored freshmen—"but she's pretty tied up. You still talk to your old friends?"

Oh, right. Every day. "Um, I'm not what you'd call a social butterfly."

"Really? You don't act shy."

"I'm not. I just like to keep to myself."

"Ha, good luck with that." She finishes off her first corn dog and crunches into the second. "I know, I know," she says, like she's expecting criticism. "I can't help it. I like to *eat*. I eat even more when I'm nervous, and I'm nervous right now. That game on Saturday? I'm singing the National Anthem."

"You've got guts," I say in admiration.

"Singing's the only time I feel good about myself, you know? Like people are *listening* to me for a change, instead of ragging on the fat girl."

We chew in companionable silence for a while. Then Cecilia informs me, "Looks like your friends are trying to get your attention."

Sure enough, Lacy, half out of her seat, beckons madly. Is there a rule that says I can't sit with anyone but them?

Cecilia studies her corn dog stick. "Better go before they get mad."

I hesitate. Of course I don't want to lose the few friends I have, but neither do I want to abandon Cecilia. "No point in moving now. Lunch is almost over."

It's kind of sad how overjoyed she looks. We chitchat about this and that till the buzzer rings. PE is next. As I gather my book bag and head for the tunnel, Cecilia lags back.

"I'm going the other way." She nods to the far doors leading directly into the gym. The sign says NO ENTRANCE. PLEASE USE CORRIDOR. "I don't like the tunnel."

"Who does?"

"Nobody. But once when I was five, my brother accidentally locked me in the garage. He *said* he didn't hear me yelling. I was stuck there for hours. I've been claustrophobic ever since."

"Yikes. I don't blame you."

She shines with gratitude. "I just don't want you to think I believe in ghosts, which I absolutely do not."

"That makes two of us," I say cheerfully. "See you there, then."

So I take the tunnel like everyone else—*I'm* not getting busted—and make a mental note to stop at the office to report another dead rat.

3 MONTHS + 25 DAYS ————

Thursday, October 30

As we survey the boxes of Halloween decorations after school, Lacy warns, "Don't expect me to climb on any ladders in my delicate condition."

Tasha hoots. "Delicate?" Thankfully she agreed to help us out *just this once*, and only because she's not swimming tonight. "Don't make me barf. Oh, wait, that's *your* job now."

"I never should've told you," Lacy hisses.

"Like you could keep it a secret? You've been spewing your lunch all week."

Lacy stifles her reply when Cecilia appears at the cafeteria door. "Jacobs. Tell me you seriously did not invite the singing cow."

"I seriously did." I move closer to Lacy. "We need her, so be nice. I mean it, Lacy."

Lacy aims her nose about an inch from mine. Unsure of

the outcome, Tasha busies herself with crepe paper streamers. Meg grabs a bag of hollow plastic pumpkins.

Seconds tick by. Lacy loses. "What-*ever*, Rinn."

Proud of myself, I wave Cecilia over. Meg and Tasha toss over "hi's" as brightly as I'd hoped. Lacy nods, and leaves it at that.

With encouragement from me, Cecilia joins in, taping cardboard ghosts and witches to the cafeteria walls. Meg and I spread orange and black tablecloths while Tasha fills plastic pumpkins with candy corn, suckers, and Tootsie Rolls. Lacy languishes, sucking a cherry Blow Pop, absently handing out strips of masking tape to Cecilia.

Mom, who agreed to stay late so there'd be an adult around, pops in twice to check on us. The second time I send her a *look* to remind her, please, this isn't a Brownie meeting, never mind the juvenile decorations. She backs off.

Tasha ducks when Lacy throws her a lollipop. "I can't eat that! I'm on a diet till after regionals."

"Really? In that case maybe you can give Cecil here some pointers." With that, Lacy pig-snorts at Cecilia.

I wondered how long it'd take her to start some shit.

Disregarding Lacy, Cecilia addresses Tasha. "Just be careful you don't develop some weird eating disorder. It's common in athletes. My dad's a doctor," she explains to me.

Lacy hoots. "So why hasn't he come up with a cure for obesity yet?" She snatches up a handful of candy corn and pitches it at Cecilia. Little orange and white cones rain down on the pumpkin display and skitter off the table.

"Knock it off!" I yell.

"Knock it off," Lacy says, mocking me. "Jeez, who croaked and left *you* friggin' queen of the candy corn?"

Tasha explodes into laughter. Even Meg giggles. Okay, that *was* a pretty funny line. I struggle to stay straight-faced, and fail miserably. Cecilia stares at me in betrayal. I quickly sober up. "Oh, ignore her. She's been nothing but a bitch since she got knocked up."

Sudden silence. I don't realize what I said till Lacy flies in my face. "Thanks a lot! And you call *me* a bitch? You think I want the whole school to know? I haven't even told my parents!"

I'm such an idiot!

"Sorry," I say meekly.

"You're sorry," Lacy repeats, dripping with spite. "Well, gee, doesn't *that* make me feel better?"

"Cecilia won't say anything. Will you?" I plead.

Cecilia smiles a strange smile. "Of course not."

The way she says it—not quite sarcastically, but not sincerely, either—worries me. Maybe I misjudged this girl.

I see it worries Lacy, too. Forgetting about me, she watches Cecilia dump the rest of the Tootsie Rolls into one last pumpkin, while Tasha and Meg shuffle decorations around. I don't think I like that smile on Cecilia's face.

Then, casually, Lacy says to Cecilia, "So I hear you're singing the National Anthem. Does that mean you're coming to the dance, too?"

Cecilia's tiny smile wavers. "I wasn't planning on it."

"Why not? No date? You mean you're singing our National-freakin'-Anthem and nobody asked you to the dance? Bummer!"

Tasha snaps, "Shut *up* already."

"Oh, well, no matter." Lacy ignores my scowl. "If you come, Cecil, we're having a séance in the tunnel. We'd love for you to join us. What do you think?"

I missed something. "What séance?"

"Just something Dino and I planned," Lacy says mysteriously.

I stare. "You're going to Homecoming with *Dino*?"

"I'm not going *with* him." An evasive laugh. "We'll just kinda be there at the same time."

I'm speechless. Lacy and Dino? Whoever heard of a cheerleader dating a stoner?

She narrows her eyes at me. "What's wrong? You jealous? Because I know he asked *you* and *you* turned him down."

Tasha hoots, "Omigod, Rinn! And you never told us?"

"Why would I?" Seriously, must they know every detail of my life?

Meg shakes her head at the pumpkin in her hands. "God, Lace. I can't believe you're back with him. What about Chad?"

"It's just for the dance," Lacy insists. "I'm not back *with* him. And I was never *with* him in the first place, I'll have you know."

Tasha blows raspberries. "Oh, so that's why Nate dumped you last year. Because he *didn't* find out you were blowing Dino. Sorry. My mistake."

Then she looks at me and covers her mouth.

"You dated Nate?" I ask faintly, hoping Lacy'll deny it.

Lacy shrugs. "We hooked up once or twice."

Meg slams the plastic pumpkin on a table. "Do you guys always have to talk about who's hooking up with who?"

"Well, Meg," Lacy retorts. "Speaking of which, you better make sure your vaccinations are up-to-date, seeing how Jared's screwed just about every girl in school."

"No he hasn't! You are so full of—"

"Shut up." Lacy stiffens. "Shut up. Shut up!" Drained of

color, she clutches her hair and stumbles away, sinking into the nearest chair. "My head's exploding!"

If her face weren't so ghostly I'd swear she was faking.

"*I need something for this pain!*" she screams, digging her fingers into her scalp.

Tasha sneers. "No drugs for you, preggo. Suffer!"

Lacy must be as sick as she claims or we'd see Tasha flying across the cafeteria by now. She rocks in place while Meg, forgetting her outburst, flutters around her with concern. Tasha, though, who knows Lacy well, watches her performance as skeptically as I do.

Cecilia asks nervously, "Rinn, maybe you should get your mom."

"No!" Lacy sobs before I can move. "Just make it go away! Oh God, it hurts. It hurts so bad . . ."

And then, just like someone reached out and hit a kill switch, the wailing stops. Lacy's hands fall to her lap. She stares at Cecilia, her face relaxing by degrees.

Cecilia stares back. In fact, we all do.

"I'm sorry I said those things, Cecilia," Lacy says softly. "I guess I'm kind of on edge."

Tasha jabs a finger into Lacy's back. "You know what, Kessler? You have some very serious mental issues."

Lacy wipes her tears. "I guess I'm just super hormonal."

"Well, you got the *first* syllable right."

Meg shushes Tasha. "Drop it. Can't you see she has a migraine?"

"Actually"—Lacy blinks in surprise—"it's gone." She fluffs out her mass of curls and forces a smile. "But I'm fine now. Totally!"

Her speedy transformation bites my gut. Either she faked this whole thing and we're *all* gullible twits, or . . .

Movement catches my eye, a shifting of shadows. I turn my head, rigid with disbelief, and watch the shadows of the table legs grow longer . . . darker . . . slithering across the floor like monstrous fingers. *What the hell, what the—?*

"Shit!" I stumble backward and bump into Cecilia.

"Ow!" Ungraciously, she pushes me off.

I blink at the floor. The table shadows remain. But now they're simply shadows.

Nothing else.

Lacy, back to her old self, regards me with amusement. "What's with *you?*"

"I . . ." Tearing my eyes away from the floor, I stare at Lacy, then Meg, then Cecilia, then Tasha, and I realize by their clueless expressions that *I'm* the only one who noticed those shifting shadows.

Nobody else. The same way nobody ever saw my shadow people, either.

This is not the same thing. It can't be. I won't let it.

"Sorry." Funny how my voice comes out so normal, so perfectly calm. "I'm tired. Let's finish this up."

———◇———

Done by six thirty, we sit around and admire our handiwork. The plan for tomorrow is for all the students to bring lunches from home and eat in the auditorium, so as not to trash our hard work.

I sit far, far away from the shadow table, but find it impossible not to sneak looks in that direction.

Nothing moves. Nothing's out of place. Nothing remotely resembles what I'd see when I'd stop my meds for a while: those dark, humanlike shapes in the corner of my vision, drifting along the walls, approaching slowly, insidiously—like the table shadows—only to leap out of sight the second I faced them directly.

These weren't shadow people. And I've been TAKING my meds.

Tasha, thankfully, stops egging Lacy on. Meg relaxes. Lacy behaves civilly. Tasha and Cecilia bond over the memories of their old gymnastics class.

I'm the only one who doesn't talk.

Watch that table, watch that table!

I flinch when thunder rumbles and the overhead lights flicker. "Let's get out of here."

"Are you scared of a wittle thunder?" Lacy teases.

I keep my eyes on the table leg shadows, black on the linoleum. Waiting for them to crawl. Certain I'll feel them if they come close enough to me.

An illusion, that's all. Not a hallucination.

"What're you looking at?" Lacy demands.

I pull my jacket out from under me. "Nothing."

The lights blink again. Lacy whispers, "Maybe it's Annaliese, trying to communicate."

Tasha rolls her eyes. "Or maybe it's—omigod—the *weather!*"

"Come on, let's check it out." Lacy jumps up and darts to the door to the tunnel.

Remembering what happened *last* time I went in there with Lacy Kessler, I shake my head. "Leave me out of it."

"Me, too," Cecilia agrees, for her own reason, of course.

But Tasha bounces right up. "Wimps." She beckons to Meg.

Meg reluctantly rises. By then Lacy has already rushed into the tunnel.

Her voice echoes from beyond the door. "Yoo-hoo, Annaliese! Where *a-a-a-re* you?" She peeks out at us. "Hurry! If we all call her at the same time, maybe she'll show herself."

"I don't believe in ghosts," Cecilia says.

"Oh, really? Then why are you hiding way over there?"

"Ignore her," I tell Cecilia. "Let's just go."

"What're you afraid of, *Cecil*?" Lacy taunts as Cecilia gathers up her jacket and book bag. "Come on in. I dare you."

Cecilia bites her lip. Why does she take this abuse?

"You *dare* her?" I repeat. "What is this, kindergarten?"

Lacy nails me with a knowing beam. "You're not afraid, are you, Jacobs? Even though the last time we went in here"—she emits an apologetic giggle—"you almost ended up dead."

I'd like to smack that evil grin right off her face.

Cecilia asks, "What'd she do to you?"

"Can we not talk about this?" I say loudly.

"Really!" Meg agrees. "I don't think we should be goofing around in there." She stares at me, silently begging me not to bring up what she'd said about the tunnel, how it tried to choke her somehow.

I smile back loyally. "Nobody believes that Annaliese stuff, anyway."

"Cecilia does," Lacy purrs. "That's why she never takes the tunnel. That's why she's too scared to come in here *now*."

I wait for Cecilia to confess that she's claustrophobic, not that it's any of Lacy's business.

Then I wait for her to march off, too smart to be drawn into this devious game.

Cecilia does neither. Instead, she walks away from me and breezes past Meg and Tasha. When Lacy serenely moves aside, Cecilia, chin up, marches into the tunnel.

Abruptly, Lacy slams the door. I spring forward in alarm "What're you doing?"

Cecilia's shout from the tunnel echoes my own—*"What are you doing?"*—followed by the sound of hammering fists. "Let me out of here! Lacy! Let me out of here NOW!"

Collapsing into laughter, Lacy and Tasha, and yes, Meg too, lean all their weight against the metal door. Lacy presses her lips near the crack. "Hey, Orca! This isn't the only way out, you know."

"You guys are not funny," I yell. "Let her out!"

"Oh, please. All she has to do is go out another door."

I grab the first arm I reach—Tasha's—and yank with all my might. Tasha, no longer laughing, doesn't resist my tug. Meg, shamefaced, slinks away from the door next. "She's claustrophobic! What's wrong with you guys? Why do *you*"—I direct this at Lacy—"have to be such a bitch?"

"Me?" Lacy shoves me smartly. "Why are *you* such a *freak*, Jacobs?" Then she slashes her index finger significantly across her throat.

I can't move a muscle.

"What happened to your neck?" She hushes Meg's horrified protest with a flash of her hand. "Tell us. We can keep a secret."

Distantly I'm aware of Cecilia's persistent pleas, her thumping fists. Somewhere among my racing thoughts, I wonder, too, why she doesn't run for the next exit; the locker room door, for instance, is only steps away. I want so badly to shout this to Cecilia, but Lacy's venomous eyes immobilize me.

"Who cut your throat?" Her words chill me like ice sliding down my chest. "It wasn't you, was it? *Was it?*"

A thunderclap splits the air. Everyone reacts but Lacy; her cold stare stays fastened to my neck. Luckily my own leap into the air clears my confusion; as the rumble fades away, I notice a terrible silence.

I grab Lacy's sweater. *"Move!"* I pull so hard, the momentum sends her colliding into a table. Pumpkins roll. Candy splatters.

I open the door to a blast of frigid air. Somehow I thought I'd see Cecilia immediately, curled up on the floor in a hysterical ball.

"Where is she?" Tasha asks over my shoulder.

"Cecilia?" I step into the tunnel, then stop, wisely distrustful. "Watch the door," I order Tasha. "You guys pull the same thing on me I'll break *all* your necks."

Tasha nods. I glance toward the north end of the tunnel, past the gym. Beyond the murky void I spot a dim slant of light—the open door of the auditorium.

I back out, rubbing goose bumps. "She made it out."

"Well, of course she did." Tasha won't meet my eyes.

Meg whispers, "We only meant to scare her."

I fight the urge to scream in her face. How could Meg, of all people, do that to Cecilia? "Well, I guess you succeeded." I turn to Lacy now, slumped in a chair, head down, shoulders shaking. "Do you think this is funny? You terrorized her!"

"Leave me alone," she moans. She's crying, not laughing. "My migraine's back. Oh God, it hurts so *baaad . . .*"

"Good," I snap.

I race out of the cafeteria and out the front door. Oh, I hope

Cecilia heard me trying to get her out! Otherwise she'll never speak to me again.

Outside, it's a downpour, and I see no sign of Cecilia. The wind swallows my breath when I shout her name. All I hear are the rustling trees, and gusts of rain splattering the sidewalk.

A car rolls by, wipers slapping. Power lines bob. Street signs rattle.

Where is she? Where?

Then I spot a figure plodding across the square. I bound down the steps and splash across the street. "Cecilia!" She keeps walking. Rain drips into her eyes, but she barely blinks it away. "I'm so sorry that happened. Are you okay?" Slipping in the wet grass, I stop her with my hand. I'm surprised she doesn't punch me.

Hugging herself, Cecilia whispers something through chattering teeth.

"What? I didn't hear you. I said, are you all right?"

Her lips move again but I can't make out the words. I lean closer and put my ear next to her mouth. Finally I hear it, when she repeats it a third time: "I c-can't talk."

"You can't talk?" I echo.

Cecilia nods, and crumples against me with a sob.

3 MONTHS + 26 DAYS ———

Friday, October 31

What were you doing in that tunnel, anyway?" Mom clanks my juice glass in front of me and passes my pill bottles.

"We weren't *in* the tunnel. Lacy locked *Cecilia* in."

"Well, I can't believe you let it get so out of hand."

"Me? I'm the one who told them to leave her alone!"

"Honey, I'm proud of you for making friends with Cecilia, and for trying to include her. But why didn't you come get me when the trouble started?"

I almost choke on my pills. "Oh, *that'd* go over great."

"Or you and Cecilia could've left."

"You mean choose, right?" I say angrily. "Say good-bye to my new friends so I can go hang out with the one person none of them like?"

"If your *friends*"—Mom stretches out the word in an irritating way—"are truly your *friends*"—oh, God, she does it again—"then why can't they accept Cecilia? Why does somebody always"—her voice climbs in pitch and volume—"have to be left out?"

I cringe when she snatches my cereal bowl, slams it in the sink, and whacks on the faucet. Rays of indignation radiate from her silhouette like heat from an asphalt road. "Mom, what's with you? Are you having a nicotine fit?"

"You know what's with me! You know how I feel about bullies."

"Well, I'm not a bully. I *am* friends with Cecilia. But I like Meg and Tasha, too, and—" *Okay, maybe not Lacy, but how can I stay friends with the others and not with her?* "Oh, why do there have to be all these stupid rules?" I burst out. "You know, you can hang out with this person, but not that one, because the others'll get mad. It's so unfair!"

"Yes, it's unfair. And no, it'll never change."

Sullenly I say, "Maybe I'll go back to the dark side, then. Maybe I'm better off without any friends. At least that was easier than *this* stupid shi—— uh, crap."

Mom turns from the sink. "I can't tell you what to do. And no, I can't tell you not to hang out with Lacy. I just want you to think things over a bit." She kisses my hair and reaches around to hug me. "I'm proud of you, honey."

"For what?" *Because I haven't tried to cut my head off lately?*

"For everything. For being you."

———◄◎►———

I have no idea how to face Cecilia. Mom's right, I should've done more to stop it. Yet, to be fair to me, Cecilia walked into that tunnel by herself. Nobody hog-tied her. Nobody threw her in.

Why did she do it? To take Lacy up on her dare? Why does Cecilia care what Lacy Kessler thinks?

I know why: because, like me, she wants to belong. God knows *I* don't want to go through another year with no friends. When I was sick, I didn't care. I do care now.

Vowing to make things right, I get dressed, grab my stuff, and bounce out the door. Although the sun shines through the naked branches, it's twenty degrees colder today. Frost cakes every surface.

Nate, in a Cincinnati Reds jacket, his glorious chestnut hair hidden by a hunter's cap with furry earflaps, rocks in the porch rocker, perfectly at home. "Trick or treat!"

I try not to look so thrilled to see him. "No band practice again?"

"Game's tomorrow. If we don't have it down by now, we never will." He jumps up. He looks happy to see me, too, which makes me even happier. "So, did you guys get the cafeteria all fancied up last night?"

"Yes, and that frickin' bombed." Briefly I rattle off the details. "And when I found her on the square, she couldn't talk to me. Her voice was *gone*."

Nate, disgusted, shakes his head. "About Lacy. I guess I should've warned you."

"Warned me that she's a witch? I figured that out the first day."

"So why hang around her?"

"How can I not hang around her? She's Meg's friend, and I like Meg." Though not so much last night. Remembering something, I add defensively, "Anyway, from what I hear, you used to hang out with her, too."

He eyes me. "Meaning?"

"Meaning I know you hooked up."

"Hooked up as in 'going out,' which we did, or as in 'having sex,' which we did not?"

Relief washes over me. "You didn't?" *He didn't!*

"Cripe, Rinn, gimme credit for a brain."

"So why did you stop 'going out' with her?"

"Because she cheated on me the whole time."

"Right, with Dino. Uh, Tasha mentioned something," I add at his sharp look.

"My fault, for not knowing better. They've been messing around since middle school. Sneaking around, really, since Lacy thinks she's too good for him. But that doesn't stop her from . . . well, you get the picture."

"He's sort of her Homecoming date. Unofficially, that is." *Poor clueless Chad.*

Nate smiles crookedly. "Anyhow, it's not like we were serious." He squeezes my hand, lifting my mood a hundred percent.

I smile at our entwined fingers as we hop down the steps.

◄◦►

According to King Solomon's announcement over the PA, the no-cut-through-the-gym rule will not apply during the Homecoming dance. In fact, the tunnel is forbidden tomorrow night, for our "own safety," he says. Either he caught wind of Lacy's planned séance or he thinks we'll use it for an orgy den.

Cecilia and I reach the art room at the same time. "How's the voice?" I ask anxiously.

She clears her throat as if testing it. "Fine now."

"Good. I was worried."

"I bet." With that, she stalks away.

Okay, I get it: she's mad as hell.

I trail in and take my ceramic bowl/candleholder/whatever off the shelf. Meg, pale, her un-made-up eyes shadowed, strolls in last and drops into place.

"I didn't sleep much last night," she offers, though I didn't comment.

Guilty conscience, I hope. "Why not?"

She lifts a shoulder. "My ears again. No biggie."

My candleholder looks fabulous now that it's painted—smooth, dark red, only slightly lopsided, with my name etched into the bottom. I decide to skip the glossy finish so I can take it home tonight, find a candle, and place it on the porch for the trick-or-treaters.

"Are you mad at me because of what happened with Cecilia?" Meg murmurs.

"I'm madder at Lacy," I say truthfully. "Sick of her, too."

"Rinn, you really don't know her that well."

"Maybe I don't want to."

"I've known her forever. If she acted like that *all* the time, do you think I'd stay friends with her?" I flash her a *hell-if-I-know* look. "Okay, she's bitchier than usual. But that's because—"

I hold up a hand. "I get it already."

"Well, good. Because I don't appreciate having to defend my friends." Meg's dirty look surprises me. "And why did *you* have to open your mouth about you know what? To Cecilia yet! She's not even part of our group."

I glance at Cecilia, hoping she didn't hear. "I don't know. I was mad. It just slipped out."

Pause. "Guess we all have our bitchy moments."

"I guess so." We exchange forgiving smiles, and then I brandish my candleholder. "I think I'll bring this to the séance."

Just like that, Meg shuts down. "Right. That séance."

"I'll protect you," I joke. She rubs one ear and says nothing. Firmly I add, "Meg, it's just a *tunnel*. And it's just a game, okay?"

She nods, casually.

I don't think she believes me.

◄◦►

After school, I catch Cecilia on her way out, to try to make up with her one more time. Before I say two words, she faces me. "Look, Rinn. I think it's cool that you're not so much like other people around here. But I can't be friends with you if you're gonna be friends with *them*. I don't need this crap, and I don't need to be anybody's project. No hard feelings, okay?"

I'm stunned by how deeply that hurts. "You weren't my project."

"Whatever. If hanging out with the clique bitches is so important, well, more power to you. I feel sorry for you, Rinn," she adds, walking away. "Really sorry."

Me, too. And I'm not altogether sure why.

◄◦►

"My house," I argue when Nate wants us to hand out candy from *his* porch. "It's my first Halloween here."

"Uh, that might not be such a good idea," he warns.

"Why?"

"Well, there's this tradition around here . . ."

"Oooh, you're scaring me already." I pretend to quake. "Forget it, farmer boy."

"Suit yourself. But you better have some decent candy, see? None of those Nyquil suckers. We like chocolate round these parts, Snickers 'n' stuff."

"I got it covered."

My art project sits proudly on the porch railing, a spicy scent drifting up from the candle I inserted. Two hollowed-out pumpkins, also with candles—Mom's traditional jack-o'-lantern, and mine more sinister with slanted eyes and a screaming mouth—perch on either side of it.

We drag the glider to the edge of the steps, where we sit and pass out candy to clusters of kids dressed like witches and ghosts and Disney characters. After a time, Nate pops a mini Mounds bar into his mouth, chews, and then states, like he's been pondering this, "We'll have fun tomorrow night."

"I never went to a school dance before," I confide.

"Why not?"

Simple: because I couldn't. No dances, no school programs, no plays, nothing. I was too afraid people were watching me, talking about me, possibly following me around with devious intentions. Would they poison my food if I looked the wrong way? Plant a tracking device on me so I could never escape?

I've already told Nate so much about me—do I really want to scare him off for good? So I smoothly reply, "Nobody cute ever asked me."

At that split second, my evil screaming pumpkin flies off the railing and splats on the ground. A dark figure in a sinister mask races through my yard, shrieking, "Can Annaliese come out and play?"

Nate jumps up. "Beat it, you moron!"

The ghoul howls and dashes down the street. I stare, outraged, at the empty space. Why didn't he pick on Mom's pumpkin instead?

Nate vaults off the porch steps. "Nice!" He kicks the shattered pumpkin, then hops back up on the porch. "Hey, I forgot. Rumor has it, someone else asked you to Homecoming."

"Yeah. Dino." I roll my eyes. "Can no one around here keep their mouths shut?"

"Was it supposed to be a secret?"

"Why? You jealous?"

The glider squeals as he sits back down, *much* closer to me than he sat before. "Maybe." The huskiness in his voice transforms my heart into a fluttering moth.

A new group of kids, clearly too old for trick-or-treating, halt in front of us: Leatherface, waving a plastic chainsaw, Michael Myers in his hockey mask, and a Grim Reaper. They stand and stare, saying nothing.

I shake my bowl of candy bars. "No need for violence. I've already been warned: no crappy suckers."

Silence.

"How about a Twix?" I dangle one invitingly.

Nate snickers, joining in. "What's the capital of Delaware? Who was the last president of the Soviet Union? What is—?"

"—the square root of one thousand, three hundred and seventy-five?" I shout.

Still no answer.

"Weirdos," I murmur.

"Just wait."

I do. Eventually Leatherface asks in a spooky voice: "Can *Aa-a-ana*-liese come out and play?"

"Told ya." Nate nudges me.

I jump up and plunk down the candy bowl. These dudes are creeping me out! "Why don't you go harass someone else?" Michael Myers chuckles. "Fine. I'm siccing my dog on you."

Nate says under his breath, "You don't have a dog."

"They don't know that." I open the front door, whistle sharply—and screech when a brick crack-lands on the porch, missing me, Nate, and my imaginary dog by inches. "HEY!"

Laughing, the ghouls sprint off, costumes flapping, shoes slapping the sidewalk.

"I'm calling the cops!" I scream. "Willful destruction of property!"

"Don't bother. Mrs. Gibbons called the cops every Halloween. They never catch 'em." I stare in disbelief. "I told you, it's a tradition. People stand outside and ask if Annaliese can come out." He pulls me down on the glider. "I sort of hoped they'd forget about it this year, seeing as how the old lady's . . ." He glances up at the big amber moon. "Dead now."

I think of that room upstairs, the one with the canopy bed, where, presumably, Annaliese once slept. "They tormented Mrs. Gibbons? After what she went through? *You* didn't, did you?"

"If I say yes, would that change your perception of me?"

"I'm not sure I have a perception of you yet." *Other than the fact that I think you're very, very cute and a whole lot nicer than some people around here.* "Losers!" I shout as Nate slides an arm through mine. But now that I know I won't be slaughtered by a mob of monsters, I laugh outright. "What a hoot! Admit it, Nate. They scared the bejesus out of you, too."

Nate frowns. "Hoot? Bejesus?"

He deflects my fist. Then, just like in the movies, he leans closer and closer till our lips nearly touch—and whispers to me in the sexiest way imaginable, "Dang, surfer girl. You're fittin' in here just fine."

3 MONTHS + 27 DAYS ─────────

Saturday, November 1

Meg and Tasha show up in the morning to take me shopping at Barney's. It's *so* last minute, I doubt I'll find a thing, and I'm having hideous visions of showing up in *Mom's* old prom dress.

"Lacy wanted to come," Meg says, "but she's got another migraine and wants to shake it before the game."

I'm glad Lacy didn't show. I'm in no mood to be nice to her.

"Chad finally e-mailed her," Meg adds as we walk toward the square. "He says he's going to send her a plane ticket to Okinawa."

"What?" Tasha yelps.

"He wants to marry her. Really! Now she just has to tell her parents."

"Or elope."

"She can't elope to Japan unless she has a passport," I remind them. "And she needs their permission to get one. To say nothing of getting *married*."

"Maybe Japanese laws are different," Meg says hopefully.

"Who cares, if she can't get there?"

"Why are you always so negative?"

"I'm not, I . . ." Fine, forget it. I don't know how old this Chad dude is, or what the age of consent is, here *or* Japan. But I suspect he's in for a buttload of trouble.

We cross the square and walk down Main Street, while Tasha describes the fight she had with Millie. "She pitched a fit! She practically threatened to disown me. But I said, too bad, I'm going to the dance and no way can she stop me."

Meg pats her back. "Good for you for sticking up for yourself. She pushes you way too hard."

"Maybe," Tasha admits halfheartedly. "But, really, she just wants me to be the best. *I'm* the one who wants to go to the Olympics. My folk have been saving up for it for years. But I'm *not* missing Homecoming. Now she's mad as hell."

We reach Barney's Consignment Shoppe at the south end of town, between the Lutheran church—Lacy's dad is the pastor there, Meg informs me; no wonder Lacy's so nervous about telling her parents she's pregnant—and the Army Surplus. I roam the cluttered aisles for fifteen minutes, growing more and more desperate. Nothing but halters, spaghetti straps, and plunging necklines!

Then I spot it: black velvet, with long sleeves and a high collar. My friends watch doubtfully as I pull it on over my clothes. Okay, it's kind of roomy, and too long, and it stinks of mothballs—but other than that, it's perfect.

I posture in front of the mirror while my friends offer comments:

Meg groans. "It's ancient. You can't be serious."

"What's that smell?" Tasha fans her nose.

"Didn't Annie Oakley wear this to a funeral once?"

"Yeah. Her *own*."

Their hysterics cause some creepy dude in a red bandana to glare at us over a barrel of shoes. Torn, I finger the ruffled collar, soft with age. Do I love it because I love it or because it'll cover my scar? I stare into the mirror, running my fingertips down the row of pearly buttons. My gray eyes shine back. My black hair blends into the dress. I look . . . *otherworldly*. It's the only word to describe it. "I love it. It's mine."

After the elderly clerk, maybe Barney himself, rings up my purchase, Creepy Red Bandana Dude blocks our exit. "You gals gettin' ready for the shindig tonight?" He reeks of booze and motor oil. "Well, don't get too friendly with the boys, don't drink and drive"—*drive where?*—"and don't take no chances stirrin' up old Annaliese, now."

"We won't," Meg says courteously. Then she ducks one way and Tasha ducks the other way, leaving me alone with Creepy Red Bandana Dude.

"Monica Parker's kid, right?" Recognition sparks in his bloodshot eyes. "Tell'er her old friend Joey Mancini said hey. Joey, from high school. Tell her to come on down and see me sometime."

Mancini? This drunk, trashy old guy is Dino's dad? I smile politely, dodge around him, and catch up outside with Tasha and Meg. "*Wow*, what a freak."

"Tell me about it." Tasha fake-shudders as Mr. Mancini stumbles outside. With one long evil leer, he unsteadily heads off. "Weirdo," she adds, giggling.

"Stop it!" Meg barks.

"What? He didn't hear me!"

"Not that—this buzzing!" Meg bats at her head. "It's like a *bee* flew in my ears."

"Or maybe a roach," Tasha says unhelpfully. "I heard they like to do that."

"It's not a roach!"

I flash Tasha a look. "Meg, maybe you should go to the emergency room."

"No! That'll take hours. I can't miss the game." Cupping her ears, she adds irritably, "Come on, let's go. I've got warm-ups in one hour." She starts off ahead of us, the crisp wind tossing her pale ponytail.

Tasha nudges me. "Something's not right. I'm worried about her."

Me, too.

———<o>———

Not being a football fan, I didn't want to come to this game. Plus it starts at 2:00, the witching hour for my meds. But with Nate marching, the least I could do is show up.

The band crosses the field, playing "Hang on, Sloopy." Cheerleaders leap, chant, and shriek, threatening the first-row spectators with flying feet and pom-poms. Nate, a big hunk of gorgeous in his scarlet and gold uniform, whacks his drum as the band struts for the sideline. I wave wildly. I doubt he sees me.

Beside me in the stands, Tasha remarks, "I can't believe Lacy made it."

Me, either. Only an hour ago, between her migraine and morning sickness, Lacy had her head in a toilet bowl. Now her toes kick to unbelievable heights, and she flips up her pleated skirt every chance she gets. I wonder how much longer she'll be able to squeeze into that uniform?

Up at the microphone, Mr. Solomon drones a welcome to the Kellersberg Vikings. "And now our own Cecilia Carpenter will sing the National Anthem for us."

As Cecilia joins him on the platform, a girl behind me yells, "MOO!" I send *shut up* to her and her hee-hawing friends, then hold my breath and silently cheer Cecilia on.

Cecilia smiles shyly and opens her mouth: "Oh say can you *seeee* . . . by the dawn's early *liiight* . . ." *Liiight* ends with a guttural note, like she needs to hawk up a loogie. "What so *proud*ly we hail . . ."

Off-key, off-key, oh, she is sooo off-key!

Tasha nudges me. "Oh, man, what's *with* her?"

Snickers and snorts abound from the less mature onlookers. Others exchange sympathetic glances. Baffled, I listen as Cecilia bravely continues, and *nothing's* in tune, not one single note. The harder she tries, the worse she sounds.

When a rumble rises, Cecilia cuts off. Silent, she teeters at the microphone as the audience—mostly kids, but plenty of parents, too—grows noisier by the moment. I want to scream *Shut up! Can't you see she's embarrassed?*

Finally Mr. Solomon steps forward. He swings his arm around Cecilia and leads her away. She stumbles once, and Moo Girl behind me announces, "Ya know, if she busts through that stage it's gonna take a crane to pull her out!"

My instinct is to ignore her; Cecilia's too far away to hear. Besides, she already made it clear she wants nothing to do with me. Why start a fight on *her* behalf?

Then I think about all Mom's antibullying lectures.

I remember how I felt when people made fun of *me*.

So I turn around. It's Lindsay McCormick, that girl who works in the school office. "You think that's funny?"

Laughing too hard to answer, Lindsay buries her face into her tank-sized boyfriend.

"Gotta problem?" Tank inquires without malice.

"No, I think *you've* got the problem," I reply.

As soon as I turn back, Lindsay toes me in my spine. I manage to resist the impulse to rip off her foot—but if she kicks me again, she'll be very, *very* sorry.

—◄◦►—

Halftime. The home team's ahead. Jared O'Malley scored four touchdowns already.

After ten minutes of cheers, backflips, and flashes of thigh, the squad springs effortlessly into a human pyramid. I remember reading in *Time*, or maybe *Newsweek*, that schools all over the country are banning these dangerous stunts. Guess no one in River Hills reads *Time* or *Newsweek*.

I don't see it happen because Lindsay McCormick takes this opportunity to grind her toe into my kidney. I whirl around. "You do that again and I'll . . . !"

Just then a collective gasp of horror rises up from the crowded bleachers.

—◄◦►—

Tripping down from the stands, Tasha and I make it to the sideline in time to hear Meg protest, "I'm okay, I'm okay!" She wrestles away from the burly medics the school keeps on hand for these games, though normally for the players. "I just lost my balance."

"Lost your balance?" Lacy shouts. "You *creamed* me!" Although it was Meg who free-fell from the top of the pyramid, it's Lacy who received the brunt of the impact: bloody knees, a fat lip, and definitely a bruised ego. "We've done that stunt a bazillion times! What the hell is wrong with you?"

"I don't know! I, I've been dizzy lately, and—"

Coach Koenig towers over Meg. The rest of cheerleaders scamper smartly out of the way. "Dizzy? And you didn't tell me?"

"It comes and goes," Meg stammers.

The coach puffs out her cheeks. "You had no business performing today and putting everyone at risk. What were you thinking?" Meg stares at the ground. "That's it. You're out."

Meg's face jerks up. "You can't kick me out. I'm captain!"

"Well, I say you're out for the game. And if you don't bring me a doctor's note saying you're fit to perform, you're out for good."

"But I'm fine!"

"It's *not* fine to lose your balance in the middle of a stunt. You have one week to bring me that note. Got it?" Meg recoils as Coach Koenig blows her whistle. "Anyone who's hurt, get back here on the double. The rest of you, back in place!"

"You can't kick me off!" Meg screams.

Lacy springs over to Tasha and me. "Do you believe this? I'm gonna kill her!"

"Just be glad nobody really got hurt," I snap.

"She was walking funny, right? And when I asked her about it, she's all, 'Oh, I'm fine, I'm fine.' But she kept messing up.

116

Everyone noticed! Then she blows the pyramid. She landed right *on* me."

"Those stunts are dangerous," I say. "People have been paralyzed, even killed."

Lacy slams me with a murderous look. "Oh, Rinn. Shut up."

She bounces off after the second whistle blow. As Coach Koenig propels a tearful Meg away, Tasha worries, "I hope Lacy's okay. I mean, if Meg *fell* on her . . .

Right, the baby. I didn't think of that.

Because I'm sick of Lindsay McCormick's foot, and Nate can't see me from the field, and Tasha finds football as infinitely boring as I do, we mutually agree to ditch the game altogether. Current score: River Hills 33, Kellersberg 0. It's a no-brainer anyway.

———◄○►———

"Wow," Nate remarks when I open the front door.

My skirt twirls around me when I waltz in a circle. Mom hemmed it so I could skip high heels, which I hate, and wear my black ballerina flats. "Not too goth-queenish, is it?"

"No, I think you look . . ." He clears his throat, and then slips into his farmer-boy persona. "You look mighty fancy there, Miz Rinn. *Mighty* fancy."

It's so cute that he's too embarrassed to say I look nice. He looks mighty fine, too, in a suit and tie, instead of his usual flannel and denim.

"Where's your mom? Don't we get a lecture about keeping our hands to ourselves?"

"Already at school. She's chaperoning." God knows I tried to talk her out of it.

Nate groans. "So's my dad."

Great! Mom and Mr. Brenner in the same place for an entire evening? Generally they avoid each other at all costs. I hope there's a fire hose handy.

Because it's cold and rainy—when is it ever anything else?—I wear my sneakers and change into my flats at school. I stash the Keds in my book bag along with my candleholder and hide it under a table. I didn't mention the séance to Nate yet. Will he think it's stupid? Juvenile? Will he lecture me about sneaking into the tunnel when Mr. Solomon ordered us to stay out of it this weekend?

Tasha, with her pixie cut sculpted up with too much gel, in a dress scarily similar to a First Communion frock, joins us. Lacy follows, in red satin and assorted bandages. And Dino, of course, who just "happens" to be with her.

He grins at me, ignoring Nate. "Hey, Rinn." He looks nice tonight, too. Clean, even.

"Hey, Dino."

"Hey, Dino," Nate echoes pointedly.

"Nate."

They regard each other with hooded eyes, two gunfighters out of one of Nana's old-time Westerns. Thankfully Meg appears with Jared O'Malley. I smile with relief. "Meg! You okay?"

"Yeah." Meg tugs up a dress strap. "I'm fine." She smiles serenely at my dress. "You look awesome in that. I take back everything I said."

"Thanks." Though now, surrounded by naked shoulders and rainbow gowns, I feel like I'm auditioning for a *Rocky Horror* revival.

Nate tucks my arm under his in a gentlemanly gesture. "C'mon, let's dance."

———◁◦▷———

"But I want you to come," I later beg. "Please, Nate?"

He shakes off my hand. "We're not even supposed to *be* in that tunnel."

"Ooh, scared we'll get caught, you big baby?"

Nate blinks. "You know, I didn't come here to argue with you. We're supposed to be having fun."

Stubbornly I say, "A séance *would* be fun," and then sigh when he sets his chin. He's probably right. Besides, *I* don't want to get into trouble, either. "Never mind. I'm sorry I called you a baby."

Nate smiles. "And I'm sorry I called you an immature little twit."

"Wait. You never called me that."

"Reckon I just thought it, then."

He takes me into his arms and sweeps me across the gym. Halfway back, we run into Lacy. She smiles at Nate, her bottom lip puffy under scarlet lipstick. "Rinn, I need you a sec."

Nate releases me. "Go ahead. I'll get us something to drink." He heads off, undoubtedly glad for an excuse not to socialize with Lacy.

Lacy's eyes pounce after him in a way I don't like. "Nine o'clock in the boys' locker room. It's the only way we can get in without somebody seeing us. And don't forget that candle."

Already nervous, I admit, "I don't think Nate wants to do it."

"So? Ditch him."

"I can't do that."

"Well, make up your mind. But if you chicken out," she warns, "do *not* give us away."

I nod. Do I really want to do this séance thing? Badly enough to risk ticking off Nate?

Yes, I do—and I know why.

Because I live in the same house where Annaliese grew up.

I pass her bedroom every day, not that there's anything left of her. Only that dusty canopy bed slated for the Salvation Army, and the dresser Mom plans to haul up to my room one day.

I bathe in the same clawfoot tub. I eat my Cocoa Puffs in her kitchen. I see the same view through each window that Annaliese used to see.

Does that make us kindred spirits? Maybe.

Or maybe a part of me *wants* to believe in ghosts.

———◦———

I wish I could be up front with Nate, to say, *I want to do this séance thing and I'd really like you to come.* But he already said no. He doesn't want *me* doing it, either. Why won't he admit it might be fun? That burns me up.

What also burns me up is this: a few minutes before nine, when I'm chatting with Mom, I notice Nate talking to Lindsay McCormick—yes, the bitch who mooed at Cecilia—and her big sweaty boyfriend, Tank. When Lindsay appears to say something incredibly witty, Nate and Tank laugh so hard I can hear them over the music.

What are they laughing at? I glance self-consciously at my toes peeking out below my hem. Are they laughing at my ancient, mothbally dress?

Are they laughing at *me?*

Oh, stop. They're not even looking at you.

True. Yet . . .

Another burst of laughter travels across the gym. The tacky, glittering disco ball hurts my eyes. Colors spin, painting people's faces, rendering them inhuman. I watch my spread fingers rapidly change color—first red, then gold, then green, then blue . . . red, gold, green, blue . . . redgoldgreenblue . . . *redgoldgreenblue . . . !*

I shake my head hard, and I squint at the clock: 9:05. I wave at Nate. He lifts one finger, motioning for me to wait. Wait for him to finish blabbing with the hag who kicked me? Not likely!

Vindicated, I dart back to the cafeteria and fetch the candle-holder from my book bag. Back in the gym, after a quick glance around—I'll *die* if anyone sees me—I bypass the girls' locker room and pull at the door to the boys'. It sticks.

"Who's there?" someone asks, muffled.

"Rinn," I whisper back.

The door opens. A hand yanks me in. Dino leaps at me with a "BOO!"—speaking of immature twits—while Lacy grouses, "What took you so long? We thought you bailed."

"Well, I didn't. I'm here."

So are Meg, Tasha, and Jared O'Malley. Dino's goofy grin tells me he's thrilled I showed up. Jared, Meg's date, a husky red-head, squeezes my hand too hard when we're introduced. Meg smiles vaguely. Tasha whispers, "Yay, you came."

Lacy takes charge. "Let's hurry up and get in there before some loser wants to pee."

Single file, we enter the tunnel. As the door clanks behind

us, I hear Meg's quick intake of breath. I take an experimental breath myself. Just plain, musty air.

Jared produces a roll of twine and a pocket knife. "What's that for?" I ask.

"I gotta tie the doors shut."

I'm starting to regret this adventure. "Oh, no you're *not*."

Lacy scoffs. "Just the locker room doors. People are using the *bathrooms*. You want them to barge in on us?"

"They can barge in from any door," I remind her.

"No, they can't," Tasha says traitorously. "The chaperones are watching."

"Except for the locker room doors," Lacy adds. "Who wants to sit *there* all night? Anyway, we have to make sure no one sneaks in and interrupts the paranormal process."

So Jared, his suit coat straining across his shoulders, cuts pieces of twine to knot around the metal handles of the double doors, first to the boys' locker room, then to the girls'. I notice with relief that some of the lights have been replaced, but Jared runs down and kills the switch.

Darkness descends. Then a flashlight springs to life in Dino's hand. He swings it around, the yellow beam peppered with dust motes. Shadows jump crazily in all directions.

When Jared returns, Meg squeaks, "Why is it so cold in here?"

He slings his arm around her. "Atmosphere, baby. I'll warm ya up in no time. Woo-*hoo*!" His shout bounces off the walls, hollow, vibrating.

Lacy, relishing her part as medium extraordinaire, leads us away from the locker room doors. Pricked by anxiety, I watch her draw a large circle on the concrete floor. *Has Nate missed me yet?*

"Give me that candle," Lacy instructs. "Then everyone sit down in the circle and join hands."

Tasha wrinkles her nose. "We should've brought our coats. This floor is filthy!"

Jared, at least, offers his suit coat to Meg. Happy I'm not wearing a skimpy formal, after all, I hand over my candle-holder, jammed with one of Mom's lavender votives. Though I try to position myself between Tasha and Meg, Dino, slick as a fish, shimmies in beside me.

He takes my hand. "So where's your boyfriend?"

"Waiting in the gym." At least I hope he is.

Lacy lights the candle with Dino's Bic and places it in the center of the circle. "First of all, whoever wants to back out better say so now instead of waiting till the middle of it and then you screw us up."

Dino snorts. "Who believes this crap, anyway?"

"You don't have to believe. You just have to stay still, and very, very quiet. No negative energy. Just relax, breathe deeply, and concentrate on the flame. Concentrate. *Con*centrate . . ."

The cold floor nips me through my dress. Wondering how the others can stand it in those thin, fancy gowns, I settle back uneasily and focus on the candle.

Minutes pass. I hear the distant thump of the deejay's speakers. The normalcy of it feels strangely comforting.

"Nothing's happening," Jared gripes. "Anyway, I smell pizza."

"I smell dirt," Tasha says.

Dino elbows me. "*I* smell four cute, horny chicks. How 'bout you?"

I shrug. "I smell lavender."

Meg says nothing. Lacy grabs the candle. "Maybe we're too far away from her. Let's try the pool room."

I pat Meg's arm when she lags back. "It's a *game*," I say in her ear.

"Keep telling me that," she murmurs back.

The lock to the pool room door has yet to be repaired. "Tie it shut," Lacy commands Jared.

"No!" Meg clutches my hand. "Don't *trap* us in there."

"Okay. I'll do the auditorium instead." Jared unrolls some more twine.

Meg's anxiety is contagious. "Forget tying the doors," I argue. "Who's gonna come in from the auditorium? Everyone's at the *dance*. And there are chaperones everywhere."

With an exasperated "Fine!" Lacy leads the way into the pool room. She flips the light switch, but nothing happens. I can't see the pool at all. She draws a second circle and places the candle as before. "Okay, let's sit and start over."

This floor is much dirtier than the floor in the tunnel. Still, we obey. I try to ignore a cramp in my calf. I try not to think about any critters scurrying over me in the dark. Most of all, I try not think about Nate. I'm sure he's figured out by now that I've ditched him.

Concentrate . . . concentrate.

The lavender fragrance grows stronger and stronger. And then—

Dino farts.

"Sorry, sorry!" he yelps, not sounding sorry to me.

"Sweet!" Jared howls.

Tasha doubles over laughing. Even Meg cracks a smile. I

pinch my nose. Lacy's green eyes flash dangerously in candle-light.

"Hate to tell ya, cuz." Jared, addressing Dino, points at Lacy. "But if you wanna get lucky later, that ain't the way to do it."

Lacy's lips part in outrage. I bet she'll go to her grave denying she and Dino ever hooked up. Then, ignoring Dino's hungry grin, she flings back her hair and glares around. "Well, now that our circle's been drained of any positive energy, *will you all please shut up? Or we'll never make contact."

The laughter fades. Minutes tick by. Meg leans into me. I stare at the flame, a dancing orange entity. After the way Nana died, you'd think I'd be petrified of fires.

"We are calling to the spirit of Annaliese Gibbons," Lacy croons. "Annaliese, are you here with us tonight?"

I shut my eyes. All is silent. I can't even hear the deejay back here.

"We're your friends, Annaliese Gibbons. We know you died here. We're sorry you died. And now we are asking you to speak to us somehow."

Come on, Annie, it's me. I live in your house, remember?

Meg's hand tightens over mine. Dino's feels hot, slick. I slit my eyes to see Lacy rocking, Tasha and Meg hypnotized by the candle, and Dino and Jared glazed with boredom.

The fence creaks gently beside us. My arm hairs prickle. Nana used to say that when your arm hair stands up it means someone took a walk over your future grave.

Who walked over mine?

"Annaliese," Lacy calls in a high, eerie voice. "*Aaaannaliese,* come to us. Come to us *nowww . . . !*"

The overhead lights flick on for a split second and then blink right back out. Yes, the same lights that only a few minutes before *didn't work at all* when Lacy hit the switch.

"REDRUM! REDRUM!"

We all shriek, even Dino. This makes Jared, the culprit, laugh all the harder. He may not look much like Dino, but after this little trick it's perfectly clear they're related.

"You dumb shit!" Tasha screams. "I almost peed my pants!"

Jared ducks to avoid Lacy's right hook. "What's wrong with you guys? It was a joke!"

Dino—who, frankly, screamed louder than I did—leans over me to pinch Meg's leg. "What's a'matter, booboo? *You* sittin' in a puddle?"

When Meg squeals, Jared lunges at Dino, knocking over the candle, snuffing the flame. A river of hot wax slides through my fingers as I scramble out of the way. I shake my right hand, and then stop, riveted with disbelief: there's too much wax on the floor.

Way too much wax for a votive that's been for burning ten, maybe fifteen minutes. It rolls between my fingers, coating my hand, dripping down my wrist into my sleeve. My nostrils siphon the scent of lavender, pungent enough to make my stomach churl.

"Don't!" Lacy shouts when Dino switches on the flashlight. "We're almost there! Can't you feel it?"

"I'm cold," Meg whines.

Tasha nods. "Plus it stinks in here. You guys smell that?"

I breathe in deeply, but nothing can penetrate the scent of the lavender wax. Curious, I dip a fingertip into the puddle. *Hot! And so much of it. Like a huge candle that's been burning for hours . . .*

"Clorox," Dino says wonderingly. "Like, from a swimming pool."

Jared shakes his head. "You mean chlorine. And I don't smell—"

With no warning whatsoever, Dino drops the flashlight and grabs my candleholder, jumps up, and hurls it over the fence. "Here ya go, bitch!" he roars over my shrill protest. "You wanna screw with us? Huh? *You wanna screw with us?*"

Swearing, Jared yanks back on Dino's belt, throwing him off balance. Dino crash-lands beside me. His jerky hands start smacking his own face. "Oh, shit. Ow! What's *burning* me?"

"Ha-ha," I retort as Lacy rescues the flashlight. I'm not falling for another dumb prank.

Faces surround me, eerily illuminated. Lacy's breathing hard, and so are Tasha and Dino—slow, enormous breaths, with flared nostrils as they inhale . . . what? *What are they smelling?*

I sniff. Yes, there's the lavender from the candle, sickly sweet and powerful. But nothing else.

I turn to Jared, the only one *not* sucking in air. "Do you smell it now?"

Before he can answer, the lights flicker again—on, then off—and then spring on altogether, washing the pool room with a blinding florescence. Everyone screams, even the guys. Then the lights black out again.

So does the flashlight.

In the pitch-black Lacy whispers, "Don't move. Don't scare her away."

Squelching panic, I pat the floor around my knees. "The lighter!"

"I said don't move!"

"Can you smell it?" Tasha marvels. "The chlorine? Oh my God."

Someone, Meg, I guess, grabs my waxy hand as a new chill rolls over us in a subzero wave.

No one else moves. All is silent again.

Chest tight, I wait for something to happen. For Dino to make some smart-ass remark. For Jared to scare us half to death again.

For someone, anyone, to break this hollow, awful silence.

My numb fingers can no longer feel Meg's. In the unfathomable darkness, in this deadly cold, I imagine the vapor of my breath curling from my lips.

"Try the f-flashlight again," I say through chattering teeth.

No response.

"The flashlight, Kessler!" Jared bellows, jumping heavily to his feet.

Nothing. Nobody else moves. If it weren't for all the shallow panting, Jared and I might as well be alone in this room.

"*Shit!*" Jared explodes. The next sounds I hear are his feet thumping away, followed by the clank of a distant door.

Wrenching free from Meg, I fumble around till I find the flashlight. When I slide the switch, the smoky beam swings over the faces of my friends.

Meg, Lacy, Tasha, and Dino. Faces frozen. Eyes unblinking. Mouths stretched in soundless screams.

My back ripples with horror. "Wake up."

Nothing.

I aim the beam directly at Lacy's face. She doesn't so much as blink.

Mannequins. They look like damn mannequins!

The flashlight beam wavers in my unsteady hand, causing more monstrous shadows to jump from the walls. "Wake up!" I point the jerky light at each of them, one by one. "What're you *doing*?"

My unresponsive audience stares back, unseeing. I rise slowly, dimly aware of the funny sounds I'm making. My shoes slip in the splattered wax—*it's wet, omigod, how can it still be wet?*—as I stumble to the door and out of the pool room. I run down the tunnel toward the locker room, forgetting in my panic that Jared tied the doors shut. *How do I get out, how do I get out?* I stand, paralyzed with confusion, trying to figure out which way Jared went . . .

Then I remember the auditorium. I double back and throw myself out.

———◇———

I spot Mom dancing with Mr. Brenner, of all people. Under normal circumstances I'd gawk at the sight—but all I can think of are the frozen faces I left behind.

Unless I imagined it. Is that even possible?

Music pounds my ears as I wrestle my way through the dancing couples. "Mom!"

She breaks away from Mr. Brenner. He doesn't look happy about that. "What?"

"I need you! Hurry!" When Mr. Brenner steps forward, too, I add, "It's personal," because if what I saw *was* a hallucination, I sure don't want him to know.

I rush her off after she murmurs an apology. She balks at the auditorium entrance. "Why are we going in here? You said it was, ah, personal . . ."

"No, it's worse!" I race down the aisle to the stage. Mom follows me to the steps leading up to the tunnel entrance. "In there." I point. "In the pool room."

"The pool room?" she yells. "What were you doing in there?"

I plop down onto a stage step as she disappears into the void. Hugging my knees, I pray I imagined it. As bad as it'll be if I *am* hallucinating, that won't be half as bad as—

I hear Mom's faraway shout: "All of you! Out!"

Mom, they can't move! Something's wrong with them!

I raise my face in shock at the thud of multiple footsteps, and Lacy's petulant complaint: "I *knew* she'd rat us out."

She stomps out first, perfectly fine, followed by Tasha and Meg, and, lastly, Dino. Mom, bringing up the rear, actually shoves him when he dawdles. "What part of 'no one allowed in the tunnel' do you people not understand?"

"We were just goofing around, Mrs. Jacobs," Dino protests.

I push myself up. Except for Meg, they all look pretty hostile. Meg just stares at the floor, one arm tucked through Tasha's. "Are—are you guys okay?"

Tasha tilts her head. "Why wouldn't we be?"

Dino, the epitome of innocence, faces off with Mom. "Are we in trouble, Mrs. Jacobs? I mean, we weren't making out or nothin'."

"Well, I'm glad to hear that," Mom barks. "What *were* you doing?"

Lacy flutters her lashes. "Just talking. It's so noisy in the gym."

"Well, get back there right now. All of you!"

Meg and Tasha flee. Lacy reluctantly follows. Dino,

undoubtedly to prove that *nobody* orders him around, takes his time sauntering out.

Mom spins around. "I can't believe you did that. *Anything* could've happened."

"I thought you didn't believe in Annaliese," I croak.

"I'm not talking about ghosts. That room is dangerous. The roof could cave in! Why do you think they're going to tear it down? Didn't you hear any of the announcements?"

I try to look appropriately chagrined. This lasts about one second. "Mom, something weird happened—"

Mom sniffs my breath. "Were you drinking back there?"

"No! We were just—" *No, no, don't mention that séance!* "Talking, like Lacy said. But then everyone, I mean everyone but *me*, they all . . ."

Stared into space? Wouldn't speak to me?

Embarrassed, I stare at the carpet. "Never mind. It's nothing."

What if they were kidding around? What if they planned this whole thing?

"Rinn, my God, I thought something happened to you."

She doesn't have to spell out what she thought that might be. "Sorry."

We both look up at a sound in the back of the auditorium. Mom calls, "Look who finally turned up," and propels me up the aisle toward Nate. "I believe this is your missing date?" She tweaks my arm and then sails back to the gym, instructing Nate: "See if you can keep her out of trouble the rest of the night."

"Trouble, huh?" Nate folds his arms. "Why am I not surprised?"

If my face gets any hotter I'll have second-degree burns. "Sorry I dumped you like that."

"You did the séance thing."

I nod. "Are you mad?"

"Oh, please."

He heads toward the gym. I follow slowly. Once there, I glance around for Meg and the others.

"If you're looking for your friends," Nate says, "they already left."

"Left?"

"Yep. You ditch me for them, and then they ditch you. Ironic, huh?"

I tilt my head. "Are you mad at me or not? Because if you are, then say so, okay? Instead of, like, dwelling on it for the next six months."

"Rinn, I'm over it."

But he doesn't sound like it.

3 MONTHS + 28 DAYS

Sunday, November 2

She calls to me from above while I'm trapped in the depths of the pool: "Corinne! Corinne!"

Nobody calls me Corinne. Only Mom, when she's mad, or making a point. Or my teachers, when they're trying to get my attention when my chin lands on my desk at 2:00 p.m.

The water strangles me as I struggle upward. "Where are you?" I scream through my burning lungs.

"I'm here . . . up here . . ."

At last I bob to the surface, spitting and choking. There, I turn my face to the sunlight—how did I get outside?—grateful to be alive. Grateful that somebody saved me.

A hand grasps my hair from behind. Ragged nails dig into my scalp, pulling me down, down, down, dragging me back underwater.

The disembodied voice above me shrills with laughter.

———◇———

"Just a dream, just a dream." Mom strokes my hair.

I fight to hide my irrational annoyance. "I know it was a dream. I'm not five."

"Honey, if these nightmares are waking you up again—"

"Just this one," I lie.

"—maybe you need your meds adjusted."

"No, I don't!"

"I think you do. And I'm the mom, so I win. I'm going to call that new doctor and *insist* he get you in sooner. And you need someone to talk to—"

"Mom, *no*." Oh, I've rehashed my whole life so many times and with so many doctors, sometimes it doesn't feel like my own life anymore.

"About Nana," Mom clarifies. My muscles tighten. "Honey, it's only been three months. I *know* you're suffering. Me, too," she adds softly. "Maybe we could both use a bit of intensive therapy."

I hug my head, knowing it's futile, that Mom'll get her way in the end.

If Annaliese was above me in the dream, then who was pulling me back underwater?

Nana?

Oh, God . . . Nana . . .

Mom pats my leg. "Try to go back to sleep. We can talk in the morning."

I chuck the pillow aside. "I dreamed about Annaliese. They say she haunts the tunnel and that's why everyone hates to go in there. You know about that, right?"

Mom hesitates. "I've heard some things."

"So we had a séance last night and *that's* why we were in

there. And we kind of got carried away, and it was pretty scary, and, well, I guess I kind of freaked out. That's why I had that dream. It's got nothing to do with my meds."

"A séance," Mom repeats, like she got stuck on that one sentence and heard nothing else. *"Why?"*

"It was just a game."

A game? That's a lie. You SAW what happened.

"You knew her, right?" I ask Mom when she takes too long to answer.

She draws back. "Vaguely."

"So what happened? How'd she drown?"

"Ah, I don't think this is something we should be talking about now. Unless you want another nightmare."

I catch her as she starts to push up from my mattress. "I'm okay now, honest. I'm just curious, you know?" Deviously I add, "If you don't tell me, somebody else will."

"There's nothing to tell," Mom says crisply. "Nobody knows how it happened. Her grandmother reported her missing when she didn't come home from school. They found her the next morning. Poor Mrs. Gibbons never got over it."

"Was she swimming by herself? They always say not to do that."

Mom shrugs.

"Well, was she swearing a swimsuit?"

"Street clothes," Mom admits. "The same ones she wore to school that last day. We weren't allowed to use the pool after hours, but sometimes we'd sneak in. She had a bump on her head, so the police thought she fell in by accident. They interviewed everyone. Nobody saw a thing."

Or nobody admitted it. "Were you friends with her?"

"We had classes together. We weren't really friends."

Something tells me Annaliese wasn't the cheerleader type. "Didn't they wonder if she was murdered? You know, with that bump and all."

Mom slaps my hip. "Well, thank you very much for that pleasant idea. Now *I'll* be having nightmares." She springs up before I can stop her. "Go back to sleep, unless you want me to make us a pot of coffee."

I stretch out with my hands under my head. "No, thanks. I'm still tired."

After she blows me a kiss and leaves, I turn Annaliese's story around in my mind. If the tiles are wet, you *can* slip and fall into a pool; I've done it myself, twice, with our pool in La Jolla—stoned the first time, careless the second. So it's not impossible.

Is it true that if someone dies a violent death, their ghost can come back and haunt the place where they died?

I remember the frozen faces of my friends last night. Can a ghost do *that*?

Wait. I don't believe in ghosts.

But I do know what happened last night.

◆

I decline Mom's invitation to drive to Westfield to pick up some decent, affordable groceries. As soon as the SUV pulls off, I dial Tasha's number, hoping to feel her out about the séance. Before we exchange five words, she invites me over. "Lacy and Meg are here. Hurry up!"

I do. But when I get to Tasha's house, no one's talking about the séance; instead, they're discussing yesterday's game, and Meg's ill-timed fall.

"I can't believe Koenig kicked me off the squad," Meg moans.

"Not for good," Tasha reminds her. "Just till your doctor okays you."

"What if he doesn't? What'll I do then? Cheering's all I care about!"

Unfazed, Tasha retorts, "You heard what Rinn said. Those stunts are dangerous. You'll never catch *me* trusting my life to a bunch of ditzy pom-pom girls."

Lacy sticks out her tongue. "No, you just leap headfirst from a fifty-foot board and pray your skull doesn't smack the cement."

I cringe, picturing Annaliese tripping, whacking her head, tumbling into the pool with a scream nobody hears . . . gasping for breath . . .

Lacy nods curtly. "What's with *you*, Jacobs?"

I wet my lips. "Is everyone okay?"

Tasha blinks. "You asked us that last night."

"I mean . . . you know . . . the séance."

"Oh, that. A waste of time."

Lacy pokes Meg. "But we sure scared the hell out of that big jock boyfriend of yours. Where'd *he* disappear to? What a pussy."

Meg's wan smile reveals nothing. Tasha says with a snicker, "Too bad Dino farted and spoiled the whole mood."

Frustrated, I shout, "I'm talking about what happened *after* Dino farted."

"Nothing 'happened,'" Lacy growls, "because *somebody*

had to run crying to her mommy. We got busted. We left. End of story."

"That's not the end and you know it." My confusion blossoms as they all exchange looks. "That's not the end of the story," I repeat loudly *because I wasn't hallucinating!* Now, in the daylight, with time to think about it, I know I'm right. My "real" hallucinations were always vague, distorted. I remember every vivid detail about last night.

It happened.

Lacy lifts her brows. "So what is the story?"

"You guys acted . . . well, weird!" How *do* I describe their dead faces and frozen limbs? "You sat there like zombies, not moving, not talking—"

Amused, Lacy interrupts, "Whatever you're smoking, Jacobs, I wish you'd share it."

"Why are you pretending nothing happened? You *said* you smelled chlorine and then all of you went blank!"

Tasha interjects. "I smelled dirt. And that candle."

Why is she lying? I heard her *say* she smelled it. I seek out Meg, lost in her own world, absently rubbing one ear. "Meg?"

Frowning, she drops her hand. "I don't know what you're talking about."

"Well. So much for that." Lacy thoughtfully twirls a curl. "Hey, guys, did you see Rinn's mom dancing with Nate's old man? Whoa, better watch out—you might be dating your own stepbrother one of these days."

"That's not incest," Tasha assures me kindly.

"Not technically," Lacy concedes. "Just gross."

Okay, now the truth is quite clear: either they honestly *don't* remember what happened, or they've already made a pact not to discuss it with me. This second idea makes the most sense, I decide. And for this I ditched Nate?

I'm glad I never took off my jacket. "Whatever. Go ahead, play your stupid games. But next time, leave me out of it."

As I charge out, I hear Tasha ask, "Jeez, what got into her?"

3 MONTHS + 29 DAYS

Monday, November 3

I'm mad. And frustrated. And ready to scream.

First thing this morning, I catch Dino near his locker. It's almost comical how he looks both ways, like he wants to make sure I'm actually speaking to *him*. "I need to talk to you about Saturday night."

Dino affects his bad-boy slouch. "Yeah, what about it?"

"You guys were goofing around, right?"

"Uhh . . ."

"At the séance, Dino. Before my mom showed up."

He loses the slouch. Confusion clouds his face. "You mean when I threw the candle? Look, I'm sorry about that—"

I stomp impatiently. "No, Dino. *After* the candle and *before* my mom. What happened in there?"

A long, long silence. Then he answers slowly, as if carefully choosing his words, "I guess I fell asleep. It's kind of a blur, y'know?"

"A blur," I scoff. "Fine. Forget it."

Boldly he catches my sweater as I whirl away from him. "Hey, hey, wait! Why'd you ditch us, anyway? And run for your mommy?"

"You know damn well why." I pull free and smooth my sweater down. "Oh, and by the way, my candleholder? I spent *days* working on that thing. Thanks for nothing."

"I can get it back for you," he offers, "and we can glue it or something."

"Right, get it back how?"

"I can hop that fence. I done it before," he boasts.

Irritably I say, "It must be in a thousand pieces by now." Funny how I didn't realize till now how attached to it I was. That candleholder was first thing I'd ever made with my two hands. Lopsided or not, even Mom said she liked it.

"Look, I said I was sorry. I'll get it back, I swear." He shoves hair out of his eyes and smiles tentatively. "I really, um, like you, y'know? I guess you figured that out." His toe scrapes the floor as he avoids my stare. "I mean, I know you're with Brenner and all. But I keep thinkin', if he hadn't gotten to you first, maybe you and me . . . ?" He shrinks at my look and plaintively adds, "I'm not really a jerk, honest. I just like to goof around."

"Whatever." Obviously he's not going to tell me a thing about last night. All he wants is, well, *me*. Talk about nerve. "Forget it. See you around."

I stalk off.

———◄○►———

Cecilia ignores me both in art and chorus. Does she plan to stay mad forever? Or is she too embarrassed to talk to *anyone* after she massacred the National Anthem?

I hope it's number two.

Approaching Dino was a waste of time. It occurs to me maybe I'll have better luck with Jared—I know *he* saw what happened—but he's nowhere around. Is he avoiding me?

And other than an occasional "hi," Nate's barely spoken to me since the dance.

At lunch, with the cafeteria humming around me, I rest my chin glumly in one hand. Then I sit back up and sniff my fingers. Lavender?

This is the same hand that skidded through the wax Saturday night. Hot, wet wax, when, as cold as that room was, it should've dried the second it hit the floor.

My hand itself looks perfectly normal. I sit there, sniffing suspiciously, while Tasha blabs about the regional diving competition coming up in a couple of weeks. Lacy whines that her head hurts again, and that Chad hasn't sent her that plane ticket or answered her e-mails. Meg, keeping elbows on the table and her hands over her ears, mumbles occasionally so they'll think she's paying attention.

Lacy zeros in on my compulsive sniffing. "What—are—you—*doing*?"

Cheeks warm, I reach for my Snapple. I've taken three baths since Saturday. I wash my hands constantly. *How can I still smell the wax on my fingers?*

Dismissing my nonreply, Lacy continues, "I hope Chad's not, you know"—she laughs weakly—"dumping me after all this. We even picked out baby names—Chad Junior for a boy and Chantal for a girl. Or maybe Chandra. What do *you* guys think? Chantal or Chandra?"

She can name it Osama or Guadalupe for all I care. Slowly

my right hand creeps back up. *Sniff . . . sniff.* Confused, I frown. *Now* all I can smell is my pencil and a hint of soap.

No lavender.

"Is anyone listening to me?" Lacy asks petulantly when no one offers an opinion.

Meg massages one ear. "I can't hear half of what you're saying over all this buzzing."

"Well, go see a doctor already! We're sick of hearing about it."

Tasha objects, "Speak for yourself. All *you* talk about is that loser, Chad. I bet he dumped you already and you're too dumb to see it."

Time stands still at our private table, while the cafeteria bustles with conversation and activity.

"What did you say?" Lacy asks slowly. Tasha, apparently rethinking the situation, pokes a straw into her milk carton. Lacy's disbelieving eyes roam the table. "Do you guys really think that?"

Meg scooches her chair closer. "Nobody thinks that! Don't even listen to her." She glares at Tasha. Tasha then cocks one eyebrow at me, silently asking: *Care to chime in?*

I shake my head. I am *so* staying out of this.

Lacy crumbles. "Oh God. She's right! Why else would he ignore me?"

She looks so, well, *tragic*, my resolve to stay mad at her, and the others, dissolves. It doesn't mean I'm ready to forgive them for that séance prank. But Lacy's on the verge of a serious wig-out. To say nothing of being sixteen and pregnant in a stuffy town, with a preacher for a dad, no less. In the old days they used to write books about this stuff.

So I say, "I think you should e-mail him again and ask him straight out. If he says yes, then you can deal with it, right? It's the only way to find out, instead of aggravating yourself to death." *And the rest of us, too.*

Lacy blinks away tears. "Maybe you're right." She surprises me with a grateful smile.

The bell rings and we gather up our stuff. Meg asks Lacy, "Are you gonna be okay?"

Lacy nods. "I guess, if this headache ever goes away."

As Meg and I head off in the same direction, she confides, "Jared's acting all weird now, like he doesn't want to be around me. I tried to talk to him but he keeps blowing me off." Her face falls. "God, if I don't get back on that squad I don't know *what* I'll do. I'm auditioning for a cheerleading scholarship in April. How's it gonna look if I'm not on a team anymore? Or if Coach Koenig won't give me a recommendation?"

"Lacy'll get kicked off, too," I remind her. "Sooner or later that coach'll catch on that she's"—I drop my voice, taking no chances—"you know what."

"I know. And I'm worried about her headaches. What if it's something serious, like a brain tumor?" She rushes on while I examine this ghastly idea. "She says she's had a migraine every day since we—" She stops, stricken.

I stop, too, ignoring the jostles and rude comments. "What?"

"Remember the day she jumped you in the tunnel? When the air got all funny? *That's* when. That's when my ears started ringing, too." Meg squeezes her books and starts walking again. "It's a known fact that weird things happen in that tunnel. It just never happened to me before." She taps one ear. "Not like *this.*"

What weird things? Before I can ask, Meg sprints ahead and disappears. I slow down, my brain spinning with improbable ideas. I go into that tunnel, too, sometimes twice a day. If there's something "wrong" in there, why haven't I felt it? Why didn't *I* notice the funny air? Why didn't *I* smell chlorine during that séance and morph into a mannequin?

Unless that chlorine thing was part of the joke, too.

The warning bell rings. I'm practically alone in the hall. I break into a run and reach my English classroom one second before Ms. Rasmussen closes the door.

Maybe it's *all* a joke, one they planned from day one. A conspiracy designed to trick Corinne Jacobs into wondering if she's losing her marbles again.

And, like before, everyone's in on it. Everyone!

———◇———

Maybe Mom's right: maybe my meds *aren't* working. Because there's a word for this. It's called P-A-R-A-N-O-I-A.

Not that I think anyone's poisoning my food or following me with a camera. Been there, done that. This is not the same.

So far I've come up with three possible scenarios:

1. The séance was a setup. Freaks in this school think it's funny to pick on the new girl, same way they think it's funny to stand outside and scream "Can Annaliese come out to play?" This scenario means I'm not paranoid. Only suspicious. For good reason!

2. The séance was *not* a setup. Everyone did zombie out, but they have no memory of it.

145

Therefore, I'm not paranoid because what happened *really happened.*

3. The séance was for real and everyone knows it. But they won't discuss it because
   A. they don't trust me,
   B. they don't like me, or
   C. they're playing it down because they're plotting to get me alone after school, duct tape my mouth, and throw me over the fence so Annaliese can rip out my throat with her ghostly teeth.

Okay. Now *that's* paranoid.

3 MONTHS + 30 DAYS ———

Tuesday, November 4

For the holiday program," Mr. Chenoweth announces, "I'll need a couple of soloists." He smiles ingratiatingly around the room. "You get ten bonus points just for trying out."

I don't need the ten points. Hello, it's chorus?

"Pass," I say when he calls my name.

"C'mon, Rinn, I know you have a nice voice. And your mom tells me you play the guitar." I groan inwardly. "Why don't you bring it in this week? I've got an idea."

Thanks, Mom.

When Cecilia's turn comes, she also passes. Heads swivel in surprise.

"I need a break," she explains. "I always end up with a solo, so maybe it's time"—she kicks my chair—"to give someone else a chance?"

Disappointed, Mr. Chenoweth says, "Well, if you're sure," and glances down at his list to bellow out the next name.

I steal a glance over my shoulder.

Cecilia smiles at me.

———⟨◦⟩———

I catch up with her as she heads toward the sidewalk after school, hunched under a polka-dot umbrella in today's relentless drizzle. "Why didn't you try out today?"

She keeps walking. "You were at the game. You saw what happened."

"But that was a fluke. Even professionals screw up. I mean, that crowd was huge, right? And then you had that problem that day . . ."

"What day?"

"The day we decorated the gym. When you lost your—" I stop on the sidewalk.

"Voice." Cecilia stops, too.

Yes, yes—when she lost her voice!

"Crap," I whisper. I can't believe the words even as they fall from my lips. "We locked you in the tunnel and you lost your voice!"

"Thanks for saying 'we' instead of blaming it all on Lacy. Not that I care," Cecilia adds, speeding up. "I'm sure it was her idea."

"Forget that! Listen! Something weird's going on."

"You mean aside from you talking to me when I asked you nicely to leave me alone?"

Rainwater splashes my legs as I break into a jog. For a big girl, Cecilia's fast on her feet. "Wait! I have to tell you something important and I can't do it here." I point to Millie's Boxcar Diner. "Let's go in. Please," I beg as she lags back.

Disgruntled, Cecilia agrees. I choose a booth by the front window, away from Millie's counter. I don't need her listening in and then blabbing it all to Mom.

Millie slaps down our hot chocolate and, without asking, a plate of her famous onion rings. "Well, I think this is first time you stopped in here without your mom. What's the occasion?"

I whip a random book out of my bag. "We have homework to discuss." The second she's out of earshot, I lean forward eagerly. "Tell me what happened when you were locked in the tunnel."

Cecilia frowns. "Why?"

"You tell me first. Then I'll explain it."

"Forget it. I don't trust you."

"I know," I say miserably. "I wouldn't trust me either if I were you." Relief rushes through me when Cecilia grins at my statement. "I apologized and I meant it. And if it makes you feel any better, Lacy's not too thrilled with me for sticking up for you."

Her grin vanishes. "You want a medal for that? Or just a pat on the head?" I wait patiently. She sighs. "I told you, I'm claustrophobic. What do you *think* happened?" She dunks the whipped cream down into her cocoa with a spoon. "You don't know what I go through. I can't shut my bedroom door. I can't walk into a closet. I can't even pee at school because of the stalls." She ducks to take a sip. "You have no clue."

Do I tell her? Do I dare? If she doesn't trust me, how can I trust her?

"I get it," I assure her. "Just tell me what happened in the tunnel."

Beads of perspiration dot Cecilia's wide forehead. She swipes them away with her crumbled napkin. "She slammed the door and I couldn't get it open. I heard you guys laughing. At first, all I wanted was to get out of there so I could kick your asses! Then I panicked. It—it's hard to describe," she fumbles. "At first I can't breathe. I'm *sure* I'm gonna die. But after that passes, it's like I end up on this higher plane. I'm kinda out of myself, but not quite, you know? I still know what's going on." She crunches an onion ring. "There's a name for that, um . . ."

"Depersonalization," I recite.

She doesn't ask how I know this. "Anyway, it usually happens on its own. But that time it didn't. I couldn't stop screaming. At least not until—" She bites her lip.

"Till what?"

"Till the air got in my mouth."

For a minute I listen to the clatter of silverware and china. Millie's joking with Edna, the lady who helps her out here. A jukebox plays Reba McEntire. The canvas awning outside thumps erratically in the wind.

It all seems so normal.

"Greasy air," Cecilia clarifies. "*Thick*. Like Crisco or something."

"What did it smell like?" I whisper.

"Bleach."

My lips grow numb. "That's when you lost your voice."

She nods. "I couldn't scream anymore. My whole throat closed up. I can't remember what happened next, except I somehow got out and . . ." Cecilia strips the breading off an onion ring, rendering it naked. "Well, my voice came back, but it's not the same. I—I'm tone deaf or something. I can't *sing* anymore."

"That's why you messed up at the game. And why you

didn't try out for a solo today." I add, more awestruck than afraid, "It stole your *voice*, Cecilia."

"What?"

"The tunnel."

"Annaliese, you mean?" Cecilia throws down her napkin. "Oh, give me a *break*."

"But Meg says weird things happen in there . . ."

"Yeah, stupid things that happen to stupid *people*." Ignoring my protests, Cecilia stands, wriggles into her roomy coat, and jerks her chin at the leftover onion rings. "It's on you."

————◄○►————

Later, unable to sleep, I get up to make another list:

1. Lacy got headaches after she went into the tunnel. Plus she went Rambo on me.
2. Meg's ears started ringing after she went into the tunnel. She fell on the ground in front of hundreds of spectators doing a stunt she's done a thousand times.
3. Cecilia lost her voice after she went into the tunnel.

Laid out in front of me, it's not much evidence. Three coincidences, all with explanations. Lacy's headaches could be from stress or hormones. Meg's ringing ears might be a medical thing. Maybe none of this has anything to *do* with the tunnel.

But Cecilia's voice baffles me. How do you turn tone deaf overnight? It makes no sense.

What also makes no sense is that people use that tunnel

every day. Has anything bad happened to anyone else? Nate might know. I bite my thumbnail, undecided—*is he hugely mad at me, or just a teeny bit irritated?*—and then dial his number without thinking any further.

"You know what time it is?" he asks sleepily.

"Sorry. I just want to know one thing: *why* is everyone so afraid of that tunnel?"

"What do you do? Lie awake at night and think of this stuff?"

"Seriously. You should see them after gym, banding together like buffalo. Do the boys do that, too?" I guess his silence means yes. "Meg said some weird things have happened to people in that tunnel. Is that true?"

"Flukes. Coincidences."

"Oh, really? Like what?"

Nate yawns. "Oh, like a kid'll come out of the tunnel and, I dunno . . . get sick all of a sudden. Or have an asthma attack. Or lose a report or a library book. Or punch his girlfriend, say, for no reason at all."

I snicker. "A library book, huh? Wow, what a tragedy."

"Yeah, well." He sounds more awake now. "One teacher we had last year, he went into the tunnel to break up a fight. He had a drinking problem, I heard, but he'd been sober for years. He stopped at a bar after school, got drunk, and ran his car into a storefront."

Now that's more interesting. "What else?"

"Um, the way the lights never work? Bennie changes those bulbs all the time and they never last. And one time . . ." Nate grunts like he's changing position. I hear a TV turn on in the background. "Okay, this one's for real. This girl brought a kitten to school once, to see if anyone wanted it. She had it in this box, and she walked through the tunnel with it. When she came out the other end, the cat was dead."

"You are totally making that up," I say around the heart in my throat.

"Hey, you asked me, I told you. Don't blame me if you can't sleep tonight."

I decide to call his bluff. "Who'd it happen to?"

"Lindsay McCormick."

So much for bluffs. "It was probably diseased."

"Probably," he agrees. "A fluke, like I said."

I hesitate, happy that he's talking to me even though he just scared the pants off me. "So you're not mad at me anymore, because of Saturday night?"

"I'm talking to you in bed at one in the morning. How mad can I be?"

I picture him there, in what, flannel pajamas? Underwear? Nothing at all? The sudden rush of heat leaves me weak. "Okay, good. And, uh, good night."

I quickly hang up.

——◄◦►——

A crash wakes me from a dream I forget as soon as I open my eyes. In the small slant of light from the streetlamp outside I can see the beams of the ceiling. What the hell was *that*?

I tiptoe restlessly from window to window. I check out the school—no visible lights—then peer at Nate's house across the street, dark except for a TV flickering upstairs. Is that his room? Is he still awake? Should I call him back and say: *Hi, I can't sleep, thanks to your nasty dead-kitten story. Wanna come over for popcorn?*

Lightning flashes, followed by thunder. I heave the heavy window up and press my nose to the wet screen, breathing in the night. The storm draws me in. I quiver in its magnetic pull.

My alarm clock says 2:44.

What time did Mrs. Gibbons hang herself?

What was she thinking about before she did it? Was she thinking of Annaliese?

Was she remembering how, every Halloween, kids throw stuff at her house and yell for her dead granddaughter?

Did she miss Annaliese? Does Annaliese, even now, miss her, too?

If Annaliese were alive, she'd be Mom's age now. Maybe she'd still be living here, sleeping in that canopy bed.

Maybe she and her grandmother would plant flowers together. Play checkers. Laugh at TV shows. Count fireflies on a summer night. *All the things Nana and I used to do.*

I hear them now: Annaliese, saying, "Grandma, I love you the best."

MRS. GIBBONS: *No, you don't. You love your mother the best.*

ANNALIESE: *If my mother loved me, she wouldn't have sent me away.*

MRS. GIBBONS: *She only wanted to keep you safe.*

ANNALIESE: *I don't care. I love you best, more than anyone else.*

MRS. GIBBONS: *I think she might be sad if she knew you felt that way.*

ANNALIESE, *slyly: Then we'd better not tell her, right?*

But maybe Annaliese's love for her grandmother won't be enough. She'll come home one day, call for her grandmother, and no one will answer. She'll wander from room to room, scarching, confused. She'll reach the attic stairs and walk up them, one by one, still calling for the person she loves more than her own mother—

—only to discover a tipped chair.

A discarded slipper.

And her grandmother, black and bloated, swinging by her neck from a beam.

"Rinn! Wake up!"

I choke off in the middle of my bloodcurdling scream, tearing at my throat with my nails till Mom pries my hands away.

The sun is up. Somehow I'm back in bed.

She rocks me gently. "It's okay, Rinn. It's just another bad dream."

4 MONTHS EXACTLY ─────

Wednesday, November 5

Mom doesn't mention the anniversary, but I know it's on her mind. She keeps staring at the phone this morning, like she's dying to call Frank but doesn't want to do it with me around. She knows I'll ask to speak to him.

Like me, she's afraid he'll say no.

I'm not sure why I don't call him myself. What's the worst he can do, hang up on me? Hanging up would be a blessing compared to a lot of things he could do.

Like ask me *why*.

Why did you sneak out your window that night?

Why did you leave that lamp burning when you knew it was dangerous?

Why did you lock your door so she'd think you were inside?

Why didn't you call 9-1-1 when you first saw the flames?

Why didn't you save her, Rinn?

Why didn't you save my mother?

One thing I learned is that, even if you're certifiably crazy, you can't always use it to excuse the things you do. Prisons overflow with mentally ill convicts. Proving you're nuts won't give you a free pass.

For four whole months I've tried to answer these same questions, and I keep coming up with the same pathetic excuse: *because I was crazy.*

I snuck out of the house because the Voices told me to *RUN!*

I left the kerosene lamp burning because I didn't think ahead.

My door was locked to keep out imaginary intruders, not to trick Nana into thinking I was inside.

I didn't call 9-1-1 because I didn't, at first, realize the flames were real.

And I didn't save her because only a crazy person could watch a house burn down without trying to save anyone inside.

Nobody understands. Not me, not Mom. Least of all Frank.

I know I'm the main reason for Mom and Frank's separation. After Nana died, Frank didn't want me anywhere near him. They'd argue when they thought I couldn't hear.

But I did hear. I heard Frank admit to Mom that he couldn't trust me to stay on my meds, and that the next time I went off, who else would I kill? How he couldn't look at me without remembering how his mom died. How he thought I'd be better off in boarding school—undoubtedly on another continent, if Frank had his way.

I heard Mom plead with him to meet me halfway. To not make her choose between the two of us. To give me one more chance to prove myself worthy of his trust.

Some days, like today, I wonder if she made a mistake. Mom could be back in La Jolla with Frank now, with their parties and Jet Skis, vacationing in Aspen with elderly rock stars.

Me, I'd be—well, who knows where I'd be?

I stumble through class after class, answering when called on, smiling when spoken to. The dark sky outside the windows, the pattering of rain, only enhance my depression. I wander to lunch, where I listen to Meg, Tasha, and Lacy angst about the same old, same old. I wonder how they'd react if I put *my* two cents in: "Yeah, I'm angsty, too. Four months ago I set fire to a house and killed my grandmother. Then, two days later, I tried to commit suicide."

Would any of them bat an eye?

◄○►

Nate's not waiting for me after school; he left early today to help his dad with an emergency furnace repair at one of Luke's rental properties.

At my locker, though, is Dino, reeking of pot. He'd been kicked out of English by Ms. Rasmussen, so I can imagine how he'd spent that time. "Hey, Rinn."

I shrug, not knowing what's safe or unsafe to say. The last thing I want to do is encourage this guy.

"You keep an eye out for Bennie, I'll get that thing back for you now."

I slam my locker door and zip my jacket up to my chin. "Dino. It's not *that* important."

"Yeah, it is," he argues, leaning in close enough to breathe on me. "C'mon, I checked—there's nothing going on here tonight. It'll take me five minutes. Ten, tops."

Secretly, I'm kind of flattered that he's so determined to make amends. "I already told you, it's probably broken. Besides, how will you get over that fence?"

"I can hop it, easy."

I hesitate.

Dino adds earnestly, "All you gotta do is watch for Bennie. I'll be in and out. C'mon, Rinn. Lemme do this."

I must be stupid. But if my candleholder isn't completely shattered—it *is* rock hard, and I didn't hear it break when he threw it—maybe it'll be worth it. Maybe it's only chipped. "Aren't you afraid to go in there?" I navigated the tunnel today, with company as always, but no way am I ever stepping another foot into that pool room.

Dino laughs, a little too hard and a little too long. I translate this as *Hell yeah, I'm scared, but I ain't telling YOU that.*

"Meet me in the auditorium in ten minutes," he instructs, and dashes off.

I unzip my jacket and pretend to rearrange the stuff in my locker. Behind me, the noisy, after-school crowd thins out till only a trickle of kids is left behind. Lockers slam. Mr. Lipford waves as he passes by, heading out with a couple of teachers I don't know. Doors bang shut, echoing in the distance.

When the last of the kids disappear, I slip on my book bag and walk off, nonchalantly, through the deserted halls. Dino's waiting in the auditorium, crouched on the steps to the tunnel. "Come in with me and just keep an eye out. You see Bennie or anyone else, let me know."

"Let you know how?" I demand. "Because I am not going all the way in."

"Just yell hi to them or something. Loud, so I'll hear ya. Then *you* get outta here."

Nobody's fixed the pool room door yet. Dino produces a flashlight from his own book bag and slips inside. I hover at the threshold, eyeing the tall metal fence in the bouncing ray of light. The gate—with a sign that reads KEEP OUT! VIOLATERS WILL BE SUSPENDED!—is sealed shut with the same padlocked chain. I view the links at the top of the fence, all of them twisted and exposed, forming a wall-to-wall row of jagged spikes.

Well, this just proves it: Dino's dumber than I am. "Dino, forget it. You'll kill yourself."

"Bull," he says cheerfully.

He tucks the flashlight into the waistband of his jeans, and he reaches up to curl his fingers around the links. Rust rains down as he heaves himself up with a grunt. His shoe snags a link, then another, then another, and—as easily as he predicted—he scales the swaying fence. I watch him lift a slow, a cautious leg over the jutting metal links. One false move and good-bye family jewels.

Arms quivering under his weight, he struggles for a foothold, finds it, then eases the other leg over. Then he drops to the ground on the other side. "YES!"

When his jubilant shout dies away, everything is silent. And dark.

And very, very cold.

I step back from the doorway. "I'm going to wait out here." Already busy swinging the flashlight in search of my candle holder, Dino doesn't bother to reply.

A hint of lavender—my imagination?—lingers in the tunnel. I remember the séance, and what happened, and how everyone, even Dino, is lying about it, and I start to get angry all over again. Anger, though, is a useless waste of energy. So I breathe deeply in and out to calm myself down, thinking that, one way or another, I'll find out the truth.

I hug myself against the chill, feeling exposed and abandoned in the dim yellow light, the murky tunnel stretching before me. What am I doing here, *alone*—Dino doesn't count; he's too busy showing off, hunting for his prize—after what happened on Saturday? If something happened to me, right now, what good would Dino *be*?

Squeak . . . clank . . . squeak . . . clank, clank . . .

My heart practically explodes from my chest till it dawns on me what I'm hearing: Bennie's janitor cart, rolling through the auditorium. Hastily, I shut the pool room door and then screech, "Hi, Bennie!" as I leap out of the tunnel and down the four steps. *Get outta here,* Dino ordered. Well, I'm doing exactly that.

Bennie glowers suspiciously from beneath his orange knit cap. "What're you doing in there? Why ain't you gone home?"

"I forgot my book bag." A spur-of-the-moment fib. "I'm, um, on my way out now."

He doesn't ask why I'm *here*, miles away from my locker and the door I normally use. Then again, why would he? He can't possibly track everyone.

Bennie shuffles down the aisle, past the stage, and pushes open the rear emergency exit. No fire alarm sounds in spite of the warning sign. "Might's well go out here. You just live over yonder."

No, no! Now what? Hopefully Dino heard me yell. Hopefully he's lying low. Better yet, he got *out* of there, too.

"Okay, thanks." Casually I stroll out the door and into the backyard of school. My feet sink in crispy mud. Through the bare, swaying trees I spot the roof of my house. I could be home in thirty seconds . . . but what about Dino? As much trouble as he's always in, he'll probably get suspended if Bennie catches him in the pool room. And what if Dino blabs that I helped him out? Or started to, anyway.

No, I decide. If he's as obsessed with me as Meg says, I doubt he'll drag me into it. He wants to be my hero, not get me in trouble. *At least I hope so . . .*

Impulsively, I turn and tug at the door, already inventing another excuse to show my face to Bennie again.

I'm locked out.

4 MONTHS + 1 DAY ─────────

Thursday, November 6

Dino's not in homeroom today, or in any other of the classes we share. I guess this means Bennie busted him, after all, and ratted him out to Mr. Solomon.

Selfishly, I hope he found my candleholder first.

The temperature drops drastically during the day and the streets are coated with white by the final bell. Nate and I slush home together, and he promises to return with a shovel to clear out the driveway.

"Want some help?" I ask, not that I've ever shoveled snow. Or *seen* it, till now.

"No, it's my job." Snowflakes melt on his face. "Dad pays me."

"Oh. Well, in that case, carry on."

I hop inside, kick off my shoes, and sling my jacket over the brass hook in the foyer. When I hit our voice mail, I hear Frank say, "Monica, call me back when you get a chance."

My heart hurts at the sound of his voice. Hardly thinking it through, I pick up the phone and dial. I guess Frank notices the caller ID because he says without a hello, "Hey, I didn't expect to hear back from you till tonight."

"It's me."

"Rinn?" Silence. "Well, how're you doing? Where's your mom?" he asks without awaiting my first reply.

"She's not home yet. I heard your message so, um, I thought I'd call you back."

"Oh."

More silence. I try again. "I haven't talked to you in forever."

"I know." I picture him running his hand across his balding head, fingering his long gray ponytail. "How's the new school?"

"It's cool. I made some friends. I'm in the chorus, too."

More silence.

Frank doesn't care if I made friends or that I'm in the school choir. Why am I babbling? I feel those *well, I gotta go* vibes zinging through the receiver. "Frank?"

"Yeah, Rinn?"

I'm sorry. I'm so sorry! I didn't mean for it to happen.

But how many times can I say I'm sorry without hearing "I forgive you"? He's never said that to me. I doubt he ever will.

"I miss you," I say instead. I shut my eyes, expecting him to slam down the receiver.

He doesn't. "Yeah, uh, me too. Have your mom call me when she gets home."

"Okay."

"Bye, Rinn."

"Bye, Frank."

I throw myself facedown on the sofa. Part of me knows it's time to move on. Does the rest of my life depend on Frank's forgiveness? Do I honestly want to be fifty years old, still saying I'm sorry, hoping he'll love me again?

But if he never forgives me, why bother *making* it to fifty?

A few minutes later Nate bangs on the front door, crusted with snow, wearing that same grotesque hunting cap. He holds out a soggy plastic bag. "Your newspaper. It was buried."

"You could've left it on the porch."

"Actually . . ." Nate stomps snow off his big rubbery boots— probably called "galoshes" in this neck of the woods. "I was gonna ask if you want to go riding."

"In the snow?"

"The horses don't care. Anyway, we can ride in the barn."

I start to beg off, because yes, I'm in a rotten mood. But then I see how hopeful Nate looks. Why does he like me so much? Because obviously he does. I guess I'm not used to being "liked" by guys who don't immediately try to jump my bones.

Nate studies me. "You have that look again."

"What look?"

Cold fingers touch my cheek. "Like you want to cry."

"Well, I don't." Impulsively, I catch his hand. "But I do want to go riding."

His smile melts me. "Yeah?"

"Yeah. Except I need to know one thing." Biting back a smile, I point to his ugly hat. "What'd you do? Scalp Sasquatch?" I dodge away from his outraged response, hunt up paper and a pen, and scribble a note for Mom.

<hr>

After riding for several hours in Rocky Meadows' indoor ring, and another hour hanging out in the paneled lounge with the moth-eaten bear rug—the owners are in Florida till Christmas, so it's kind of our own private hideaway—we say good-bye in Nate's driveway and I run across the street.

Mom swoops down. "It's eight o'clock! I was worried sick!"

"I left you a note," I protest.

"I didn't see a note."

Spotting it—the wind must've blown it from the kitchen table when she opened the back door—I snatch it up. "You didn't look very hard." I thrust it in her face. "Well?"

"Well, what?"

What did she think I was doing all this time?

I know exactly what she thought. "Go ahead. Say it!"

"Say what?"

Furious at her fake facade, I shout, "You still don't trust me! No matter what I do, no matter what I say, you're just like Frank. You'll *never* trust me again, ever."

"That's not—true!" Mom swings her back to me and clutches her hair. "Oh God, oh God, I need a cigarette so bad!"

Why am I so mean to her sometimes?

"No, you don't," I say, hoping to make up.

"Yes, I do. You have no damn idea."

Stung, I snap, "Smoke, then! Who cares?" Halfway to the stairs I remember something. "By the way, Frank called."

"I know. I spoke to him."

"Yeah, well." I stomp off. "So did I."

————◄○►————

The phone rings an hour later. I'm lying on my mattress, listening to the piano music drifting up through the register. I love that Mom's playing again. Sadly, I think of Nana's piano, a family heirloom brought over from Europe on a steamship. Then I remember what it looked like after the fire: charred wood, blackened ivory, a jumble of glowing red strings.

Feeling *very* antisocial, I ignore the ringing phone and just stare at the beams and listen to the wind rattling outside. Snow! Fricking snow, one week after Halloween. This whole town'll be on Prozac by Christmas.

Mom appears at the top of my stairwell. "Rinn, honey. Something's happened."

"Is it Frank?" Of course I think of him first. He's much older than Mom, plus he drinks and smokes. He's also been on my mind all day.

Mom kneels beside my mattress. "That was Mr. Solomon on the phone. You know Dino wasn't in school today, right? Well, apparently there's been . . . an accident."

My shoulder blades crawl. "What kind of accident?"

"Honey, Bennie found him in the pool room after school today." Mom hesitates. "Dead."

I think I heard her wrong. *"What?"*

"No one's sure what happened. But I guess he was there, uh, all night."

All night? Bennie didn't chase him out yesterday?

He never got out at all?

My voice quavers. "He died in the pool?"

"By the pool, Mr. Solomon said. He couldn't give me any more details." Mom drags a wrist over her eyes. "Oh, poor Bennie. I can't even imagine how . . ."

I fly to my window. Through a curtain of snowflakes I make out, in the dark, the flashing lights of two police cars, a fire truck, and an ambulance. The entire safety force of River Hills, no doubt.

"Oh my God." I yank off my nightshirt and reach for the jeans I wore earlier, the legs stiff and reeking of horses. "Oh my God!"

"Wait! You are not going out there."

"He was my friend, Mom!"

Friend? You liar. You never gave him the time of day. You left him behind yesterday.

Defeated, I drop back onto my rumpled mattress. Why didn't I keep my mouth shut and wait quietly when Bennie showed up? Or go into the pool room *with* Dino?

I moan. "But what happened to him?"

"I don't know, honey. I honestly don't."

I cover my face as Mom pulls me close.

4 MONTHS + 2 DAYS ———

Friday, November 7

School is canceled. I watch the building from my bedroom window, not sure what I'm hoping to see. Then, disgusted by my own curiosity, I force myself to get dressed.

Millie, of course, finds out the details first. As Mom and I start on our second pot of coffee, she blows into our living room in a flurry of perfume and leftover cooking grease. Tasha follows, hugs me, and wails, "I never knew anybody who died, unless they were *old*!"

Same here. I hug her back as Millie tells Mom, "I talked to Claire. You remember Claire, from the team? Well, she's an EMT now and *she* says it looks like that kid climbed the fence and then snagged his leg at the top, and"—Millie glances at Tasha and me—"couldn't get loose."

Ashen, Mom whispers, "That poor boy."

"Bennie's beside himself, I hear." Millie fishes a Kleenex from her purse and blows a bubbly honk. "They think his heart gave out, what with him hangin' upside down for so long, stuck like a piece of meat."

Upside down? "Why didn't he call for help?"

"Maybe he did. But Bennie swears he didn't hear nothin', and he was there till five. Not many other folks around, maybe a teacher or two. Nobody heard nothin'." Jamming her tissue back into her purse, Millie adds briskly, "We can't stay. We're off to the Aquatic Center. With weather like this, I bet we get the whole place to ourselves." She bristles at Tasha's rude snort. "I told you, no point in wasting an opportunity. It's bad enough I let you miss Saturday!"

"And I'll never hear the end of it," Tasha mutters.

"That's *right*." Millie points a red fingernail at Tasha. "You mess up at regionals and I'll *never* be able to hold my head up again. All those nice people who've donated to your fund? The whole town's rootin' for you and you know it, missy. And don't forget, your daddy's driving in special just to watch you." Tasha's dad is a trucker and on the road most of the time. "You want to disappoint him?"

Sour-faced, Tasha ignores this. She squeezes me again. "I'll call you later if I don't get back too late." Millie hauls her off before she can even zip up her jacket.

Mom says in disbelief, "I love Millie, but what is she thinking? A boy just died!"

I wish Tasha and I could've hung out tonight. I bet Tasha wishes the same thing.

The idea of Dino hanging helplessly upside down, suffering for hours, makes me sick to my stomach.

So do the *other* crazy thoughts darting madly through my brain. Thoughts I can't share with Mom, or anyone, really.

Except maybe . . . ?

I grab the phone and dial Nate's number.

———◄◊►———

He obediently appears ten minutes later. After he endures Mom's condolences, I push him toward the stairs, ignoring Mom's warning to "leave your door open, please!" I don't *have* a door to my room, just the one to the stairwell.

Nate surveys my Precious Pewter walls. "Cool color."

"Way cooler than that boring white you slapped on."

"It was all new drywall. At least I *painted* it."

"Why didn't you leave the walls the way they were?"

He hesitates. "Uh, it was some pretty ugly wallpaper."

I watch him admire my band posters, all originals and most of them signed by the artists. Frank always gives—*gave*—these to me for special occasions. I flip in a CD for some background noise in case Mom decides to be nosy.

"Pink Floyd?" Nate guesses after the first few notes.

"David Gilmour. He played with Pink Floyd before he went solo."

He points to my Led Zeppelin poster: "Stairway to Heaven." "Where'd you get this stuff?"

"My stepdad's a music producer. He's retired now, but he knew all these people."

"Seriously? You meet any of 'em?"

"Yeah, some. But rockers, they're just people, you know? Mostly I was in bed whenever anyone came around." *Or sneaking off, doing my own thing.*

David Gilmour warns through my speakers that *there's no way of out of here*, that we're *here for good.* Frank loves this song.

So do I. Listening to it now, I feel better, if not braver. I sit on my mattress and motion for Nate to join me.

He does, maintaining a safe distance. "You want to talk about Dino? You okay?"

"Yeah. You?"

"Yeah, I just—I just can't believe this happened."

"Me, either." I hesitate. "Nate, I have to tell you something. But you can't laugh at me. And you can't blow me off as 'crazy.'"

Nate nods seriously. "What happened to Dino? I don't think it was an accident."

Already he's skeptical. "Sure it was. I mean, if Dino wanted to kill himself, there are easier ways."

"I'm not saying he killed himself. Just listen, okay?"

<hr/>

At first Nate says nothing when I explain why I think the tunnel is evil. Not only the tunnel but the pool room, too. Maybe he wonders if I'm delusional. Or where the nearest escape route is.

"Nate, it's exactly like you told me. Everything bad that happens to people happens *after* they're in there."

Nate says wearily. "I never should've told you that stuff. Those are *stories*, Rinn. Urban legends. Whatever."

"What about the dead cat?"

"You're the one who said it might've been sick in the first place."

"That's before I put it all together." I inch closer to him. "Look, we're in the tunnel, right? And Lacy goes nuts and attacks me. Then she starts with the migraines. Meg's ears ring constantly, plus she's different, Nate. She's *down* all the time.

Then Cecilia gets locked in there and now she can't sing. Now look what happened to Dino."

Nate stays silent.

"You don't see a pattern here?"

"We all use that tunnel," he reasons. "All of us, every day."

I blow out my breath in increments. "Why'd I know you'd say that?"

"Because it's true. The rest of us are fine. *I* never noticed any funny air. And hey, what about Bennie? He's in there more than any of us, cleaning and stuff. Why doesn't something happen to him?"

I study my folded hands. I forgot about Bennie.

Nate slides closer, too. "You're talking about earaches and headaches and people losing their voices. But then Dino dies? That's a pretty big leap."

"Maybe he saw something."

" 'Something'?" he repeats. "A ghost, you mean?"

"Yes, a ghost!" I rush on over his explosive sigh. "That séance, Nate. Before that, it was like you said: things happened to people, but nothing serious, right? Aside from that drunk teacher, I mean. But then we had the séance, and—oh, I don't know! But what if we did something in there? Released some kind of power?"

Something strong enough to hurt. To kill, even.

Nate responds with an incredulous head shake. Stubbornly I insist, "You weren't there. You didn't see how *eerie* it was, how they all sat there like dummies. Not moving. Not talking. Then when I ran for help, they strolled out like nothing happened."

"They were playing you, Rinn."

"I thought of that, too. Except now Dino's dead."

"Yeah, Dino's dead. But you can't tell me that has something to do with that séance." Nate pats my leg. "Look, all those things, they're like random nothings. Shit happens, surfer girl. Every day, every minute."

His touch, through my jeans, quenches my frustration. I throw up my hands, resigned. "Fine—I'm crazy."

"Look," he says impatiently. "We all make jokes about Annaliese. But to believe in ghosts and think they can actually hurt you? What do you think this is? A Poltergeist movie?"

I remember the shadows in the cafeteria that day, the way they didn't match up to the table legs. My imagination? Or something supernatural? *Either way, it sucks.*

"What sucks?"

Holy crap, did I say that out loud? I think fast. "Okay, say ghosts do exist. Then why Annaliese? Why not my grandmother?" My voice breaks, frustrating me more. "Why can't *she* come back? Why can't people be haunted by the people they love? Not by stupid people we never met."

His hand creeps up my leg, reaching for mine. I watch, entranced, as he takes my fingers and presses them to his lips. Then Nate, who possesses radar far more acute than mine, drops my hand one millisecond before Mom pops up.

"Not to intrude," she calls sweetly over Gilmour's guitar. "But your dad's looking for you, Nate."

Muting the music with the remote, I wait for Mom to leave us alone to say good-bye. When she doesn't, Nate politely excuses himself and clomps off downstairs.

"Well," Mom notes, "I can see he likes *you*."

I smile. "I like him, too." My glow fades when Mom's

forehead pinches with disapproval. "Spare me the lecture. I've heard it before."

"For all the good it did. This is your *bedroom*, Rinn." Ignoring my blaze of indignation—*is she always going to suspect me of screwing around?*—she disappears back down the stairwell.

4 MONTHS + 3 DAYS ———

Saturday, November 8

Barton's Funeral Home is packed, even with people you wouldn't expect to show up. Like some of the football jocks, because of Jared, of course. Tasha, Lacy, and Meg are all here. Nate, too. Even Mr. Solomon and most of the teachers.

Dino's dad, in an outdated black suit and minus the bandana, looks strangely calm. I figure out why when I smell the liquor on his breath. His wife, Deb—silent, unfocused—hangs on his arm like she's drugged on downers. Maybe she is.

In front of the casket, Mr. Mancini's dark eyes, identical to Dino's, meet mine first. Then they rest on my mother's out-stretched hand.

"Joey, Deb," she says. "I am so sorry."

He accepts her shake with his own grease-stained hand. "Monica, Monica . . . been a long time, ain't it? Y'know, I told your little girl here to tell you I said hi, to stop by sometime. She ever give you my message?"

Mom looks at me. "I forgot," I say reluctantly. It's true. I never thought about Creepy Red Bandana Dude again.

Mom extricates herself from Mr. Mancini's grip. "You've already met Rinn?"

"Yep." He flashes yellow teeth.

I nod back. Then, impulsively, I touch Mrs. Mancini's sleeve. "I'm sorry about Dino."

Dino's mom, thin and plain, works her mouth like she wants to smile and can't remember how. Mr. Mancini chuckles humorlessly. "Me, too, honey. Now I gotta run that damn garage all by myself." He shoves his hands into his shabby suit coat. "Monica Parker. Well, well."

Mom's smile never wavers.

Mr. Mancini sways, knocking his spooky wife off balance. Uncaring, she fiddles with a sweater button. "Know what my momma used to say to me, Monica? 'What goes around comes around,' that's what she said. Reckon I'm just now figurin' out what she meant by that."

Mom, after a dreadful pause, murmurs some nicety. Then she draws me away, leaving the Mancinis to mingle with the next victims in line.

"What was that all about?" I hiss. "What did he mean?"

"It's a saying, Rinn."

"I *know* it's a saying."

"I have no idea what he meant."

"And what's wrong with *her*?"

"Car accident, ten years ago. Joey was driving drunk. He

spent two years in prison for it. Poor Deb was in a coma for nine months."

So this is Dino's family: a drunk, obnoxious dad and a brain-damaged mom.

I should've been nicer to him when I had the chance.

Mom brightens as Nate and Luke Brenner approach. So do I.

"Closed casket," Nate notes with some relief.

Nana had a closed casket, too, although at the time I'd wished it was open. I even asked Frank to lift the lid so I could see for myself that people weren't lying to me, that she really did die from the smoke and not from the flames. Frank's reaction to that made *me* want to crawl into that casket.

Nate notices my shudder. "What's wrong?"

I will not panic. I'm sick of being such a baby. Sick of popping a pill when things get to be too much.

I unclench my clammy hands. "Too stuffy in here."

Nate weaves me around the milling visitors. Tasha waves, but I'm too distraught to wave back. On the way outside we pass Lacy, too, slumped and sullen, hemmed in by her parents. I ignore her as well.

On the freshly shoveled and salted porch, Nate opens his jacket wide, draws me in, and folds the leather around me. I forget my panic. I forget I'm at a wake, pretending to grieve for a dead boy I didn't care for much. Engulfed by Nate's warmth, sheltered by his arms, I'm exactly where I want to be at this moment. When his lips touch my hair, I lift my face. Like magic, those lips find mine and my arms slide around his waist. We kiss, and we kiss, while I wonder, dazed, why I can still feel the rock salt crunching under my boots.

By now I should surely be floating to the sky.

4 MONTHS + 4 DAYS ————

Sunday, November 9

It's a cold, bleak, wet day for a funeral. After Reverend Kessler, Lacy's dad, delivers the final blessing, one by one we drop roses on the casket. Bennie Unger, his neon orange cap squashed over his head as usual, squints at me. I wave halfheartedly. He then wipes sleet off his face and lumbers over to toss his flower at Dino's casket. He misses.

I huddle by a tree while Mom and Mr. Brenner talk to the Mancinis. I don't think Dino's father had a chance to hit the bottle today; he looks haggard and miserable. Mrs. Mancini, as lifeless as yesterday, drifts through the snow like a rag blowing in the wind.

Lacy stands with her family, her shoulders convulsing, tears dripping endlessly. I know she and Dino had a thing going on, but I never expected *this* reaction out of her. Before I can decide whether or not to walk over, I notice Mr. Mancini pass something to Mom. Over the wind, and other conversations around me, I make out two words: "Dino" and "pool."

Then he collapses, sobbing, to his knees in the muddy snow. Dino's mom picks at her gloves, ignoring the anxious onlookers who gather around her husband.

Stomach fluttering, I trudge off toward the cemetery gate. All I want is to go home, grab a book, and crawl into bed. But Nate sloshes over and catches my hand. "Hey."

I know by his smile that he's thinking about how we kissed. My mood spikes. I smile back and squeeze his hand. "Hey." That's as far as it goes, because Mom and Luke hurry to join us. I drop Nate's hand and ask Mom, "What did Mr. Mancini say about the pool?"

Mom shifts her Jimmy Choo boots while Luke shakes out a cigarette. "Oh, that. Well, what he said was"—she gazes longingly at Luke's Newports—"he knows why Dino was by the pool that night." With great care, Mom rearranges her scarf before reaching into her coat pocket. She hands over the mysterious item, adding in a peculiar, distrustful tone, "They found this in his pocket."

Speechless, I finger the broken ceramic shard. It's the base of my candleholder, my name plainly carved into the jagged red disk:

Rinn Jacobs

I know it wasn't my idea that Dino climb that fence. But I didn't go out of my way to discourage him, either. Yes, he did tell me to leave if anyone showed up. But what if I'd stayed?

Aside from what happened to Nana, I've never felt so guilty. Or so afraid.

———◦———

There are "doings" going on back at Barton's, coffee and cookies, nothing fancy. But Lacy begs Meg, Tasha, and me to come home with her instead. "I gotta talk to you guys in private. No boys allowed," she adds to Nate.

I hesitate. Mom and Luke are a half a block ahead of us, heading toward the funeral home. But Nate says, "Go on, go. I'll let your mom know. Call me later?"

I nod, deflated, cupping the pottery shard in my coat pocket.

"So what's up?" Meg asks as we turn to head toward Lacy's street.

Congested from crying, Lacy croaks, "I'll tell you when we get there. I have to show you something."

Lacy's house is unoccupied except for one fat striped cat stretched across the center hall stairs. Lacy boots him out of our way. "I told my folks I have a headache. They're so used to hearing me say it they don't even question me anymore."

This is the first time I've seen Lacy's room. Surrounded by lace, fluff, and various shades of pink, it's like plunging head-first into a cotton candy machine.

As soon as we settle, Lacy starts sniffling again. Meg hugs her. "Aw, Lace. We know you're sad about Dino. But if you don't stop crying you *will* get another headache."

"I'm not crying over Dino! I'm crying about Chad! I e-mailed him again, like you said." She throws me an accusatory glance.

"He still didn't answer me. So I kept *on* e-mailing him, like a thousand times. Then last night"—Lacy reaches for a stack of papers on her desk—"I get *this*."

She hands the first sheet over. We crowd around to read the message: *Hey, sweetie, sorry I missed all your e-mails. Some of the guys and me got a few days off and went to Shanghai. Don't worry, I been thinking about you every second! I'll read the rest of your e-mails and get back to you ASAP! Love, Chad*

"But that's good," Meg proclaims. "It means he's not blowing you off."

"Wait." Lacy thrust a second paper at us. "Then *this* one came this morning."

No "*Hey, sweetie*" this time. Instead: *Well I finally finished going through your last 39 e-mails. Let me just say that I'm glad I found out NOW what a crazy bitch you are before I did something stupid like MARRY you. You sure that's my kid? I want proof— because you're SICK! You need a shrink! Am I the only person who ever told you this? I can't believe you wrote that stuff. All I can say now is: do not EVER contact me again. FYI, I reported this to my C.O., who says he'll notify your family if you write me again. P.S. Keep the damn ring.*

"What?" Meg howls. "You e-mailed him thirty-nine times? What did you *say*?"

Lacy, face scrunched, hands over the rest of the papers, all but one. We pass them around, and it's pretty dramatic stuff: Lacy begging Chad to answer her, demanding to know where her plane ticket is, pleading with him to tell her if he still loves her or not. Nothing bad enough to make her look "sick"—only possessive, frantic, and *really* annoying.

"Man," Tasha breathes. "This is, like, stalker stuff."

Instead of reacting, Lacy simply hands over the final paper. "This is from Wednesday. This is the last time I wrote him."

You asshole! How dare you ignore my e-mails? What are you doing over there, screwing some Japanese slut? Well, FYI I have a NEW boy-friend now and he's way hotter than you in EVERY WAY! Believe me, I know cuz I've been fucking him for YEARS! BTW if you think I'm having any baby by you, think again, freak! I don't care if I have to jump in front of a train! I wish you were dead! I HATE YOU, YOU BASTARD! Good-bye forever.

Speechless, we all pass it around. Then Meg ventures, "Um, why would you write this?"

"I didn't! I mean, I know I *wrote* him that night. But I pretty much said what I said in all the others. B-but *this*"—she slaps the paper—"is what he *got* from me." She draws herself up, rigid with suspicion. "You guys didn't do it, right? I mean, Meg's got my password, and—"

Meg gasps. "I'd never! None of us would."

Lacy slumps back against her pink wicker headboard. "I know. I—I just had to ask. I keep trying to figure out how this happened. But it's my e-mail address, right? And it's in my sent mail, so I know I sent it—I just don't know why! I swear to God I don't remember *doing* it." She cries harder, her words barely coherent. "I had a headache that night, the worst one ever. It hurt so bad I just wanted to die! And now I hope I do. Because I *can't* lose Chad. I'd *rather* be dead!"

"Don't say that," Meg pleads. "You have to think about the baby."

Lacy can't, or won't answer. For a minute or two all we hear are her hysterical sobs. I yank a fistful of Kleenex from a pink crocheted box and hand it over.

"You're right," she blubbers, mopping her face. "I do love my baby. It's all I have left."

"Everything'll be fine," Meg soothes. "We'll even throw you a shower. We'll babysit and everything!"

Lacy's eyes shine. "You will?"

"Sure. You just have to, you know, tell your folks about this, Lace."

"Omigod, they'll kill me! I'd rather kill *myself*." She slaps Meg away. "Leave me alone, all of you! Just, just go away . . ."

Tasha argues, "You can't say you want to kill yourself and then expect us to go away."

"Oh yes, I can!" Lacy's unexpected rage petrifies me. "I guess I'll just have to wait till you bitches aren't around."

Meg ignores that. "You don't want to die."

"You don't," Tasha echoes. "No dude's worth that."

From an unfathomable distance I hear myself say, "Maybe she does."

Three stunned faces whip in my direction.

"Are you nuts?" Meg cries.

I stare into Lacy's moist, venomous eyes. "I know you feel like dying. But don't try it. Because if you screw it up, Lacy, it'll make everything worse."

I drag down my turtleneck to display, on purpose, the scar they're too polite, or too afraid, to ask me about.

"Trust me," I say quietly. "I know."

———◄◦►———

"Open it!" I tried to dodge around Frank to reach the casket myself. "Open it! Please, I have to see her!" I wanted to see for

myself that Nana didn't burn to death, didn't lie there screaming while flames devoured her flesh

Frank shoved me away, his eyes filled with hate. Nobody
ever looked at me like that before. Nobody's looked at me like
that since. "Get the hell away from her!"

The jolt knocked the fight right out of me. Mom stepped
forward with a strangled sound—and that's when I felt myself
reaching that plane. The same plane, I know now, that Cecilia
seeks whenever she's trapped in a closed space with no hope
for escape.

Tucked safely up where no one could reach me, I watched
the scene play out below. Mom, in a sleeveless black dress and
an elegant chignon, dabbing her eyes. Frank, in a suit and tie,
his ponytail neat, beard expertly trimmed, looking decep-
tively like an anguished old man.

I saw myself, too, in shorts and sandals and a grungy tank
top, not the dressy black suit Mom brought home from Nei-
man Marcus. My hair, unwashed for days, reeked of smoke and
salt water and glittered with sand.

I saw how people veered around me, embarrassed. Because
they already suspected I put Nana in that flower-draped casket?
Because they knew of my reputation for being surly and unpre-
dictable? Or because I looked so filthy, and possibly smelled
worse than I looked?

I couldn't distinguish the murmuring of the guests from
the Voices in my mind. The good Voice soothed me. The bad
ones taunted me.

I moved away from my parents. Like walking on a sponge,
my sandals sunk inches into the floor with each awkward step.

People smirked, suspecting I was stoned, but I had to move. Only constant movement kept the worst of the Voices at bay.

I weaved around people, strangely alert though I'd already gone three days without sleep—pretty typical of me. I liked strolling the streets or the beach all night. I knew where the stoners hung out, who'd share a blunt or a beer. I knew who was safe. I also knew who might hurt me.

If the police picked me up for breaking curfew—or worse—Frank usually convinced them to let him take me home, or back to the hospital for another "evaluation."

I had no boyfriends, only guys I slept with for dope. No girlfriends, either. The last one I lost because I'd picked open her back door and hung out for two days while she and her family were vacationing in the Bahamas. I lost the one before because I hooked up with her boyfriend. I don't remember *why* I hooked up. I pretty much hated the dude.

To this day I don't remember a lot of things.

I do remember the beach, and watching the smoke billowing from Nana's cottage.

I remember asking Frank about the piano, and Frank's horrific rage.

I remember all the psychiatrists. All the pills I flushed. All the times Mom pleaded with me to *take them, Rinn, please, just take the pills!*

But the pills made me too groggy to function. And, like I told Nate, I missed the highs. I missed feeling invincible. Sometimes I even missed the shadow people and the Voices, the only friends I had left when even my teachers learned to keep their distance. If you're forced to live your life in a lonely stupor, then tell me: What's the point of living at all?

At Nana's funeral, I *was* on drugs; Frank made sure of it. Although what he crammed down my throat didn't stop the Voices, it did make me understand Nana was dead, that her funeral was real, and that I, Corinne Katherine Jacobs, was responsible for it all.

I was drugged on the outside, but wild and frantic inside, like a snake trying to shed a skin made from glass. *I had to get out of there.* I swiped Mom's cell phone from her purse, hid out in a bathroom stall, and punched 4-1-1 to get the number for a cab. At that precise moment, several ladies walked in.

This was what I heard:

". . . they need to lock her up and throw away the key."

"Monica will never stand for it."

"Poor Frank. To think he raised her as his own. Did you hear her out there?"

"I'll bet he's ready to slash his throat."

"Or hers." *Chuckle, chuckle.*

"That girl's not right. Don't they have places for kids like that?"

"Sure they do. And Monica better wise up before they *all* end up dead."

Toilets flushed, water ran, and then the automatic hand dryer drowned everything out. By the time the motor stopped, the women were gone.

Alone again, I dropped the phone in the toilet with a thunk and a splash.

Monica better wise up before they ALL end up dead . . .

Haunted, bones clanking, I waded off through the invisible sludge, thinking: *This is how they want me to spend my life. Walking in quicksand. Terrified I'll murder the rest of my family.*

Downstairs, caterers darted to and fro, arranging lunch meat and pickles and loaves of bread. The bread knives looked sharp. The Voices raged like the surf on Nana's beach, the words garbled, yet perfectly clear nonetheless.

I knew what to do. But there was no place private enough to do it.

So I left, and slapped back home in my sandals, sun-burned and exhausted by the time I arrived. The cold house smelled unfamiliar, the home of strangers. Halos of color danced around the lights, magnified by my double vision.

The phone rang, scaring the shadow people from the walls.

"It's okay," I said to them, and to myself.

At Frank's desk I printed out a note and propped it next to a picture of me.

The phone rang again, and again, and again. Then stopped. Calmness descended.

It's okay. It's okay.

I cracked open a pack of replacement blades for Frank's razor. I filled the tub in the master suite and turned on the Jacuzzi. Dying on the beach might've been nice. Lying in the sun and tasting the salty wind while your blood seeps away into warm, swirling sand.

Too late for that. I'm already here.

I climbed into the water in my shorts and tank top. People do this naked on TV, but I couldn't take the chance Frank might find me first.

The razor sparkled in my surprisingly steady hand. Those women from the rest room must've followed me home; they circled the foaming tub, repeating the same truthful words:

Poor Frank. And to think he raised her as his own.

I'll bet he's ready to slash his throat.

Or hers.

Detached, I whispered to Frank, "I'll save you the trouble."

I reached up and dug the razor blade into my neck. It was easier than I'd thought. Kind of like slicing into a not-quite-ripe pear.

You really need to die, Rinn. You really do. It's okay.

I drew the blade downward. I felt no pain.

Then I tilted my head to one side and watched the water turn red.

———◁◦▷———

"My mom found me, not Frank. She'll never get over it. I was in a psych ward for a month. My whole family's screwed up. Is that what you want?" I ask Lacy.

Lacy says nothing, only stares at her lap. Tasha confides, "We wondered how you got that scar. My mom said not to ask you."

Meg reaches for my hand. "We won't say a word. Right?"

"Right!" Tasha rests her own hand on Meg's. "So what are you? I mean, what do they call it?"

"Bipolar," I admit.

Tasha nods. "Oh, that's really popular now. Like autism, right?"

Scandalized, Meg huffs, "Do you *ever* think before opening your mouth?"

I smile, anyway. "It's okay. I'm glad you guys know." *Though I'm not so sure about Lacy.* "It's so hard keeping it a secret."

"Does Nate know?" Meg asks.

"Yes. He still likes me, though."

"Duh!" Tasha squeals. "Like, nobody can tell?"

My smile expands. They really *don't* care. But can I trust them not to spread the word around school? What are the chances of my secret staying safe with, say, Lacy?

I peek over. Lacy hasn't said a word. Is she mad because I hijacked the attention away from her? That wasn't my plan. I only wanted her to know that killing yourself isn't as simple as you think.

Lacy sucks in her breath. But instead of speaking, she doubles over, her face contorted. Before any of us can ask what's wrong, I spy the blood on the quilt under her jeans.

———◆———

We huddle outside in a torrent of crystal-sharp sleet as the Kesslers' salt-crusted car fishtails off down the street. Meg and I stayed behind while Tasha ran back to Bartons' to discreetly fetch Lacy's parents. Lacy pleaded with us to hide those printed-out e-mails. I buried them in my purse while Meg, half-panicked, deleted Lacy's entire mailbox.

When Ma and Pa Kessler burst in, their state of shock lasted approximately five seconds. Then Reverend Kessler bundled a whimpering Lacy out to the car, blowing off my ambulance idea. Mrs. Kessler warned, rather than requested, "Do not say a word about this to *anyone!*" before flying out after her husband and daughter.

"All she cares about is what people think," Tasha says now. "I bet she comes home and sews scarlet *A*s in Lacy's underwear."

Tears shimmer on her dark lashes. This surprises me;

Tasha's the *first* one to jump all over Lacy about, well, whatever Lacy's current drama happens to be.

"And she just now said that baby's all she has left," Tasha chokes out. "God, how could this happen?"

Meg's tears fall freely. "It's my fault. Remember? I fell on her that day."

"That was ages ago," I argue, hoping I'm right. "It would've happened before now." When I move to hug her, Meg sidesteps closer to Tasha. Hurt, I add nonetheless, "Meg, these things happen. *You* didn't do it."

"Yes I did. I never should've cheered that day. I knew I was sick. I *knew* I was dizzy!"

"Stop!" Tasha snaps. "Rinn's right. It was an *accident.*" Shivering in the next blast of wind, she motions to us. "C'mon, it's freezing out here. Ma shut down the diner for the day. Let's go raid the kitchen."

———◄○►———

At the Boxcar Diner, with the CLOSED sign on the door, surrounded by warmth and the smell of brewing coffee, I burst out, "I think it's Annaliese."

Tasha frowns. "More ghost stories. Yay."

"Forget it," Meg says darkly. "I'm not in the mood."

"You started it. In the hall the other day?"

"Started what?" Tasha demands.

I point at Meg's hands, playing with her ears as usual. "See?" I tell Tasha—and then I blurt out everything I'd told Nate the other night. "And I *heard* about that alcoholic teacher, and Lindsay McCormick's cat."

Tasha quips, "I heard she killed it herself. Probably ate it, too."

I look at Meg. "If your ears made you dizzy and that's why you blew that pyramid, what if Lacy's migraine made her write that letter?"

"That's stupid," Meg says uneasily.

"You know something happened in there. You said so yourself!"

Tasha stares. "Wait. *What* happened?"

Meg ignores her, raging at me instead, "Yes, and now I'm sorry I said it! I should've known you'd blab. God, Rinn—is *no* secret safe with you?"

I flush. "Telling Cecilia about Lacy was wrong. But we have to tell Tasha this because *she* was there, at that séance. She has a right to know, in case—" I stop, afraid to jinx us by putting the idea into words.

Tasha gets it. "In case something happens to me? But I'm fine. So are you and Jared."

"Jared left in the middle of it," I inform her.

"You didn't," Meg says icily. "At least not until you ratted us out."

Her wary, too-familiar expression unnerves me. "Whatever." I fold my arms on the counter and rest my chin. I'm tired of defending myself.

"Listen, Rinn." Meg pats my shoulder, a forgiving gesture. "You're the one who lives in Annaliese's house, right? If she wants to haunt someone so bad, why doesn't she haunt you?"

"Because she drowned at school. Don't people haunt the places where they die?" I think of Nana's burnt cottage. *Does her ghost haunt that? That beach? Or is Nana simply . . . gone?*

The coffee's done. Tasha lines up three mugs. "In movies, maybe. If they die a violent death."

"Or," Meg adds softly, "if they have unfinished business."

I watch Tasha swing the carafe, pouring out one, two, three cups of steaming coffee. Meg's "unfinished business" lingers like the smell of burnt toast. She stares at the wall, her hands locked to her ears. Ice-cold cat claws tap the back of my neck.

Something's wrong with her. It's not just her ears.

"You guys want something to eat?" Tasha asks. I shake my head. "Meg?" When Meg remains mute, Tasha slams a hand on the counter. "Hey, are you deaf?"

Meg jumps. "What?"

Oh my God, that's exactly what I'd do when I was listening to the Voices.

The cat claws dance harder, faster.

"I *said*—" Tasha begins with enormous patience.

"Never mind!" Meg slides abruptly off the stool. "I'm going home."

"Why?" Tasha and I ask together.

"I told you, my ears are *killing* me! I can't even hear what you're saying half the time." Agitated, she bustles into her coat. "And you know what else? Dino's dead, Lacy lost her baby, and Jared *dumped* me—and you guys are sitting around here talking about ghosts! GOD!" she screams as she slams out of the diner.

"Jared dumped her?" I repeat to Tasha.

"Pretty much. He won't even tell her what he's so mad about. Or *if* he's mad."

"Pig," I say absently. I *must* talk to Jared the first chance I get. Thinking back, he did start avoiding her right after that séance. Is he embarrassed that she knows what a chicken he is?

Or is it something else?

Tasha ducks around the counter to claim Meg's stool. "Hey, that ringing in her ears? I looked it up. It's called tinnitus."

I recognize the word. "Yeah, rockers get that, from listening to all that loud music."

"So do old people when they start to go deaf. Swimmers get it, too." She makes a face. "Nice to know I've got *that* to look forward to."

"What can you do for it?"

"Depends on what's causing it. She's seeing some doctor tomorrow. I hope she gets that note so that stupid coach'll let her back on the team, or we'll *all* be listening to it till the end of the year."

I stare at the row of untouched coffees. Wind rattles the diner windows and sleet sprays the glass like handfuls of rice. It's almost dark; the yellow globes of the streetlights blink on all at once. "Do you ever wonder about her? Annaliese?"

Tasha hesitates. "Sometimes."

"My mom won't talk about her."

"Mine, either."

"Don't you think that's odd?"

"Yeah, considering how she gets off on talking about everyone *else*." A weak giggle, and then Tasha taps my shoulder. "Come home with me. I gotta show you something."

———◁◦▷———

At the Luxes' house a block away from the diner, Tasha opens the door to a den—"Ma's junk room," she calls it—crammed with decades of memorabilia. "I swear she's a hoarder in the making. She never throws *anything* out."

While I'm wondering why she dragged me here—*not to help her clean, I hope*—she fishes around till she finds a big box marked *HS STUFF!* Inside are yearbooks, scrapbooks, note-books, and photo albums. There's even a cheerleader's uni-form. Shrink-wrapped, no less.

"You want to know about Annaliese?" The top half of Tasha disappears as she roots around in the box. She emerges with lint in her hair, and tosses me a scrapbook. "Check it out."

Newspaper clippings, all in chronological order. The head-lines alone tell Annaliese's story, each in ten words or less:

DEATH OF LOCAL GIRL STUNS QUIET COMMUNITY

CORONER RULES GIBBONS'S DROWNING DEATH ACCIDENTAL

DOZENS TURN OUT FOR CANDLELIGHT VIGIL

ANNALIESE GIBBONS REMEMBERED AS "SHY AND SWEET"

SADLY, NO WITNESSES TO ANNALIESE'S LAST MOMENTS

"HOW COULD THIS HAPPEN?" GRANDMOTHER DEMANDS ANSWERS

OFFICIALS AGREE: GIBBONS'S DEATH TRAGIC, NOT SUS-PICIOUS

GRANDMOTHER OF DROWNING VICTIM THREATENS LAWSUIT

RIVER HILLS SCHOOL BOARD UNDER PRESSURE TO SHUT DOWN POOL

These stories were published the year Annaliese died. A later one announces the school board's decision to drain the pool, blaming a "lack of funds to maintain the upkeep" and "a reluctance on the part of students to swim in the pool respon-sible for a classmate's death."

"Annaliese's grandmother sued," Tasha says flatly. "So good-bye, pool."

I wave at the mountain of memorabilia. "I can't believe she hung on to this stuff. My mom threw everything out, even her yearbooks."

Tasha snorts. "She only keeps it so she can remember how popular she was, so she can throw *that* in my face, every chance she gets."

I flip farther through the scrapbook, scanning later stories:

ANNALIESE GIBBONS: TEN YEARS LATER

SCHOOL BOARD TO VOTE ON FATE OF H.S. POOL

VANDALS STRIKE POOL TWICE IN TWO WEEKS

AFTER ANNALIESE: NEXT GENERATION WONDERS—IS POOL HAUNTED?

Then one last story published a few months ago: STATE OF THE ART MEDIA CENTER TO BE BUILT ON POOL SITE.

"This is some great stuff," I murmur.

"Take it with you. Take the yearbooks, too."

"Your mom won't miss them?"

She waves expansively at the surrounding mess. "Are you kidding me?"

———◦———

"I was just about to send the cadaver dogs after you," Mom says as I stomp off snow and kick my boots into the hall closet.

"I went to Lacy's with Meg and Tasha. Didn't Nate tell you?"

"He did. You could've told me yourself, though." Mom first eyes my socks, wet from the slush I dragged in from the foyer. Then she eyes my pile of junk. "What's all that?"

"Stuff from Tasha." Hugging it, I dodge past her and race up the steps.

"Wait!" she calls. "Don't you want to talk about today?"

I pretend not to hear. No, I don't want to talk about Dino. Nor do I want to tell her what happened at Lacy's. Not because of Mrs. Kessler. I'm just not in the mood.

Mainly, I don't want her to see what Tasha gave me. I have a funny feeling she won't like me digging into her past. Before tonight, I never thought much about the fact that she threw out her high school stuff. True, she's a neat freak. But don't most people hang on to their yearbooks?

Too many bad memories? Like . . . maybe memories of my dad?

River Hills High is an anthill compared to my schools back in California. The skimpy yearbooks prove it. Mom, of course, looks flawless in every shot. What's it like to wake up to perfection every morning? I wake up a greasy, bushy-headed mess.

Truthfully, I hardly think about my real dad. And because Mom got pregnant *after* she left town, I doubt I'll find him in any of these books. All I know is that his parents were from Mexico, and that his first name was unpronounceable, so Mom called him "Jay" for short.

I wonder: Did Jay, like me, wake up a mess every morning? Did he eat Cocoa Puffs for breakfast? Did he love horses? Would he paint his room gray? Did I inherit his crooked tooth?

Was he mentally ill? Did I get that from him, too, like my teeth, my black hair?

Page after page, just in case, I study every boy who looks faintly Latino, but all the *J* names are ordinary, decidedly nonethnic: John, Joshua, James, and Joseph . . . as in Joseph Mancini, who looks hot in his senior picture, in a sexy Al Pacino–Hollywood Mafioso kind of way.

I whap the book shut, horrified at my lurid thoughts about Dino's dad. After a deep breath, I thumb through the other yearbooks. There's Nate's dad, a younger version of Nate in his senior picture. Ruggedly cute. *No* crooked eyeteeth.

The grainy newspaper picture of Annaliese didn't do her justice. In the color yearbook photos I see her hair was long and light brown, her eyes pale blue. In her sophomore photo a smile lights up her face. By junior year, the year she died, the smile is gone. *That* picture's marred by a big red *X*, plus someone scrawled the word "SKANK" in the margin.

"Ni-ice, Millie," I grumble. "What'd she do to you?"

I hear Mom's climbing footsteps. A quick flip of my comforter covers the books. I know Mom'll stroke out if she sees the Annaliese scrapbook. She'll say my interest in her is unhealthy, morbid, and that reading this stuff will give me nightmares. *Which it might.*

I make it to the top step in time to body-block Mom's admittance. "I'm getting ready for bed," I lie, flinging my sweater over my crackling hair.

"Are you okay? I thought I heard you talking to someone."

Maybe she thinks I'm hiding Nate up here. God, I wish. "No, just to myself. In a good way," I add hastily, squiggling out of my skirt. Trying to look dignified in my camisole, tights, and underpants, I meet her gaze. "May I have some privacy, please?"

"Rinn, I haven't seen you since this morning. I think we should talk."

"I'm tired. Can't we talk tomorrow?"

"I know it's been a hard day for you, honey. I don't even know where you've been."

"I told you where I was." I roll down my tights as I talk, then kick them off. This leaves me in nothing but my underwear. Mom still won't budge. "Mom, please. I did not want to hang around and watch people cry all day. None of us did. So we just took off."

Mom doesn't look pleased. "Fine. We'll talk tomorrow." When she hesitates, I cross my arms and grab the hem of my cami. That message she gets, and reluctantly leaves.

Maybe I *should* change rooms. A real door would be nice. Preferably one with a lock.

4 MONTHS + 5 DAYS ———————

Monday, November 10

I can't sleep. I keep thinking about Dino, how I was the last one to see him and nobody even knows that because I'm too afraid to say it. And Bennie saw me come out of the tunnel that day. What if he thinks I had something to do with it?

When I'm not thinking about Dino, I'm thinking about Lacy. *Why* did she write that terrible letter to Chad? Was she sleepwalking? Or was she simply mad because he didn't answer her e-mails, so she told him off, then lied about it?

I don't think she lied. I believed her. We ALL believed her.

And when I'm not thinking about Dino and Lacy, I'm thinking about Annaliese.

At 4:00 a.m. I give up, turn on my lamp, and pull out her scrapbook.

ANNALIESE GIBBONS: TEN YEARS LATER rehashes the story about how an early gym class found Annaliese dead in the pool. How witnesses saw her walk into the auditorium after school, but no one saw her come out. No one saw her again till they found her dead.

Disconcerted, I read on:

SCHOOL BOARD TO VOTE ON FATE OF H.S. POOL—boring stuff about how the pool room poses a danger because the roof is bad, plus stupid kids keep sneaking in.

VANDALS STRIKE POOL TWICE IN TWO WEEKS—kids again, spray-painting walls, breaking bottles, smoking weed, and most likely fornicating. Because fire regulations won't allow Principal Solomon to lock the tunnel itself, he puts a fence around the pool, a lock on the door, and threatens disciplinary action to any offenders.

Riiight. Like any of that works.

AFTER ANNALIESE: NEXT GENERATION WONDERS—IS POOL HAUNTED? Interviews of students who believe in "the ghost of Annaliese": *"I never get the flu, but I felt her watching me—and then I barfed!" "It's so cold in there." "It smells funny sometimes." "I can't explain it but it gives me the creeps." "I tripped for no reason and broke my nose!"*

Last of all, written last spring: STATE OF THE ART MEDIA CENTER TO BE BUILT ON POOL SITE. One staff member interviewed said, *"I have mixed feelings. I know it's useless the way it is— but a child died there! You know, some people believe her spirit lives on. I happen to be one of them. So is Annaliese's grandmother, my dearest friend. I'd much rather see a memorial built."*

The name of that staff member jolts me: Miss Roz Prout, former school secretary.

"Holy freaking hell," I whisper.

Maybe it makes sense that Mrs. Gibbons believed that Annaliese's spirit hung around. Maybe it comforted her. But how many adults *believe* in ghosts? Did Miss Prout see something, feel something? Is that why she left in such a hurry?

I find Annaliese's junior-year picture again. She stares, unsmiling, back from the page.

"Ghosts don't exist," I tell her. "You're a joke, like everyone says."

Whichever way I move my head, her pale eyes follow me.

"You're dead, Annaliese. Get it? You do—not—exist!"

As I start to close the yearbook, a name jumps out: Unger. Not Bennie, but maybe his older brother. I remember how Mom said Bennie's been working at RHH for years. He's there *all* the time. Early in the morning. Long after school lets out.

If Annaliese's ghost does exist, would Bennie know?

———◄○►———

I tell Mom about Lacy before school. "Don't say anything, though. Her mom wants to keep it a secret." Maybe around here they stone you to death or something.

"If she lost it, Rinn, it's probably for the best," Mom says after a moment. "Lacy's young. She has her whole life ahead of her. Believe me, it'd be a disaster."

I stare, unsure of how to take her un-Mom-like lack of sympathy. Does she regret having me? When she had to drop out of college, did she consider *me* a disaster?

She's never said that. But I wonder if she thought it.

———◄○►———

Looks like half the student body took a mental health day; the halls are quiet, sparsely populated. A grief counselor, imported from Kellersberg, spends the day in the cafeteria reading

Deepak Chopra. Meg, who missed morning classes because of her doctor's appointment, shows up in time for lunch.

"What'd he say?" I notice how chalky she looks.

Meg stares at the table. "He says my ears are fine."

"How can they be fine?" Tasha yelps.

"I don't know, but they are! So he thinks it's neurological. They're doing a test on Saturday, an MRI or something. And he *won't* give me a note for Coach Koenig because I'm still dizzy." Meg slaps the table hard. "My mom told him that. *I* was gonna lie, but *she* had to open her big mouth!" Tears shimmer on her lids. "If they don't find out why, I guess I'm off the team for good."

Gently I say, "But if you *are* dizzy, Meg—"

"How can I try out for a scholarship if I'm not even on a team? Do you think it's crazy for me to want to be a professional cheerleader? Like, for the Dallas Cowboys?"

"Well, no," I say honestly. "Anyway, maybe this'll just go away."

"Yeah," Tasha agrees. "Maybe you just have a bug."

"I hope so." Meg swipes at her tears and attempts a smile. "I love you guys." After a moment she adds, "I called Lacy yesterday. This morning, too. Nobody's answering at the house."

"Same here," Tasha says. "I wonder what's going on."

The three of us lapse into uncomfortable silence for the rest of the period. Tasha says nothing about her regionals this weekend, and neither she nor Meg bring up Dino. They pick at their lunches while I finger, discreetly, that piece of pottery through the fabric of my purse. After handing it over to me, Mom never mentioned it again. If I talked to her about it, would she say it's not my fault? Because that's how she is.

She's said "it's not your fault" to me more times than I can count.

Even when it was.

⟨◦⟩

On impulse, I stop at the main office after lunch. This is Mom's lunch break, I know. I also know Lindsay McCormick fills in for her at this time.

Today Lindsay is buried in a copy of *Twilight*. With a "*Yeek!*" she jumps like a hamster when I wham the bell on the counter. "You don't have to ring that when I'm sitting right here!"

"Sorry," I say, though I'm not—that was *funny*. "Is my mom around?"

"She's at lunch, as you well know."

"Can I ask you something?"

"No, I'm not breaking into the computer to change your grades." At my incredulous look, Lindsay explains, "That's what you guys usually ask me to do."

"Really?"

"Yeah." Lindsay relaxes. I wonder if she remembers I'm the person she kicked at the football game. "Sometimes they offer to pay me."

I point to her book. "Is that any good?"

"Yeah, it's awesome. You wanna borrow it? I already read it twice."

"Thanks." Encouraged, I take it and pretend to rustle through the pages.

Lindsay reverts to her normal, bitchy self. "Well? What do you want?"

I hug the book. "I just wanted to ask you about something I heard. About a kitten you brought to school?"

She scowls. "Don't tell me you believe that lie that I killed it myself?"

"No. I just want to know if it really happened. See, I'm new here, right? And people sometimes, well, try to freak me out . . ."

Lindsay twists her mouth down. "Maybe you're hanging around the wrong people."

"Just tell me, yes or no?"

Her smirk disappears. She picks a chip of polish off her thumbnail. "Yes."

Oh, God. She's messing with me, too.

"He was *so* cute. Black, with white paws. Coach Koenig wanted to see him, so I came in early and took the tunnel to the locker room. She played with him, but he had fleas, so she changed her mind. So I took him back through the tunnel—my mom was waiting in the car so she could take him back home—and when I came out, he was dead."

I barely trust my voice. "Do—do you think the tunnel did it?"

"Well, *I* didn't do it," Lindsay says impatiently. "And Coach Koenig didn't do it. That only leaves one person." I notice how she avoids saying Annaliese's name. "And you know *how* I know? Because when I looked in the box and saw he wasn't moving, I took him right out. I shook him and stuff, but yeah, he was dead. But—" Lindsay stops. She rubs her arms roughly.

"But what?"

"He was already stiff, like he'd been dead for hours. Stiff

and cold. Just like all those rats we keep finding lately." She nods at *Twilight*, pressed viciously into my chest. "Enjoy the book."

———◀◦▶———

I'm so creeped out by this revolting story, I think of nothing else the rest of the day. I'm *still* thinking about it after the last bell, when I notice some noisy jocks hanging out in the cafeteria. Yes, Jared's there, but sitting off to one side, mostly ignoring his obnoxious buddies.

He half rises at my cautious approach. "Hey," I say.

Jared nods. He doesn't say hey back. He looks like he wants to *run*. The cloud of testosterone peaks at a critical level as the rest of the guys notice my presence. The booming laughs and dirty jokes cease. Elbows nudge.

I lower my voice. "I have to ask you something about"—I don't want to say *séance*—"that night."

Jared's flash of alarm hardens to irritation. "Look, I'm busy here."

"Aw, jeez, O'Malley!" One of his teammates. "Be nice to the girl. Ya never know when you'll need a quick piece of—"

"Do you mind?" I snap back. "This is private."

At that, Jared jumps up and hustles me a safe distance away. A red stain mottles his hefty neck, working its way up to his angry face. "I *said* I'm *busy*, so make it fast."

Forget the preamble. "You saw them, didn't you? At the séance. You saw what happened to them."

"I don't know what you're talking about." But his eyes dart.

"You *saw*," I insist. "That's why you ran." I catch his wrist as he turns—a thick, clammy wrist, cool to the touch. "Jared, it's okay. I saw it, too. I just had to be sure—"

Jared knits his reddish brows menacingly. He leans close, *too* close. "Yeah, I saw it. And I'm telling you now, you say one word about it, I'm gonna deny it, okay?" He jerks his wrist free. "Just stay away from me. You and the *rest* of those freaks!"

As he jogs back to his friends, two thoughts strike me at the same time. One, that this may explain why he broke up with Meg—*is he afraid of her? Does he think she's a freak because she froze in the pool room?*—and two, this is exactly the proof I'd been hoping for!

What happened in the pool room was not a joke. Not a hallucination, either.

It happened exactly the way I *saw* it happen.

I wait for a wave of relief that never comes.

4 MONTHS + 9 DAYS ————

Friday, November 14

At breakfast Mom says that Lacy's mom called the school. Lacy's taking some time off for "health reasons."

Then she sets a soft-boiled egg down on the table in front of me.

I stare at the cracked white lump, nestled in a ruby-red egg cup. I recognize this cup; Nana gave me a set of four for my thirteenth birthday: "For your hope chest, Rinnie," like people do that anymore. Three broke. This is the last one left. I don't even remember packing it.

"She's staying with relatives in Columbus," Mom adds.

"Why?"

"I'm sure I don't know."

Disturbed, distracted, I try to peel my egg. I don't like soft-boiled eggs, and I have no clue why Mom, out of the blue, bothered to cook me one. Guess I'll stall till she leaves and pitch it down the sink.

Silent, Mom sponges down the counter while I toy with bits of shell. She rinses her fingers, picks up a towel, and halts to nod down at my inedible breakfast. "What are you eating?"

I pretend to study it. "Hmm. Looks like a soft-boiled egg to me."

"You hate soft-boiled eggs."

Confused, I ask, "Why'd you make it for me, then?"

"I did?" She glances at the stove, at the pan of murky warm water. "Oh, well." Playfully she fluffs my yet-unbrushed hair. "See you at school."

I throw the egg in the trash.

Something weird is going on.

———◁◦▷———

"Do you ever ask your dad about Annaliese?" I ask Nate on our way to school.

"Ask him what?"

"Well, anything. Did he know her? Did they hang out? Was he around when she died?"

Nate stops walking, though he hangs on to my hand. "Is this all you can talk about?"

"It's not *all* I talk about," I protest, wondering if it is.

"Excuse me. Maybe only ninety percent of the time, then."

I shake my hand free. "Sorry I'm so *bor*-ing lately."

"C'mon. Don't do this."

"What am I doing?"

"You're obsessing."

"I'm not obsessing. I'm interested."

"Well, I wish you'd get over it."

"Why? Am I not paying enough attention to you?"

Nate's jaw tightens. His chestnut hair blows straight up in a gust of wind, or maybe with fury. "I'm just sick of hearing about Annaliese, Annaliese. I'm sick of hearing about *ghosts*. Can't we talk about something normal?"

"Normal?"

"Yeah, normal."

Coldly I reply, "If you want normal, Nate, you *really* picked the wrong girl," and march off ahead of him.

———◄o►———

Ugh, what a day. Meg's home sick. Tasha's on her way to Cincinnati for her regionals tomorrow. Cecilia ignores me again. Plus I forgot about the history paper due today, because—I admit it—I can't get Annaliese out of my mind.

After PE, when everyone gathers to race through the tunnel, I lag back for the first time. Only when the echo of hysterical giggles fades away do I wander over, alone, to the tunnel entrance.

It's just a dumb corridor.

How scary to think that we all walked through here the other day, not knowing Dino was there on the other side of this wall, hanging upside down, dead for hours.

I gasp when a lightbulb noisily fizzles out. Like Nate said, these lights *always* pop out. Bad wiring, maybe. Amazing that this place doesn't go up in—

Don't even think it.

I step close to the pool room door, trying to ignore the chill penetrating my sweater. "Annaliese?" I whisper through the crack.

Pipes clank. I hear a scrabbling sound near the bottom of the door. Another rat?

"Annaliese?" The scrabbling stops. "Hello?"

Silence.

I back away. *There's nothing in there, nothing in there, nothing in there . . .*

My left shoe sticks to someone's discarded gum. Bricks pass in a blur as I walk rapidly to the opposite end of the corridor, counting the burned-out lightbulbs: seven in all. When I reach the cafeteria door and the reassuring chatter beyond, I jubilantly leap out and blink in the light.

There—I did it!

Take THAT, Annaliese.

———◁○▷———

With my stomach knotted up all morning, thanks to the egg episode, plus my fight with Nate, I decide to skip lunch and seek out Bennie Unger.

I discover him scarfing down a sandwich in the custodian's closet.

"I know you," he says through a mouthful of bread and bologna. "You're Corinne."

"How do you know my name?"

"I know everybody here." He pops open a Thermos, digs a couple of pills out of his pocket, and washes them down with whatever's in that bottle. It smells like V8. "I get fits sometimes," he explains. "I gotta take medicine so I don't fall out."

I fidget, hoping he doesn't fall out anytime soon.

He pulls off his ever-present knit cap and points to the dent in his skull. "They took out a piece of my brain. I was puttin' on a roof with my brother and I fell right off."

Stifling a shudder, I wait till his cap's back on. "Can I talk to you?"

Bennie doesn't seem surprised. In fact, he acts like he *expected* me to show up here today. This, in itself, is spooky weird; I've barely exchanged five words with him, ever. Not that I'm a follow-the-herd kind of girl, but it's supremely uncool to hang out with the school janitor.

I dive right in and explain everything. How Lacy clobbered me. How both Meg and Cecilia felt that oily, smelly air creep down their throats. I explain about the séance, and the wax, and how everyone froze up. "I think something happened. I think we . . ." *Unleashed something?*

"You think you all called her up," he states matter-of-factly. "That Annaliese girl."

"You do believe in her. That's why you told us that day— 'there's nobody there *now*.' Right, Bennie?" Half of me hopes he'll say no.

Bennie peers around the cluttered closet like he's checking for video cams. "This ain't a joke, right? I don't like people laughing at me."

Whatever crap I've gone through the past few years may be nothing compared to what Bennie's had to endure. "I'm serious, Bennie. And I'm not gonna laugh."

Bennie shifts to the other foot. "Okay. I ain't never *seen* nothin' . . . but she's there, all right. She's been there a long time. *You* didn't call her out." He shakes a chastising finger. "You all weren't supposed to go in there, anyhow."

"How do you know she's there if you haven't seen her?"

Bennie hunches his sloping shoulders. "Same way you know. You just *know*. Anyhow, Miz Prout told me, too."

"Miz Prout?" I repeat.

"Yup. She'd take her lunch and go sit by the pool every day." He pats his oversized key ring with pride. "I'd let her in there myself and clean out a place for her to sit. She always said, 'Thank you, Bennie.' She sure liked her peace and quiet. She'd sit in her folding chair and eat her lunch and read for a spell. Then she'd get up and leave. That's before she got sad."

"Sad how?"

He cracks his knuckles, one by one. "She used to take pills every day, just like me. She'd drink 'em down with her lunchtime coffee. Then one day she says to me, 'Bennie, I'm tired of taking these pills.' And then, I reckon, she didn't take 'em no more."

"What kind of pills?"

"Well, they must've been happy pills, 'cause then she stopped being happy. She'd cry sometimes. And she'd walk around that pool, just walk, walk, walk, like she didn't have no other place else to go. I'd hear her talkin', too. Talking to *Annaliese*." He scratches the back of his cap. "I reckon she was one of those ladies who sees things, like with crystal balls and stuff. Only she didn't have no crystal ball."

Entranced, I ask, "Was she a medium?"

"Yeah, sort of regular size. But not as big as Miz Gibbons. *She* came here, too. Miz Prout brought her once. Good thing Mr. Solomon didn't know."

"Why'd she bring Mrs. Gibbons?"

"So they could call up Annaliese 'cause Miz Gibbons missed her so much. She was a sad lady, too. *Real* lonesome."

I ponder this. Did Miss Prout believe she could communicate with Annaliese? So she brought Mrs. Gibbons along to "visit" her dead granddaughter?

I ask Bennie this. He only shrugs. "Beats me. But it was pretty soon after that when Miz Prout went away. Then poor old Miz Gibbons—" He makes a vague jerking motion above his head.

"Bennie, do you know why Miss Prout left town so fast?"

"Yep. So Annaliese couldn't find her."

"What do you mean, f-find her?"

Bennie industriously wraps up the remnants of his sandwich. "Like she found you girls. And like she found that boy, Dino." A regretful headshake. "He acted mean, but I never wished him no harm. Nope, not like that."

The end-of-lunch bell rings, I have to get to English, but something else nags me. "You said Miss Prout 'told' you about Annaliese. What did she *say*, Bennie? Exactly?"

Bennie frowns, thinking hard. "Oh." He brightens. "She said 'Be sure to take your medicine, Bennie.'"

"Why'd she say that?"

Bennie smiles broadly. "'Cause then I can't see nothin'. Then Annaliese can't touch me."

———◀◦▶———

Nate and I make up after school. I apologize for my snarky attitude. Nate apologizes for his rudeness and for not being more sensitive to my Annaliese fixation. Then he invites me to his house to do homework.

Luke and Mom, I've noticed, are spending more time together, too. Tonight, in fact, they're having dinner at some fancy restaurant in Kellersberg. Nate and I avoid this subject while he diligently works on a German paper, and I sweat buckets of blood over my algebra problems. I'm not sure which is the biggest shocker: That Mom and Luke no longer want to rip each other's throats out? Or that Mom trusts me enough to let me hang out with Nate, at night, in an empty house, without supervision?

I surrender in the middle of my second page of problems. "If I tell you something about Annaliese, will you flip out again?"

Nate drops his pen. "This is the part where I'm supposed to be more sensitive, right?"

I relate what Bennie Unger told me. "So he thinks if he takes his seizure meds, Annaliese can't hurt him."

"Need I remind you, surfer girl, that Bennie's not all there?"

"He's there enough. He *believes* this stuff. So did Miss Prout and Mrs. Gibbons. Were *they* missing part of their brains?"

"Well . . ." Nate thinks. "Miss Prout was an oddball. She'd deal Tarot cards right in the office, and read fortunes and stuff. And *obviously* Mrs. Gibbons had problems. Anyway, how do you know Bennie wasn't making it up? Nobody talks to him. You gave him a captive audience."

"He was pretty convincing." But I'm thinking: *Tarot cards?*

Nate pushes his book aside. "Let's watch TV. It'll get your mind off this stuff."

"I hate TV. How many times do I have to tell you?"

"Yeah, but you never told me why."

"It reminds me of my grandmother," I admit. "We'd watch those old reruns one after another. *Bewitched* was her favorite."

"Not *Laverne and Shirley*?"

Wow! He remembers our first conversation? "No, that was mine. I liked *The Andy Griffith Show*, too. I called you Opie in my mind when I met you," I confess shyly.

He plays with my hair. "Is that good?"

"Oh, yeah. Opie's cute. If we had *cable* around here I could show you how cute."

"Maybe we could rent the DVDs and watch them together."

"That'd be cool."

So we curl up on the sofa together with the TV on.

Not that we watch it, of course.

4 MONTHS + 10 DAYS ——————

Saturday, November 15

Moving from headstone to headstone, I search for the grave of Anna-liese Gibbons. At last I find it, but the grave is open, the lid to the casket gone, and Annaliese stares up from her satin pillow. I smile. She smiles back—and then I watch in horror as her lips erupt into blisters. Her face blackens and curls, torched by invisible fire, till all that remains is a raw, leering skull and the stench of cooked meat.

———————◄o►———————

Haunted by the nightmare, half-dead from a cold, I stumble downstairs for something to clear the Play-Doh out of my nose. Mom hands me a blister pack of cold tablets. "Nate was look-ing for you already, but I told him you were sick. I heard you sneezing all night."

I moan. "I feel *awww*-ful." And if I feel awful, Nate's bound to get it, too. Last night was lovely.

I swallow the tablets with my regular meds. "No riding for

you today," Mom warns. "Stay in bed. I'm going to pick up some groceries. You want anything?"

Too sick to shake my aching head, I crawl back to my room, burrow under the covers, and sleep until the phone rings later in the afternoon.

"There's nothing wrong," a voice says in my ear.

"What?"

"With *me*. I got the MRI results today. There's nothing wrong—which means there's nothing they can do." Meg hiccups. "Tasha's out of town, and I had no one else to c-call, and oh, God, I can't b-believe this is *happening* to me."

"You want me to come over?" My feet are already on the floor.

Ignoring my offer, she cries out, "How can they say there's nothing wrong? This buzzing is *killing* me. Oh God, my ears hurt so bad, *sooo baaad*—"

In the background a woman chides, "Meg, please don't be so dramatic."

"*But they hurt!*" Meg screams, nearly cracking *my* ear.

"I know, but the doctor said—"

"Who cares what he said? I can't fucking *cheer*!"

Hearing Meg drop the F-bomb—to her mom, no less—sets off a terrible alarm. The Meg I know never uses that word. "Meg?"

"For that, young lady"—her mother's voice moves closer—"you can hang that phone up right now."

"*I'm using this goddamn phone!*" Meg screeches back at her.

"I *said*—"

I hear a smack against flesh. Then the sounds of a tussle. The phone drops.

"Meg!" I shout. "Meg, pick up the phone!"

"Stop! What are you doing?" Meg's mom screams in the distance. "What the *hell* are you doing?"

More scuffling.

"No!" Meg's mom, gasping, hysterical. "Stop! Oh God, no! *No-o-o-o!*"

Moans. Inaudible cries. Panicked sobbing.

And then . . . a terrible quiet.

"Meg," I shriek. "Meg, I'm coming over right now!" As I start to hang up, I hear the clunk of someone picking the phone off the floor. Steady breathing whooshes in my ear. "Meg? Did you hear me? I'm on my way!"

"Don't bother," Meg whispers, eerily calm. "I'm fine. Really."

Gently, she hangs up.

◄○►

Nate answers the door to my frantic pounding. As he savagely scrapes ice from the windshield of his jeep, we hear the approaching sirens.

I freeze. "Forget the car!" And I race off, my feet skidding in yesterday's slush that turned to ice overnight.

Taking the well-plowed streets instead of the treacherous sidewalks, it takes us less than five minutes to reach the Carmodys'. By then, the police and ambulance are there.

Nate hauls me back, trapping me in his arms. "Wait!"

Hugging him to me, I watch in horror as paramedics carry a stretcher out of the house. At first I think it *must* be Meg, then realize it's not—it's a woman bundled in blankets, oxygen strapped to her face. "Is that her mom?"

Nate nods, rigid with disbelief.

"What happened?" I cry out as a police officer shuffles us out of the way.

The cop ignores me and mutters into his walkie-talkie. I struggle, but Nate grips me tighter. As they load Meg's mom into the ambulance, the front door opens again.

It's Meg. In handcuffs.

Trees and houses and cars spin around me. I lunge again, taking Nate by surprise, breaking free of his arms. I dodge the officer and stumble up the icy drive. I'm an arm's length away from Meg when another cop grabs me. Close up, I notice the blood on her clothes, on her arms, even on her face. "Meg! What—what happened?"

Meg rolls her heavy-lidded eyes toward me. "I told her to stay away from me. I *begged* her to. But she just wouldn't listen." She balks as the cops hustle her toward the squad car. "No! Wait! I have to tell her something."

The cops pause. The guy holding my arm lets me move an inch closer. Meg looks right into my face and smiles her old familiar smile, though her eyes remain flat, devoid of any life.

"The buzzing's gone. I'm okay now, Rinn."

———◦———

I spend the afternoon on the sofa with my head in Nate's lap. Mom doesn't mind. She and Luke sit pretty close themselves.

Why did she do it? Why? The question pecks at my brain with a ragged beak.

"Maybe we need more coffee," Mom suggests, probably to break the silence.

Luke objects, "Maybe we need something stronger."

"Wine?"

"That'll do."

He follows Mom into the kitchen. I hear the clatter of glasses, the pop of a cork, hushed voices, and the scraping of two chairs. I hear the click of a lighter, once, then twice. Mom's having a cigarette? I'm too upset to care.

Nate tucks hair behind my ear. "You okay?"

"I just wish I knew why she did it."

"People snap," he says, like I don't already know this.

I sit up and scooch back till we're side by side on the sofa. "She said her ears hurt. She was crying, Nate, crying with pain. But then, after she did it, the ringing went away." I hug myself. *Like that's what it took. Like hurting someone was the only way to get it to stop.* "The way Lacy's headache went away after she wrote that letter."

"What letter?"

I tell Nate about the letter, and about Lacy's miscarriage.

He doesn't say I'm crazy. He says nothing at all.

4 MONTHS + 18 DAYS —————

Sunday, November 23

The headline in the *River Hills Journal* reads: Local Girl Arrested in Domestic Dispute. I skim it only for the facts I care about: that Meg's mom is in serious condition, but there's no question that she'll recover. And that Meg's in jail, on suicide watch. She hasn't been charged yet.

Millie has a cell phone. Nobody gets a signal around here, but Tasha says they use it when they're out of town for practice or competitions. Mom tries the number this morning, fearing the Luxes might read this and find out about Meg before anyone can tell them in person.

I can't imagine how Tasha's going to take this.

But Millie's phone flips right to voice mail. "I don't get it," I say as Mom hangs up a second time. "Regionals were yesterday. You'd think Millie'd be calling CNN, at least."

"It's strange," Mom admits. "I thought for sure she'd call last night and let us know how Tasha did."

Personally I'm glad we can't reach them by phone. Some things *need* to be said face-to-face, and I think telling someone her best friend's in jail is one of them. Especially when you have to tell her why.

I can't stand hanging around the house and thinking about Meg. Nate, when I call him, agrees, and we decide to spend the day at Rocky Meadows. This time, though, after we ride, we work; I help him turn out the horses, muck out the stalls, sweep the stable, and refill the water troughs. By the time the last horse is back in and happily fed—hours later—I'm caked with mud and manure, my jacket is ruined, and I'll probably end up with pneumonia on top of this head cold. But at least it took my mind off Meg for a while.

We pass Millie's car on the way back, parked in front of the Boxcar Diner. But the restaurant's lights are off and the CLOSED sign hangs on the window.

"What gives?" I wonder.

Nate suggests, "Bet they're out celebrating Tasha's victory," as he backs the jeep into his drive.

"Bet not." *Not if they heard about Meg first.*

Unafraid of my germs, he kisses me good-bye with warm, salty lips. When I open my front door a minute later, it's Millie I hear first, agitated and hysterical: "How could this have happened? How? I'm just sick about it. *Sick,* I tell you." As I creep toward the kitchen, she wails, "Oh, Mo, what'll we do? What do we do *no-o-w-w?*"

In the kitchen, Millie's sobbing on Mom's shoulder. Mom pats her. "C'mon, Millie. It could be worse, *much* worse."

I marvel at Millie's over-the-top reaction. Shaking and

gasping, she clings to my mother, stretching Mom's sweater halfway up her back.

"It's okay, Millie," I say from the doorway. "Meg's mom'll be fine. The newspaper said—"

I cut myself off as Millie rears up, and Mom throws me a warning frown two seconds too late.

"I know that," Millie snaps. "I can read the paper, too. I'm talking about Tasha, dammit. All our plans! Everything!" She clutches Mom again. "Oh, what're we gonna *doooo*?"

"Honey," Mom says over Millie's sobs. "Tasha's upstairs. Why don't you go keep her company?"

Confused, I nod, back out, and run up to my room. Tasha is stretched out on my mattress, studying her fingers. "What happened? Tell me!"

"I blew it," she says, with no emotion. "I blew regionals. They disqualified me."

"How? Why?"

"I don't want to talk about it."

I sit down beside her. She doesn't look at me, just watches her fingers making designs in the air. "I thought . . . I mean, when I heard your mom . . ."

A disbelieving scoff. "You thought she was crying about Meg, right? Like she cares about anything except *me winning*?"

"I'm sorry about Meg." Feeling awkward, I reach for her hand.

She ignores it. "I thought I could get through this, you know? But she won't stop harping on it. And then when we got back and heard about M-Meg . . ." She drops her hands and squeezes her eyes shut. "Oh God. This is the worst day of my life."

I don't know what to say. So I just sit there quietly and listen to my clock tick.

—◇—

It's almost dark by the time Millie hollers up: "TASHA! GET DOWN HERE! TIME TO GO!"

Tasha—who fell asleep—flies up, all disheveled and confused. I've already showered and changed into a T-shirt and flannel pants. "Oh no," she whispers. "Please tell me it's a dream." Pushing past me, she swipes her coat from the floor and staggers toward the steps.

I follow her down. Millie, now composed, levels steely eyes on her daughter. "I hope you enjoyed the visit. It's the last one you're gonna get for a while."

"Millie," Mom begins, stepping forward.

Millie continues, prodding Tasha toward the door, "I don't care what it takes. I don't care what it costs. Soon as we get home I'm callin' Nancy, you're getting back on that diving board, and—"

"No!" Tasha stops. Maybe I only imagine her look of sheer terror; it's gone in a flash.

Millie then turns those cold eyes to *me*. "Did she tell you what happened? Huh? Did you tell her, Tasha?" Losing it again, she ignores Mom's protests. "She got halfway up that damn ladder and stopped. Stopped! For no reason! Her coach had to climb up and *peel* her off."

"It wasn't my fault," Tasha whimpers.

"Oh no? Whose was it?"

Tasha whirls on me, her face taut, beseeching. "I froze. I

was fine at first, and—and then I *froze*. I don't *know* what happened but I couldn't move, I couldn't look down . . ." She faces Millie, fists clenched. "I was scared, Ma! I thought I was gonna *die*."

"Die?" Millie splutters. "I'll give you die. You think I've been draggin' you around all these years for my health? All those lessons? All that money? *Do you think this a game?*"

"Please stop yelling at me," Tasha begs. "I tried. I swear!"

"You humiliated me. And you humiliated your daddy," she adds cruelly. "He lost two days of pay to make that extra trip, and for what? To see you hangin' on a ladder, making a fool of yourself?" She shakes her head in disgust. "This whole town was behind you. Oh, sweet Jesus, how'll I face anyone tomorrow?"

Stricken, Tasha stares at her mom. So do I, in utter disbelief. Mom, on the other hand, plows between them at last. "Millie! Stop it! Leave this poor girl alone, or I swear—"

But Tasha, unexpectedly, erupts back to life to add her own bitter two cents. "That's right, Ma. That's all you care about. 'Oh, my wonderful daughter, the high-diving champ,'" she mimics. "You want me to be perfect, right? So people'll talk about *me* instead of talking about *you*. Because you're a fat, ignorant whore and everyone knows it!"

With that, Tasha slams out of the house. Millie, after a single stunned moment, marches after her. No good-bye, nothing. She slams the door twice as hard.

I've never seen Tasha that worked up. I've never even heard her talk back to Millie.

And I've never heard a mother talk that way to her daughter. Mom never did, no matter how nasty *I* was.

Mom, her face troubled, stares at the front door. Then, "Are you all right?"

I guess so, though I feel shaky and weird, and very sorry I was part of all this. "I won't say it," I promise. She hates when I call Millie names. "But you know what I'm thinking."

Mom nods. "In this case, I think you're right."

4 MONTHS + 19 DAYS ———

Monday, November 24

All people talk about in school today is Meg. *Nobody* can believe what happened. Worse, the more people who blab the story, the more twisted it becomes; by third period they've got Mrs. Carmody disemboweled with her throat slashed from ear to ear, and Meg chained to the wall in some unspeakable dungeon.

Idiots.

At lunch, I flag down Tasha. She joins me silently and drops her tray on the table.

"You doing okay?" I ask.

"I'll live." When we hear someone say "Meg" at the next table, Tasha curls her mouth into half a smile. "Nobody's said a word about me getting kicked out of regionals. They're all too busy making Meg out to be some kind of homicidal maniac."

"Nobody said anything to me, either."

"Well, it's just a matter of time." She rolls her hot dog

around with the tines of her plastic fork. "Maybe my mom'll smother me in my sleep and save me from all the shame."

Firmly I say, "She was awful to you yesterday. Even my mom said so." Not in so many words. But it was perfectly obvious she wanted to throttle Millie.

"Whatever. I'm just sick of listening to her. She keeps saying I screwed up on purpose, and I *didn't*, Rinn. Why would I?"

"I believe you. And your mom'll get over it."

"Doubt that. Anyway, I'm to the point now where I don't care if I ever *see* a pool again." I watch her cut the hot dog into pieces, arrange them in a row, and then, one by one, flick them off her plate. "Oh God, oh God, I miss Meg so much."

"Me, too." Believe it or not, I even miss Lacy right now.

"You know, I've been thinking . . ." She glances stealthily around. "What you said after Dino's funeral. At the diner, remember?"

Wisely, I wait.

"You said something might happen to me on account of that séance."

"I didn't say it to scare you," I say quickly.

"You didn't. I just didn't believe you at first. But since I blew regionals so bad . . ." She pushes her mangled lunch away. "You wanna know a secret? I don't even care that I blew it."

"What do you mean you don't care?"

"Just what I said."

"Tasha—"

"I don't! I'm, like, totally over it." She giggles, but it's a strained, unnatural sound. "So you know what I'm thinking now? I'm thinking maybe, just *maybe* . . . Annaliese's getting to me, too."

I consider my untouched lunch, a wilted boxed salad. "Don't joke about it."

"I'm not joking, Rinn. I mean, Meg attacked her *mom*. Really? Meg, of all people? How crazy is that?"

Thrilled that she's not teasing me, that maybe she finally gets it, I exclaim, "That's what I've been saying all along. Things *happen* to people. You guys did zone out on me. Jared saw it, too. He admitted it. That's why he broke up with Meg, I think. He's scared of her now."

Tasha blinks. "You talked to Jared about this?"

"Yes, but don't bother asking him yourself. He already said he'd deny it." I pretend not to notice her flicker of skepticism. "And now, ever since the séance, things are happening to *us*."

"Well, some of us," she agrees. "I mean, after all . . . nothing's happened to *you*."

———◁◦▷———

"Millie invited us over for Thanksgiving," Mom says as we're throwing dinner together.

I roll greasy meat loaf mix between my hands. "That's nice."

"Actually, I got the impression she invites the whole town. I guess it's something of a tradition around here." She cocks her head, staring at the loaf pan in her hands. "I'm worried it might be, uh, a difficult holiday for us . . ."

I finish her thought: "Because Frank won't be here. Yeah, I get it."

"We'll call him," Mom decides.

"He won't talk to me."

"I think he will."

I grab the pan, drop the meat loaf in, and punch it into shape. "Whatever."

While the meat loaf is baking, I hang out in my room and play my guitar. Mr. Chenoweth asked me to play "My Sweet Lord" for the Christmas concert, and I picked up the music today after school. Mom shows up after a while and watches me strum. "Very nice."

"Thanks." I wonder what's next.

"I called that new psychiatrist today. He said he'll let us know if there's a cancellation before January. And in case of an emergency, there's a crisis center we can contact."

I stop strumming. "What e-*mer*-gency, Mom?"

"Honey, you just seem so down lately. I understand, after what happened to Dino, and now Meg, but—well, I'm worried about you."

Oh, crap. Here we go.

"Mom, I'm not having a crisis. Yes, I'm upset. Isn't that normal? Can't I be *normally* bummed out without you dragging me to a shrink?"

Taken aback by my snappishness, Mom hesitates. Then: "Rinn, you'd tell me, wouldn't you, if something else was bothering you? Or if you feel, well . . ."

"Suicidal?" I scoff. "Please. Once was enough."

I know she's just being my typical worrywart mother. But a psychiatrist, especially now, is out of the question. I'd have to watch every word I say, be careful not to slip up. Even then, knowing shrinks as well as I do, he might find a way to drag it out of me that I, Rinn Jacobs, believe in ghosts.

Ghosts that can hurt you. Ghosts that can make you sick.

Ghosts that force you to do things against your will or stop you from doing the things you love best.

Not just any ghost.

Annaliese.

4 MONTHS + 20 DAYS ——————

Tuesday, November 25

The phone rings as I head down for breakfast. Mom grabs it. "Hello?" I can hear Millie's shrill babble as Mom holds the receiver safely away from her ear. Noticing me, she bunches her forehead. "Nooo, I didn't know. Yes, I'll ask her." More frantic chatter. "Mil, don't worry. I'll *ask* her."

"Ask me what?" I demand after she hangs up.

"Tasha gave you some yearbooks? And one of Millie's scrapbooks?"

My stomach sinks. "Uh, yeah." *And Tasha promised me she'd never miss them.*

"Well, Millie wants them back."

"Okay," I say casually, rooting around for cereal. Mom forgot to buy Cocoa Puffs. In fact, there's no cereal left at all. "What am I supposed to eat?" Not another soft-boiled egg, I hope.

Mom ignores that. "What were you doing with them?"

"Just looking. I never saw *your* yearbook," I add defensively. "I was curious, that's all."

"Is that why you took that scrapbook, too?"

"I didn't *take* it. Tasha let me borrow it." I feel like a traitor.

"She had no business doing that. Those books belong to her mother."

"Fine! Okay! I'll give 'em back." Wow, you'd think I committed a federal offense.

"Bring them to me," Mom says sternly.

"Now?"

"Now."

Ticked off, I march upstairs and dig the yearbooks and Annaliese's scrapbook out from under a pile of clothes. Then I march back down and thrust the stack at my mother.

She thumbs first through the yearbooks, then through the scrapbook. Then she repeats the whole process, examining every page. "Is this all?"

"Yes!" I viciously pop bread into the toaster. "I don't see what the big deal is."

"You didn't find any pictures? Anything in an envelope? Because Millie swears she's missing some pictures." I shake my head. "Are you sure they didn't fall out?"

"There were *no pictures*! Why would I lie?"

"I'm not saying you are," Mom says patiently. "But Millie's beside herself."

"What are they? Nude pics of the cheerleading squad? One of those *Girls Gone Wild* things?"

She presses her lips shut. Then: "She didn't say. But they're very important to her."

My toast pops, barely browned. I slam the lever again.

"Well, I don't have them and I don't know anything about them."

Mom stacks the books on the table, Annaliese on top. She fingers the cover like she's reading Braille.

When she says nothing else, I paste on a cheery smile. "Mom, I'm not traumatized. I just wanted to find out about Annaliese. *You* didn't tell me much."

"It was so long ago," Mom murmurs. "I try not to think about her. It's over and done with. I'd like it to stay that way." Before I can question this, my toast pops again, this time black and crispy. Mom scowls. "We need a new toaster." Then she grabs her coat from the hook in the back hall and gathers up Millie's books. "I'll drop these off to her now. See you at school, honey."

———◁◦▷———

"It was the weirdest thing," I tell Nate on the way to school. "She completely freaked out. And she wouldn't even tell me what kind of pictures they *were*." I grab his arm when I slip on a sneaky patch of ice. "I mean, I know she was kind of wild, but— Nate, what if they're porno pics? And they're floating around town?"

Nate laughs as he steadies me. "Your mom? Nah. She'd never be that stupid."

She got knocked up with me. That was pretty stupid.

"Want to go riding after school? Dad and I are off for our annual hunting trip Thursday, and, well, I won't see you till next week."

"Thursday's Thanksgiving. What about Millie's pig fest?"

"Oh, don't worry. She already sent over a truckload of goodies."

"I can't believe you *hunt*," I complain. "How can you watch those poor little bunnies bleeding to death?"

"They don't bleed to death, Surf. I'm a pretty good shot."

"And I'm so not impressed."

———◦———

No PE today because the teacher's out sick. Apparently there's no such thing around here as a last minute substitute. So Tasha and I sit in the back row during our impromptu study hall, avoiding the eagle eye of Mrs. Schimmler. Tasha calls her Frau Schimmler; she has her for German.

"Did your mom find the pics?" I whispers.

"Nope, and she was up all night tearing the place apart." Tasha props her German book up on end so Schimmler will think she's studying. "Man, she went *ballistic* on me. You'd think we ripped off a Picasso or something."

"*You* said she wouldn't miss that stuff."

"Well, now she's planning some dumb reunion. That's the only reason." She lowers her voice when Schimmler clears her throat. "Anyway, who cares? She's gonna be even madder at me tonight."

"Why?"

"Because I made up my mind. I'm not competing anymore." She recites this monumental decision so casually, my jaw drops. "I'm tired of it, period. And I'm telling her that tonight."

"But what about the Olympics? You told me a thousand times—"

Tasha sticks out her tongue. "Kid stuff. I'll never make the Olympics. Just like Meg's never gonna cheer for Dallas."

"You can't just quit because one bad thing happened."

"Oh yes I can," she snaps.

It's happening to her, too. I can feel it.

"Tash," I whisper. She buries her face behind her book as Mrs. Schimmler sniffs the air, searching for the source of the whispering. "You said yourself you think Annaliese might be getting to you. But now that we *know* what's happening, maybe we can stop it."

Tasha snorts without trying to be discreet. Schimmler cracks her palms together. "Silence back there!"

Tasha won't look at me. I sigh, open Lindsay McCormick's *Twilight*—I'm halfway through it—and pretend to read, but my churning stomach makes it hard to concentrate. Tasha blew *one* crummy competition, so now she's giving up diving forever?

Is it because she's upset about Meg? Could that be clouding her thinking?

I hope that's it. And not something else.

———◦————

After horseback riding, I laze on the couch in the stable lounge while Nate nukes water for cocoa. "Who's taking care of the horses if you're gonna be gone for four days?"

"Got a couple buddies from school lined up." He hands me my cocoa and sits down. "How's Tasha doing?"

"Okay, I guess." I don't mention Tasha's decision. "She's upset about regionals. And about Meg, of course. She doesn't really talk about her, though."

"Neither do you," he says gently.

I sip from my steaming mug. No, I don't. But that doesn't mean I don't remember the blood on her, or how she stared at me with that strange, dead expression. "You don't want to hear what I have to say, anyway."

"Which is?"

"That what happened to her makes one *more* bad thing that's happened around here."

Nate groans. Before I can jump all over him for his maddening indifference, he takes my mug away and then jumps on *me*, pulling me to the floor. He rolls me onto the big dead bear by the fire and kisses me lightly.

Then, less lightly.

Breathless, overwhelmed, I forget to be mad at him.

———◁◦▷———

When things start to get *wa-a-ay* too hot, I reluctantly pull my cardigan back on. Nate watches with one of his hands resting on my knee.

It's too soon.

How unlike the "old" Rinn Jacobs to think such a thing.

His teasing fingers trail further up my thigh. "Are we finished here?"

"Yeah, it's late. I need to get home and—"

The rest of it hits me like a bullet to the brain: *TAKE MY PILLS!*

Why didn't I put it together before this?

"I'm stupid. I am so, so stupid!"

"Little hard on yourself, eh, surfer girl?"

"Nate, it's the pills! Miss Prout sat by that pool every day and never said a word about Annaliese till she stopped taking her pills."

"What pills?"

"I don't know! Antidepressants? Bennie said she cried a lot after, and talked to herself, and then she got all hung up on *Annaliese*." Words tumble out of me. "And Bennie takes stuff for seizures! You said yourself he hangs around the tunnel and nothing happens to him. Nothing happens to me, either. Because *I* take stuff, too."

It makes so much sense! All those mind-altering drugs to block out the Voices, to jolt my brain chemicals into alignment—how could anything, even a ghost, penetrate that fortress?

"Like a safety shield, a gate," I muse. "Bennie and me, we're perfectly safe."

"You're perfectly out of your skull." Nate adds in a sexy growl, "I mean that, of course, in the most adoring way."

I stare at the popping embers in the hearth. "What about Jared?" Disgusted at my indifference to his attention, Nate scoffs, but with a tight, evasive expression. "What?" I tug his T-shirt and then straddle his lap when he ignores me. "You *know*, right? What does Jared take?"

He rests his chin on my shoulder. I feel his muscles relax, and then I know, at last, he's crossing over to my side. "Jared's ADHD. He's been taking stuff since kindergarten."

"I knew it!" Then I'm speechless, stunned by the clarity of the situation. The pure, absolute understanding of what I need to do next.

Nate grasps my chin. "Don't even think about it."

"Aha! So you *do* believe me."

"Who cares? Don't you dare stop your pills."

"But what if it proves . . . ?"

"Proves *what*? That you don't have a brain in your head? I mean it, Rinn. Promise me." At my disbelieving look, he warns,

"You want me to tell your mom? You want her to count every pill?"

"Then do something for me," I beg. "I want to get back into that pool room."

"Why?"

"To prove I'm immune. But I need you nearby in case . . . well, just in case."

Nate drags his shirt down over his head. "No way."

"If you *don't* believe me, what are you worried about?"

"Oh, where do I start?"

"You don't have to come in with me. I don't want you to, anyway." Yeah, just what I need: something to happen to Nate. "Just watch and wait. Tie something around me in case you have to pull me out."

"Tie something? No. No way."

"Nate, *please.*"

Rigid, he moves away from me then. "I'm not gonna be a part of this, Rinn."

When he gets like this, I know better than to argue.

"Okay," I say casually. "It's a dumb idea, anyway."

But even when he breaks down and smiles, satisfied with his victory, my mind is already racing with possibilities.

4 MONTHS + 21 DAYS ————

Wednesday, November 26

Last night, I knew the exact moment Tasha broke the news to her mom: probably sixty seconds before our telephone rang. Mom spent an hour comforting Millie, assuring her it's not the end of the world, to give Tasha some time, and maybe it's a stage, yadda yadda.

Needless to say, I went to bed early, kind of sorry I wasn't there when the bomb dropped to offer Tasha some support. On the other hand, who wants to witness *that*?

In school, Tasha's surprisingly upbeat for someone who might be written out of her parents' will by the end of the day. "It went fine," she insists at lunch when I ask her about last night. "She took it better than I thought."

Could've fooled me. I wonder why she's lying. Or *if* she's lying. Maybe once the initial shock wore off, and she talked to my mom, Millie had second thoughts. Maybe she and Tasha made up?

"Well," I say. "I'm proud of you, Tash." *As long as you did this on your own, and not because of Annaliese.*

Tasha beams. "Thanks." Then, "God!" she shouts, stretching her arms over her head. "I'm alive again! No more killing myself seven days a week. Ha! Now I can do anything I want. *Eat* anything I want." She gasps, slapping a hand over her mouth. "Omigod, Rinn—I can even *date* now!"

"I thought you said all the boys around here suck," I tease.

"They do, but who cares? At least I'll be doing something else." She jiggles in her seat, positively glowing. "Stay after with me and help me clean my lockers out. I've got, like, a thousand swimsuits to pitch. We can have a bonfire!"

———◦———

Nate kisses me good-bye at my own locker; he and his dad are leaving for their trip almost immediately. "I'll miss you," he assures me.

"I'll miss you, too."

"You can come along," he offers with a wink. "I've got a big enough tent."

I can't tell if he's joking or not. "Thanks, but no thanks. Have fun." I don't understand that whole shooting-animals-for-fun thing. Then again, I eat meat. Who am I to judge?

I'm staring longingly after Nate when Tasha, brandishing a black trash bag, rushes up behind me. "Got this from Mr. Lipford. C'mon!"

First we do her hall locker. I thought we'd be done in five minutes, but Tasha's a *slob.* Not only is her locker crammed with stuff like swimsuits and towels and flip-flops and rubber caps—all handy for the days when Millie drives, uh, *drove* her to practice directly from school—but also months and months of old homework, used notebooks, and a hundred candy wrappers.

"My secret stash," she whispers, though there's no one around. "My mom never lets me eat this stuff at home."

I count eight swimsuits in all, half of them blue and white, the colors of the Kellersberg Diving Team. When I hold open the bag, Tasha doesn't so much as flinch as she dumps them all in.

"*Hasta la vista*, baby," she croons, flinging armfuls of all the regular old locker trash on top of her swim stuff. When her locker is relatively clean, she stops me from tying the red plastic drawstring with, "Wait, not yet. I've got to do my gym locker, too."

"Can't you do it after vacation?" The halls are dead, the lights already dimmed. Everyone booked out of here as fast as possible today, to get a head start on their four-day weekend.

"C'mon! It'll just take a minute." She dances off, and I follow awkwardly, lugging the bulky trash bag. She's gonna owe me for this.

Her gym locker, also packed, positively *stinks*. I hold my nose while Tasha rips out all her extra clothes, *more* towels and swimsuits, and a pair of damp, moldy sneakers. I open my mouth to make my opinion of this known—and then a distant sound makes us freeze in unison.

"What was *that*?" Tasha whispers, staring at the door to the tunnel.

I relax, realizing. "Probably Bennie. No biggie."

"Shouldn't we check?"

"Check? Why? We're not even supposed to *be* here."

Tasha ignores this. Tiptoeing in a playful, exaggerated way that, sadly, reminds me of Meg the day she first showed me around school, she pushes open the door and steps into the tunnel. *"Yooo-hooo!"*

"Are you high?" I demand, hoping I know her better than that.

"Yeah, I'm high. High! High!" Evidently pleased with the echo, she shrieks, "High, high, *hi-i-i-igh*!" Then, in a normal tone, "Oh! Hi, Bennie."

I knew it. I stomp in after her. Bennie, down by the pool room door, points in our direction. "You girls ain't supposed to be here!"

"We know," I call back. "We're just on our way—" I shut up as Tasha, with no warning, skips down the hall toward Bennie. Maybe she *is* high. I hope it's on freedom.

I hurry after her. Bennie doesn't look pleased at our intrusion. "You ain't supposed to *be* in here," he repeats. "You're supposed to be home."

Tasha eyes the open door to the pool room. "So, Bennie . . . what're you doing in there?"

"I'm fixin' to put a new lock on this door." He holds up a shiny new dead bolt to prove it.

"About time," she chirps. "I mean, now that Dino's dead."

Bennie gapes. So do I. But before I can call her on this, Tasha darts into the pool room.

"Hey!" Bennie shouts. "Nobody allowed in there!"

"No kidding," Tasha merrily calls back.

The last thing I want to do is walk into that pool room again. Already a blanket of cold air drifts through the door, wrapping me in icy tendrils.

Poor Bennie's so beside himself, he drops the dead bolt on his foot. "She's gonna get me fired, all right. Mr. Solomon, he's still here. He's not gonna like this one bit, not one bit!"

"I'll get her," I promise.

After all, if I'm right, and it's my meds, I'm safe anyway.

If I'm wrong, I'm screwed.

At first I can't see her. The lights, what's left of them, flicker and hum overhead. It's like being in a fun house, strobe lights and all. I scan the length of the fence and spot her halfway down. "Tasha, what're you *doing*?"

"Omigod, look at this!" Her voice trembles with excitement. "Hurry! Omi*god* . . ."

Wary, I advance, aware of Bennie's heavy footfalls behind me. I reach her, and stop, and stare at the hole in the fence. My throat swells. My hands turn to ice. The rusted metal links have been clipped away, forming a rectangular passage. The fence sags on either side of this hole, the raw, jagged links threatening anyone stupid enough to slide through.

This is how they got Dino off the fence. They had to cut part of it down.

If I look at floor, will I see dried blood smeared on the tiles? Or did Mr. Solomon make Bennie mop it up?

Holding my gaze firmly up, I turn to Tasha who, without warning, slips through the hole, barely scraping the sides.

Okay. Now I'm *mad*. "Hey!"

She turns back, face shining. "How did they do this? How?"

"Do what?"

She waves her arms in two wide arcs as if embracing the black pit only yards in front of her. "*This!* Are you blind? How'd they keep it a secret?"

Bennie, puffing hard, plants himself beside me, his fists raised, though more comical than intimidating. "You crazy girl! You get outta there *now!*"

Instead, Tasha pirouettes around and runs farther away, careening around the corner of the empty pool. "This is amazing!" she cries. "I can't believe it!"

Then she throws off her coat, kicks off her boots, and jumps onto the ladder of the diving board. The ancient rungs creak under her weight.

"*Tasha!*" Unthinking, I throw myself through the fence, but something yanks me backward. "Let go!" I scream at Bennie before I realize it's my jacket, hooked to the fence. I struggle madly, but all that does is grind the nasty iron link into my shoulder blade.

Bennie, who can't get around me, curses as ferociously as me while he twists my jacket, trying to free me. The fence rattles in my ears as I stare, transfixed, at the pool straight ahead with no crisscrossed links to hinder my view. *What are you doing?* I scream, maybe out loud, maybe not, because all I can hear is the thunder of the fence.

Tasha reaches the top of the ladder.

I wise up at last and barrel out of my jacket, leaving it behind.

She steps onto the diving board and walks purposefully forward.

I stumble around the pool, barely avoiding the edge.

She bounces gently, as if testing the springboard.

Reaching the ladder, I grab a rung and shake it fiercely, knowing I'll never make it up there in time. "Tash, stop! STOP!"

I can't see her from down here, yet I imagine it perfectly.

Tasha, gracefully raising her arms.

Tasha, arching her back.

Tasha, lifting her heels off the board.

Tasha, singing out, "Oh, I can't *wait* to tell my mom I changed my mind!"

The rush of wind from her body brushes my face.

4 MONTHS + 22 DAYS ────────

Thursday, November 27

I wake up when something crawls through my hair. Nate catches my batting hand. "It's okay. It's me."

It's 7:12 a.m. Is this a new habit of his, sneaking into my room? I'm too miserable to be flattered. Plus I'm wearing SpongeBob boxers and a yellow T-shirt. Not the sexiest nightwear in the world.

Nate works his fingers through my knotted hair. Then he slides in next to me, staying on top of the covers. Our noses touch. "My mom's downstairs," I warn with a hiccup.

"Nope, she called Dad. She wanted to check in on Millie and didn't want to leave you alone."

"I thought you were going hunting. Why are you *here*?"

"We just got done packing the truck and we heard the sirens. We canceled the trip. My dad said to keep an eye on you." He squeezes his right eye shut and bugs out the left. "So that's what I'm doing."

Tasha's dead. I should not be staring at Nate's gorgeous hazel eyeballs, remembering how we made out at the stable.

Your eyes are the windows to your soul, Nana once said.

I swear I can see it: Nate's soul. I stare up at him till his mouth lands on mine. He yanks back the covers without breaking our kiss and wraps himself snugly around me. I dissolve into a hot puddle as he smooths my breasts and casually toys with the drawstring of my shorts. Not untying them. Merely testing the waters.

Tasha's dead and I'm horny. How very, very wrong.

He gets a load of my attire. "Whoa, SpongeBob?"

"My mom bought 'em." Weakly I drag up the sheet. I'd like to curl into a ball here and never move again. "Nate. It wasn't suicide."

"She jumped in."

"But it wasn't suicide."

"Did you . . . ?"

I know what he wants to ask, and that he's afraid to ask it.

"I didn't see it," I say softly. "I covered my eyes. Then Bennie grabbed me and dragged me down to the office. Mr. Solomon called 9-1-1."

And I couldn't stop screaming. I screamed so much, my throat's raw this morning.

"She jumped in," I say loudly. "She dove in. B-Bennie saw it. He said she landed on her h-hands."

I hide my face, glad I didn't see it. But I'll never forget that rush of air. Or the sound she made when she hit the bottom of the pool.

"I don't know *why* she did it," I say through my fingers. "But I told you what she said. So it wasn't a suicide."

"This is crazy!" he explodes. Like me, he's trembling. "First Dino. Now Tasha? What the *hell* is going on around here?"

"You already know," I whisper.

This time he doesn't argue. He only holds me tighter.

"Nate . . . what we talked about . . . I still want to do it."

"And I still say it's stupid."

"If she's there, we have to *know*. You'll help me, right?"

Nate blows out his breath. "Rinn, it makes no difference what Tasha said. Bennie *saw* it. Nobody pushed her in."

I shake my head stubbornly. "It's not just what she said. She *saw* something, something Bennie and I didn't. And she was happy, Nate. Happy! She wasn't thinking about dying." I draw his head closer to make him look me in the eye again. "It was Annaliese. Don't you believe me yet?"

"I don't know," Nate says thickly. "Rinn, I swear. I don't know *what* I believe."

———◄❍►———

Mom is back by midmorning. By then Nate and I are downstairs, sitting at the dining room table, though nobody ever sits there and we're not even eating.

"How's Millie?" I ask.

Mom throws her coat onto a chair. "A wreck. Bob drove in this morning." Tasha's dad. "He's with her now." She hugs me from behind with cold arms. "How are *you?*"

"Okay." I look at Nate. "Can we go riding?" Mom stares at me, aghast. "Mom, I can't sit around and do nothing." I remember how Xan, and all the hard work at the stable, took my mind off of Meg, if only for a while. Maybe it'll do the same with Tasha. "And you can go back to Millie's," I add.

I know she wants to be with her. I would, if Millie were *my* friend.

Besides, all she'll do is fawn over me. Ask me a thousand times how I feel, if I want to talk, if I need a shrink. On and on. I don't think I can bear it.

Nate squeezes my knee under the table. "I'll take good care of her, Mrs. Jacobs."

"Well, I suppose it's all right. But don't be all day," she warns, reaching for her coat again. "And if I'm not here when you get back, come down to Millie's."

Hand in hand, Nate and I walk to his jeep. For once, the cold winter air feels good on my face. The sky is blue, not gray. Even the sun's out for a change.

It's a beautiful day. I wish Tasha could see it.

4 MONTHS + 24 DAYS

Saturday, November 29

At Tasha's funeral, while I'm standing at the grave site—*I was just here for Dino, how is this fair?*—it occurs to me I'm the only person not crying. I rarely cry—not even when I was screaming in Mr. Solomon's office—but I never thought much about it, or even wondered why.

Now it's perfectly clear: I don't cry like other people for the very same reason I can't be "touched" by Annaliese Gibbons.

The drugs. They silence the Voices. They chase the shadow people away. They keep me down enough so I don't get all manicky and do stupid things like hook up with strangers, break into houses, or try to grab hold of a police officer's gun.

They also keep me *up* enough so I don't want to cut my throat again.

Yes, the drugs make me safe—but they numb me, too. I can't cry when I'm sad. I can't always laugh at the funny stuff, either. Things that used to excite me don't excite me as much. My guitar, for instance. I'm playing it now because Mr. Chenoweth socked me with that part, but I'm not exactly loving it. I just do it.

Of course I'm glad I'm not sick anymore. Glad, too, that Mom trusts me enough to take those pills on my own. But sometimes those same old doubts creep in, and I wonder: if I'm numb all the time, how is that living? Maybe I'd *like* to cry over a sad movie, or because someone hurt my feelings.

Or because I'm standing in a cemetery two days after Thanksgiving, knowing it's Tasha in that shiny pink casket. Don't normal people cry when a best friend dies? Maybe *not* hearing and *not* feeling things like other people is crazier than hearing and feeling things everyone else *doesn't*.

And watching bad things happen to your friends, one after the other, and not being able to help because you *can't understand what happened to them first* because you're a NUMB, PATHETIC, DRUGGED-UP FREAK is unfair.

And frustrating.

And incredibly scary.

Annaliese exists! Even Nate can't deny it. But if nobody finds out what she wants—and of course she wants something, isn't that why ghosts hang around?—who knows what terrible thing might happen next?

I have to figure it out. Yes, it has to be me. Nobody else cares enough. If I'm already labeled crazy, I have nothing to lose.

So, as soon as Nate and I do what we need to do, I'm stopping my meds.

———◦———

"No, you're not," Nate says.

"Yes, I am." This argument's getting old.

"Rinn. You are not."

"You have nothing to say about it."

The funeral's over. Like lobsters in a tank, we're among a hundred other townspeople packed into the Boxcar Diner.

"Not all of them," I say. "Just the mind-numbing ones. I'm only telling you this so you can let me know if I get goofy."

"Goofier than usual? How will I *tell*?"

I ignore his sarcasm. "Trust me. You'll tell."

A commotion breaks out. Millie, physically restrained by a bald, frantic man I'm guessing is Tasha's dad, screams at a cowering Bennie Unger. "You! This is your fault! It was your job to keep those kids away from that pool. *Why did you let them in?*"

"I d-didn't, Miz Millie," Bennie stammers. "It just—it just happened."

"Just happened, my ass! You were *there*—why didn't you stop her?" Breaking free of Mr. Lux, Millie lunges for Bennie. I automatically hide my eyes, a new habit lately. "What kind of moron *are* you? I'm gonna have your job, you hear me?"

It takes half a dozen people to wrestle her away. Bennie, sobbing unashamedly, grapples for the door and stumbles outside. As the diner falls into a prolonged, sickening silence, I think: *See? Even Bennie Unger can cry.*

4 MONTHS + 26 DAYS ———

Monday, December 1

Honey, do you want to stay home today? I doubt many people'll show up."

"You're going," I point out.

"Well, I have a job."

"Aren't you allowed to be sad?"

"Yes, I'm allowed. But if I wallow today, then I'll want to wallow tomorrow, and the next day, and then, who knows?"

A funny thing for Mom to say. Mom never wallows. The closest she got to wallowing over Tasha was late last night, when I heard her playing Chopin. A sad piece, one she played over and over, and the more she played, the more she messed up. I think she's exhausted from spending so much time with Millie.

Bleary-eyed, Mom slops milk into my juice glass, forgetting I don't drink milk, that I never drink milk except over cereal. It sits untouched as she scoops away my empty bowl. Where's her makeup? Did she even brush her hair? She's going to school like that? She looks like a—well, like a *hag*.

"I might be late tonight," I say nonchalantly.

She doesn't ask why. "If I'm not here when you get home, I'll be with Millie."

"Okay."

I follow her to the foyer. She pulls on her coat, flinging her messy hair away from the fur-trimmed hood. When I step forward for my usual good-bye kiss, she dodges away out the door.

What's *that* about? Is she mad at me?

Hurt, I wander back to the kitchen to shake my pills—my last dose—out of the bottles.

—◁○▷—

First thing in homeroom, Mr. Solomon announces over the PA: "As you know, we're all grieving the death of Tasha Lux." Half the girls burst into tears. I stare at my desk as he goes on and on—and then I hear him say, "For those of you who keep ignoring my warnings, listen up: that pool room is completely—off—limits! If I find out anyone's been in there or tampering with the lock, you'll be immediately suspended, and most likely expelled. I hope I've made myself clear."

Rats. Now what?

"If I had my way," he continues, "I'd block off the outer corridor"—his fancy phrase for the tunnel—"completely. But with no other exit from gym, the fire marshal won't allow it. Now I know some of you are, er, a bit uneasy about walking through there in light of recent events. Therefore, I'm lifting my ban on cutting through the gym. All I ask is, if there's a class going on, you'll keep to one side and not cause a disturbance."

Well, Cecilia Carpenter should be happy about that.

—◦—

School's tough. Another grief counselor sets up shop in the cafeteria. Students and teachers alike drift through the day in tears. At lunch, when I approach my vacant table, I'm struck by the most depressing truth of all: all my friends are gone.

No Meg.

No Lacy.

No Tasha.

I'm alone.

I see Cecilia chattering with Stacy Winkler, the student council chick with the overalls, and with Pat Schmidt, apparently recovered from mono. Cecilia, no doubt remembering our unpleasant meeting at Millie's diner, pays no attention to me.

I ditch the whole scene and check the custodian's closet. No Bennie, either.

Next, I head to the office. "Mom, is Bennie here today?" I just want to check on him. As bad as I feel, he must feel ten times worse. Especially after what Millie said.

Mom stares at her computer screen. "I haven't seen him."

"Is he sick?"

"How would I know?"

"Duh, Mom. Isn't it your job to keep track of us?"

She raises her head, but looks past me, not at me. "Aren't you supposed to be on your way to a class?" Then she picks up the ringing phone, dismissing me entirely.

———◀◦▶———

Last night, Nate and I planned to meet after school today. I know he didn't believe I'd go through with this. Now he asks incredulously, "Didn't you hear the announcement?"

"Yes. But you said you'd help me."

"Well, not to get myself expelled in the process."

"Fine, I'll do it myself." I stalk off, secretly hoping he'll follow. He does, of course.

I think I love this guy.

———◀◦▶———

We wait forever, till no one's around and most of the lights have been turned off for the night. We hang out in the wood shop, isolated in the basement, where I carefully choose my weapons. Then we sneak back upstairs and into the tunnel.

"You're crazy," he just *has* to say.

"Tell me something new."

"Where'd you learn how to pick a lock?"

"You probably don't want to know."

Breaking and entering is a lot harder than it looks in the movies. I ignore the new DANGER—DO NOT ENTER sign and examine the pristine lock, probably the same one Bennie dropped on his foot. Nate grudgingly keeps lookout while I insert my hooked wire and a tiny screwdriver into the lock. My technique sucks; I bet my old friend Carlos could jimmy this in ten seconds. Whenever I get one pin to pop, another one drops back down.

Twenty minutes later I've gotten nowhere. Sweat drips. My knees hurt. At the doorway of the locker room, his impatience mounting, Nate carries on a soliloquy. "You sure you can do this? Seriously, pick a lock? Who knows how to do *that*? California, my ass. I bet you're from the Bronx . . ."

I jam the wire for the ninety-ninth time, cussing the stubborn pins. "I know what I'm doing. Quit distracting me." *Jiggle, push . . . jiggle, push.* I'm about to give up when I hear a satisfying click. "Ha!"

"Sweet." He does sound impressed.

We cringe at the frigid air as the door swings open. I also came prepared with a flashlight and clothesline. Nate watches with distrust as I tie the rope to my belt loop and hand him the other end.

"Whatever you do," I say, breathless, "do *not* come in after me."

"I don't know why you're doing this," he snaps. "You were *in* there with Tasha. Did anything happen to you then? No? So what's the point?"

"I was only there a few minutes." I know this is true because I gave it a lot of thought. From the time I followed Tasha into the pool room till the moment she sprang off that board—five minutes, tops. It only felt like forever. "I want to make *sure*. So give me, like, fifteen minutes—"

"Ten."

I decide it's not worth it to argue. Ten uninterrupted minutes *might* be enough time. "Okay, then. And if nothing happens to me, it'll prove my theory."

"If nothing happens, it proves Annaliese doesn't exist."

"Whatever. You stay right here and hold the rope. And don't forget to pull me back if, you know, something attacks me, ha-ha." My feeble laugh dies at his furious expression.

"One dumb-ass move, you twit, and I'm yanking you in like a walleye."

"Ooh, I love it when you talk sexy."

Like an Eskimo stepping out of a warm igloo onto the frozen tundra, I walk into the pool room; I have plenty of rope, twenty feet at least.

"Don't come in," I yell back, like I haven't warned him a dozen times.

"Yeah, yeah." Nate tugs on the rope. "Ten minutes, surfer girl. I'm timing you."

Trailing the clothesline, I move toward the fence. The beam of my flashlight dances on the crisscrossed wires, casting light and shadows over the pool beyond.

Pool? Don't you mean the black pit of death?

Did they make poor Bennie clean THAT up, too?

Nauseated, I pause. Then I swing the beam along, till it touches the hole in the fence.

I swallow hard. I'm not sure I can do this . . .

No. I have to.

I shine the light on my watch. It's only been two minutes.

Anticipating a panic attack, I slow my breathing. My fingers stiffen in the chill. My teeth chatter, but to try to stop them will only tense me up. I let them chatter, and keep breathing, and waiting . . .

Breathing.

Waiting.

My breath billows out, visible in the beam. Senses on high alert, my teeth clanging like cymbals, I move as close as I dare to the missing section of the fence, gazing through it from one end of the pool to the other.

I feel nothing. I smell nothing. I see nothing that vaguely resembles a human form, ghostly or otherwise.

What did Tasha see? What secret was she talking about?

Water drips. I hear faint, intermittent thunks, possibly from the furnace. Wind whistles through the crack in one of the tiny windows. Is that why it's so cold in here?

I peer at my watch again. I'm at the five-minute mark.

I take one step closer to the gaping hole, shuddering as I remember how it grabbed my jacket, how I couldn't get away, how Bennie couldn't get past me . . .

Shut up. Don't think about Tasha. Concentrate on Annaliese.

"Annaliese?" I whisper. "Are you there?"

"Rinn?" A faraway Nate, waiting in the tunnel. "Time's almost up."

No it's not. I have at least four more minutes. Annoyed, I flap the rope to show him I'm alive—*stop bugging me, farmer boy*—and turn back to the pool. "Annaliese? Are you real? Are you in there somewhere?"

Drip . . . clank . . . drip.

Nothing. Absolutely nothing.

"Rinn! RINN! Get back NOW!" He jerks the rope so hard, my belt loop snaps. The clothesline sails away from me, whipping through the air like a John Wayne lariat.

Angry, I trudge back to the tunnel. "You said I had *ten* minutes—"

He yanks me through the door without a word. I trip and land on my hands and knees. Disregarding my choice of words, he lifts me up again and heaves me into the locker room.

I forget to be quiet. *"What the hell are you doing?"*

Nate slams the door. "I said let's go!"

I balk, but he hustles me through the locker room, the gym, and the cafeteria so fast, all I see is one big blur. Finally, in the main hall, I free myself, resisting the urge to kick him into Christmas. "What is *wrong* with you?"

"Why didn't you come when I called you?"

"You didn't have to assault me!"

Livid, I start for the doors, but remember I left my book bag behind. I whirl around and bolt back the way we came, with Nate thundering close behind. It occurs me that heading into a confined area with a maniac on my heels might not be the smartest move in the world.

"Don't touch me!" I snarl when he catches up in the gym.

Shocked, he raises his hands in surrender. "God, Rinn. What's *with* you?"

"You're chasing me. When people chase other people, it usually ends badly."

"I'm sorry, but—just don't go back there." He moves forward. I step back at the same time. "I'm not gonna hurt you." Panting, we glare at each other. Then Nate asks carefully, "You didn't hear it, did you?"

"Hear what?"

He gestures toward the locker room. "If you're screwing with me, Jacobs . . ."

"I'm not! I didn't hear anything. What did *you* hear?"

"I'll tell you outside. Let's go."

"My book bag!"

"Get it tomorrow."

"No! My name's all over it. I am not getting kicked out."

Torn, Nate hesitates. "Okay. But *I'll* get it. You wait here."

"Don't forget the rope. And my flashlight!"

He dashes off, stranding me in the shadows. I hop from foot to foot, eyes glued to the wall clock with the big red second hand. *Sixty seconds . . . two minutes . . . five minutes . . . seven.*

What's taking him so long?

Why did you let him go back there alone?

Finally I can't stand it. I take off, and bump right into him as he veers out of the locker room. Aggravated, he thrusts my book bag into my chest. "All your junk fell out, by the way."

"I hope you got it all," I pant as we race back. "I hope you didn't leave something behind with my *name* on it." No answer. We rush to the main doors where Nate collides to a stop. "What're you doing?"

"You seriously didn't hear it?" I shake my head. He eyes me for an eternity. "I couldn't tell what it was. It was kind of a voice, but not *really*. It—it's hard to describe."

"What did it say?"

"Nothing. It just kind of . . . howled."

"You mean like a dog?"

"Maybe wail's a better word. Like it was trying to scare us away." Nate cracks his knuckles smartly. "But not like a person. *Jesus*, Rinn." He rakes impatient fingers through his hair, and then stops, astonished, and stares down at his hand.

His fingers are wet.

With my heart punching the walls of my chest, I stand on tiptoe to examine his hair.

Ice crystals, like crushed glass, coat the top of his head.

4 MONTHS + 27 DAYS ─────

Tuesday, December 2
"Experiment: Day #1"

Drugless, I make it through the school day without a glitch. All I notice is that when 2:00 rolls around, I'm awake, not groggy, and my brain works faster.

I wonder how long it'll take.

All day I wait for Mr. Solomon to scream over the PA that someone broke into the pool room again. Yes, once you pick a dead bolt you can't relock it, of course—a fact I forgot about till it was over and done with. But I know Nate shut that door; nobody'll notice it's unlocked unless *they* try to get in. With Bennie MIA, that might take a while.

I doodle Annaliese's name on a folder.

I have no plan. Shouldn't I have a plan?

I print her name a second time, and then smear it with my thumb before anyone sees it.

Annaliese. Where are you?

How will I know when it's time to find you?

4 MONTHS + 28 DAYS ————

Wednesday, December 3
"Experiment: Day #2"

In my dream, Annaliese is playing the piano, and I'm sitting there watching her like it's the most natural thing in the world . . .

Then I open my eyes, and it's dark, and the music is real, not part of my dream. I peek at my clock. Why is Mom playing the piano at 4:00 a.m.?

I smell cigarette smoke.

I sneak downstairs. Mom fumbles a few notes, and backs up again. She misses. She tries again, and again. Not once does she get the tune right.

"Mom?"

Ignoring me, or possibly not hearing, Mom continues to bang out the same awful notes. I walk up behind her and touch her shoulder. She slams her hands on the keys with a thunderous crash. "My God, Rinn! Don't ever sneak up on me in this house again!"

In this house? Would sneaking up on her be less heart-stopping in any other house?

"I didn't sneak up. You just didn't hear me." I point to her overflowing ashtray where smoke drifts up from a smoldering cigarette. I spy the pack: Millie's brand. I said nothing the night she smoked with Luke, but now I feel I have to. "Why are you smoking? You were doing so good."

She grinds out the cigarette. "Don't nag me. I needed one. It's been a hellish week."

Wisely I don't point out that she likely smoked twenty, not one. She absolutely reeks, and she looks tired and haggard. "Why are you up so early?"

"I couldn't sleep. And I can't seem to get this piece *right* anymore." Querulously, she shakes the sheet music as if to wake it up. "Make me some coffee, will you?"

So I make the coffee, the whole time listening to Mom struggle with the tune. I wonder, *Did I dream about Annaliese because I heard Mom playing in my sleep? Or is Mom playing the piano because I dreamed Annaliese was playing?*

It's a funny thought, though not out-and-out "crazy." Wondering if I should keep track of these weird ideas, I swallow my birth control pill and wash the psych meds down the sink.

I know what to watch for. I'll pay very close attention. Nate promised to help me.

I'll be perfectly fine.

4 MONTHS + 29 DAYS ——————

Thursday, December 4
"Experiment: Day #3"

We get our schedules for next semester. I make some changes, like switching two classes so Nate and I have the same lunch period. This eating alone depresses me. Today I sat with two girls from PE, but all they wanted to talk about was Tasha: "You were there, right?" *Like they're blaming me.* "Did you see her fall?" *Like I want to talk about that.* "You guys were friends. Didn't she say anything? How could you not know she wanted to kill herself?" *Like I knew she planned it, which she didn't, and I never said a word.*

Rinn—everything that happens is not your fault.

Then why do I feel like it is?

Because you're crazy, Rinn. It's what crazy people do.

I jump up in the middle of their conversation—and mine—and throw my lunch away.

5 MONTHS EXACTLY ———————

Friday, December 5
"Experiment: Day #4"

I'm sad about Tasha. I'm missing Meg like mad. But I'm not nervous, I'm not *lethally* depressed, and the only Voice I hear in my head is my own. Either I don't need those stupid meds, after all, or I haven't been off them long enough to make a difference.

Think about it, though: what if I'm *not* bipolar? What if it simply went away? If you believe what you read, or those TV evangelists, people are cured of terrible illnesses all the time.

Why not me?

This morning, again, Mom doesn't set out my pills or remind me to take them. Does she *really* trust me?

Or does she no longer care?

Either way, the pills go down the sink.

———◁○▷———

I skip lunch and hang out in the library, worrying again about the pool room door. Bennie's still not back. Does that mean no one discovered the broken lock? Would they report it to Mr. Solomon if they did? Would he fix it immediately?

I agonize over this for, like, half the period.

It has to be locked! Nobody else can go in there! It's too dangerous!

I ditch the library, cut through the auditorium, and dart into the tunnel. Since Tasha died, *nobody* uses it. Even the jocks steer clear.

I hesitate, remembering, with a shudder, those ice crystals in Nate's hair. Funny how we've both been too afraid to bring that up.

Then I grasp the knob. The metal stings my fingers.

Wait for Nate. Do not try this by yourself.

Unlocked, as I'd feared, the door knobs turns easily.

Is that chlorine I smell?

I open the door an inch, wondering why I'm doing this, yet powerless to stop.

Fearless Rinn, Nate once called me.

"I know you're there," I call softly, vaguely aware of my burning fingers.

With an audible *whoosh* the knob wrenches out of my hand The door slams shut.

Throat parched, I bolt out of the tunnel and back to the real world.

The slick sensation of candle wax scathes my hand the rest of the day.

5 MONTHS + 1 DAY ————————

Saturday, December 6
"Experiment: Day #5"

You look different," Nate observes. "You wearing makeup?"

"Yep. Deodorant, too," I drawl. "I even warshed my pits jest for you."

Nate joins in. "Well, hayull, you clean up *real* good. I reckon I might have to ask you out on a date real soon."

"You mean when you pay my way and everything?"

"Yup. How about tonight?" he asks in his regular voice.

I consider this. I'd so love to do something besides sit around and be sad. Is there a protocol to follow when a good friend dies? Like, no dating for a month? No laughing for a year? "There's nothing to do around here on a Sunday night."

"We can drive to Westfield, catch a movie. Maybe sit in the back and throw Milk Duds at people."

My stomach flips when Nate's smile assures me that Milk Duds aren't all that's on his mind. "Wow, you farm boys sure know how to show a gal a good time."

We skip the Milk Duds, but we do sit in the back. I must be more depressed than I thought; I keep wondering, what right do I have to enjoy myself? How can life breeze along like nothing terrible happened? It feels so very wrong.

It takes Nate less than a minute to wear me down. I feel safe with him, and he holds me tighter than ever, like he needs this as much as I do. We kiss till my cheeks are raw from his stubble. Luckily the movie's awful; only ten other people in the theater, and none of them close enough to see what we're doing with our hands.

So why do I feel someone's eyes on me?

Ridiculous! No one's paying us any attention. Yet more than once I have to sit up and crane my neck in the dark. That man there, two rows ahead of us—wasn't he farther away a few minutes ago?

"What's the matter?" Nate asks.

I shake my head and go back to kissing him. Under my shirt, his hands are warm on my skin. Sliding the hem of my cami out of my jeans. Gliding up.

Slut, slut, you are such a slut, that's all you are, you'll never change, will you, Rinn?

I tell myself I'm not hearing that, that the man two rows down can't possibly know my name. Still, the nasty whispering continues: *Look at you, you make me sick, you slut, you bitch, don't you know I can see you, that EVERYONE can see you? Oh yes, we're watching . . . we're watching you, Riiinnnn . . .*

"Stop it!" I shout.

Nate jerks. "Huh?"

Heart ripping through my chest, I stare ahead.

The man is gone. All I hear now are the actors laughing on-screen, and snickers from two kids way down in the first row.

"God, Rinn," Nate says gruffly. "I thought you—I mean, I thought we—"

"I wasn't talking to you."

Nate looks around briefly. "Um, then who?" I shrug help-lessly. Technicolor lights flash in Nate's eyes, rendering them unreadable. "*O*-kay. So, is this what you meant by goofiness?"

"I'm fine," I say weakly. "Sorry."

Fine? I think about the pool room door, how the knob burned my hand, how it slammed shut by itself. If I tell Nate about *that*, will he think it's more of that "goofiness" I warned him about?

He kisses me again before I can make up my mind.

◄◊►

It's snowing hard by the time the theater lets out. Usually Nate lets me drive the jeep, but no way will I navigate these icy roads in the dark. After a slow, treacherous ride, it's after midnight when we get back. Although I don't have an official curfew for weekends, Mom may kill me; I thought we'd be home by eleven.

Our good-night kiss lasts approximately ninety seconds.

Inside, I find that our previously neat, quaint living room has morphed into a giant ashtray. Mom, on the sofa, puffs on a cigarette and stares at a late night talk show.

"Sorry I'm late," I announce. "It took forever to get home." I wait for the lecture, but Mom says nothing. "What's wrong?"

Mom's eyes swivel to touch on mine. She blows out smoke.

I can't resist. "Mom, you need to quit smoking. It's totally disgusting."

"Don't worry, honey." She taps off a cylinder of ashes. "I won't burn down the house."

I sway. *Did she really say that to me?*

WOULD she say it?

I retreat to my room, with its comforting Precious Pewter walls, and wipe the sweat off my shaky hands.

5 MONTHS + 2 DAYS ————

Sunday, December 7
"Experiment: Day #6"

I don't sleep all night.

I lie there for hours thinking about my Klonopin downstairs, how just one teensy pill would knock me out for a while. How two might let me sleep peacefully till morning. Three could render me unconscious till noon tomorrow.

Four or five would carry me through till Monday. I could skip *all* of today—what a great idea! Because if I don't get some sleep, my head'll explode.

When I shut my eyes for the millionth time, I see Annaliese's face for the millionth time.

What kind of a friend would Annaliese have been? The kind who'd be nicer to Lacy, who'd accept her for who she is?

Who'd call 9-1-1 when she knew something was wrong at Meg's instead of running first to Nate, wasting valuable time?

Who could've read Tasha's mind, and kept her out of the pool room altogether?

Who wouldn't have abandoned Dino.

Who would've rushed back to the cottage the second she saw those flames and dragged her unconscious grandmother to safety?

I had those chances. I blew them every time.

Annaliese had no chance to do anything, right *or* wrong.

I turn on my lamp and rummage around for a compact. Flicking it open, I aim the dusty round mirror at my face. I stare hard at my eyes, those flat gray disks. The longer I stare, the lighter they become, growing paler and brighter till they shine like silver coins.

Is that you, Annaliese, hiding inside me?

What would you be like if you'd lived? Did people like you? Hate you?

Were you smart in school? Mediocre, like me?

Were you in love with someone?

I think you were. You looked sad in that yearbook, but I know you were just lost in another world, thinking about him, counting the minutes till you'd see him.

Whoever he was, he loved you. Yet he let you die.

I hear her reply: "Yes, he did. And I hate him for it."

My words, my voice. But I don't know why I said it.

I throw the compact across the room.

———◆———

Sleep. Who needs it? By 7:00 a.m. I've unpacked all the boxes I've ignored for weeks. I've also alphabetized my books, changed my sheets, organized my CDs, and showered and dressed. Next I consider all my random piles of clothes, and I decide I'm sick of living out of laundry baskets. I sort and stack every item by color and season, then gallop downstairs to ask Mom about Annaliese's dresser. She *said* I could use it.

I find a note on table: *At Millie's. Will probably take her to out to lunch. Be good!*

Millie again. I crumple the note. Be good? Really?

I enlist Nate's help in moving the dresser. It's hard navigating the narrow staircase, plus we knock a hole in my wall once we get it to the top.

"Nice going," I observe, though it's not entirely his fault.

He falls on to my mattress with exaggerated pants. "Now what?"

"Now you can help me clean this thing up"—I nod at the dresser, a cherry wood box with four roomy drawers—"and put my stuff away. *Or . . .*" His eyes grow huge as I unbutton the top button of my shirt. "We can have sex."

"What?"

I unbutton the second one, then the third. Nate watches, transfixed. "My mom's taking Millie out to lunch. We've got plenty of time." The fourth and fifth buttons pop open. I slide my arms out of the shirt, wondering why he's looking at me so funny, and why I feel like I'm acting a part in a movie. *Cut! Print!* "Well?"

Speechless, he waits till I drop my jeans. Then he leaps off my mattress as if jabbed by a branding iron. "Stop." My hands falter. I can tell he's trying hard to concentrate on my face, not my thong. "Maybe it's not such a good idea to jump into this. Y'know, like it's nothing special."

Hotly I ask, "Who said it's not special? You were all *over* me last night."

"Yeah, I—" He steps forward as I yank up my jeans, but stops at my warning glare. "Look, don't get mad. But when you told me to watch out for 'goofiness,' you weren't all that specific. So I did some research and, uh . . . this is one of the signs."

"What is?"

He flips one finger to me, to himself, and back at me. "You know. *This.*"

I flap my shirt at him. "Whatever. Thanks for your help. You can go home now."

"Rinn—"

"*Good-bye*, Nate."

If I were a crier, I'd be bawling my eyes out. *I can't believe he said no! How could he say no?* Facedown on my mattress, I dig my nails into my pillow, hating Nate.

Hating myself more.

———◦———

I wake up from a dead, overdue sleep to the sound of car doors slamming outside. Woozy and disoriented, dying of thirst, I grope my way down to the first floor in time to hear Millie whimper, "I'm being punished, Mo. Punished!"

"That's ridiculous," Mom objects. From my perch on the steps I hear her fill the tea kettle and drop it on a burner. "You know it's not your fault."

"Then whose is it? My child *killed* herself. How can I live with that?" Millie's wretched sobs drown out Mom's comforting words. "Why didn't I know? Why didn't I see it coming?"

"Because you can't always see it. Didn't they tell you that at the support group?"

Millie half snorts, half sobs. "Support group, my ass. They have no idea. *You* have no idea."

"I do have an idea. You know I do."

Don't talk about me, Mom. Please—don't say it.

I creep through the living room, then through the dining room.

"It's not the same thing. You just don't know!"

"Then *tell* me, Mil."

A brief silence. Then Millie asks warily, "Where's Rinn?"

"I don't know. Upstairs. Millie, please, why do you think you're so different? What do you mean *punished*?"

All I hear is mumble, mumble. I tiptoe closer and peek around the edge of the kitchen door. There, I see Millie snuffling into her hands.

And Mom, blanched and rigid, one fist pressed to her mouth.

What did Millie just tell her? Why did I have to miss it?

Mom's ESP kicks in. She zooms right over. "Rinn! Are you eavesdropping?"

Millie emits a small moan at this. I feign innocence. "No. I just need a drink of water."

Mom points firmly to the sink. "Then get it and go."

I snap back, "Well, you don't have to be so nasty about it!"

"And *you* don't need to be skulking around, listening in on conversations."

Embarrassed, infuriated, I spin around and stomp back the way I came. Upstairs, I slam the attic door and run up to my room. There, with a shriek, I dive onto my mattress.

It feels so good to scream that I do it again.

Then again.

And again!

Nobody cares.

5 MONTHS + 3 DAYS ———

Monday, December 8
"Experiment: Day #7"

Once again my unstoppable thoughts keep me awake all night. I roam the house, at a loss for anything to do. I even slip outside and stroll around the block, enjoying the stillness of the dark cold night.

I stop at the school, and sit on the steps to watch the clouds drifting over the moon. But all the same thoughts and memories race through my brain, over and over, over and over—like not one, but a *zillion* songs stuck in your head at the same time. When a car slows at the curb—*rapists, serial killers, scoping me out*—I jump up and run home.

I make coffee, throw on clothes, and blast my radio full volume—*how do YOU like being woken up in the middle of the night, Mom?*—but with no effect. At last I leave for school, earlier than usual to avoid Nate. I'm not sure if I'm mad because he turned me down, or mad at myself for coming on to him. Why did I *do* that? I haven't the foggiest.

By 11:00 I decide I owe him an apology. At 12:00 I change my mind. By 1:00 I've not only changed it again, I'm also seriously considering getting back *on* my meds before I try to jump someone else's bones. Mr. Chenoweth's, say.

But after school, embarrassed all over again, I rush home without even looking for Nate.

Hyper in spite of so little sleep, I zip through my homework, blowing off biology, and spend the evening in exile, listening to Frank's favorite old songs on my iPod. Has he called here lately? If so, Mom never mentioned it.

Call him, Rinn.

What if he hangs up on me?

Take a chance!

I can't. I'm afraid.

Because you're a big fat baby. You're pathetic. Pathetic!

My thoughts spin faster and faster: I think of Frank, and then Nate, and how I took off my clothes—*why did he turn me down? Am I ugly? Is he gay? Does he secretly hate me?*—*and Mom didn't care that I didn't eat tonight, or all day, really, and she hasn't figured out I'm not taking my meds, does she care, no she doesn't, and Millie's being punished, she was mean to Tasha, and I miss her, miss her, and Meg, too, Meg, Meg, and I should practice "My Sweet Lord" but I can't think straight, oh, crap, I can't sit still, maybe a Klonopin, no, no, remember Annaliese, Annaliese, oh Nana, where are you and why did you leave me?*

———◇———

By 3:00 a.m. my room's immaculate, every stitch of clothing meticulously folded and placed in my drawers—no, in *Annaliese's* drawers. Then I cradle my guitar and sing "My Sweet Lord" under my breath, praying for the strength not to pop a pill.

I hear music again, and it's Mom, trying to play "Für Elise." Who'd guess that she studied music in college, that she might've played professionally one day if Señor Jay hadn't knocked her up? She hits the same two notes over and over. I grit my teeth till my jaw aches, then switch on the radio—loud—and haul my biology book out. I read four straight chapters, and, amazingly, absorb every word about autotrophs, heterotrophs, and photosynthesis.

"A*ha!* See?" Jubilant, I kick the book aside. With all those poisonous chemicals purged from my system, I can think more clearly, comprehend things better. Even biology!

Pleased, I dress for school at 4:30 and pack up my book bag and my guitar; Mr. Chenoweth's holding our first rehearsal for the Christmas concert tonight. As I swipe on lip gloss, I notice in the mirror the reflection of my wall and that ugly chip in my paint job. I remember asking Nate about the new drywall, why he didn't leave the walls as they were.

He'd said, "It was some pretty ugly wallpaper," and left it at that.

I drop the plastic tube, crouch on the floor, and pick at the dent. Inside the crack I see a hint of flowered wallpaper, so I dig till it's big enough for me to notice something else. Is that *handwriting* in there? *I have to see!*

Downstairs, I slip past Mom and her mangled Beethoven, and ravage the jumble of tools she keeps under the sink. Armed with necessities, I rush back. After a few pounds with a hammer and jabs from a screwdriver, the crack transforms into a book-sized hole. Distantly I'm aware of that David Gilmour song—"There's No Way Out of Here"—drifting from my speakers.

"No way out, huh?" I whack my tools in time with the music. "That's what you think."

Pound, pound, pound with the hammer. Then jab, twist, and flip with the screwdriver. Bit by bit I fling out chunks of drywall, haunted by Gilmour's words, the same surreal strains of his guitar playing over and over . . .

When at last I step back to study the hole, made bigger by breaking off pieces with my hands, I can easily read the writing on the faded flowered wall.

Bible verses.

Lyrics to a hymn everybody in the world knows: "I once was lost but now I'm found."

And *ANNALIESE, ANNALIESE* scrawled a thousand times over.

Behind me, Mom shouts, "Rinn! What're you doing?" over the deafening music.

I blink.

I'm standing there at the wall, coated in gray dust and flecks of chiseled drywall. Some pop song blasts from my radio—not Gilmour at all—and my bedside clock says 6:07.

"Corinne Katherine Jacobs. Will you please explain why you're knocking down *walls*?"

Suddenly, I'm incredibly happy. *This* person sounds *exactly* like my mom—not that sullen, nocturnal stranger who can't play Beethoven, and smokes, and throws out nasty hints about burning down houses.

I point triumphantly to the mutilated wall. "Mom, look

what she wrote! Annaliese's name, and all these Bible verses, and—"

Mom steps closer. She's dressed for school. I smell soap and shampoo, and, from downstairs, the aroma of coffee. "Honey. What's going on?"

"Nothing! I just wanted to see what was under the drywall."

Exasperation flashes. "Do you have any idea what it'll cost to repair this?"

"Mom, don't you get it? Mrs. Gibbons was trying to *communicate* with her. She did it at school, too. In the pool room, with Miss Prout!"

Screwdriver poised, I move toward the hole—*funny how it's so much bigger than I thought*—but Mom catches me. "Stop!" She points to the enormous mess on the floor. "You pick up the pieces. I'll bring up the vacuum. And don't you dare touch that wall again. Are you five years old, Rinn?"

She stomps downstairs. Confused now, I stand there and stare at the hole.

It's as tall as me. Maybe three feet across.

What the hell did I just do?

———◄○►———

"The goofiness has started," I murmur to Nate at my locker. "The real deal."

Thank God he's speaking to me. "What'd you do?"

"I tore down a wall. Well, not a whole one, but—"

"Which wall?"

I narrow my eyes. "One of the ones *you* covered up."

"Oh, that," he says noncommittally.

"Why didn't you tell me Mrs. Gibbons wrote all that stuff?"

"'Cause I didn't want you freaking out?" Nate nods at my neck as I gear up to tell him off. "Look, you're the one who told me about *that*. How was I supposed to know how you'd react?"

Guess I can't blame him for that.

"Okay, so you knocked down a wall. That's goofy," he concedes. "But is it crazy?"

"Well, there's that time warp." I explain how I lost two hours. How I heard the same song playing over and over as the twelve-inch hole I'd planned turned into a cavern. "I swear I was only at it, like fifteen minutes. I started at four. When my mom came up it was *six*."

"Okay. That's crazy."

"And what I did . . ." I falter, knowing I have to face this. "To you. The other day."

Nate smiles. "Under any other circumstances, I'd definitely take you up on it."

Cheeks hot, I press on. "Anyway, I think we need to do this now, *today*, before I do something worse. Maybe after school? After rehearsal?" Because Nate's in the orchestra, he'll be there, too.

His smile fades. "I guess. But it's still a bad idea."

"Well, if you don't want to, I'll go by myself, then." I pray he doesn't ask how I plan to hang on to both ends of the rope.

"Like *hell* you will."

———◦———

Nate waits in silence while I tie the clothesline, around my waist this time since I can't trust my belt loops. "I don't suppose I can talk you out of this."

I haul the flashlight out of my book bag. "I'll be okay. Just pay attention."

Without warning he shouts, "No, *you* pay attention!" He drowns out my *shush* with, "Ghosts don't exist, Annaliese doesn't exist, and I have *no—idea* what the hell you're trying to prove here."

Shocked by his nasty tone, I retort, "You had ice in your hair. Ice! And you've been too damned scared to even talk about that! So don't lie to me and say you don't believe in ghosts."

He stares me down, speechless with fury. That's how I know: *he's hiding something.*

He's been hiding it since the last time we were here, when he came out of the locker room with frozen hair.

Nate shoves me. "Do it, then. You get *five* minutes this time."

I stick out my tongue and test the door. Still unlocked. Nobody's been here.

I step over the threshold into the pool room. At first I notice nothing different; it's as dark and as cold as the last time I was here. Now, though, it's perfectly silent. No clanking furnace. No whistling wind.

I inhale slowly, experimentally. The air reminds me of a muggy summer night. Much colder, of course.

A scent brushes my nostrils with my next deep breath.

Chlorine.

I didn't smell this at the séance. Everyone else did, though.

As I nervously aim the flashlight at the black pit—through the fence this time; I'm not going near Dino's hole—the tickle of chlorine evolves to a bitter sting. I rub my nose and glance back, searching for Nate's shadow. I think I see it. At least I hope it's him.

My tongue toys with my lips, all slick and greasy like—baby oil? I tilt my head, acutely aware of the foul, heavy air caressing my face.

Is this really happening? Is it?

When I first hear the sound, I automatically suspect Nate.

He's messing with your head. He wants you out of here.

When I hear it a second time, I know I'm wrong.

A human sound, part sigh, part wail, drifts up from the dark hole. Soft and insistent, the haunting cry curls around my head, stirring the mysterious substance that, unbelievably, feels like it's seeping into my ears. I swat wildly at the air, shooting circles with my flashlight.

The floor vibrates under my feet as the muted wail blossoms to a menacing howl.

Something's happening, something bad—but when I try to shout a warning to Nate, the oily substance chokes me off, slithering down my throat, cutting off my air.

A cloud of something dances nearby. Not smoke, not exactly. More like a fog.

A thin, pale fog rising from the edge of the pool.

My knees buckle and I sink by degrees, floating through a barrel of bitter molasses. Pressure flattens me. I can't breathe.

I can't breathe!

I'm going to die in this horrible room like Dino and Tasha.

"There's no way out of here," David Gilmour sings inside me.

Nowayoutnowayoutnowayoutnowayout . . . !

The unearthly howl peaks, and then cascades into a torrent of hysterical laughter.

I should've listened to Nate.

Why didn't I?

Why . . . ?

———◄◦►———

I open my eyes to the fluorescent lights of the locker room ceiling. Four rows of lights, when there should only be two.

"Are you awake? Can you hear me?" A bolt of pain stabs my head when Nate crushes me, kissing my face, my hair. "Oh God, oh God, I thought you were dead! You hit your head when you fell." He offers me his bloody hand as proof.

"I—I think I'm okay," I squeak.

"You passed *out*!"

My head hurts worse when I force myself up. I touch my wet hair, look at my hand, and whimper. For someone who slashed her neck in a Jacuzzi, I don't do well with blood.

"How many fingers do you see?"

I push him away. "You didn't go in, did you?" It all rushes back to me. "Please say you didn't."

"I didn't. I dragged you out with the rope."

Thank God! "Did you hear it?"

As soon as I ask this, I'm sorry. What if he says no? What if those hideous sounds and that funny fog were nothing but the hallucinations of a crazy girl who ditched her meds for the past seven days?

Nate presses his cheek against mine. His face is wet, and not from my bloody hair.

"Yes, I heard her," he says, all muffled against me.

Her, he said. Not *it*.

Now I know he believes me.

<hr>

Mom falls for my idiotic story about slipping on some ice. "Idiotic" because it was in the forties today, a heat wave for Ohio in December. No ice left anywhere.

It bothers me that she believes this tale. The fact that she doesn't insist on X-rays, or try to keep me awake so I don't lapse into a coma, or ream Nate out like it's all *his* fault, bothers me more.

I think of a book she used to read to me ages ago: *Are You My Mother?* Today that story rings all too true. A funny WTF sensation gnaws me as Mom parts my hair to examine my gash for, oh, maybe one second.

"You'll be fine," is her disinterested remark. Then she lights a cigarette—her old brand, not Millie's, which means she's buying them now—and turns to face the kitchen window.

Nate, after a dubious glance at Mom, pushes my jaw back in place. "I'll call you later, okay?"

I stagger after him to the front door. "Don't say anything to anyone. Promise me?"

"Ha. No chance of *that*."

No chance of telling? Or no chance of promising? Without clarifying, he kisses my forehead, swears he'll call me later, and then he's out the door.

I notice the bare stove and no sign of dinner. Not that I'm hungry, but still. "Aren't you cooking tonight?"

"No." Mom stays glued to the window. "You can order a pizza if you like."

"We *can't* order a pizza."

"Then make a sandwich," she snaps. "You're sixteen! Why is it *my* job to feed you?"

Flabbergasted—*what's wrong with her, what's wrong with her?*—I leave her hunched into herself. Upstairs, I throw a bath towel over my pillow and carefully rest my head.

I know exactly what I need to do: get back on my meds and do it NOW! But that would involve walking all the way back downstairs. Between my head and my iffy stomach, I doubt I'd make it.

Besides, I'm afraid of that woman in the kitchen.

I'm afraid of my own mother, who's never been afraid of me—not even when I hit her, cussed her out, called her horrible names—though I gave her every reason.

My wall creaks. Not like the usual settling of this old house, but a prolonged, rasping creak, like it's deliberately trying to draw my attention. *Do ghosts travel?* Immobilized by the idea, I stare at my Precious Pewter wall, hypnotized by the big raggedy hole.

The hole stares back.

Then it speaks.

"I once was lost but now I'm found," we recite in unison.

Both voices, mine and the hole's, aggravate my headache, making me retch. My ears feel plugged, like I've spent hours underwater. A stinging sensation lingers in my nostril.

I address the deadly beam above the foot of my mattress. Somehow I know without being told that this is the beam Mrs. Gibbons hung herself from.

The Hanging Beam.

"She laughed at me," I tell Annaliese's dead grandmother. "I heard her. And I saw her friggin' *ghost.*"

We found her.

It's true.

Annaliese exists.

5 MONTHS + 4 DAYS ————

Tuesday, December 9

I do sleep, finally, but wake up during the night with the same raging headache, exacerbated by Mom's butchering of "Liebe-sträum." Once again, she can't play for shit.

Every—single—night she does this! I'm sick of it. *Sick!*

"Will you stop banging that thing?" I shrill from the landing. "If you're gonna play it, then play it! Quit fucking up every song!"

Mom's hands fall. She whips her face in my direction.

"I'm the crazy one, Mom. Not you. *Not you!*"

"What's the matter with you?" she whispers.

I shout, "Can't you *guess* what's the matter? Do you even give a shit anymore?"

I stumble back upstairs, grab my iPod to block everything out, dive onto my mattress, and glare at the Hanging Beam till I fall back asleep.

————◄o►————

My alarm doesn't go off, Mom doesn't wake me, and I don't regain consciousness till noon. Sore, vaguely confused, I slink downstairs in time to hear Mom say my name on the kitchen phone.

Talking about me. Why is she always talking about me?

I edge into the kitchen, fingering my matted hair. "Was that Frank?"

"Yes, it was Frank. And no, he didn't ask to speak to you."

"He hates you. You murdered his mother."

"You are no longer his daughter."

"He wishes you were dead. You SHOULD be dead."

"You should've died in that fire. Not Frank's mother."

"Not Nana."

My frozen gaze sticks to Mom's face. Her lips never moved.

Is it still a hallucination if you *know* you're hallucinating?

If you cut your throat when no one's around to see it, do you still bleed red?

Do you bleed at all?

Keeping a wide berth, I sidle around her to grab my meds. She says nothing. Neither do I. I rarely understood what the Voices said to me before. I never recognized them as belonging to anyone, either. But this time I did.

It was my mother's voice.

I sleep straight through till 9:00 p.m., then I wash down my nighttime meds with a Pepsi I open myself. I return to bed without stopping to pee. My head lump feels like a mushy kiwi.

Wasn't Nate supposed to call me? Or was that yesterday?

5 MONTHS + 5 DAYS ————

Wednesday, December 10

Next time I open my eyes, it's morning again. Immediately I realize I desperately need to pee, not to mention take a shower. The bump pokes out of my greasy hair, crusted with old blood.

Should I go to school? Is it Wednesday or Thursday? I squint at my wall calendar. Each month features a different rock album cover—Frank gives me these for Christmas—and December is Aerosmith's *South of Sanity*. Ha, very funny.

I hug my knees and try to focus. At least I don't feel like screaming at Mom again, and I don't hear any voices whispering in the wall.

Yet something's not right.

In the shower, Steven Tyler screeches *"Dream on! Dream on! Dream on!"* in my head as I gently rinse shampoo from my hair. Did Mom really say I'm not Frank's daughter? That I, not Nana, should've died in that fire?

No no no!

Dripping wet, wrapped in a towel, I run up to my room and halt in front of the hole. I stare at the random Bible verses, written in Mrs. Gibbons's squinchy handwriting.

At the endless columns of lyrics to "Amazing Grace."

At Annaliese's name written over and over by the lady who killed herself here.

I drop the towel, snatch up my book bag, and heave it at the hole as hard as I can. Then my hairbrush. Then a dictionary. Then my smooshed-up pillow and the bloodstained towel. Dust splatters. Loose chips of drywall fly. I snatch up my CD player, too, but luckily think twice. "You won't win, you bitch. I'm onto you now. I'm gonna figure you out if it kills me!"

"Where are your *clothes*? And who are you talking to?"

CRAP!

"Myself," I say, shivering.

"Oh." Mom smiles a peculiar smile. "I do that, too, sometimes."

—◄◦►—

"I didn't hear you playing last night," I say at breakfast.

"Good. I tried to keep it down."

I ask nonchalantly, "So, why do you do that?"

"I can't sleep." Mom slumps in her chair like she has no plans to ever move out of it. "In fact, I think I'll take today off. I haven't slept in days. Not since Tasha's funeral."

And looks like you can't play the piano anymore, either.

That niggling sensation kicks my stomach again.

When did Mom start getting so weird? After Tasha died? Or after I stopped taking my meds? If it's the meds, maybe I'm only imagining her weirdness.

But I didn't imagine the piano playing. And I'm sure Nate noticed how strange she acted when he dragged me home with my head split open. I'd better ask him to be sure.

Back upstairs, I dial his number. "What?" he barks without asking who it is.

"Well, isn't that a nice way to answer the phone?" Silence. "You said you'd call me," I add awkwardly. "You didn't."

I wait for him to explain. All he says is, "I know."

"Nate, I—I think we should talk about what happened at school. And there's something really important I have to ask you about my mom."

"Are you back on your meds?"

"What? Yes. Why?"

"Good. Keep taking 'em. Because seriously, Rinn, you're making *me* crazy now."

This stings. "How am I making you crazy?"

"This *ghost* shit, Rinn."

"But you were there. You heard her." A nasty idea dawns. "Or were you humoring me?"

Nate says curtly, "I'm going to the stable."

"Wait, what about school?"

"What about it?"

I forget my indignation. "I'll come with you. Wait for me!"

"No," Nate snaps. "I don't want you there."

He hangs up on me.

———◇———

Miserable now, I watch from my window as Nate, in a camouflage jacket and that ugly fur cap I tease him about, tosses a rifle into his jeep and roars off down the street.

He's not going to the stable. He's going hunting. Why'd he lie?

One thing I know: *I* can't go to school today, either. I am way too messed up. If I'm hearing voices in my wall, what'll I do if the blackboards or lockers strike up a conversation?

I also know I can't stay here with Mom. If I start yelling at Annaliese again, it won't take her long to figure out I've been skipping my meds.

Or will it?

Funny how her hovering used to annoy me so much. Now I miss it like crazy. It's like she's been taken over by aliens, like that *Invasion of the Body Snatchers* movie I once watched with Frank. I ragged on the idea that aliens would waste time spinning pods, waiting for people to fall asleep. After all, they're *aliens*. Why not land, conquer the world, and be done with it?

Because, Frank said, it's better to do that gradually, insidiously. Then by the time people catch on, it's too late to fight back.

Forget aliens. What about Annaliese? Why does *she* want to hurt people?

I dig up the worn, crumpled list I started ages ago:

1. Lacy got headaches after she went into the tunnel. Plus she went Rambo on me.
2. Meg's ears started ringing after she went into the tunnel. She fell on the ground in front of hundreds of spectators doing a stunt she's done a thousand times.
3. Cecilia lost her voice after she went into the tunnel.

To which I've since added the following:

4. Dino died in the pool room.
5. Lacy wrote a nasty letter to Chad, didn't remember writing it, and lost her baby.
6. Meg stabbed her mom.
7. Tasha dove into that empty pool.

The first three things happened before the séance. The last four, after.

I scribble more:

8. Miss Prout went crazy hanging around that pool.
9. After she dragged Annaliese's grandmother into her happy medium act, Mrs. Gibbons killed herself.
10. That alcoholic teacher (maybe related).
11. Lindsay McCormick's cat (definitely related).
12. I ALMOST died in that pool room.
13. Mom doesn't act like Mom anymore.
14. Now Nate's changing, too. Why did he lie? Why not SAY he was going hunting?

But Nate wasn't at the séance. Neither was Mom. Mom doesn't even use the tunnel; she stays in the office all day and only comes out for lunch. I bet she hasn't even seen that pool room since high school—

Wait. That's not true.

Something claws at my neck.

That damn séance! Who did I run for when they all zoned out on me? I ran for Mom. She did go in there that night, to chase everyone out.

I crumple my list. Oh God. That's it! Okay, maybe it took a while for Annaliese to "get" to Mom. But my mother's a strong person. She wouldn't make it easy.

This time it *is* my fault. But how could I have known?

<hr />

With Mom not at school to realize *I'm* not, either, I decide to hike over to Rocky Meadows myself. Nobody's there to mind, only a caretaker who now knows me by sight. Exhausted after the two-mile walk, I stumble when I notice Nate's muddy jeep. He's here, after all? I thought he went hunting.

Unnerved, I slog up the long driveway. What'll he say when I show up uninvited, and undoubtedly unwelcome? I don't understand why he's so mad at me in the first place. Like it's *my* fault there's some lunatic ghost on the loose?

I walk through the stable, glad to be out of the wind and muck. Every stall stands empty. No shuffling of hooves or munching of grain. No welcoming whinny from Xan. Funny, Nate never turns them all out at once; not every horse gets along with the others. Ginger, for instance, loves to bite Xan's hindquarters if she gets right up behind him, and he's twice her size.

No sign of Nate in the stable. I leave by the rear door, squinting in the sunshine flashing through a patchwork of gray clouds. When I hear the distant, restless nickering coming from the fenced-in paddock behind the barn, I stop.

Something's wrong. The horses know it, too.

Heart thumping, I dodge into the barn and tramp through

the carpet of dirt and sawdust. Then, as I duck back outside, I hear a horrific sound: the metallic slam of a rifle being loaded.

I'm already running when the *CRACK* splits the air, followed by the acrid smell of gunpowder.

Nate snarls, *"Damn!"*

Panicked whinnying. The rustle of massive bodies. Stomping hooves and snorts of alarm. Desperate to escape the danger, the horses crash about the paddock in a brownish blur. Nate, over by the fence, slams another round of ammo into the rifle and then points the barrel at the creatures.

The shotgun explodes a split second before it leaves his hands. My flying body slams him into the mud, knocking the breath out of us both. Nate, first to recover, flips me over and pins me to the ground, screaming obscenities.

"Stop it!" I scream back into his damp scarlet face. *"Nate, stop!"*

He shuts up and stares at me. His hot, ragged breath reeks of bleach. Sweat rains down as he violently shakes his head, and then abruptly releases me. He rolls away and flings an arm over his face.

Side by side we lay on the cold earth. Mud splatters us through the fence, kicked up by hooves. I imagine the horses, with indignant snorts, discussing the incident among themselves. Wondering what would possess the boy who loves them so much to try to do such an unthinkable thing . . .

Possessed.

Slowly, I turn my head to the side. Aside from his heaving chest, Nate doesn't move, and the rifle's a safe ten or twelve feet away. *This must be a dream. It can't possibly be real life.*

As minutes pass, and wetness leaks into my jacket and jeans, Nate's panting slows so much I wonder if he's breathing at all. I whisper his name, afraid to touch him. His arm drops away from his mottled face. Tears trickle into his ears. "Nate, get up."

He *could* get up. He could jump up, grab the gun, and shoot the horses, anyway.

Or shoot me.

He could do anything he wants, something totally unexpected—because *he is not Nate Brenner!* Nate would never do this.

Squelching my fear, I shove his head. "*Talk* to me, Nate."

Nate blinks at the sky. Then, very slowly, turns to face me. Will he hurt me? Should I run? No, because then I'd have to take the rifle with me, too. And if I can't outrun him . . .

"Rinn?" He says my name, softly, wonderingly, like he thought I was dead and now he's shocked to see I'm not.

Sobbing, he reaches out to touch my cheek with his icy hand.

———◇———

"You know what would've happened after I shot them?"

I'd started a sort-of fire in the fireplace in the lounge, but the puny flame does nothing to warm us. Nate's teeth chatter so hard I can barely understand him.

"You have to get out of those clothes," I say bossily, poking the logs.

Nate wrenches the poker away and grips both my hands. He's so cold, so cold, his fingers don't feel human. I shiver as he transfers the chill to me. "I would've shot myself. I had it all figured out. I'd put the gun in my mouth and hit the trigger with my toe. Right over there." He nods at the couch. "I was gonna write you a note, but then I thought, maybe not." I wince as he squeezes my hands harder. "Maybe it'd be better if I—"

"Shut up! You didn't do it. You're still alive."

"Am I?" A dead, flat whisper.

Twisting free, I dig two musty blankets out of a bin and dump them on the floor. "Take your clothes off," I order, "and sit *down*."

Rigid, Nate gazes wordlessly into the growing fire, so I pull off his sodden jacket and unbutton his shirt myself. When I reach for his belt buckle, he pushes me away, kicks off his muddy jeans, and sits down like a good little boy. Nearly faint with cold, I strip down to my underwear, too, then kick the mangy bear rug aside and spread our clothes out to dry. I can't figure out why we're both so cold, why the heat from the fireplace hasn't reached us yet.

I crawl onto the couch and drag the blankets over us. "Don't worry. Mutual body heat's the best way to prevent hypothermia."

Nate's marble lips press my temple. "I was gonna do it. Seriously."

"Why?" I whisper, cuddling close.

"Because I love them. Because that's what she wants."

———— ‹◦› ————

We almost do it. We come so very close.

I saw this coming before I took off my clothes. Maybe I saw it the second I met him. Still, I never dreamed it'd happen like this, with both of us shivering and scared under two smelly blankets. We kiss and touch, and I'm glad to say that it's *not* because I'm a crazy girl who can't control herself. Or because he's a guy who tried to destroy so much and now needs to be reminded that everything's okay.

We stop in time. It's enough for now. Slick with sweat, I fling off the blankets and dress quickly, all awkward and exposed, my heart fluttering like bird wings.

None of this makes me forget there's still a rifle outside, plus a paddock full of horses that nearly lost their lives. What if I'd gotten here five minutes later?

What if I'd been the one to find Nate with that gun barrel in his mouth, his blood and brains sprayed all over the couch?

"I'd hate you forever," I hear myself say.

Nate understands. "It didn't happen."

I curl my legs under me and rest my head on his bare shoulder. His chest glistens; he's warm, so warm. I touch the line of dark fuzz creeping down his stomach.

"And I'm not suicidal," he adds tonelessly. "Not like when *you* tried it." He touches my neck. "It's . . . it's not the same."

I snuggle closer, enjoying the heat. "I know. It was Annaliese. Maybe I could lend you some drugs," I half tease. "Then you'd be safe."

"Says you. Seriously, how many people at school even take that stuff?"

"You said Jared—"

"That's one. But the whole student body? Except for the people she targets? Gimme a break. We'd all be running around with guns."

"The people she targets," I repeat softly.

Oh. My. God. That's it!

The idea explodes like a supernova. "You're right. She's selective. She *chose* us."

"Why?"

"I don't know! But I'm sure of it."

Nate lets my message sink in. "Okay, then *how* did she 'choose' us?"

"The séance?"

"You said Cecilia wasn't there. Neither was I."

"You're right." I sigh, more puzzled than ever. "Now if you'd gone in the pool room *with* me, I'd say that's when she got you, but—"

Nate fidgets strangely. Dread punches my gut.

"You didn't, right? You said you *dragged* me out."

He observes the fire like it's the most fascinating thing in the world. "The first time we tried it, before you stopped your meds? And I ran back for your book bag?" Nate hunches over. "Rinn. Something was *there*."

"What?" I breathe, already afraid of the answer.

"I'm not sure. But the locker room, it looked different somehow. I saw shadows where there shouldn't have been any shadows. Like in the middle of the floor, and—and up by the ceiling. And the regular shadows were . . . wrong." Nate flushes. "Don't laugh."

I'm not even close to laughing. "Did they move?"

"Uh, yeah. That's what took me so long."

"Eight minutes," I remind him.

"That's 'cause *I* couldn't move. It scared the hell out of me."

I remember the night I stayed late to decorate for Homecoming: those table shadows, how they slithered and changed before my eyes. Not my imagination *or* a hallucination. So why am I not happier? Because now I'm wondering if Anna-liese floats around the whole school. *Do* ghosts travel? If so, how far?

Was Annaliese ever actually in my room?

White around the mouth, Nate continues, "Rinn, when I said I dragged you out? I lied. You fell, I saw the blood, and I kinda freaked out. I did pull the rope, but I couldn't move you. It's like . . ." His Adam apple dances. "Like something was hangin' *on* to you, keeping you from me. So I ran in and got you. I had to," he insists as I gawk in disbelief.

"No, you didn't! Nate, you promised!"

"What'd you expect me to do? Leave you in there?"

"Oh, big hero. Thank you *soo* very much." I kick angrily at the blanket. "You know, if you'd told me what happened the *first* time, with the shadows and stuff, I wouldn't have made you help me."

Nate sneers. "Oh, right. Like you'd go alone."

"I could've gotten someone else."

"Like who? Meg? Lacy? Tasha?" I shrink back at his nasty laugh. "Oh, wait. Meg's in jail, and Tasha's dead, and Lacy's, well, who knows? So who's left, Rinn? Huh?"

"Okay, I get it. You don't have to be a jerk about it."

We sit there, side by side, as the fire spits and crackles. I hear the horses outside, but they're happy horses now, not trampling around all wild-eyed with terror. Nate gets up, pats his clothes, and pulls his jeans up over his flannel Scooby-Doo boxers. And he laughed at my SpongeBobs?

He buttons his plaid shirt, then picks up the poker and jabs the fire. "Okay, think. Why us? Why not the other three hundred kids in school?"

"She takes things from us, like Cecilia's singing. She took Chad away from Lacy. Then she took Lacy's baby."

Nate knocks a log aside, an explosion of orange. "Go on."

"She took away Meg's cheerleading. She stole her personality. She made her attack her mom." Hyperventilating, I force myself to slow down. "She took Tasha's diving away—"

"And her life," he says curtly. "Dino's, too."

"She almost took *yours*."

The mental picture of Xan and Ginger, dead on the ground, surrounded by the bloody carcasses of their stable mates, makes me moan out loud. Nate drops the fire iron and kneels on the couch, drawing me close again. He smells like horses and gun smoke. *Not* chlorine.

"It's all part of her plan," I say into his chest. "Everything we love she wants to take away from us. The parts that makes us happy. The part of us that's *us*."

She changes people. She changed sweet, happy Meg into someone capable of murder. She changed my mother into someone I barely recognize.

"The part that keeps us strong," Nate agrees.

"It's the degree I don't get. I mean, what happened to Cecilia and Meg and Lacy was bad enough. But Tasha and Dino are dead, and you almost died, too." *And you could've taken me out with you.* "So if Annaliese can kill any time she wants, how does she decide . . . ?"

I stop, remembering his words: *the part that keeps us strong.*

Superstitious that Annaliese may somehow overhear, I whisper, "She sucks our strength. She doesn't care whose strength, as long as she gets it. Because it makes *her* stronger. And maybe, if she sucks too much of it"—I press my mouth to Nate's ear— "we die."

Nate kisses me hard, his hands roaming over me with a quiet desperation. Like this is all he's ever wanted to do in his life and now he's afraid he'll never get another chance. After what happened out in the paddock only a couple of hours ago, how can I feel so safe with him?

Safety, I know, is nothing but an illusion.

We're not safe.

Nobody is safe.

5 MONTHS + 7 DAYS ———————

Friday, December 12

It's taking way too long for my meds to kick in. I sleep for a couple hours and then I'm up the rest of the night. I change my sheets again, finish reading *Twilight*, and rearrange my posters to cover the talking hole. Now it's Kiss and Joan Jett and Lynyrd Skynyrd instead of Bible verses and *Annaliese, Annaliese.*

While waiting for my alarm to go off, I practice my Christmas piece. This time my notes twang hopelessly off-key. After I drop the pick twice, I wonder: is this the beginning of the end for me, too?

Skin crawling, I stuff my guitar into the case and zip it with a ragged squeal. It's 5:53—seven more minutes till my alarm goes off. I wander in restless circles, then stop and stare up at the Hanging Beam. It hangs lower than the others, an easy reach; no wonder Mrs. Gibbons chose it. I drag over my desk chair and hop up on the seat. Balancing in my socks, I stretch out my arms, but fall a few inches short of touching the beam.

Even so, tossing a rope up there would be simple enough. Then you drop the noose over your head, tighten the knot under your chin, and—

I leap off, choking for breath before my toes leave the seat. The chair topples sideways with a crash that stops my heart.

What am I doing, what am I doing . . . ?

WHAT THE HELL AM I DOING?

———◇———

Each time I ended up in a psych ward, they made me sign a daily contract.

Now, when my trembling hands allow me to hold a pen, I open a random notebook and write, from memory: *I, Corinne Jacobs, promise not to hurt myself for the next 24 hours. If I feel I'm losing control I promise to tell someone immediately.*

I scratch out "the next 24 hours" and write instead: *EVER.*

———◇———

On the way to school I think of something. "Shouldn't we warn people to stay out of the pool room?"

Nate laughs bitterly. "Didn't Solomon already do that? It didn't stop *you.*"

"Yes, but I couldn't lock it again. Now anyone can get in. I think we should tell Mr. Solomon so he can go in there and lock it."

"Oh, sure." Nate affects an excited falsetto: " 'Guess what, Mr. Solomon? Somebody picked your lock. Not me, of course. I just found it by accident.' Oh no, that won't look suspicious at all."

"What about an anonymous note?"

"Why not cut words out of a magazine and paste 'em together? Like a serial killer."

"You're not very helpful. Maybe my mom can lock it. I bet she can get a key."

"And what're you gonna tell *her*?"

"The truth?"

"Hate to say it, surfer girl. That's a bad idea, too."

"I know." I sigh. "Lately, that's all I have."

5 MONTHS + 8 DAYS ———————

Saturday, December 13

I'm lying in bed in the dark with my eyes wide open. I hear the tree outside, knocking the house, and a brand-new snowfall hissing across my windows. So what *do* I say to my mom? First, I can't let her know it's me who picked that stupid lock. Second, how do I explain why I'm afraid something might happen to someone else? If I say it's a matter of life and death, she'll think I'm off my gourd again.

And *thirdly*—since Nate insists that's a word—if Annaliese does travel, and the whole building is cursed, why am I wasting so many brain cells worrying about this?

With a sigh, I flip over, and then—

BANG!

I squeeze my eyes shut, my knuckles mashed to my teeth. I recognize that sound because it's such an *ordinary* sound: the sound of a chair falling over.

The same sound I heard yesterday. Only then *I* knocked it over.

Creak . . . creak . . . creak . . .

The grinding of a rope swinging from the Hanging Beam.

Creak . . . creak . . . back and forth, back and forth.

This isn't happening. I am dreaming again.

With my breath puffing from my lips in shallow bursts, I open my eyes and peek up at the moonlit ceiling.

Nothing there. No rope. No swinging corpse.

Giddy with relief, I flip on my lamp, scramble up—and freeze.

There, on the floor, I see my chair—the same one I picked up yesterday after standing on it for some *sick, unknown reason* and pushed back under my desk—lying on its back, four legs pointed sideways. On the vinyl-cushioned seat, imprints of two bare feet fade away before my eyes.

Real feet. Toes and everything. Feet much bigger than my own size sixes.

"You're not really here," I whisper. *Whoever you are.*

No answer.

When I was little, I thought a monster lived under my bed, something with claws and fangs and foul, fiery breath. When my fear kept me awake, I'd scream for Mom and Frank till one of them showed up to promise me I was safe.

Feeling ridiculously immature, I hold the covers to my chin and call, "Mom? Mom!"

But Mom doesn't answer, not even when I call her a dozen times.

I don't hear a sound, not even the piano.

———◁◇▷———

When I smell coffee brewing, I inch my comforter away from my head. Yes, the chair's still there, a ghoulish monument. Tripping over my bare feet, I fly down to the kitchen. Mom, startled, sloshes coffee. "What? What happened?"

Good! She can tell something's wrong.

"My chair fell over last night for no reason at all." *After it walked from my desk to the foot of my bed, that is.*

"Well. Isn't that odd?"

Surely she doesn't mean this as a serious question. "Do you think this house is haunted?"

"No, Rinn. Do you want toast or a bagel?"

"I'm telling you, that chair fell by itself!"

"Maybe it broke. Or the floor's crooked. It's a very old house."

Or maybe Mrs. Gibbons tried to hang herself again.

I lick my lips. "Mom, when's Bennie coming back?"

"I don't know. Why?"

"Because . . . because somebody needs to check that pool room door." When Mom stops, a bag of bagels in one hand, a bread knife in the other, I anxiously push Meg and *her* kitchen knife out of my head. "I think it's unlocked. I mean, I *know* it's not locked."

"And how do you know that?"

I hate that I have to lie. "Um, I just heard that somebody broke in there again."

She views me with increasing suspicion. "Why this sudden interest in the pool room?"

"I—it's because—" I can't say it.

You have to. HAVE to!

So I rush upstairs, grab my list of "Annaliese things," then race back to the kitchen and hold it out. Mom skims it and hands it back.

"Well? Do you get it?" I ask hopefully.

"Toast or bagel? Last chance. Though the bagels might be a bit stale."

"Mom, everything on that list is true! She hurts people."

"She?"

"Annaliese! It's like everything you're good at, everything you love, she steals it away. Or if there's something you shouldn't do, something you're trying *not* to do, she takes away your willpower. She makes you fail. She sucks your soul out till there's nothing left!"

Mom sinks into a chair and watches me intently. She's listening. Listening!

"She killed Dino and Tasha. She could've just played with them, like she played with Cecilia and Meg—"

" 'Played with'?"

"Took their strength. Like she took away your music. The way she made you start smoking. She takes thing from people— but she *killed* Tasha and Dino."

Calmly Mom asks, "What, exactly, do you think she took from *you*?"

"Well, nothing yet." Though my guitar skills seem to be lacking lately. "But that's because of my meds. She can't reach me when I take them, but she *can* when I *don't*. Somehow they keep her out. Mom, it's true!"

Mom's eyes narrow. "Oh, really. And how did you find *that* out?"

Fish-mouthed, I flop around in my own trap. Mom rises,

stalks to the counter, saws a bagel with the knife, and slaps the halves into the toaster. The lever slams like a guillotine.

"How long have you been off them?" she asks without turning.

I play with the salt shaker. "I'm not. I only stopped them for a few days."

"You stopped them," she repeats.

"I had to! I had to find out for sure."

"Find out what?"

"If Annaliese is real."

I hold my breath. Mom sighs, shakes her head, and returns to the table. She sinks back into her chair and takes my hand without hesitation.

Thrilled that she's hearing me out, I rush on, "That's why you have to talk to Mr. Solomon. He has to make sure that room stays locked. He has to, to *seal* it or something. And the tunnel? Mom, that's not safe, either. Annaliese is dangerous! She is! And I think she's getting stronger . . ." *Because she found me last night. She came into my room.*

Though her fingers remain entwined with mine, Mom's voice floats over from an unexpected distance. "I can't believe you stopped taking your meds, Corinne. You promised me. You promised Frank. After what happened to Nana, how could you be so *stupid*?"

Starkly confused, I recoil. Mom, back at the counter, taps the same knife impatiently on a plate. Jaw fixed, face creased, she glares at the toaster as if willing it to pop before she smashes it on the floor.

Yet she's *also right beside me,* speaking in sync with the "other"

Mom: "I'm so sorry, honey. I'm trying to understand all this, but—"

"Mom?" I glance fearfully from the Mom at the sink to the Mom holding my hand.

I'm hallucinating. I never should've stopped those pills. Now they don't work at all! I'm doomed.

"This is what I get for trusting you," says the Mom at the sink . . . while the Mom at the table says earnestly, "I can't ask Mr. Solomon to seal that door, not without—"

"—this was a bad mistake, bringing you here. You're sick, and you know it, and you won't take your goddamn pills. Oh, yes, the doctors warned me. It's never going to end—"

"—a *sensible* reason. Honey, you need to be truthful or I can't *help* you."

"—for us, will it? How much more can I take? How much? *How much . . . ?*"

Chlorine spirals up my nose. I yank loose and slap both hands over my face. "Shut up. Both of you! *SHUTUPSHUT-UPSHUTUP!*"

————◄○►————

Wearing only my SpongeBob pajamas, I fly out of the house to crouch beside the garage. Is this part of it, too?

Is this Annaliese?

Or ME?

I can't tell, I can't tell!

"Rinn!" one of the Moms shrieks from the back door. "Get in here! It's freezing!"

I can't. I'm afraid.

I shiver against the splintery garage wall, my bare feet burning holes in the dazzling new snow. The back door slams and muffled clomps draw near as Mom—or whoever—marches over.

I flail my arms. "Don't touch me!"

"Rinn! Stop it!"

I shrink away, afraid to look, as she swoops me into a ferocious hug. I smell cigarettes and chlorine, but the anxious eyes that meet mine are my mother's eyes. Still, I want to hit her, to fight her off. I want to run, run, run, but I'm not even dressed, and where would I run to?

No place is safe.

Instead, I let this Mom hug me and wipe my tears on her robe—tears, *real* tears, for the first time in forever—and lead me back into the house.

————◖◗————

Believe it or not, I'm relieved to see my desk chair where I left it: ordinary and benign, just a knocked-over chair with no ghostly feet imprinted in the seat. Even if I did imagine those footprints, at least I know the chair really *fell*. It would've been worse to find it back by my desk where, in a normal world, it would've stayed all night.

Gathering courage, I lift it upright and then whip my hand safely away.

Nothing happens. The chair simply sits there.

I pile every blanket I can find on the turret floor, far away from the Hanging Beam, and stay there all day, not reading, not thinking. When Mom shows up later with Pepsi and a tuna sandwich, I pretend to be asleep. I don't want to have to guess which "Mom" this really is.

There were *two* of them this morning. One said "goddamn," a word my real mother never uses.

Forget the pool room. Forget the tunnel.

Annaliese can reach me no matter where I am.

5 MONTHS + 9 DAYS ———————

Sunday, December 14

Calmer by morning, I call Nate. He and Luke are on their way out to visit relatives in Cincinnati. At least they're not hunting, I think, though I can't imagine Nate *ever* picking up another shotgun.

So while the guy I am now madly in love with is missing in action, I finish an English paper, paint my toenails blue, and jam on my guitar. I leave my room once during the day to pee, grab an apple and a bottle of water, and take my meds. Mostly, I sleep. I do manage to get through "My Sweet Lord" without missing a note.

Take that, Annaliese.

You too, Mom. Both of you.

Around midnight, I notice the lavender scent seeping up through the iron latticework of the heat register. Mom, burning a candle so late? In a surreal daze, I walk downstairs to ask her to blow it out. Honestly, I *hate* that smell now.

The candle, however, sits unattended on the steamer trunk table, which means Mom left it burning when she went to bed. *Is she trying to burn down the whole freaking house?*

The thought nauseates me.

Remembering the séance and that massive puddle of wax—*hot* wax, when the rest of the pool room felt deadly cold—I *poof* out the candle, run back upstairs, and curl up in my turret in my nest of blankets.

I don't turn my light off.

5 MONTHS + 10 DAYS ————

Monday, December 15

Well, hi, stranger," Mom greets me. "It's about time you came up for air."

I fake a smile and steal a look around for any sign of that "other" Monica Jacobs. Mom watches, her thoughts perfectly clear to me: *Hmm, darting eyes. Rinn must be paranoid again.* I'm sure she noticed I didn't eat her tuna sandwich, either.

She shakes out my meds for the first time in ages. Is this a Fake Mom trick? Or has Real Mom decided she'd better start divvying them out again?

She withdraws her hand as I reach out. "Promise me."

"I promise." Trust me: I *know* I'll have to take these the rest of my life, and no, I will never be stupid enough to stop them. Funny how this knowledge no longer makes me angry and resentful. Instead, I find it liberating.

They'll keep me safe from Annaliese. But they'll also keep me safe from myself.

"Swear," Mom suggests. "Swear on your grandmother's soul."

Like the word "goddamn," this is something Real Mom wouldn't dream of saying.

I recite it, anyway. "I swear on Nana's soul."

She hands me the pills. I examine each one before washing them down.

"Good girl," the Mom says with a wooden smile.

I'd bark for her if I were in a better mood.

The phone rings. Mom ignores it. I pick it up, and it's Millie. But Mom shakes her head.

"It's *Millie*," I stress, waving the receiver.

"I don't want to talk to her now."

Flabbergasted, I whisper, "What should I tell her?"

"Tell her to go to hell!" Mom shouts back.

I don't have to repeat the message; Millie hears, and hangs up immediately.

And Mom's already out the door.

———◆◇◆———

I don't know if Mom broke the news, or if someone else discovered the pool room wasn't locked—but Mr. Solomon's rant over the PA lasts longer than homeroom. He does all but threaten to post an armed guard at the door. Plus, he adds, when we return from winter break, contractors will be tearing the whole pool room down. Therefore, the tunnel itself will no longer exist. An emergency exit will be constructed in the gym.

My wave of relief leaves me giddy. No pool room! No tunnel, either!

Thank you, thank you!

It's another lonely day for me. I spend lunch in the library, wishing again that I'd been smart enough to make more friends. After school, we rehearse with Mr. Chenoweth for the concert this Friday, the last day of school before Christmas vacation. Cecilia's a bit friendlier now, and we chat a bit. Nobody else goes out of their way to talk to me, though.

I'm driftwood again.

————◆————

When Nate and I walk home after rehearsal, I consider telling him about the creaking rope I heard the other night. And the toppled-over chair with the disappearing footprints. Not to mention my two Moms.

But Nate picks up his pace—it's below 20 degrees and snowing hard—and I have to struggle to keep up. As we round the corner of our street, a vicious gale slaps my breath away. Snow crystals sting my watery eyes.

"I hate snow!" I shout. "I hate this stupid, frickin' Ohio weather. I want sun. Sun! Stop laughing at me," I add when his shoulders shake with laughter. I snatch that awful fur cap off his head and fling it to the curb. "You bunny killer, you."

My boots leave the sidewalk when Nate spins me in a circle. His hot breath thaws me. He kisses me hard, forcing my mouth open, meeting my tongue. My knees melt and he has to hold me up. He laughs again when I stick my cold hand down his shirt. He does the same to me.

Maybe I'm not driftwood, after all.

Maybe I'm me again.

5 MONTHS + 11 DAYS ———————

Tuesday, December 16

I know my drug levels are back to normal when I actually nod off in class. No rehearsal tonight; Mr. Chenoweth has an emergency dental appointment. Eager for a nap, I rush home without Nate, who cut out early to drive to the stable to plow a foot of new snow. I can't believe people in River Hills think nothing of this weather, that they drive around with chains on their tires and throw snow-shoveling parties.

I do need sunshine. Or at least a tanning booth.

Puffing ice through my teeth, I push open my front door—and there is Frank, sitting with Mom on the sofa. He's holding a beer, Mom a glass of wine.

I stare, mesmerized.

"Hey, Rinn." He grins through his trademark gray beard. "How's it goin'?"

"You're here," I say stupidly.

Mom smiles, too, but thinly. "He flew in just this morning."

"Why?"

Frank downs what's left of his beer in a one gulp. "A couple of reasons."

I kick off my boots, slink into the dining room, and drop my book bag in its usual place. I notice the official-looking papers spread over the table, and a manila envelope with the name of a San Diego law firm.

Shocked, I face them. "You're getting divorced?" So much for Mom and me *ever* moving back to La Jolla, where it's warm and sunny and people don't put chains on their cars.

So much for us being a family again.

Mom tenses visibly. "It's just a legal separation for now."

Frank scratches his beard, pats his leather jacket for a cigarette, and lights up. Mom, on cue, lights one of her own. Frank glowers. "When did you start smoking again?"

"I don't remember," Mom admits.

I butt in, "You said this was temporary. You said you guys needed time to *think*."

"We have thought about it," Mom says quietly. "And it might be temporary, though I'm thinking"—face pained, she directs this at Frank—"maybe it's better to just go ahead and end it."

I twist my fingers, realizing I guessed the truth from the start: when Mom said we all needed some time apart, what she really meant was that Frank needed time away from *me*. To do what? To decide if he still wants to be my dad?

"What about me?" I ask.

Mom and Frank speak at the same time, uncannily reminding me of that two-Mom business. Frank wins. "Uh, we both think it'd be best if you stay here with your mom."

Well, duh. "What about vacations? Summers?"

"It's too difficult," Mom says tersely. "The logistics, I mean."

Frank's flash of surprise isn't lost on me. "Monica, I don't think we—"

"Besides, honey," Mom interrupts, "we really just got here. We should wait till you're more settled in before we start jerking you around."

"I am settled in." Well, unsettled, actually, with a frigging ghost on the loose. Does this mean no more beaches? No more jamming with Frank? I don't even get to see my old room one more time? A room *without* a Hanging Beam, thank you.

"You need a routine," Mom says. "Maybe later down the line we can work something out, but for now, no. I'm sorry."

"You don't want me to visit." I aim this at Frank. "I know you hate me."

"Hate you?" Frank repeats, unhooking his wary eyes from Mom.

"Yes!" That's when I lose it, with no warning whatsoever. "You hate me for everything. For what I did to Nana. For ruining you and Mom." Tears, real tears, spring from my eyes again. I guess I haven't been back on my meds long enough to keep this from happening. "I kept all my promises! I take my meds, I go to school, I stay out of trouble. Tell him," I plead with Mom. "Tell him it's true."

A pall settles. Mom stubs out her half-smoked cigarette. She starts to speak, but again Frank beats her to it. "Rinn, listen. This, the whole separation thing is between me and your mom. It's got nothing to do with you."

"Liar! I said I was sorry a million times and I am. *I am!* How many times can I say it?" He frowns at the floor. "See? You can't even look at me! Because every time you do you think about

Nana. Every time I walked into a room, you'd walk right out. You hardly said a word to me for three whole months!" The words fly from my lips, uncontainable. "You wanted to send me to boarding school. You wanted me out of your life! *That's* why Mom and I left. Because no matter what I say, no matter what I do, *I'm* the one who killed Nana. And I'm sorry. *I'm so sorry!*"

I sink to the floor, sobbing into my knees. A minute or so later I sense a heavy presence and catch a whiff of tobacco and aftershave. It's Frank, now crouching beside me. Just the smell of him makes me cry harder.

"Rinn." He rests his big hand on my arm. "I don't hate you. I never hated you." I shake my head, a pathetic protest, and he plops down on floor like a big furry bear. "I loved my mom." He pulls me into a hug. "I *loved* her. And I miss her like hell."

"Me, too," I whimper.

"The only thing I thought about all this time was *me*." He rocks me hard in his arms. "I couldn't get my head around the fact that my mom was gone. I was all torn up, and yeah, I was pissed. But not because of what happened to your grandma. Because . . ."

He breaks off. I realize with pure shock that Frank, big, tough *Frank*, the dad I loved and looked up to almost my whole life, is crying right along with me, though not as sloppily.

"Because of *how* it happened. Because I sent you there, knowing you were sick, knowing we were taking a big chance. I gave up on you, darlin'. I mean, hell, I'm your dad! Dads fix things, right? But I couldn't fix *you*. So I just threw you away." Frank's thick fingers brush my turtleneck collar. "Right when you needed me," he finishes, choking up again.

I shake my head. "You didn't throw me away. I loved Nana.

I could've stayed there forever if—if I hadn't messed everything up."

"You didn't mess up. I messed up. We *both* messed up,"
Frank adds with a meaningful look at Mom. No response; she
sits there like an ice sculpture, hands folded in her hap. Frank
hugs me tighter. "What happened, darlin', was not your fault."
He pushes my face up. "You hear me? You were sick. It *wasn't*
your *fault*."

God, God, God, I waited *so* long to hear this. As I gaze up
into his weathered face, something clutches my heart with
hands bigger and warmer than his. *He means it. He does!* I fall
back into his chest, marveling at this odd, delightful sensation
growing inside me. Hope, maybe. Or something like it.

But before I can decide, the smell of Frank disappears. In
its place, something more familiar, more sinister: *chlorine.*

I sit up and meet Mom's accusing stare. Her features blur;
am I seeing double again? The taste of pool water sears my
tongue. I cover my mouth and focus hard on *one* of the two
shimmering faces of my mom.

The one that chills me the most.

The one that stares back with smug recognition.

"You can't fool me," I scream through my fingers. "You are
not my *mother!*"

5 MONTHS + 13 DAYS ─────────

Thursday, December 18

Frank's staying at a motel in Westfield so he can hang around for tomorrow's concert. Mom didn't ask him to stay with us. I doubt Frank would appreciate her all-night piano pounding. Yes, last night she did it again.

Now, creeping exhaustedly downstairs, I hear Mom on the phone, voice husky from cigarettes and her own lack of sleep: "—told you, she's been like this for days . . . Of *course* she's depressed about her friends . . . Yes, she's taking them—I watch her every morning."

Liar. You never watch me anymore.

Mom says sarcastically, "Oh, I'm so glad you've had a chance to *think* about it, now that our daughter's so convinced you hate her guts! . . . Oh, please. Don't go there."

Go where? What does he want? I remember Frank's surprise when Mom said I won't be visiting him. Her idea? I doubt she consulted him.

"How would I know? I told you what she said, all that stuff about ghosts stealing souls and killing off her friends. *You* heard what she said to me yesterday. She's delusional, Frank."

"No, I'm not," I whisper.

Mom's voice rises. "What do you mean I'm not trying? I've been trying for *weeks* to get her in! . . . You did what?" Silence. "When? Okay, well . . . thank you, then."

Spotting me, she jumps, hangs up on him, and delivers a phony smile.

One face. One smile.

"What did Frank do?" I ask.

"He took it upon himself to find you a new doctor. Your appointment's on Saturday. He agrees," she adds before I can argue, "you need therapy. Something more than a handful of pills every day."

"The pills work," I protest.

"*When* you take them."

"I take them! I take them!"

"Then maybe they're not the right ones. If they worked that well, you wouldn't be so tempted to go off them."

Crap, crap, crap. I can't see a psychiatrist now! If I slip up and say one careless word about Annaliese, I'll never again see the light of day.

"I swore I'd take them. On Nana's soul you made me swear, and I did, remember?"

Mom swings around from the sink. I duck, expecting, I don't know—another monster posing as my mom? "I know you did. But it might not be enough."

"I'm not delusional," I say calmly. "You think I am, but I'm not."

Mom stares at me for a long time.

Then she turns and walks away.

"She touched you, too, Mom," I whisper. "You just can't see it."

◄◦►

One thing I learned from being in psych wards is this: when people say you're delusional, the best thing to do is to *shut up* about your delusions. Otherwise they lock you up twice as long.

I shouldn't have said "I'm not delusional" to Mom because— *what if I am?*

What if everything I've seen, heard, and believe is just part of my illness? Even the double vision could be a side effect of the drugs. Except "double vision" doesn't normally include another whole human being.

No! I know exactly what happened that day in the kitchen.

I felt my mother holding my hand. Yet I also saw her at the toaster, yammering away.

I saw them both on the sofa yesterday, one watching resentfully as Frank comforted me.

Doubt stabs me. What if Mom's right and the pills *aren't* enough? Or what if I need a higher dose? Obsessing over this, I sneak back to the kitchen after Mom leaves for school and shake out a extra tablet of everything.

Then *two* of everything. Do I dare do this myself?

I finger each tablet.

Tempting . . . *so tempting.*

Then: "I'm not that stupid," I say to Annaliese. "You don't know me one bit."

She *wants* me to overdose. She thinks no one'll be surprised.

Maybe she's right. People will say: *Yeah, Rinn Jacobs. She's always had problems. We all knew it was a matter of time before she tried it again.*

Is that how Annaliese hopes to get rid of *me*?

Livid, triumphant, I cram the pills back into the bottle. "Sorry, bitch. Today you lose."

The phone rings. It's Frank again.

"Mom's already gone," I say.

"It's you I want to talk to."

I grip the phone, fingers cramping.

Gruffly he says, "I want to say two things. One, that I'm a sorry excuse for an old man. You know I love you, right?"

I nod, though he can't see me.

"Second, I don't know what's going on, but we're gonna get through it, okay? You just do what your mom tells you, and you'll be fine, I promise. It's never too late. We're not giving up without a fight. You got that?"

"Got it." I smile though sudden tears.

"See you tomorrow. Love you, darlin'."

"I love you too, Frank."

———◄○►———

We have our last rehearsal after school today. The concert's tomorrow.

Nate's not here, I haven't seen him since this morning, and Mr. Chenoweth has a few choice words for the people who didn't show up. I shift restlessly, wishing the rehearsal were over so I could just go home. Now that my high from Frank's saying he loves me wore off, all I can think of is Nana. I keep trying to conjure up her face in my mind, but it's hard, so hard. Like even her memory is now being stolen from me, piece by piece. Soon there'll be nothing left.

Would she forgive me, too, if she knew how sorry I am?

Rehearsal ends at last. As I hoist my guitar case, Cecilia wanders up. "Hey. Are you nervous about tomorrow? I am."

I'm glad Cecilia's talking to me again, though I'm sure it's because she feels sorry for poor friendless me. Maybe she hopes *we* can be friends, now that I no longer hang out with the girls who harassed her. Well, Lacy did, not that Meg and Tasha discouraged it.

"A bit," I admit.

Behind us, the auditorium doors clank open. It's Bennie Unger, lugging a cardboard box.

"Bennie!" I say happily as he reaches us, somewhat out of breath. "Where've you been?"

"Hey, Rinn. Hey, Cecilia. I just come back for my things. Mr. Solomon, he was nice enough to give me some vacation. But then they had this meeting, and now I can't come back here no more."

"He fired you?" I howl as Cecilia demands, "*Why?*"

"He said I wasn't keepin' a good enough eye out on things. Because of Dino, you know. And what happened to your friend." He observes me sadly. "He says Miss Millie's right. So now it's time for me to go." And with a matter-of-fact "Bye now," Bennie galumphs past us and vanishes through the rear exit of the auditorium.

Cecilia folds her arms severely. "Well. That sucks."

Yeah, it does. Now what'll he do with his life?

——◇——

Snow flutters down like talcum powder as I bypass my house and skid across the street to Nate's. Both his jeep and his dad's Buick sit in the driveway. Hoping I'm not ratting him out, I say to Luke when he opens the door, "Is Nate okay? I didn't see him all day."

"Yeah, he felt sick, so he came home." Luke steps aside to let me in. "Actually, I'm glad you stopped by, Rinn. I'm kind of worried about your mom."

I stall by pretending to struggle with a boot. Has Luke been seeing two Monicas, too?

He holds my elbow to steady me. "Is something going on? She's not herself lately."

"What do you mean?" I ask innocently.

He gestures vaguely. "She's touchy. Preoccupied. I don't want to pry, but . . ."

"She's got a lot on her mind. You know, with Millie and all." Though Mom's definitely steering clear of Millie these days. Either they had a fight, or else she's just Millied out. I decide not to mention Frank at all, because . . . is *Luke* the reason Mom's dumping Frank so fast?

Luke shoos me off, oblivious to my suspicions. "Nate's upstairs, but don't get too close. You might catch something." Right. I'm so sure he's concerned with *germs*.

Nate's asleep on his stomach, one cheek buried in a pillow. He snores. How cute! I sit down on his bed and rest a palm on his back. "Nate?" I duck my head to kiss him, and—

With a roar, Nate leaps up and dumps me flat on the floor. He lands on me hard, knocking the wind from my lungs, straddling me, grinding me into the rug. When I shriek, he releases one of my shoulders—but only to silence me by clutching my throat.

I can't breathe. I can't fight. I clutch his steel wrist, trying to pry away his fingers. Fetid air tinged with bleach scalds me with each ferocious pant from his mouth. He rams a knee between my legs and mashes my neck harder, completely unaffected by my digging nails.

Golden specks flash. My vision dims as I desperately search the contorted face hovering inches above my own—*oh my God, his eyes! Where are his eyes?*

All I see are two black murderous holes reaching deeply into his skull.

——◦——

Someone drags me into a sitting position. A glass presses my teeth. I swallow water, and moan at the burning in my ravaged throat.

When my vision clears, I focus on Luke, who keeps repeating my name. When I finally croak an incoherent reply, his expression dissolves to one of relief. "Can you breathe?"

Breathing just fine—well, gasping, really—I push him away in search of Nate; he's sitting, head down, on the edge of the bed, his hands dangling between his knees. Someone's feet thump closer and closer, and the next thing I know Mom flies in. Did someone call her? How much time has gone by?

"What happened?" she shouts, falling down next to me.

Nate answers in an eerily impersonal tone. "I—I had a dream someone snuck in here and tried to kill me."

Mom screeches, "So you decided to kill my daughter instead?"

The sheer volume of this is enough to jerk Nate back to life. "No! I swear I don't know what happened. But Dad woke me up, I had Rinn on the floor, and . . . and . . ." He stares at me in horror, unable to go on.

"Monica." Luke stands; the fear on his face electrifies my spine. Seriously, adults should *never* act this scared in front of their kids. "*Look* at him. He had no idea what he was doing."

"The hell he didn't. Look at *her*!"

I can't see for myself, but I'll take her word for it. My stomach hurts where Nate sat on me. My neck throbs like it was stung by a hoard of African bees.

Nate pleads, keeping his eyes on me, "I'd never hurt Rinn, not on purpose. You've got to believe me."

I stare back into those eyes—*yes, real eyes, not holes, just his own hazel eyes*—and mouth back: *I believe you!*

Mom prods me to my feet. Robotically I obey, with no energy to resist. "I ought to call the police!" She directs this at Luke, who makes a protective move toward Nate. "Your son assaulted my daughter. God *knows* what else he might've done. Oh!" she cries out. "How did I ever think we'd be happy here? How did I think we could be friends after what you *did* to me?"

"Me?" Luke snarls. "What about you? You never fooled anyone, Monica. Why don't you take a good look at *yourself* for a change?"

I balk, but Mom hauls me to the door. "You keep away from my child. Both of you!" Ignoring my whimpers, she hustles me downstairs and across the street, minus my boots or jacket. Back home, she forces me into a dining room chair and yanks off my wet socks like I'm a toddler who tripped into a puddle. One lands on the floor, the other in the living room.

"Mom!" My raspy voice startles me, but at least I can speak.

"Stay away from him, Rinn. I mean it."

Stay away? How? He lives across the street.

I force the words past my burning vocal cords. "He *was* sleeping! I—I guess I scared him or something."

"Really? And what were you doing in his bedroom?"

We face off. I can't explain to her how innocent it was. As far as Mom's concerned, nothing that has to do with boys and me is ever innocent.

She rages on. "I thought you'd stopped all this nonsense, all this sleeping around with boys who you don't even know. Do you think I appreciate strangers telling me my own daughter's a slut?"

Speechless, I squint as her face shimmers, then blurs. When she speaks again, it's from the *kitchen* this time: "Tea and honey might help. But maybe an Urgent Care . . ."

As she moves about, rattling mugs and spoons twenty feet away from me, the first Mom grips my shoulder. "I should *let* Frank take you back to California." I wriggle away as Mom # 2 runs water into the kettle, calling, "Honey, why don't you lie down on the sofa? This'll only take a minute."

Surrounded by chaos, I scream THE TRUTH at her—and promptly fall out of my chair.

◄◦►

Why did I think people only faint in the movies? I just did it twice in less than an hour.

I wake up on the sofa, draped in an afghan. Voices drift from the kitchen:

". . . he said it was an accident, that he was sleepwalking."

"It happens." It's Frank. "I'd give him the benefit of the doubt. Did she hit her head?"

"I don't think so."

"Then why'd she pass out?"

"I don't know! She started screaming at me, saying I'm not her mother, that I'm driving her crazy, and trying to kill her, and that she's *on* to me now and—oh, who knows what she said!"

I swallow delicately. *God, that hurts.*

"Frank, she thinks furniture moves in her room. She tore up that wall. She never sleeps. She sneaks around the house all night—one night she even *left*—and I hear her talking to herself. What *else* am I supposed to think?" Mom finishes hysterically.

You're supposed to think I'm crazy. That's what Annaliese wants.

I open my eyes when Frank towers over me. "How ya feeling, darlin'?"

I touch my scar, surely bruised by now. "Please don't let Mom call the police on Nate."

"She won't." Frank smooths the hair off my sweaty forehead.

Nearby, Mom lets loose with a long, throaty chuckle.

"Did you hear that?" I whisper, every muscle wired. "It's not me, it's her! There's something wrong. Can't you see it?"

His puzzled face tells me he doesn't know what I'm rambling about, that he didn't even hear that terrible laugh. Only *I* can hear her. Annaliese planned it that way.

"Your mom loves you, Rinn," Frank says thickly.

"Not anymore."

"You remember what I said on the phone? We're going to help you. You're gonna be *fine*. You believe me, right?"

Why should I believe him when he refuses to believe me?

Hopeless, helpless, I make myself nod because it's the answer he expects.

5 MONTHS + 14 DAYS ⸺

Friday, December 19

Nate totally, absolutely, avoids me in school. Maybe he's afraid Mom'll make good on her threat to have him arrested for assault.

I hate her. I hate Frank, too, in a way, for not believing me.

Most of all, I hate myself because I can't convince them about Annaliese.

Against my better judgment, I tried once again to explain it last night. Mom and Frank got all quiet and shifty eyed—cardinal signs that they believe I've lost my grip on reality.

Today Cecilia nudges me in the lunch line. "What happened to your neck?" Because in spite of my usual turtleneck, Nate's bruises glow purple on the underside of my jaw.

"I tried to hang myself last night." Dumbfounded, Cecilia almost drops her tray. I don't know where those words came from or why I said them. My heart skips two beats. "Sorry. Bad joke."

Cecilia grabs her plate of tacos and escapes without another word. I send hateful vibes to Annaliese, wherever she is. Probably quite close, enjoying every minute of her game

I cut PE and hide out in the library so I don't have to parade my purple neck in front of the class. It's *cold* today in school—problems with the ancient furnace, according to the homeroom announcements—and I keep my extra sweater buttoned all the way up. Rooting curiously through the paranormal section, I stumble upon a book called *Spirit World*. Luckily Mrs. Harper, the librarian, is too absorbed in the *National Enquirer* to hear my stifled exclamation.

I bury myself between the shelves, skim the index, and flip to page 126.

One of the greatest myths about ghosts is that they are stationary. While it is true the majority of spirits remain "at home" so to speak, there are also recorded instances of ghosts traveling from place to place. While traditional spirits may attach to one location and remain there for years, even centuries, a more stubborn spirit will occasionally attach to objects, animals, or people. Because of this phenomenon, moving away from a "haunted house" is no guarantee one will no longer be haunted. One such incident involves a family in Greenwich, Connecticut . . .

I slam the book shut. This time Mrs. Harper notices. "Rinn Jacobs. Don't you have gym at this time?" It's sad when even the librarian knows your schedule.

I do not check out the book.

So tonight's the concert. Although my voice, by some miracle, is perfectly fine, I'm so jittery and depressed I'd like to skip the whole thing. I doubt Mr. Chenoweth would let me live that down.

I beat Nate to the main doors after the last bell and plant myself in his path.

"Rinn," he says sorrowfully. "Just go away."

"No."

"Jesus Christ! Did you forget about last night?"

"You were sleepwalking."

"What if I wasn't?"

I eye him. "You said you didn't remember." Nate shakes me off, forcing me to chase him to the sidewalk. "You *said* you didn't remember jumping on me."

He sags against a utility pole. "Rinn."

"What? *What?*"

"I lied. I do remember."

He sinks down to the icy curb. I do the same.

"I remember," he repeats. He tucks his hands into his armpits and stares across the street at the no-longer-green village green. Snowflakes gather on his lashes. "I remember everything. Waking up. Seeing you. Throwing you on the floor."

"But—"

"I remember choking you. I—I remember how your neck felt in my hands, and—and how I wanted, I dunno . . . to *break* you, I guess." Nate bows his head, his words muffled by the splashing tires of a car picking its way along. "So, no, I wasn't asleep. I was awake. I was awake the whole time."

My hand touches what I know are the imprints of Nate's fingers on my neck. I try to ask, "Why?" but nothing comes out.

He understands. "I don't know why. But I meant to kill you, or at least hurt you really bad. And *then*"—he swallows hard enough for me to hear—"I'd do it." One fist smashes his palm. "What I said I'd do to myself after I shot the horses."

When his shoulders quiver I realize he's crying. It breaks my heart, yet I'm too afraid to touch him, to comfort him in any way.

He meant to do it. He meant to hurt me. He'd have succeeded, too, if Luke hadn't heard the commotion. The same way he would've shot Xan and Ginger and other horses if I hadn't decided, on a whim, to head out to the stable that day.

But why? Supernatural or not, everything has a reason.

Nothing in life is as random as we'd like to believe.

The answer rams me like a wrecking ball. Forgetting I'm supposed to be afraid of him, I clutch his arm. "You're supposed to die. You're meant to die."

He doesn't acknowledge this. He doesn't argue, either. Maybe he already figured it out.

Nate is *meant* to die, the way Dino was meant to die, and Tasha was meant to die.

And maybe the same way *I'm* meant to die.

———◦———

Now that kids are walking around us and throwing funny looks, I prod Nate up off the curb. I speak rapidly on the way home, my brain in overdrive. "It's not enough for Annaliese to hurt us like she did Lacy and Meg and Cecilia. Something's *different* about us. She really wants us dead."

Nate mumbles, "Man, I gotta stay away from you," which makes me wonder if he's listening. "I can't trust myself."

"You have to resist her."

"I want to. I'm trying. But I *don't know how!*"

I stomp my foot. "What goes around comes around." Dino's dad said that.

"What's that supposed to mean?"

"It means there's a lot more to Annaliese that we don't know about yet. We know she's after us, but why? What does she gain?"

Nate thinks. "Strength. You said strength."

"She doesn't have to kill us for that. She can get it from anyone. Even from a *cat*."

He kicks at the snow. "Maybe there is no Annaliese. Maybe it's only us."

"No!" I say fiercely. "I saw your face when you were choking me. And your eyes—" I break off, nauseated at the memory of those unearthly black holes. "Nate, it wasn't *you*."

We stop in front of my house. Snow hurls down so hard and fast I can barely see my front door. There's a storm warning in effect, Mr. Solomon said. Mr. Solomon, who fired Bennie when everything that happened was Annaliese's fault.

I wrap my arms around Nate. After an uncertain moment, he holds me, too. No matter how hard I hug him I can't stop him from shaking. "They're supposed to tear out the pool soon. If that's her home base, or whatever you call it, do you think she'll just leave?"

"Maybe. Or maybe it'll piss her off more."

The idea of Annaliese being "more" pissed off is the last

thing my frazzled nerves can endure. We don't even know why she's pissed off *now*.

Nate bends down for a quick kiss. "Look. I'm sorry. But we can't be alone together. Not anymore." He twists away from me. "I love ya, surfer girl. But please—don't trust me."

"Nate!"

"I mean it. Stay *away*."

———◀◦▶———

Dressed in the black vintage frock I wore to Homecoming—who says you can't wear the same prom dress twice?—I throw myself down at my desk. I have to figure this out. I am *not* losing Nate!

Chewing my lip, I copy over all my notes about my friends and what happened to them. Then I add my most recent ideas:

15. Nate loves me. Yet he tried to kill me so he could kill himself. He did the same thing with the horses. Annaliese wants to steal what he loves the MOST. That way he will want to die.

16. First, Mom couldn't play the piano. Then she started smoking, staying up all night, etc. Then she started saying terrible things to me. SHE CHANGED! Is this Annaliese too? Is she stealing my mother?

My pen halts in shock.
YES! YES!

I scribble more:

17. Worse, Annaliese makes me hallucinate. I see
    my Real Mom but I see a Fake Mom, too. It's
    the FAKE MOM who says those things.
    Annaliese wants people to think I'm crazy. She
    wants ME to think I'm crazy. She makes me
    say crazy things. It's like if she can't kill me,
    she'll do the next best (or worse) thing.

"Why?" I ask Annaliese. "Why won't you tell me *why?*"

She doesn't answer, of course. But I imagine a dark, secretive smile.

With a second surge of inspiration, I flip the paper and start a new list, leaving out Meg, Cecilia, and Lacy. I hate to say it, but they're incidental. Instead of killing them, Annaliese only toyed with them, stealing from them what they loved the most. Did what she steal make her stronger than ever?

I write the names carefully, reverently—

1. Tasha
2. Dino
3. Nate
4. Me

—and try to figure out what we four have in common.

It takes less than five seconds for the winning buzzer to go off.

Trembling, I fill in the blanks:

1. Tasha = Millie Lux
2. Dino = Joey Mancini
3. Nate = Luke Brenner
4. Me = Monica Parker

Mom, Millie, Luke, and Joey.

All of them friends from high school.

You never fooled anyone, Monica, Luke said last night. *Why don't you take a good look at yourself for a change?* What did he mean by *that*?

I snatch up my phone. Nate doesn't answer right away and lets it flip to voice mail, making me suspect he knows it's me. After four more tries I wear him down; he picks up on his end and breathes into my ear.

"I know you're there, Nate."

"You're relentless, ya know?"

"Sorry," I say meekly, not sorry at all.

"So what's so important you couldn't wait, like, two more hours?"

"Remember what your dad said yesterday, about how my mom thinks she has everyone fooled?" I hope he remembers. He was pretty out of it last night. "Will you ask him what he meant?"

"He's still at the office."

"He'll be home for dinner, right? And he's coming to the concert? Ask him as soon as he gets home. Then let me know."

"Well, it's not the kinda thing you bring up over pork 'n' beans." I hiss impatiently, and Nate relents. "Okay, okay. God, you're *such* a—"

"Pain in the ass," I finish with an uneasy laugh.

"Yep. See you at school."

"Good." Before he hangs up, I add shyly, "Oh, in case you're wondering? I love you, too."

"You don't look much like a rock star in that getup," Frank notes when I waltz downstairs with my guitar.

"It's a Christmas concert," I say coolly.

Mom scrutinizes me, too. "A bit heavy-handed with the mascara, don't you think?"

Okay—Real Mom. But I can't let my guard down. "Do you want me to take it off?"

"Of course not. It's your face." She clears her throat, maybe sensing my suspicion. "Oh, and I'm washing your scarf. Let me find another one . . ."

Frank rubs frost off the window. "Whoa, it's sure comin' down. Up to fourteen inches tonight, I heard. Tell me again why people live in Ohio?"

Because they kill their grandmothers. And their fathers send them away.

Another time I might've said this out loud. Instead, I smile, remembering his hugs. "I better get going. Mr. Chenoweth wants us there early."

"We'll be on time," he promises. He shrugs into his jacket and puts on the hat and gloves he was smart enough to pick up. "Think I'll head out and shovel the drive so you girls don't end up snowed in till spring."

Mom, hunting for my extra scarf, jokes, "You? Shovel snow?"

"Watch me, babe."

"Well, just do me a favor and don't drop dead in my driveway."

Frank growls, Mom giggles, and I burn inside my chest at the familiarity of this. Suddenly all I want is to stay home and hang out with my parents—*both* of them. I want to jam with Frank, to listen to his stories about Billy Idol and Madonna and Bono and Van Halen. Or we could play Scrabble—Mom always wins—or rent a DVD and pop popcorn and laugh till we hurt. All the fun things we used to do together . . .

Before you got sick, Annaliese whispers, *and spoiled it all.*

I hate you, Annaliese.

Boots on, I clomp into the kitchen, flip open the cupboard— and stop, confused by the empty space on the shelf. "Where are my pills?"

Mom walks up behind me. "It's only five. Why are you taking them now?"

Because I want to make sure I'm safe tonight. "I might be tired later. I don't want to forget."

"Well, my goodness," she purrs in my ear. "It looks like they're not *heeere.*"

I gag on the chlorine that gusts out of her mouth. Cold air radiates from her body, causing goose bumps to ripple over my own.

It's her: the Fake Mom.

The imposter.

The one who stole my mother's soul.

I refuse to turn around. "Go. Away."

"Go where, *hmm?* Back home with Frank? I'd like that. I'm sure we can find a nice place for you, too. A cozy asylum for troubled teens?"

I clench the counter and stare at the aluminum basin. One dried-up noodle rests in the drain. "Mom. Mom, listen. I know what happened to you."

Her words caress me in the soothing tone she uses when I'm sick, or depressed. "What happened to me, honey? Tell me. I'm interested."

Don't let her scare you!

"You—you went into the pool room that night. That's when she got you."

Her laughter tinkles, frighteningly Mom-like. It sounds so *much* like her, I almost give in—but I'm too afraid to face her.

"See, Corinne? Pills won't help you. For people like you it's like swallowing candy. And how do you know those were really your pills? I could be feeding you sugar. I could've switched them any time. Or I could be poisoning you. Did you ever think of that?"

I cover my ears. It doesn't help.

"Would you *like* to go back to the hospital? Remember what it was like, after you slashed your neck? All those kids screaming and crying? You didn't feel very safe there. Remember how terrified you were?"

Yes. But not as terrified as I am now.

"What about those shots they gave you when you wouldn't behave? How they tied you down, and all you could do was lie there and scream like everyone else." Her chuckle skitters like electricity over my scalp. "That's when you *really* wanted to die. Weren't you sorry you didn't do it right in the first place? One millimeter deeper, and bingo! You'd be dead." A disapproving laugh. "Silly girl."

My voice returns at last. "Shut up. You're not Mom. You are *not* my fucking mother."

Fake Mom clucks. "Oh, here we go again. Should I call Frank back in so you can repeat that for him?"

She leans closer, closer, dripping invisible bleach. I smash my hands over my face to suck in as little as possible.

"I almost forgot. I have a present for you." I whimper as she pries one hand free and slaps something into my palm. "Keep it safe. Keep it handy. You're going to need it very soon."

She folds my fingers over and squeezes hard, only releasing them when I cry out with pain. My hand flies open, revealing a shiny new razor blade. Blood trickles through my fingers, plopping into the sink.

I wrench around to scream, "*Get the hell away from me!*" only to see Mom, with my coat and scarf, walking toward me through the dining room.

She freezes in place. "Honey, what happened?"

The odor of chlorine still permeates the kitchen. It didn't fade when the Fake Mom disappeared. This can only mean one thing.

It's coming from the "real" one.

Chest pounding, hiding my hand, I head straight for her and jerk my coat away. Ignoring the scarf, I drop the razor blade into a pocket, grab my guitar case, and slam out of the house into a torrential whiteout. Frank, busy shoveling, doesn't notice me.

I wonder if he'll notice the trail of blood in the snow.

◄◊►

I rinse off my hand in the locker room as Cecilia hovers. "You cut it on *what*?"

"A razor blade." Gingerly, I pick it out of my pocket.

She recoils. "You know we're not supposed to bring weapons into the building."

"It's not a weapon. It's a means of suicide. My mother gave it to me. Except she's not my real mother."

"What?"

Shut up, Rinn. Shut up!

I can't shut up. I can't keep it inside me! Cecilia, unfortunately, is the only one around. "It's hard to explain. She looks like my mom. But she's an imposter, sort of."

Cecilia stares. "If she's not your mother, who is she?"

"I don't know. But at the Homecoming dance, some of us had a séance, and something—something awful happened. Everyone smelled that chlorine, same as you. Then everyone *froze.* I couldn't wake them up. Jared and I ran out, because he was fine, too, and my mom went in there to get everyone out. But she hasn't been right since! Same with Meg and Lacy. Plus it happened to *you.*" My speech picks up speed as she edges away. "And Tasha and Dino—wait!" I shout as she reaches the door. "Listen!"

Cecilia stops, one hand planted on the door.

"Things happened to other people, too. Like Nate. And Miss Prout! *That's* why she left. To get away from her."

"Get away from who?"

"From Annaliese!" I explode.

Cecilia waits a beat. "Do you hear yourself? You're talking crazy."

"You lost your voice. You *mouth* the words now. I see you do it." Frustrated at her stubborn headshake, I step forward, blade in hand. Cecilia's face crumbles in panic. Quickly, I hold out the razor blade. "Here, take it."

"I'm not touching that!"

"Please!" *I can't keep it. I can't trust myself.*

"No." She yanks open the door. "I don't know what you're babbling about. You're not making any sense."

"But—"

"I'm not listening to you anymore. Leave me alone. *Get away!*"

ANNALIESE

So I guess my name won't be on Cecilia's Christmas card list. And Nate's already avoiding me, though he insists it's for my own safety. How much longer before *everyone* decides I'm a psychotic freak? How long before the whole school hates me?

Why did I think Cecilia would believe me? Seriously, who would?

Nate believes me.

Marginally cheered by that knowledge, I wrap the razor blade in paper towels and tuck it into the pocket of my dress. I hate the idea of strolling around with it, but I can't leave it unattended in my coat pocket, either. I picture a traitorous Cecilia handing my coat over to King Solomon. *Yep, that girl's got my number, all right.*

A cacophony of tuning instruments fills the auditorium. Nate's assembling his drums and cymbals, joking around with friends. He spots me, finishes up, and cautiously approaches. I must look terrible because he asks, "What happened now?"

"Let's talk."

"Okay. But not alone."

I follow him uphill to the secluded, but not isolated, last row, and immediately burst into tears. I definitely liked it better when I couldn't cry; the fact that I now cry so easily reinforces my suspicion that Fake Mom was telling the truth—I've been swallowing sugar pills. But how can sugar pills look and taste like the real thing?

Annaliese is winning. I'm paranoid beyond belief.

"I'm scared. My mom hid my pills. Then she gave me a razor blade and told me to kill myself." All color drains from Nate's face. "Look, I'll show you—"

"You have it on you?" He stops my hand. "Jesus, don't."

My throat aches. "She stole my mother. She's turning her into someone else. Someone mean! And ugly!"

"Maybe"—he sounds strained, uneasy—"she's turning her into the person your mom used to be."

"What?"

"Okay, listen. I talked to my dad, like you asked me to. And you might not want to hear this . . ."

"Go on. Tell me."

"Your mom was a cheerleader, right? Millie, too. My dad says they were, like, the total queen bees of the school."

"I already know that."

"Bees," he stresses. "As in bitches."

"My mom's not a bitch." Not my real mom, anyway.

"She *was*, Rinn. A bitch, and a bully, and—"

"No way was my mom ever a bully! She lectures me all the time about being nice to people." People like Cecilia, who hates me now, anyway. "Why would he *say* that?"

"She hurt people," Nate insists. "She and her cliquey little friends were nasty to everyone. My dad says they went out for a while, but he broke it off. He went to college in New York and never saw her again. But he did get a letter, like, a year later."

"What letter?"

"It said she was sorry, that she'd learned her lesson, and, um, that she hoped he'd forgive her so they could keep in touch. He didn't answer it, though."

"But why did he dump her?"

Nate says, ashamedly, "He said he couldn't stand her anymore. She embarrassed him. But when you guys moved in," he adds, "and he got to know her again, he was really shocked. He says she's changed so much he'd never believe it. He likes her, Rinn, a lot. Well, at least he did," he adds regretfully, "till what happened . . . you know, with you and me. In my room."

He means till Mom accused him of trying to kill me. But what girl's mother *wouldn't* react that way?

"If that's true," I say slowly, "then she did change, Nate. Because she's a good person now. The best mom ever. She's always stuck by me. And I've done some pretty bad things."

Nate shrugs. "Well, that's good, then. That she changed."

Realization dawns.

"Changed," I repeat faintly. "Something changed her, from what she *used* to be like. And now something else is trying to change her back."

Annaliese, you soul-sucking bitch—I will not, will NOT let you take my mother!

"People!" Mr. Chenoweth calls from the stage. "Everyone down here on the double!"

Nate urgently catches my wrist. "One more thing. My dad . . . uh, when he broke up with your mom? He didn't just 'break up,' Rinn. He dumped her for someone else."

He hooks an elbow around my neck and whispers her name as Mr. Chenoweth bellows, "That means you two love-birds up there!"

Nate releases me. "Break a leg, surfer girl."

———<◇>———

Cecilia, who usually stands on the tier behind me, trades places with someone at the last second. I don't know what excuse she gave Mr. Chenoweth, but now she's two rows up and five people away. When Mr. Chenoweth eyes me in a funny way, I want to scream at Cecilia: *What do you think I'm gonna do to you, up here, onstage, in front of the whole friggin' town?*

I spy Mom and Frank in front row seats, with Luke behind them. Mom smiles up at me and says something to Frank. Briefly I fantasize about us moving back to La Jolla in time for Christmas . . .

Where Annaliese, that piece-of-shit traveling ghost, might be waiting for me, anyway.

We perform the five songs we've practiced for ages. The next one is "O Holy Night" followed by "My Sweet Lord." Then Handel's Hallelujah Chorus for our grand finale.

A wave of stage fright hits me out of the blue. How can I sing in front of all these people? Why the hell would Mom hide my Klonopin? Why did Nate wait till right before the show to tell me about Luke dumping my mom for Annaliese?

I don't think I can do this. I'm petrified.

I force my tumbling thoughts aside and try to concentrate on "O Holy Night." Though I'm not all that religious, as I sing the familiar words I feel my muscles unwind, and my spiraling brain crank to a lower gear: *Fall on your knees . . . oh, hear the angel voices . . ."*

The lights flicker. Nobody misses a beat.

They flicker a second time.

Then one row of lights blinks out completely.

Performing like professionals, we finish the song to enthusiastic applause. Mr. Chenoweth steps up to the podium with an apologetic laugh. "Looks like we're having some electrical issues here. Not surprising with all that wind out there. Now I'd like to introduce to you Rinn Jacobs, who, along with the chorus, will sing 'My Sweet Lord.'"

Surreptitiously I check my hand—no fresh blood—and then head downstage to my waiting guitar. I perch on the stool, infinitely glad that Frank's here to hear me play because he's the one who taught me how to *rock out*. I strum the introduction, loving how George Harrison's breathtaking notes hum through the speakers. Though it's not a Christmas song, and not even Christian, it's one of Mr. Chenoweth's favorites. Frank's, too.

I start to sing, surprisingly unafraid after all.

Halfway through, as the chorus chimes in with the hallelujahs, another row of lights blacks out. I don't falter, but others around me trade looks. Anxiety tickles my ribcage as my slippery fingers fly over the strings of a guitar that suddenly feels like it weighs a ton.

With a *snap-crackle-and-POP*, the sound system dies. The

stage blacks out with a thump, leaving only a single row of stage lights to illuminate the auditorium. My fingers stumble. The notes, and my voice, shrink to small hollow sounds.

My vocal cords die. My hands fall limply to the strings.

Mr. Chenoweth rushes back to the podium. "Sorry, folks. I guess our 'electrical issues' are a bit more than we bargained for—"

As the last row of lights sputters menacingly, people in the audience rise and shuffle toward the rapidly filling aisles. I see Frank tugging Mom's arm.

Mom doesn't budge. She stares up at the stage, at me, instead. Watching me.

Waiting for my reaction to the sickening black holes that, moments ago, held her eyes.

My guitar topples to the floor. Trancelike, I slide off the stool and move toward the front edge of the stage. I know Frank can't see what *I* can see. All he knows is that Mom won't leave her seat. Clearly I hear him say, "Wait here, then. I'll find her."

He stands, faces the stage as if to seek me out—and that's when the last row of the lights explodes.

Sparks rain down, creating havoc. Kids leap up, tripping over chairs, music stands, instruments, and each other. A few braver ones wail, "*Wooo-OOOO! It's ANNA-liese!*" Their laughter chokes off when the sprinklers kick in, spraying ice-cold water in all directions.

No longer can I see past the stage, that's how black the room is. I can't see Frank, and that's bad. I can't see Mom and that's worse. I doubt Frank sees her, either, and that's more horrible than anything. He has no idea he's inches away from a demon.

Find him, find him, and get the hell out of here!

I slide my foot out, searching for the steps—but there's nothing but empty air under my wobbling shoe.

I hear a scream.

It's me.

◄◦►

Nothing.

No sound.

No light.

It's so dark and so quiet, I'm sure this is what it's like to be blind and deaf. *Or dead.*

No, not dead. I doubt if dead people feel this wet or this cold.

My weightless head turns in a sea of black. No lights, not even emergency EXIT signs. Somebody should sue. Those things should *never* go out.

Achy and disoriented, I kneel on the soggy carpet. I don't remember being pushed or struck. I don't remember falling. But *something* happened to me.

I do remember the horrendous crackling, the sprinkling of electrical stars. Then a lid of darkness slapped down over the auditorium. But before that?

Yes, Mom's face. That terrifying blur of white, those depthless black holes.

Where is she? Where's Frank?

Where's anyone?

My voice croaks in the void. "Nate?"

No answer.

"Mr. Chenoweth?"

Nothing.

I'm alone, but where? I have no idea.

I hobble on sore knees, flailing for something to hold on to. "Hello? Is anyone there?"

Nothing, nothing, nothing at all.

I halt at the familiar sound of a creaking door. I recognize that sound because I've heard it dozens of times: the tunnel door. Now I know for sure I'm on the floor next to the stage, probably where I landed when I fell.

Beyond that door I hear other things, too. Metal against metal, a tinny scritching. Jangling hardware. The clatter of metal pieces dropping to the floor.

A blast of icy air ruffles my wet hair. All around me, the air grows heavy, and the smell of chlorine coats my mouth like fish oil. Instinctively, I hold my breath till my lungs blaze. I'd run, but where? There's nothing around me but nothingness.

Betrayed by my body, I gasp for oxygen, choking on what feels like gallons of that vile, bitter substance. Then, seconds later, I feel the *pull.*

The inexplicable vacuum drags me off my knees and into the air. I'm moving, but touching nothing. Frigid oil ripples over my face as I sense, not see, the tunnel door growing closer . . . closer . . .

When I slam into the wall, no sound reaches my ears. Stunned, I lie flat on the floor and play dead. That works, I've heard, if you're attacked by a bear in the woods.

I don't think, however, this applies to ghosts.

Dazed from the blow, it takes me a moment to understand

that I'm *in* the tunnel next to a rectangle of light from the pool room door. The door knob rolls lazily into my hand, but when I try to grasp it my fingers won't obey. In fact, *nothing* on my body works. I'm not sure which terrifies me more: knowing I may very well be paralyzed for life or that Annaliese *knocked the whole doorknob right out of the door!*

That's when the door itself crawls open the rest of the way. Of course! What good are locks and dead bolts against a ghost? Mr. Solomon had no business firing poor Bennie. He should've taken a load of dynamite instead and blown the pool to smithereens. Screw the media center.

Struggling for breath against the wall of air, I roll my eyes toward the light on the other side of the doorway.

Not light.

Fog.

The same fog I saw that day with Nate, only brighter, more distinct. My brief gratitude at seeing *any* light at all dissolves to dismay, then horror, as the vapor grows and surges, blindingly bright, and leisurely morphs into the shape of a body.

Wavering limbs stretch into place. A neck forms and grows, broadening into a head. Silky strands of fluorescent hair float on a nonexistent breeze.

The unbearable pressure of the atmosphere lifts. Shocked to discover I can move again, I start to rise—and then scream at the twist of pain in my right wrist. That's the hand that hit the tunnel wall first. How lucky am I that it wasn't my head again?

I don't feel pain in my dreams. Not pain like this, so throbbing and vicious.

This can only mean one thing: "I'm not dreaming," I whisper.

———◄o►———

My words slip like butter through the bleach in my mouth. On my feet at last, I glance around helplessly. In the glow of that, that *thing* in the pool room, I can see through the tunnel door into the auditorium beyond.

It's not how I left it. The illuminated red letters of one EXIT sign are plainly visible. So are the beams of the emergency lights, powered by generators, I guess. I hear footfalls. Parents calling for their kids. Kids calling to each other.

Mr. Chenoweth warns: "Walk, don't run. We don't need a stampede here, folks."

I stagger gratefully toward the sounds and make it halfway through the door before that ghastly vacuum sucks me all the way back. I land hard in the threshold of the pool room.

I scream for Mom. For Frank. For anyone who can hear me.

"Give it up. Nobody can hear you."

"Wake me up, wake me up, oh God, WAKE ME UP!"

"You ARE awake, stupid."

The one thing more mind-numbing than hearing a ghost speak to you is hearing her so casually refer to you as "stupid."

"You're not real," I say, my words distorted in the heavy air.

"You wish." The shining illusion, or hallucination, or whatever she is, drifts closer to the threshold, then away again. *"You said you believed in me. What changed your mind?"*

I glance back at the auditorium. The people sounds fade, the doors leading out to the gym clang shut one last time, and now I know they've all left me behind. Alarmed, I notice how the emergency lights don't reach the pool room; they stop precisely at the tunnel entrance, leaving Annaliese's sanctuary dark, untouched.

Well, aside from *her*.

She sweeps back and forth across the room, passing easily through the fence. Her fluorescent swirl illuminates the pit of the pool. Droplets of color, sparking up at random, dance like minuscule fireworks around her drifting form.

Transfixed, I watch her drift through the fence one last time, approaching me in careful degrees. Is she as frightened of me as I am of her?

"You didn't answer me."

I forgot the question. Annaliese's features blur, sharpen, then blur again. Aside from, well, being a ghost this time, I recognize her from the pictures in Millie's yearbooks.

Not her eyes, though. These are not the same pale, friendly eyes. These depthless black orbs reveal nothing human at all.

I speak without thinking. "The windows to your soul."

She stops, though her hair continues to float in a misty halo. *"Who told you that?"*

"My grandmother."

"Can you see my eyes?"

"No," I admit.

She considers this. *"Does that mean I don't have a soul?"*

Either answer, yes or no, might be the wrong one. How easy is it to piss off a ghost? Right now she looks pretty mellow for one of the undead. Or am I thinking of vampires? Zombies?

I clear my stinging throat. "What do you want?"

"Why won't you answer my questions?"

"Why won't you answer mine? You dragged me in here."

"I didn't drag you in. You came on your own."

"Liar." Now *I'm* pissed off. "You could've killed me with that trick."

An air of amusement. *"I guess we underestimated each other, Corinne."*

"You know my name."

"I know all your names. Lacy, and Dino, and Meg, and . . ."

"Tasha," I say stonily.

"Did Tasha's mom cry at her funeral?"

"Of course she cried."

"Good. I hope she cries every day for the rest of her life."

I wet my lips and spit out bleach. "What did she do to you?"

"Why don't you ask Monica what they did to me?"

"They?"

Annaliese quivers at that. Again her features waver out of focus, then grow sharper than ever. I see a nose, a chin, and that she's small, like me, though she appears much bigger with all the surrounding vapor. *"Are you really that stupid, that you don't know who I'm talking about?"*

Of course I know: Luke, Millie, Joey Mancini, and Mom. "Are you going to kill them, too?"

"I didn't kill anyone."

"You killed Dino and Tasha. Then you tried to kill Nate."

"Nate would've done it himself once he realized he'd killed those horses. Or killed you," she adds bitterly.

"Same difference."

"And I didn't kill Dino. He slipped, jabbed a link into his leg, and fell back till he was hanging upside down. You should've heard him blubber! Crying for his mommy. Then he hung there till he died. Not my fault he was clumsy. Not MY fault he came in here." A brief

silence; I guess she wants to let *that* one sink in. *"And Tasha jumped in by herself. Why blame me?"*

"Because *you* made it happen. You made all of it happen!" Annaliese doesn't argue. This surprises me. "Why?"

"What do you care? Besides, I'm almost finished. In fact, just think . . ." Her voice takes on a taunting lilt. *"Right now your boyfriend might be cleaning out his gun, or driving around in that nasty blizzard, or—"*

Pain shoots to my elbow at my involuntary jerk. "Leave Nate alone."

"Imagine how Luke'll feel when he finds Nate with his brains blown out. Or in his car, wrapped around a tree. Mmm, *blood all over the snow. Maybe a decapitation?"*

A shower of sparks punctuates Annaliese's delight. She moves close enough to cast a glow over my skin. My arm hairs flare.

"Don't worry. It's not like you won't find another guy, right? You're just like Monica. Not me. I never even kissed a guy till Luke." She swells, radiating fury like waves from a furnace. *"But Monica? Ha! She ruined everything."*

Startled by the alien surge of heat, I back into the wall. The blackness lifts with each rising degree, revealing a pool filled with sparkling water. Bright lights. A smooth tiled floor.

The powerful odor of bleach evaporates, leaving only the clean, safe scent of a normal swimming pool.

Not a dream.

Not a hallucination.

"Watch," Annaliese whispers.

The fence disappears, and so does she.

———◦———

Now I know what Tasha saw the day she died.

She dove into an empty pool, believing this illusion was real. That somehow the pool had been secretly renovated, transformed into something beautiful beyond belief. A rational person would've realized such a feat was impossible.

Tasha wasn't rational. She'd been under Annaliese's spell.

I stare in dread at the diving board. What does Annaliese plan to show me? Tasha, en route to her grisly death?

Can she force me to watch? Will I see her land this time?

Please. Please, no.

Nothing happens. But the pool remains.

At the unexpected sound of new voices in the auditorium, and no Annaliese in sight, I make a split second decision and bolt out of the tunnel. *Free!*

But wait. There are no instruments on the stage, no tiers for the chorus. No puddles of water or abandoned belongings. The stage is lit again, but the curtains look different. Kids sprawl in the hill of seats. I don't recognize a single face.

I do recognize Ms. Rasmussen, my English teacher who also teaches drama. She's different, too, thinner, with longer hair, and what's with the outdated glasses?

As the final bell rings, she says, "Okay, have a great weekend, people. And don't forget, if anyone's interested, tryouts for *Hamlet* will be after school on Monday."

Mumbles of agreement, a few good-byes. Kids grab book bags and folders. Some head for the tunnel, others toward the gym. Unsure of what to do, I head for the gym, too, acutely aware that my right arm is now *fine*—and stop when I spot two girls in a back row.

Mom and Millie?

Yes, it's them, but much younger versions. Mom's hair hangs to her waist. Millie, easily forty pounds lighter, displays a mountain of cleavage in her tight pink top.

"You got the camera?" I hear Mom—*Monica*—whisper to Millie. Millie holds up a bulky old Polaroid. Monica smacks it back down. "Don't wave it around! What's wrong with you?"

"Chill out," Millie suggests. "And hurry up. She'll be here any sec." As Mom/Monica hesitates, she adds, "Don't worry. You just take care of Luke. Joey and I'll do the rest."

"Cool. I'm outta here." Mom/Monica hops up, revealing a short demin skirt and funky boots. Smiling slyly, she adds, "Take *lots* of pics," and squiggles past Millie out of the row.

When she halts in surprise directly in front of me, it hits me: *she sees me, too!*

I wait, immobilized.

Mom/Monica narrows the same eyes I've known for sixteen years. "What're you lookin' at, bitch?"

I'm looking at you. At my mother, at my age. And I don't like what I see.

"N-nothing," I stammer.

"N-n-nothin'," she mimics, jarring me with her unfamiliar drawl. I bet Mom worked really hard over the years to get rid of that. "I don't know you. You new?"

"Y-yes."

"So what's your name?"

"Corinne." I wait breathlessly, but she shows no recognition.

"Nice name," Mom/Monica muses. "I like it." She hefts her book bag and lifts her chin. "Now do me a favor and get your ass outta here . . . *Corinne*."

I don't need to be asked twice. With a last look at Millie, all huddled down like she's hiding, I hurry out to the gym. Funny how only a few minutes ago I thought I'd be killed by a ghost. Now I'm wondering how I ended up *twenty fricking years in the past*—and how, or if, I'll make it back to my own time in one piece.

Unless Annaliese's making me hallucinate, too, the way she made Tasha hallucinate the pool. Did Annaliese "bring" me here to kill me off, after all?

I'm afraid to budge. The next step I take may be the last move I make.

When Monica emerges behind me, I come alive and duck behind the open door. She passes without notice, sharing a significant look with a young, buff, and menacingly cute Joey Mancini.

"Luke's on his way," he mutters sideways. "Go get him, princess."

Monica springs off, her long hair flopping, and Joey saunters into the auditorium. *Which one should I follow?* The decision is made for me when I step away from the door and instantly stumble, knocked off-balance by another deadly sear of suction.

Annaliese isn't letting me go anywhere. What she wants me to see is *here*.

So I follow Joey. He and Millie exchange urgent whispers, and lapse into silence when someone else walks in.

Annaliese.

Not the ghost Annaliese. The *girl* Annaliese.

She strolls down to the front row. I flatten myself into the back wall, praying for invisibility, as Joey lopes down to join Annaliese. Millie, camera in hand, then sneaks down the side aisle, prowling catlike toward the stage. I tiptoe behind her as closely as I dare. If Mom/Monica can see me, maybe Millie and Dino can, too.

Joey's talking to Annaliese. She's so much prettier than her yearbook pictures. Not head-turning beautiful, not like my mom. But there's something, I don't know, *genuine* about her. Like, if you found yourself in the lunch room with no one to talk to, Annaliese would totally invite you over. She's so startlingly normal and so *good* somehow, I almost forget about that evil vapor in the pool room.

Annaliese jumps as Joey advances. "Leave me alone. I'm waiting for Luke."

"Want some company?" he cajoles.

"No. I don't even like you, Joey."

"Sure you do." Fast as a whip, Joey kisses her.

Click . . . buzz. Millie's camera shoots out a photo. She whips it out and places it on the edge of the stage.

"What are you *doing*?" Annaliese shouts, dodging Joey's persistent mouth.

Click . . . buzz. Click . . . buzz. Millie presses the button each time Joey's mouth hits the mark.

What the hell? No longer caring if they notice me, I open my mouth to shout my own protest—but the air turns to syrup, deadening my limbs, silencing me.

Then, bellowing curses, Joey stumbles away from Annaliese's fist with a bloody nose.

"Get away from me, you sick freak. Both of you!" Annaliese adds to Millie, now several yards away.

Millie calls merrily, "Hey, we're just gonna take some pics for Lukey baby. Y'know, so he'll know what a *slut* you are."

Joey wipes his nose on his *Hawks* sweatshirt. Then he grabs Annaliese, one hand in her hair, the other mashing her breast. *Click . . . buzz.* Millie lines the photos up side by side.

Then Annaliese breaks free. "Go ahead, take more. Get one of Dino's bloody nose! When Luke sees it, he'll *know* it wasn't my idea." She backs up, hair wild, eyes flashing danger. "He's on his way now. You better leave me alone!"

"Oh, really?" Millie taunts. "I don't think so. He's busy with *Monica* right now."

Annaliese pokes her nose up. "Liar."

"Wanna bet? You're so stupid. Why do you *think* he's not here? We told you Monica'd get him back."

Taking advantage of Annaliese's palpable surprise, Joey catches her blouse. "Don't touch me!" she screams, and punches Joey—POW! POW!—with *both* fists this time.

Joey, enraged, yanks her closer and then slams her forcefully against the wall of the stage. The sickening thump echoes. Air huffs out of her lungs.

Spellbound, I watch Annaliese slump to the floor.

Millie drops the camera. "What the hell'd you *do*?"

"I dunno," Joey mumbles, dazed.

Millie bounds over. The two of them stand, face-to-face, over Annaliese's motionless form. Blood from Joey's nose drips onto her clothes.

He wipes his face with a frantic slash. "Is she okay? Can you tell?"

"I don't know. She's not moving."

"Is . . . is she d-dead?"

"I don't know!" Clutching her head, Millie stomps in

circles. "Omigod, you stupid shit. How could you let this happen?"

"She hit me. Twice," Joey says plaintively. "It was a reflex, okay?" Then he regains his bravado. "Hey, this wasn't *my* idea. It was you and Mo, remember?"

"We told you to kiss her! Maybe grab some tit!"

Silence. What are they thinking now? That not only is Annaliese dead, but she's also covered with Joey's DNA? I wonder if they can test for that yet. If so, he's screwed. And I doubt he'll go down alone.

Or maybe they're thinking: If Annaliese *isn't* dead, what happens to them when she wakes up?

I don't know whose idea it is. I don't see who makes the first move. But Joey, without a word, hoists Annaliese off the floor while Millie rushes ahead of him to open the tunnel door. Annaliese's head strikes the wall as Joey maneuvers her limp body through the doorway. The hollow thump turns my stomach to stone.

The farther away from me they move, the more *I* can move. I guess Annaliese *wants* me to see what's happening, but only from a certain distance. Wading through nonexistent sand, exactly the way I did at Nana's wake, I trudge after them to the pool room.

I hear the splash as they dump Annaliese into the water.

"Chlorine kills evidence, I think," Millie says nervously. "It's, like, bleach or whatever."

"No shit." Joey stares at the water. "Um, what're we gonna tell Mo?"

Millie folds his dissolving hand into her own. "Easy. She never showed up. We never saw her tonight."

Then they're gone. Just like that.

Annaliese stays behind, floating facedown. Lazy bubbles burble up through strands of her hair.

She drowned, they say. Which is true.

But only because Joey and Millie threw her into the water alive.

Around me, the atmosphere chills and darkens. My new blast of panic stifles all reason, and I bolt back out of the room, running like crazy. What happens if I keep going? Will I be stuck here forever?

Then what?

My toe kicks Millie's camera, sending it spinning. With one swipe I gather the photographs from the edge of the stage—*no one can know!*—and, screaming senselessly, rip them to bits. I'm still tearing at them when that lethal grasp seizes me again, and hurtles me off into a stifling black fog.

———◦———

Annaliese's words stir the air. *"Luke promised he'd meet me there. He was going with me, now, not Monica. He dumped her for ME! And if he'd shown up like he said he would, I'd still be alive. But, nooo, he was with Monica. Like I was nothing. Nobody!"*

Curled up on the floor, I rasp, "My mom didn't do it. She never even knew what they did to you."

"She knows now. Millie told her."

"When?"

"I guess when Millie couldn't stand the guilt anymore," Annaliese snarls. *"She knows why Tasha died. And she knows why I did it."*

That day in the kitchen. Oh my God. No wonder Mom's not speaking to Millie. "But you can't blame *my* mom. Not when they lied to her."

"Monica kept him away. It was her idea to take those pictures, to make him think I was hooking up with Joey. She wanted him back, but he wanted me instead. Me! He knew she was a bitch. That's why he dumped her."

"I want to go home," I say miserably. That last unplanned trip through the air did me in. "I'll tell them what really happened. Isn't that what you want?"

"Nobody'll believe you."

"My mom will."

Annaliese snorts, a peculiarly human sound. *"You think?"*

Silence . . .

      . . . silence . . .

            . . . silence . . .

Then Mom calls, "Rinn?"

———◦———

I push up with my good arm. I see her then, wrapped in the pale ghostly swirl that, seconds ago, was Annaliese. "Mom?" It can't possibly be her. It's one of Annaliese's tricks.

But it's Mom's voice, soft and miserable. "Oh, Rinn. I loved you so much. After you left me, I couldn't stop crying. I tried to stay busy, like everyone said. I tried so hard to remember the happy times, but I couldn't. I couldn't! Honey, you were my whole *life.*"

"What're you talking about?" I ask numbly. "Mom, what—?"

"I miss you so much. Why did you leave me? Why?"

"I didn't!" I scream. "I'm right here!"

"I couldn't eat, or sleep. I couldn't even play the piano. I tried, night after night, but nothing came out right. I lost my music." Mom's voice cracks. She drops her face into her hands. "My music! The one thing I loved almost as much as I loved you."

"Mom, you're doing all that *now*. And I'm still alive!"

Annaliese scoffs. *"Oh, really? Are you sure? Or did they find you dead in that tub? Or . . . maybe dead on the floor with your boyfriend's hands on your neck?"*

Unthinking, I charge her—and slam into the fence. The thunder of the links deafen me as I scream incoherently at the hateful glow that's no longer my mother. Annaliese drifts out of range with an uneasy laugh. Even with the fence between us, I think she fears my rage.

"My grandmother suffered when I died, too. I was HER whole life. She tried to find me, in here. But I was weak back then. I couldn't reach her, not even when crazy Miss Prout tried to help her. So she killed herself. All she wanted was to see me again! And we did see each other, just for a second, and I was so, so happy! But I wasn't strong enough to keep her here."

"Yeah, well." I rub my sore arm. "You look strong enough to me."

"Ha! I am now. The rats worked for a while, but they're harder to come by. That cat worked much better. The furnace helps, lots of energy there. Electricity, too, till Bennie got lazy and stopped changing the bulbs. But that's all right, I found other ways. Easier ways."

"Like what?" Though I already know.

"Human energy, stupid. Like talent. Like physical strength." She's actually listing them like we're in class or something. *"Compassion. Sense of humor. Willpower, that's the easiest. Health, too. And lo-o-ove, of course."* She draws the word out mockingly. *"You all give it up so easily. It's pathetic, really."*

"We don't give it up. You take it from us, because you're evil." I kick the fence. "And here I was, feeling sorry for you. I almost *liked* you for a minute. So, yes, I'm stupid."

A surge of light shoots through her form, temporarily blinding me. I'm noticing now that the madder she gets, the brighter she glows, while the room itself grows colder than ever. *Sucking up energy.* What happens when she uses it up and there's nothing left?

Or if someone *takes* it from her?

"Evil? Monica was evil! She couldn't believe he wanted me instead. I wasn't a cheerleader. I wasn't pretty, or talented, or, or anything, really. But Luke liked me! And Monica couldn't stand it, so she tortured me. She told lies about me and tried to turn people against me. But guess what? It didn't work. You want to know why, Corrine? Because I was a nice person. Because people liked me."

Before I can decide how to reply to this, Annaliese sighs. I know it's a sigh because of the multicolored sparks that flitter about her face at her *whooshing* sound. Ghosts breathe? I bet they don't mention that in *Spirit World.*

Impulsively I say, "I thought you couldn't haunt people who take mind-altering drugs."

"Haunt's a stupid word."

"It's the only word I know. So, can you or can't you?"

"Not usually. I never could touch Bennie. I didn't know why till I figured it out with Miss Prout. That's one of the things they never bother to tell you."

"They? They who?"

"Just . . . they," she says secretively. *"You don't have to know who they are."* She tosses her sparkly hair, another eerily human gesture.

"Then why can you 'touch' me now? I'm taking my meds."

"Because you want me to. You opened that door, not me."

"You're so full of it."

"C'mon, Corinne. People take drugs all the time to keep us out. Then people like you stop taking them, and let us back in again. Every time that happens we hang around longer."

"Mental illness isn't about ghosts! It's a chemical imbalance. The drugs straighten it all out and, and—well, it's an illness, that's all. This is the twenty-first century, duh."

A ghostly shrug. *"Whatever you say . . . Corrr-iiinne."*

She drifts here and there, like she now has more important things on her mind. Trails of color, an electrified rainbow, glimmer in her wake. She fades a bit when she rests and that worries me. What if she tires out and disappears and leaves me here forever? Somehow I'd rather see her angry than indifferent.

"So now what?" I prompt. "Are you finished killing people off? Are you just gonna hang around here and play with shadows? Howl at the moon? Knock over a *chair*?"

A spiral of light shoots up with her laughter. *"You liked that, huh?"*

"Not really."

Silence. I wait.

Then Annaliese muses, *"I think the rope might be a good way for Monica to go."*

I clutch the fence. "You can't have her." No answer. "Do you hear me? I won't let you take my mother!"

Her sardonic laughter rings, echoless. *"I don't want your mother. It's you I want. If I take YOU, I'll get to Monica. Same way I got to Millie with Tasha, and Joey with Dino. I almost got Luke, too, that day with the horses."* Another glittery sigh. *"Too bad you butted in. Luke would never get over it! Neither would you, I bet. Pills. A razor. Whatever's handy, I guess."*

"I'd never do that to my mom."

"You tried it before."

"That was different."

"Different how?"

My arm hurts so bad it's making me cranky. No, *she's* making me cranky. I'm sick of talking to her.

Softly enticing, Annaliese continues. *"Why don't you do it right now? You still have the razor blade, right? In your pocket?"* She delivers a ghostly smirk as I try to hide my surprise. *"Please. You're so pathetically transparent."*

I switch tactics. "Look, why can't you die for real and go *be* with your grandmother?"

"I can't reach her," is her sullen reply.

"Oh, really? Is that because she knows what a conniving bitch you are? Is that why she doesn't want anything to *do* with you anymore?"

My words strike a chord. Enraged, Annaliese trembles; the floor vibrates, and I imagine it splitting under my feet. Her human form fades, disappearing into a dazzling white vortex. I start to shout "WAIT!" but stop as the radiance morphs into a different shape, one I recognize before it fully takes hold.

An old woman, her long gray hair haphazardly bunched on her head. Reading glasses dangle from a chain. She's wearing a plaid nightgown and chenille robe—the same clothes Nana wore the night of the fire.

She floats unhurriedly along the tiles. The remnants of mist trailing beneath her on the floor lengthen and solidify to form perfect human feet.

I know it's not Nana. But how can she seem so, so *real*?

Real enough for me to smell the scent of her favorite soap.

Real enough for me to notice the missing button on her robe.

Real enough for me feel her grandmotherly warmth as she smiles at me with the light of a thousand stars.

But you're not real. YOU'RE NOT REAL!

"She tells me you did it on purpose, Corinne." Nana bobs her head toward the black abyss of the pool, as if indicating a lurking Annaliese. "I don't believe her. 'My granddaughter,' I said, 'would never do that. She'd never lock her door, set a fire, and leave me alone to die.'"

Tears roll off my chin to fizzle in the lingering mist.

"Did you watch from a distance?" she asks.

Mute, I stare.

"Did you call for help?"

I know it's not Nana because the voice isn't quite right; I hear Annaliese's cruel undertones creeping insidiously to the surface. Still, I whip my head back and forth in denial.

"Did you hear my screams?"

You never screamed. You died from smoke inhalation. You never felt a thing. Mom promised!

Unless she lied to me. Unless she'd wanted me to think Nana died peacefully, not screaming in agony while the flames roasted her alive.

She's screwing with your mind. She did it with Mom and now she's doing it with Nana.

Nana approaches, holding out hands that look exactly like I remember. Her wedding ring, loose on a bony finger.

Bulging blue veins. Dirt caked around her nails like she's been gardening again . . . *gardening in Heaven.*

I stare hard at those hands, groping for the words. "It wasn't my fault."

She stops.

"It wasn't my fault," I repeat. "IT WASN'T MY FAULT!"

Something peculiar charges the air. My hair blows in an unfelt breeze and the floor shakes harder under my shoes. My arm hairs stand on end again, zapped with an electricity that can't possibly exist in this void.

Nana raises her palms, fingers spread. "I miss you, Rinnie."

It's *her* voice this time, not Annaliese's.

And she called me Rinnie, not Corinne.

Only Nana calls me Rinnie.

Vapor rises around us, crackling with fury. Before I can react, Nana steps briskly out of the fog to yank me away from the sinister swirl. She hugs me hard, and no, it's no trick—*I recognize this hug!* I sob out loud at the familiar contours of her body. Even her hair's the same, all heavy and smooth against my cheek.

"I miss you, too," I whisper, ignoring the swelling mist, the sparkling embers. I'm too overwhelmed to feel frightened, and it makes no attempt to come closer. "I love you so much! And I'm sorry, really sorry—"

"There's nothing to be sorry for." Nana strokes my hair. "And you *know* I love you, too."

Behind her, the column of vapor spins upward. Intermittent flashes of Annaliese's features mingle with a black *O* that forms in the mist, mutating at last into a tremendous mouth. *"You don't belong here!"* it shrills. *"Go away! GO AWAY!"*

Walls shudder with volcanic force. The tiny windows blow out, shooting glass through the air like crystalline daggers. Chips of the ceiling hammer down, followed by torrents of what I imagine to be ice. Distantly I'm aware of *some* kind of pain, but I'm too safe, too comfortable in Nana's arms, to care.

She rubs my back. "Don't be afraid. It's over. *You* have the strength now, Rinnie."

"What do you—?"

Another thunderous crash cuts me off. I hang on to Nana as Annaliese, enraged, flares toward the ceiling like a luminescent tornado. Sparks rain down, burning like dry ice—

—and then the suction begins to drag me backward again. I watch, powerless, as my fingers slide through Nana's . . . away . . . away . . . till I have no choice but to let go.

Whirling on Annaliese, unafraid of her towering mass, I throw myself forward. Slivers of light grip my hands with monstrous force. I squeeze her back, shocked I can touch her, that she feels like a mixture of ice, fire, and flesh. With every ounce of energy I have left, I drag her down close to me, pulling harder . . . harder . . . !

As the vapor consumes me, Annaliese's hideous black mouth widens, in terror this time. *My* pull, she knows, is far more powerful than hers. She writhes under my ferocious pants like I'm exhaling pure fire.

"Leave me alone!" I scream. Clouds of my breath swirl in and around those awful, empty eye sockets. "Go back where you came from and *leave me alone!*"

My toes fly up the ground as Annaliese shrieks with fury. For one sickening instant I can't think, can't move, and all I can see is white. My own screams echo hers as I realize we're *fused together*, that I'm trapped in this violent whirlpool of ice. Weightless, scrambling for my safety plane, I watch the sparkling colors mushroom up from below us and consume the vicious, spinning mist that is Annaliese.

In excruciating slow motion, Annaliese shrinks, absorbing the colors. Her form darkens to yellow from that infinitely painful white, and then to amber, scattering dull sparks. Her hideous eyes shrink to pinpoints, while her black mouth stretches into a monstrous cavern, growing bigger . . . bigger . . . till it devours what's left of her.

———◄o►———

First, darkness and silence.

Next, an earth-shattering explosion.

"*Nana!*" I scream.

Then I'm falling again.

Saturday, December 20
(No longer counting)

They have to dig me out.

Flat on a table under a glaring light, I hear words like "hypothermia" and "right Colles' fracture." Then more familiar terms—*delusional, psychosis*—spoken in skeptical, secretive tones.

Mom and Frank hover. My arm's on fire. I can't stop babbling.

Mom says, "Rinn, *please* settle down and let the medication work."

Frank says, "Oh, Christ, let her come out of this."

Then Nana says sternly, "*Hush now, Rinnie. Do you WANT them to think you're crazy?*"

That's when I shut up.

Monday, December 22

Blood tests show my drug levels are "therapeutic," proving to the powers that be I've been taking my meds. A temporary psychosis, the doctor claims, brought on by a concussion. The pool room roof, buried under tons of ice and snow, collapsed in the brutal fifty-mile-an-hour wind.

On the ride back to River Hills, Mom doesn't once light up. The ashtray looks as pristine as the day Frank drove the SUV home from the dealer.

I sniff discreetly. "Did you quit smoking again?"

"Yes. And buckle your seat belt," Mom adds snappishly. "I don't want my last memory of you to be with your bloody head sticking through a windshield."

I obey. "Is Frank still here?"

"No, he flew back this morning. We *told* you he was leaving."

I know. But I'd hoped the cast on my arm and my gauze

turban might persuade him to hang around till Christmas. "Do you . . . do you think you guys'll get back together?"

Mom exhales. "I don't know. I kind of *like* being on my own. I can't make any promises." My stab of disappointment fades a bit when she adds, "He wants you to stay with him next summer. Though I'm still not sure that's a great idea."

I steel myself. "Why not?"

"Because I'd *miss* you, Rinn." She takes one hand off the wheel to reach for mine—the one minus the cast. "Oh, honey. When we couldn't find you after the power failure, I was out of my mind! Then when that roof caved in, and we didn't know where you were . . ." She squeezes my fingers. "I am never letting you out of my sight again!"

Somehow I don't think she's joking.

I watch the scenery for a while, absently picking at my cast. Okay, I know Nana warned me not to bring Annaliese up. But, as usual, I can't keep quiet.

"I tore up the pictures," I blurt out.

"What pictures?"

"Millie's pictures."

The pictures that never existed. After Millie told Mom what happened, did she tell her about the pictures? That for some sick, twisted reason she'd hung on to them all these years? Probably. She'd already admitted the worst.

Mom's hand tightens on the wheel. She stares directly ahead.

"I know what happened to Annaliese," I say softly. "Just don't ask me *how* I know."

Mom replies, just as softly, "Thank you, Rinn."

———◃◦▹———

I find the broken wall in my room repaired and repainted. Nate did it, Mom said, over the weekend. My room is tidy. My guitar is safe and sound.

I'm so glad it's winter break. My arm hurts. I'd take a pain pill, but it might knock me out, and no way do I want to let my guard down tonight. With my iPod plugged to my ears, I stare at the Hanging Beam as David Gilmour sings about how *there's no way out of here*. That, once you're in, you're in for good.

I think I'm safe.

I think Annaliese is gone.

It's funny how I feel, well, *grateful* to her. Grateful that she let me have Nana back for a minute, never mind that she tried to trick me at first. I'm just happy I got to see her. To touch her. To let her know one last time how much I love her.

So thank you, Annaliese. Even though you're an evil, conniving, homicidal bi——

I jump when Nate drops down beside me. "Your mom said I could hang out a while."

I drag my earbuds off. "You mean she decided you're not an imminent threat to me?"

"Depends on how you define 'threat.'" He studies my face. "Poor Rinn. You look like a *roof* caved in on you."

I bat the one eye I can see out of. "Smart-ass."

"Can I sign it?" he asks, thoughtfully rubbing my cast.

"Yeah, if you write something mushy."

Nate rummages through my desk till he finds a red Magic Marker. With exaggerated intent, he draws a big heart and writes inside it: *Heal fast! I love you. Nate.*

I pluck the marker away and toss it aside. "Why, thanks, farmer boy."

"Shucks." He crawls under my covers. "My pleasure, surfer girl."

He nuzzles my neck with teasing kisses. I kiss him back, not teasing at all. I feel his heat, and his weight, and how much he loves me.

"Hey, in case you forgot," I tell him. "I love you, too."

He sneaks back out before Mom has the presence of mind to check up on us. Gently I trace the message he wrote on my cast. Funny how, in spite of my throbbing arm, my black eye, the stitches in my scalp, and my shattered nerves, I feel so completely and positively *wonderful*.

Downstairs, Mom begins to play Chopin's Piano Concerto No. 1. The notes float up through the vent, each one lovely and perfect.

Yes, my mom's back. My whole *life* is back.

Now that I think about it, I owe Annaliese an apology. What I said to her about her grandmother not wanting her? That was just plain cruel.

"Sorry," I say into the air. "I take it back. And I really do hope you find her."

No answer. Not that I expected one.

The Onion Ring Goddess left town. Details are sketchy, but rumor has it that with Tasha gone and her husband Bob on the road, Millie decided to shut down the diner and take an extended trip. For Mom's sake, and mine, I hope she doesn't come back.

"I'm sorry they hurt you," I continue. "And that my mom hurt you, too. But if you knew her now, you'd see how different she is. She's changed. I think *you* made her change. I think she felt bad when you died, for treating you like that."

Wherever you are, I hope you can hear me.

I burrow under the covers and try to sleep.

———◦———

I think the smell wakes me up. No, not chlorine, or lavender, or anything weird like that.

Magic Marker.

"Oh, crap." I scramble up the best I can, clutching the uncapped marker. Red ink stains my left hand and random fingerprints dot my comforter. Why didn't I make Nate put this away after he wrote his little love note?

I spot the cap on the floor and I reach for it, and that's when I notice my cast. Yes, Nate's funny crooked heart is there. But with my cast tilted sideways I can see something else.

Precisely printed letters, one line, and *not* my handwriting. I'm right-handed, you know.

My body freezes, trapped in a shroud of frost. I throw the marker aside and rub my fingers. The ink, still fresh, smears under my touch as I stare at blood-red words on my cast:

I don't believe you

A Note from Jeannine Garsee

The Unquiet is a story I'd planned to write for years, and for a very good reason: from kindergarten through the fourth grade, I attended a Cleveland public school similar to River Hills High. The wooden desks were indeed bolted to the floor, and the teachers wrote with chalk on blackboards, not with dry-erase markers. And, yes, I promise you: there was even a haunted tunnel.

Like Rinn and her friends, we weren't allowed to cut through the gym, so we'd take a long, narrow tunnel from one end of the building to the other. The tunnel wall, on one side, was made of brick or stone; the other side was a metal fence overlooking a treacherous pit. My first day there, at age five, a classmate told me the story: while workers were in the process of excavating an in-ground pool, somehow (insert vague details here) a girl was killed when she fell over the edge. For that reason the pool was never finished, and the pit remained untouched for years.

Feigning terror, we'd sometimes hold hands and race screaming through the tunnel, hoping the ghost of the unknown victim wouldn't rise up and, well, do whatever ghosts *do* to screaming children. Yet there were other times when I'd choose to travel that tunnel alone. Fascinated by the story, completely unafraid, I'd take my time and saunter along, peering through the links for a shadow, a movement, a wisp of vapor . . . anything to assure me that the ghostly girl existed. Yes, even at five, the writer inside me *wanted* to see the girl who tragically died here and now called this tunnel her home.

When my family moved away, and I began fifth grade at a brighter, newer school out in the suburbs, I often thought about that haunted tunnel. I promised myself that if I ever did become a writer, I'd find a way to bring that ghostly girl to life.

So many times while writing this story, I was tempted to pick up the phone, call that school, and ask if they'd let me return for a tour. I'd love to walk through that tunnel after so many years and see if I *could* sense something unearthly. But the fear that perhaps the tunnel no longer exists—that they'd replaced it with a media center or possibly a newer gym—always kept me from making that call. I didn't want to see anything shiny and sterile, filled with light and activity and excited chatter. Nor did I want to have to wonder what became of the ghostly girl if an army of bulldozers and jackhammers had destroyed her dark, eerie home.

Since then, I've had other, much more real encounters with the paranormal. And while this experience may have been based on nothing more than a legend invented by children, I'll never forget that tunnel, or the girl who hovered, unseen, in the shadows.

This book is partly for her, wherever she is now.

Acknowledgments

I'd like to thank the following people, because this story wouldn't have been possible without their help and support:

My first readers—Pamela Reese, Holly Snapp, Sher Hames Torres, June Phyllis Baker, Charlotte Parker, Kathie Carlson, Brian Kell, Judy Walters, Laura McCarthy, and Elizabeth Garsee.

My friends and coconspirators on LiveJournal and AWR.

My coworkers in psych who've taught me so much over the past several years, and the countless patients I've cared for who've taught me even more.

My family, of course, who once again had to put up with my seemingly endless journey through another Land of Make Believe.

My brilliant editor, Caroline Abbey, and all the other wonderful, creative minds at Bloomsbury USA Children's Books.

And to my agent, the infinitely wise Tina Wexler, who tells it like it is even when I don't want to hear it: thank you, as always, from the bottom of my heart.